SPECIAL DELIVERY

When postal worker Boyd Trevore failed to return to work that day, his supervisor didn't investigate immediately. When he didn't show up three days in a row, a "Stolen Property" report was put out on the truck, and the postal inspectors notified the highway patrol.

Two and a half weeks later, a survey engineer discovered the truck in a gully where a new development was to be built. Written on the side were the words SKELTER—DAY ONE. The truck had been towed away, washed, and repaired before they found Boyd's femur and a badly decomposed arm, several hundred yards away. . . .

LOCK YOUR DOORS.

TURN OUT THE LIGHTS.

MANSON'S CHILDREN ROAM THE LAND.

Books by Michael R. Perry

The Stranger Returns
Skelter

Published by POCKET BOOKS

SKELTER

MICHAEL R. PERRY

POCKET STAR BOOKS

New York   London   Toronto   Sydney   Tokyo   Singapore

This book is a work of fiction. Names, characters, places and incidents are products of the author's imagination or are used fictitiously.

An *Original* Publication of POCKET BOOKS

A Pocket Star Book published by
POCKET BOOKS, a division of Simon & Schuster Inc.
1230 Avenue of the Americas, New York, NY 10020

ISBN: 0-671-73496-2

First Pocket Books printing September 1994

10 9 8 7 6 5 4 3 2 1

POCKET STAR BOOKS and colophon are registered trademarks of Simon & Schuster Inc.

Printed in the U.S.A.

SKELTER

PROLOGUE

Delicta maiorum immeritus lues.
Undeservedly, you will atone
for the sins of your fathers.
—Horace

June 1970

THE DOCKET SAID SIMPLY "COUNTY CHILDREN'S SERVICES Hearing" because Judge Woolsey refused to have a media circus in *his* courtroom. If he had permitted a more detailed listing, the press mob covering the Manson murder trials down the street at the Criminal Courts Building would have smelled headlines and invaded like Patton's army. The tactic had apparently worked: The spectator gallery was mostly empty, except for the courtroom regulars—bored retirees working crossword puzzles and a few vagrants who just wanted a place to sit down.

No one was on trial. It wasn't that kind of court. The judge's task was to determine what would be best for the thirteen children who sat to his left, ranging from nine months to nine years in age. The county representative read in a monotone a report detailing the condition in which the children had been found at the Spahn Ranch, home of Charles Manson's notorious Family. In his two dozen years as a children's court judge, Woolsey had heard tales of abuse, torture, even death; but the story he heard today made all others pale by comparison.

Dr. Helen Olivera of the county began with details of conditions at the ranch, the grim reality muted through the language of bureaucracy: "improper sanitary conditions"—

1

the ranch had only one outhouse, shared by fifty or more people; "improper shelter"—the children rarely slept in the same place two nights in a row; "failure to register four school-age children in L.A. Unified School District schools." Garden-variety bad conditions, the kind of thing encountered every day by any social worker.

Then Dr. Olivera turned the page of the report, took a sip of water, and continued. "There are both anecdotal reports and medical confirmation of severe sexual abuse perpetrated against all thirteen children."

Woolsey looked down from the bench skeptically. "All of them? The youngest is what, nine months old? That would make him four months old when taken from the ranch. The court hopes that the county isn't exaggerating its case. Please approach the bench."

Olivera leaned in to the judge. "Your honor, three sources confirm that they had a practice of"—she lowered her voice—"fellating the infant boy."

"A four-month-old infant?"

Olivera nodded, then cleared her throat. "It might be advisable to refrain from reading this aloud, considering the presence of children in the courtroom."

"Motion approved."

Olivera handed the thick report to the judge. The social worker knew that its contents were bizarre, almost unbelievable; but she also knew they were true. The children at the Spahn Ranch got most of their meals from garbage dumpsters. They were regularly drugged with LSD, mescaline, marijuana. And worse, they were cajoled or forced into performing sex acts with each other, and with adults. While reading the report, Woolsey thrice called her to the bench for confirmation of the more gruesome details. The twenty-nine-year-old social worker had an ace in her hand—the most bizarre allegations had been freely admitted to by the Manson Family members themselves, as if they had no concept that anything they did was wrong. "Free love" had been used as license for unchecked child abuse.

In her capacity as a social worker, Olivera learned far more about the Manson Family than she ever wanted to know. The handful on trial for murder charges were only the tip of the iceberg: She personally had interviewed close to

2

fifty people associated with the cult, and knew of another hundred or so hangers-on from discussions with the DA and police. Most would never be tried because the tight-knit Family used tactics usually associated with Mafia organizations: witness intimidation, including two who were murdered and one who was dosed with LSD; conflicting, confusing testimony; and a large support group who were ready to say or do anything their leader demanded.

Neither Woolsey nor Olivera noticed the young man and woman with shaved heads who sat quietly in the back benches. People often came and went during the long, dull proceedings, hopping from courtroom to courtroom looking for the rare trial that provided entertainment, and the odd visitors didn't create a commotion. Rather, they just stared at the thirteen children with an intensity that could be mistaken for boredom or curiosity.

But their presence startled one participant in the trial— a boy two and a half years old who knew who they were and that they brought pain. His new jumpsuit itched his sunburn-scarred skin and he fidgeted, swinging his legs off the courthouse bench. *Red Ryder and Magick Mimi back there.* He clenched his fists in fear, and couldn't stop staring at the bad people. Then he looked at the judge, who seemed kind and serious, and might even be Santa Claus.

When the judge put down the report and took off the half-glasses he wore when reading, the murmur in the courtroom stopped and all that could be heard was the buzzing from the fluorescent lights. The judge looked at the scared and confused faces of the children, making eye contact with them one by one.

"Charles Manson's so-called Family has been accused of many atrocities. A criminal trial for murder charges is occurring as I speak, and many horrific allegations have been raised in that courtroom.

"But I feel the abuses suffered by these children may be this criminal group's most heinous legacy. A murder victim's trauma is painful, but soon ends; whereas these children will suffer the anguish of the Family's abuses for all of their lives."

A shriek emanated from the back of the courtroom, where the couple with shaved heads sat. Woolsey cast them a stern look, practiced over many years, and they momentarily quieted. The bailiff casually moved to the back of the court, in case there was trouble. He was startled to discover that both had on their foreheads an identical tattoo: a tiny, backwards swastika.

"This court orders that twelve of the thirteen children shall be placed in the custody of the State Foster Care System. I'm going to go further and absolutely prohibit visitation or contact of any kind by the previous parents and/or guardians. Further, all records shall be sealed. These children deserve to start with a clean slate. Let me go further and suggest—"

Before he could finish, Woolsey was interrupted by an outburst from the back of the room. The strange visitors stood and chanted furiously. "They're our children, they're our children, *they're our children!* They'll always belong to us!"

Woolsey slammed down his gavel. "Order!"

"They'll always be ours!"

"Bailiff, please clear the spectator gallery immediately!"

The bailiff ran to the rear of the room, opened the door, and hailed two security guards. The three, wielding nightsticks, herded the unruly couple out. As they were leaving, they continued yelling, "They'll always be ours! Ours! *Ours!*" Spectators craned their necks to see the disturbance. Woolsey pounded his gavel until order was restored.

When the room quieted down, the bailiff read the individual case numbers for each child and reviewed the technical details necessary for the hearing's legal record. Then the judge summed up the proceedings. "Twelve of the thirteen will go to foster homes. One boy, who has taken the name of Trumbo, will be permitted to join his biological father, who has demonstrated that he had no involvement with this criminal group."

The boy looked across the courtroom and saw the man he had met for the first time just a few days before. The man said to call him "Dad." He smelled of soap and aftershave and brought the boy candy and toys at Dr. Olivera's building. The boy was happy.

The judge and "Dad" talked for a bit, and kept looking

over at the boy. He straightened himself up. *Please pick me please don't leave me,* he thought. *If I cry then they'll leave me.* The talking went on forever; he could no longer hold back the tears.

"Dad" came to his side. "What's the matter, Trumbo?"

The boy stopped his sobbing. "You don't like me, do you?"

"I love you, Trumbo. Call me Dad. I'm going to take care of you from now on."

The judge laughed, and the man picked Trumbo up in his arms and gave him a big hug. "Things are going to be different from now on."

His face was scratchy, but the hug was soft. After signing some papers, the man, *Dad,* carried him out of the court-room, down the elevator and outside. On the street outside the courtroom, Magick Mimi and Red Ryder waited. The boy screamed. "No! No!"

The man whispered in his ear. "They can't hurt you anymore."

Magick Mimi and Red Ryder screamed at them as they walked to their car. "Traitors! Pigs! We'll find you! We'll find you!" Trumbo gripped Dad's chest tighter than ever and watched over his shoulder as the *bad people* disappeared from view. He hoped it would be the last time he ever saw them.

When they got into the station wagon, Trumbo smiled. "You're Daddy. You're *Daddy.* Aren't you?"

"Yes, I am. I really am."

Daddy reached over and fastened a seat belt across his tiny lap. He had never worn one before.

"This will keep you safe."

Trumbo laughed, and watched out the window as they drove away.

1

Corcoran, California
1994

THE THREAT POSED BY PRISONER NUMBER B33920 WAS APPARENT from the precautions taken to separate him from the outside world. Between his cell and free society were fourteen metal gates, three checkpoints, dogs, electric fences, razor wire, and three guard towers manned twenty-four hours a day by marksmen with standing instructions to "shoot to kill." A hundred yards of flat, vacant no-man's-land and an irrigation ditch that doubled as a moat separated the facility from the nearest road. Video cameras with motion detectors tracked every object that moved in the field; a dozen false alarms were sounded daily as the security cameras picked up large birds or cows that had wandered out of the pen. But each alert was taken seriously. No one had escaped in the prison's eleven-year history. Alive, that is.

It cost millions of dollars to put Prisoner B33920 behind bars, and a hundred thousand dollars a year to keep him there. So hated was he that he was kept in the Maximum Security Quad of the prison, in large measure so that other prisoners wouldn't kill him. Dozens had tried. This prisoner was a prize catch, a state treasure protected more securely than Fort Knox gold.

The object of these precautions sat rapt at the tiny steel table that served as a desk, scrawling onto an 8½-by-11 sheet of paper with a felt-tip pen. The guards kept the pen cap, which had enough metal to serve as a makeshift weapon. Prisoner B33920 wrote with fierce intensity, filling up every corner of the sheet with childlike letters and doodles. When he finished he hastily addressed an envelope and banged on the door that separated him from the corridor. It was made of half-inch-thick carbon steel mesh, the same material used to reinforce the president's bulletproof limousine. To compromise the door would require forty-five minutes and an acetylene torch.

He got no immediate response and shouted, "Guard!"

At the end of Hallway 8 of Maximum Security Sectional Housing Unit 3 of Corcoran State Prison, two correctional officers looked at each other. Neither wanted to fetch the letter. The older one squinted at the younger.

"Your turn."

Correctional Officer Paul Winston leisurely strolled past the other prisoners toward cell 22, trying not to make eye contact with the inmate who had summoned him. As Winston approached the prisoner, he sensed he was being stared at. He glanced up.

The prisoner's hair and beard had been clipped very short. He pressed his face into the steel mesh, distorting his face into a gargoylelike apparition. Winston tried to stare at the swastika on the bridge of the man's nose to avoid eye contact. But still, he found himself staring back at the slightly crossed eyes filled with a manic energy often described by hack journalists as "evil." An understatement. Prisoner B33920 cackled at Winston's startled expression.

"Scared ya, Paul?"

The guard looked away. No matter how many times he had seen Prisoner B33920 in the three weeks he'd worked in the Max SHU, the inmate had not lost his capacity to unsettle him. "What is it?" asked Winston, standing a safe distance away from the cell.

"'Nother letter, Paul."

"Let's have it."

Winston removed a half-inch carbon steel lock from the passage slot and slid the shallow drawer into the cell. Prisoner B33920 slipped the letter into the drawer. Winston hurriedly pulled the drawer back out, removed the letter, and replaced the lock.

"That's it?"

"Yep."

The prisoner mumbled something unintelligible.

"What'd you say?" demanded Winston.

"Nothing. I said nothing."

The guard walked toward the opposite end of the hallway, stopping halfway down to look back. The inmate still stared at him, as if placing a hex. He tittered when they made eye contact.

"Love ya, Paul. Mean it," quipped the lifer.

Winston turned around, shaken, and carried the letter to the end of the hall. Don, the older guard, waited.

"Don't let him get to you," said Don.

"He doesn't, Don."

"Oh, bullshit. You're panting like you just ran a marathon. Gimme that letter."

"I was going to take it to the censor."

"Yeah, let's us read it first. I'd like to know what the ol' nutcase is thinking about."

Don put on a pair of half reading glasses and held the letter at arm's length.

All around the border of the letter were doodles: three skewed smiling faces and crude imitations of corporate logos—Nike, Infiniti, and the NBC triangle.

J'osüf,

Got your letter. Your right about all is love and love is all. The time has come to use our true names and not the name that was given by the pig parent or the Man. Truth is still gonna be the same no matter what lies you try to create. You & them should just try to be what your meant to be and not that other. Since you asked I did your horoscope and it looks like the time is right for new things and forget the old. Expecially new things that expand on the old. Good to here that things is going so well. Yeah we do get M-Tv in the prison but I dont like it much cept the commercials like that one that says just do it with the niggers playin basketball, like that, just do it. Also like the video that goes a FACTS a FACT.

Send me more letters and stamps expecially the stamps.

peace

"Gibberish. Junk. Typical bullshit. He's found a new pen pal and is trying to freak him out."

"Yeah?"

"Yeah. He still gets tons of mail. Courts say we have to give it to him. Take it to be mailed."

The younger guard took the letter. As he started to walk away, he heard the prisoner yell at him. "You're reading my letter, Paul! I know you're reading my letter! I'm gonna tell your mother!"

Paul slammed the gate behind him and took the mail to the prison post office, shaken by the encounter with Charles Milles Manson.

J'osüf Sunn drove the orange Chrysler minivan up and down residential streets in Pasadena, looking for an appropriate place to *just do it.* Sunn was forty-two, with longish hair that was slightly out of fashion, and a deep tan. He wore a brightly colored vest over a western shirt, blue jeans, and boots. His face was rugged, with heavy lines accentuating angular features. His gray eyes were his most distinctive feature, bright and impassioned; it was nearly impossible to talk to him without being drawn in by those eyes, simultaneously inviting and threatening. He could have been mistaken for a cowboy or a camp counselor were it not for the large blue dot atop the bridge of his nose.

Sunn scrutinized the homes of the old rich. Built from stone and adobe, with large lawns tended by hired gardeners, they were rarely for sale even in the recession. The people in this neighborhood had no desire to leave it. The few homes for sale usually cost more than a million dollars apiece. This was a neighborhood where people felt above the day-to-day conflicts of ordinary life. Residents chose to live here because it was an oasis of safety, far removed from the dangers of Los Angeles. Sunn smiled. This was the perfect place to *just do it.* Jesus would have picked this place.

He parked the van in front of an old Episcopal church with a wide lawn, a spot where few people would notice its presence. Then he turned around and faced the seven silent girls sitting in the back of the van. None was older than twenty. They were pretty, white, and for the most part from well-off, troubled families. They had in common a love for J'osüf—he paid attention to them, he gave them love and listened to them and provided them with an identity, all the things that their backgrounds lacked. He gave them new names, their "true" names, divined by J'osüf as each girl moved into the Fellowship. He also slept with them, and the desire for his physical companionship was intensified by the competition. In a way, they were his harem.

Peace and Cleopatra were sisters from Seattle, the first to move in with Sunn six months earlier. Peace was seventeen, and her sister was sixteen. Both wore their jet-black hair long, and like all the girls, wove colorful ribbons through it. Princess, the Italian from San Diego, had moved in next; Panda and Fire after that; then Silhouette, the army major's daughter; and Thursday, the youngest girl in the fellowship, and somehow the saddest. Thursday's wealthy parents had gone through a terrible divorce, and before she ran away, she endured their legal threats, and knock-down, drag-out fights. All the girls wore plain, buttoned cotton dresses of muted blue, red, and orange.

Sunn leaned into the back of the van and ran his hands through Thursday's hair as he addressed the group. The girls hung on his every word. He spoke in a seductive, command-ing whisper.

"Panda has gotten us a stack of restaurant menus. That's going to be our alibi. If anyone asks you what you're doing, just tell them that you're distributing the menus. I expect that no one will ask."

He passed out the flyers, giving each girl fifty or a hundred of the photocopied flyers from a Mexican restaurant in Pasadena.

"This is a scavenger hunt, and there will be rewards, special rewards, for those who get the most prizes. I want you to divide up and put the flyers in people's doors. If no one is watching, you know what to do. Don't forget to look in potted plants, on top the doorframe, everywhere you can inspect without being seen.

"Meet back at the van when you've finished. I'll be waiting." He made eye contact with each girl, ascertaining their seriousness of purpose. Each girl blushed a little or opened her eyes wider when he looked at her. Their passion was part idol worship, part sexual desire.

He paused a few moments before he announced, still in whisper, "The game begins now."

The girls silently scattered in different directions. They went alone, except for Peace and Cleopatra: The sisters did everything together. The two had once been known as Anne and Patricia Clemens, but had done everything in their power to forget those names and embrace their new identities. They often finished one another's sentences and excitedly went about executing this new task as they ran down the quiet, peaceful suburban street.

"I'll put the flyers up there," said Peace.

"And I'll do the checking," said her younger sister.

"Right. Later we can switch."

They hiked to the end of the block and began walking up a wooded street.

Their first stop was a two-story brick home on the corner. Peace walked slowly to the porch and slipped a flyer through the screen door. Cleopatra lifted several decorative rocks around the country-style mailbox at the end of the driveway, then ran and caught up with her sister. She stood on tiptoe and ran her hand over the doorframe, then lifted the porch mat.

"Nothing?" asked Peace.

"Nope."

"Let's go to the next."

They continued working their way down one side of the street. On their fourteenth house, an oversized bungalow with a large front porch, Cleopatra yelped as she dug around in a garden next to the porch steps. "Looky here!"

She held up her prize. A house key, hidden in a fake plastic rock. "Not a very clever security system." She handed the key to her sister, who grinned.

Peace pulled a tiny pen from her bosom pocket and wrote down the address of the home on the back of one of the flyers. "Good work!"

They continued down the street, and made their way back. The two girls passed out flyers to fifty-five houses, and found three keys during their trek. As J'osüf had promised, it was remarkably easy: People were just too careless about their homes.

Hand in hand, the two happily ran back to the van, thrilled at their success in scavenging.

J'osüf sat lotus-style in the back of the van. The two leaned their heads in the window, hungry for his approval.

He stared at the ground for an uncomfortably long time before acknowledging their presence. "Yes?" he asked.

"We did real good, J'osüf," said Peace.

"Let me see."

"Three! We found three keys. Isn't that good?" said Cleopatra, breathless with excitement.

"That is good. Let me have them."

Peace handed him the three keys, and the flyer listing the addresses.

"Fine work, fine work. You may win. We must wait for the other girls to see how you did." He ran his hand lasciviously through Peace's hair. Cleopatra bristled with jealousy.

One by one, the other girls returned to the van. Most had only one or two keys, but J'osüf was nonetheless pleased. Each key was wrapped up in a piece of paper with its address written on the outside. J'osüf set the keys on a plastic drink holder in the front of the van. Finally everyone had returned except Thursday, the youngest girl. Five minutes passed, then ten. J'osüf noticed a man across the street staring out a front window at them, and he ordered the girls to sit in the hot vehicle with the door closed. Finally Thursday came back, tears running down her face.

Sunn leaped out of the van and ran down the street to meet her.

"What is it, honey, what happened?" he asked as he embraced her.

"I din't do too well. I'm sorry, I'm sorry, it's my fault, I tried."

"What's the problem?" he asked.

"I only got five. I did all those houses and I only got five keys. I'm sorry. I'll keep going if you want me to."

Sunn smiled broadly and lifted her off the ground. "You did terrific, Thursday."

She wiped her eyes dry. "You really mean it?"

"I really mean it. Let's go home. You can sit in the front of the van."

Her back straightened up. It was as if a weight were lifted from her shoulders. "Wow. Cool."

She hopped into the front seat next to J'osüf, and they pulled away from the curb.

"Why did you think five wasn't enough?"

"Well, I don't know, I just thought that maybe some of the others were getting keys everywhere. I guess it's because of how it used to be."

"I'm not like your consensus-reality parents," he said as they drove away. "We love you, Thursday. Everybody!"

The girls in the back of the van clapped their hands. "We love you, Thursday!"

A tear ran down her cheek. "It really is special being here with you, J'osüf. Everything's so much better."

J'osüf handed her some tissues and then held her hand again. He drove the van down the Pasadena Freeway, back to the place they called home. He ran his fingers gently through her hair, calming her. "It's okay, they're consensus-reality pigs, and you don't have to ever see them again. Their actions were unforgivable. But since you got the most keys, you'll get something very special tonight."

"What?"

"Wait and see. You'll be very happy about it."

They pulled off of the freeway and drove beneath an underpass into a gravel lot where they lived. Five Victorian homes were randomly scattered on the lot like an abandoned collection of dollhouses. The homes had graced a street near downtown Los Angeles until a real estate developer bought the neighborhood to build apartment buildings. A slow-growth citizens group protested the destruction of the homes, and a compromise had been struck: The developer would store the beautiful buildings until a new spot could be found. The homes had been languishing under a freeway overpass ever since, waiting for new sites that would probably never come. None of the houses had water or electricity; they were just shells.

The girls piled out of the van. Princess closed the razor-wire gate behind them. They headed for a three-story green-

and-white house, the biggest in the complex. They reconvened in the kitchen.

Sunn stood at the front of the room, near the only window that wasn't boarded up. A few couches and beds were scattered about in the large shell of a room, and the girls seated themselves in ones and twos.

Sunn closed his eyes momentarily, waiting till the entire room was silent. Quietly he said, "Food?" He opened his eyes and looked from girl to girl, waiting for a response.

Scowls fitted themselves onto all the young people's faces.

"Someone has to get it. It's about that time of day for Ralph's Market to update their produce. Any Dumpster-divers?"

"I'll go," said Fire, a brown-haired girl. Princess quickly volunteered, too.

"Good. Fire and Princess, take Panda with you. See if you can get more green vegetables this time. Any trouble from the manager?"

"Well, he's pretty much on to us. Seen us twice," said Fire.

"So tell me something I don't know." Sunn scowled. "Did you do what I told you to do?"

Princess, the redhead, giggled. "Wear a real loose dress with nothing underneath?"

"That's right. If he catches you in the Dumpster—"

"Let the dress slip a little. I already did that a couple days ago and he just stood around and chatted with us, staring at my tits like he'd been banged with a board. He used to be real hard on us, but now he talks all about compassion for the homeless and junk like that with his tongue hanging down to his toes."

"Good, good. You gotta make the system work for you. Get going now."

"Sure."

The three girls stood up and headed for the door, giggling.

"Hold it a second. Panda?"

"Yes?" A slightly chubby girl with short, flapper-style hair, Panda faced him and blushed.

"Turn around."

She slowly revolved, holding her hands uncomfortably above her head, until she was facing Sunn again.

"What'd I just tell Princess?"

"I don't know, go get some food?"

"What *else* did I tell her?"

"Um, get some greens."

"What's under your dress?"

"Eh, panties."

"Leave them behind."

Embarrassed, the girl reached under her dress and quickly pulled off the underwear, then threw them on the floor. She pulled the dress down quickly.

"I'm sorry," she said. "I was just a little shy."

"You'll remember in the future to listen to what I say."

"I'm sorry."

Sunn walked over to the girl, wrapped his arms around her, and whispered in her ear. "It's okay. I know you feel uncomfortable. You just have to get over it. It's for a good cause. I wouldn't ask you if it weren't for the good of everyone. If the grocer's perversity gets us food, then we have to do what we have to do. You're a special girl, Panda." He kissed her neck, and she smiled. "Now, have a good time." He kissed her on the lips long and slow, then pulled away.

She hung her head down low, and with the two other girls, went out the door. Sunn smiled and thought: *Hot and cold, red-light green-light, that's what keeps them in line. Can't let one girl ruin it for the whole bunch.*

The girls returned several hours later, and Sunn supervised the preparation of a "feast" made up from the cast-off food thrown in a grocery Dumpster. Princess cooked pasta over a fire in an oil drum fueled by discarded construction wood. Two others made a salad. They even had a fancy cake from a bakery's trash bin. Without electricity, the fire provided the only light. Even though they were in the middle of the city, it was like camping out every night.

After they ate, the girls grew quiet and reflective, lying back on blankets spread out around the fire. The stars were bright. Even the heavens seemed peaceful. The only disturbance was the roar of the freeway less than fifty yards away.

Thursday watched J'osüf move from blanket to blanket,

talking so quietly that she couldn't hear the conversation. He carried a knapsack and spent five or ten minutes with each girl, paying attention to her, doling out affection. Thursday could see that he was popping something in each of their mouths. He also gave them little packages. Jealousy welled up within her as he visited all six of the other girls before coming to her. She was almost in tears when he arrived.

"What's the matter?" he asked, sitting next to her.

"Nothing. Nothing at all. I just wonder why I am always last."

Sunn stroked her hair. "Thursday, I came to you last because you will get the most special thing of all. Here, eat this."

He gave her a little scrap of yellow cardboard about a half inch square; printed on it was a bright yellow happy face.

"What is it?"

"It's X. We have a very special task tonight."

She slipped the cardboard into her mouth and chewed on it. It reminded her of eating paper in kindergarten. "Should I swallow it?"

"Yes. Swallow it. It won't hurt you. It will help you see better.

"Tonight we're going to even the score with the consensus-reality people. We're going to *just do it*. I want you to think long and hard about your con-reality parents, about the hardships you've endured, and about how much we all mean to you."

"Okay." She looked up at him.

"I got an important letter today. It's time to just do it. If you're not ready, we're in trouble. Do you think you can stick by us, through thick and thin?"

"I guess so."

"It has to be yes."

"Yes."

"Okay. I'm going to give you a gift now. But I don't want you to open it until we're in the van later tonight. Now, change into those black clothes we got from a Laundromat, but also bring the clothes you're wearing."

"What are we going to do?"

"You ask too many questions for one so young. Just wait. I'm sure you'll be happy."

He handed her something wrapped in butcher paper. It was so heavy, she initially dropped it, ripping some of the paper on the ground. Something shiny and silver showed through where the paper had ripped.

"What is it?"

"You'll know later. Just hold on to it. This will be your friend."

Sunn kissed her on the back of the neck, then disappeared into the house. Thursday played curiously with the unusual package. When she thought no one was looking, she peeled back a little of the paper and examined what was inside. It was a long, sharp hunting knife. She gasped and covered it back up.

Milt Carling hadn't planned to have his girlfriend, Sandra, with him that night when he signed the divorce papers. It was a fluke of circumstance that she gave him a lift out to his old house. His Jaguar was in the shop again with electrical problems, so Sandra had agreed to give him a ride. Sandra would drop him off, go see a movie, and pick him up afterwards. But as usual, things got screwed up.

A dental surgeon, Milt had five dentists working under him. His practice was worth $2.4 million, according to the divorce lawyers. In the year since his separation from his wife, Milt had lost twenty-two pounds. He'd gotten a hair weave from the Hair Club for Men. And he'd exchanged his old suits for clothing he considered more "with it": black shirts, usually open to show his Zuni Indian jewelry, baggy pants, and cowboy boots. He was forty-one, but he tried to convince himself he was only as old as he felt.

He didn't want to fuss around with his weepy ex-wife, Pam. He just wanted to go in, sign the divorce papers, and be on his way. His girlfriend, Sandra—a raven-haired beauty who favored tight dresses and was fourteen years his junior—dropped him off at the top of the long driveway. She started to pull away when Milt signaled her to wait.

He walked to the front door and rang the bell. There was no answer. He checked over the doorframe to see if Pam had left the key as promised, but all he got from the doorframe was a splinter. He walked back to Sandra, waiting in the blue Miata he'd given her. She had cranked the stereo up high and was gnawing gum. He stared at her breasts as he spoke to her.

"Eh, Sandra, my ex forgot to leave the key."

"The cunt!" said Sandra, giggling.

"Give me the car phone. I'm not going to wait all night for her to come back."

He dialed Pam's so-called fashion consulting firm. *The money-losing vanity business I paid for,* he thought.

"Pam?"

"Milt?" she said.

"Yeah. You forgot to leave me a key!"

He heard sniffling from the other side of the phone. "I'm sorry. I've just been so upset about everything that I probably forgot. Wait a second." He heard her sob, then blow her nose. *Get on with it, you cow,* he thought. She continued. "It's my fault. I'm terribly sorry. It wasn't on the doorframe?"

"No, it wasn't," he said shortly.

"You don't have to be angry. It was a mistake. I'm almost finished up down here." Her office was twenty-five miles away, in Santa Monica. "I'll get on the road in just a few minutes. I should be there in an hour."

"And what am I supposed to do until then? Just sit out here in Pasadena? I've got things to do."

"There's another key I left for the gardener, in the birdhouse, the blue one . . . that you gave me on our eleventh anniversary . . ."

"I'm deeply moved," he said as cynically as he could muster. "Get out here fast, okay?"

Pam began a new round of crying. Milt held the phone away from his ear and rolled his eyes for the benefit of Sandra, who made "blah blah blah" motions with her mouth.

"I was hoping we could just talk a little, try to figure out what went wrong, what lessons we can learn. I feel so terrible about it all, I just don't know what to say." She wailed, *"I can't believe tonight it'll all be over!"*

"Look, did your lawyer put you up to this sob session? We had our crying time, we did everything, and now, babe, it's over. Deal with it. Just get out here as fast as you can, okay?"

"You son of a bitch!" Pam screamed, then slammed down her phone.

Milt adjusted his hair in an attempt to cover up the bald spot, then leaned down to Sandra. "The ice queen will be late, as usual, so it's going to be a while. You want to wait here or wait someplace else?"

Sandra cooed. "I always wanted to see the inside of your house. I guess this is my last chance. Do you think we could get in?"

"Sure."

She climbed out of the car, and Milt stared as she pulled the short dress down over her ass.

He quickly found the birdhouse key, then took Sandra on a tour of the house. He showed her the entertainment room he'd built in the basement, his workroom, the bedroom where he and his wife had slept side by side for eleven years. When they reached the den, he noticed that all of his hunting trophies had been removed. Panicked, he walked out to the garage. The four-point buck he'd bagged in '88 lay on the floor, dirty and abandoned.

"The goddamn nerve!" he yelled.

"What's the matter, pucker-puss?" cooed his squeeze.

"Nothing. Nothing at all." He slammed the garage door. "Let's go drink up my expensive liquor before she gets home. I cannot believe the nerve of some people."

He cracked open a bottle of single-malt Scotch and poured two doubles. Soon after, he poured two more. It had been ninety minutes since Pam had promised to come home. Sandra was getting bored.

"Can I sit on your lap, pucker-puss?" she asked.

He secretly hoped that Pam would walk in on him with this—this *fabulous babe*—on his lap. "Sure, honey." They started making out in earnest. *God, it's good,* he thought. *I'm not going to miss a thing.*

Around nine-thirty he heard the front door open. The Scotch was surging through his veins. He wanted to hurt Pam one more time before signing the divorce papers. He ignored the sound and stayed put, with his hand up Sandra's dress.

Footsteps approached. It sounded like she'd brought someone with her. He heard a man's voice. *The cunt brought her lawyer!*

"Sandra dear?" he whispered. "I think she's here. I'm going to go out. There might be some arguing, so if you want to leave, feel free."

"I love to see you arguing, Milt. It kind of, you know, kind of turns me on."

"Then by all means stick around." He winked.

Milt walked from the study into the hall.

He did not find Pam, or her lawyer, or any of her friends. Instead, he saw J'osüf Sunn and his seven teenaged devotees, standing in a semicircle in the foyer. They were dressed in black from head to toe. Their faces had been blackened. Milt didn't know what to make of them.

"Excuse me?" asked Milt. "Are you friends of Pam's or something?"

They just stared at him silently until Sunn spoke. His voice was strange, and he seemed to be mocking Milt. "Are we friends of Pam's?" He laughed. "Yes, we're friends of Pam's. Isn't that right? We're friends of Pam's!" he yelled.

The girls began imitating him. "Oh yes, we're her very best friends," said one with long, red hair. "Pam, we love her very, very much. My very closest, oldest friend!" They laughed harder.

Sunn stepped closer to Milt, who backed away. "What is this?" he asked.

Sunn moved uncomfortably close to the dentist, then struck out and grabbed Milt's earlobe and dragged Milt's head closer to his own face. Sunn licked Milt's neck, then yelled at the top of his lungs, "Down on the floor, pig!" He pushed Milt down violently.

Milt slammed to the ground. His Zuni pin flew across the room as the gold chain broke. He got to his knees. "Who are you?"

Sunn kicked Milt in the shoulder, sending him back onto the floor. "Who am I? Who are you to ask, rich pig? I said stay down on the floor." Sunn jammed his boot against Milt's head.

Sandra leaned out of the den and screamed when she saw what was happening.

"Get her," Sunn said calmly.

Three girls ran into the den and dragged Sandra into the foyer, then threw her down on the ground a few feet from Milt.

"Tie them. Fast, girls, fast!"

When Milt struggled to move, Sunn pressed his boot down harder on Milt's head. Milt felt nylon rope being fastened around his wrists. Hands spun him around. He could see two girls hog-tying Sandra, fastening her legs and arms behind her back. The end of the rope extended to the base of the staircase.

"Let me go," said Milt. "You can keep her, but let me go," asked Milt.

"Shut up, pig!" said Sunn. He kicked Milt in the jaw, destroying over two thousand dollars' worth of bridgework. Spitty blood dripped from his mouth. They moved him, hog-tying him across the foyer from his girlfriend. He was fastened to the baby grand piano he'd bought when he made his first million dollars.

"Please don't hurt me. If you want to rob this house, go ahead, I don't give a damn."

A red-haired girl, finishing the final touches on Milt's binding, laughed. "We're not robbers. We're not thieves. You consensus-reality pigs have no imagination. Just shut up and die."

Milt looked up and saw that she held a large hunting knife.

"No, please, don't, please!" he yelled.

"Shut up, pig," said the girl. She violently cut a piece of his shirt with the knife and stuffed it in his mouth, reducing his cries to grunts. "If I wanted you to talk, I would have asked you."

He continued grunting. "I'll cut your throat out if you keep it up!" she warned. She placed the tip of the knife against his trachea, then dragged it down, leaving a rivulet of blood where she had broken the surface. When he continued to struggle, she sat on his chest and placed the knifepoint against his right eyelid.

Sunn walked over to their side. "Nice job, Fire." He

yelled back to the front of the hall. "Thursday, come here. I need you."

The thin, young girl walked to his side. He put his arm around her waist.

"Who does this look like?" he asked.

"It looks like a pig to me!" she said, grinning.

"What pig does it remind you of most?"

"My consensus-reality father."

"I thought so. You want to do the honors?" he asked. Sunn took the hunting knife away from Fire and handed it to Thursday.

"How do I do it?"

"I'm not the man to tell you what to do."

Thursday took the knife from him, and while Fire and Sunn held the man down, she dragged its point across Milt's chest: once, twice, three times. They were teasing motions, each time a little deeper, and each time the pig squirmed even more. Then she plunged it straight in. It was harder to push in than she had thought. She looked to Sunn for approval. He nodded. She pulled the knife out, and blood began spurting from an artery. She pushed it in again and again until his chest stopped moving.

Then the three walked to the other side of the foyer, where the young woman in the tight dress lay facedown. "Your turn now!" said Sunn. Sandra screamed.

Pamela Carling didn't want her *asshole husband* to see her with tears in her eyes. She sat on a corner two blocks away from her house composing herself, wiping the tears from her face and putting on makeup. She took time to make up her eyes, then sprayed on some Poison—Milt's favorite perfume—before driving the rest of the way home.

She was surprised to see a Miata and an orange van parked in the driveway. *That prick brought his lawyer,* she thought. She parked across the bottom of the driveway, blocking both vehicles, then opened the garage door with the remote control.

On her way through the garage, she kicked the deer head one last time, then hurried into the house. *If he's stealing from me, I want to catch him red-handed.*

The house was eerily quiet. "Milt!" She heard the sound of people moving around upstairs. *I knew it! They're after my jewelry!*

She ran toward the main staircase, then as she passed the grand piano, she slipped on something wet and fell backwards, breaking her fall with her hand. *What the hell?* The floor was coated with something thick and gooey. She looked to her right and saw Milt's corpse, cut open like a slaughtered animal on the road. His eyes were open, imploring.

"Oh my God, oh Jesus, Milt!"

She scrambled to stand upright but slipped again. On her knees, she gasped when she recognized the substance on the floor as her husband's blood. She peeled off her blood-drenched pumps and hurled them away. *Got to get out, got to get out.*

A man's voice boomed from upstairs. "Who's here?"

Pam crawled on her hands and knees toward the closet, opened it, sat atop some old boots, and pulled the door closed behind.

A girl's voice cried out. "We see your shoes, whoever you are. Come out, come out, come out and play-ay!"

Another girl's voice yelled, "Ollie-ollie-all-come-free! You can't hide forever! Where-air-air-*are* you?"

Footsteps rushed past the closet. There were several people. Pam sucked down air as if she'd just run up ten flights of stairs. She tried to stifle the sound of her own breath by placing a hand over her mouth. She could not imagine what might have happened. Then she heard singing, to the tune of "Kum Ba Yah."

> "Time to die, pig, time to die!
> Time to die pig, time to die!
> You can't hide, pig, you can't hide.
> Time to die, pig, time to die."

Pam held a hand over her mouth to muffle her sobbing. Through the crack in the closet door she could see three girls in her living room. They tipped the couch forward; then threw a lamp down on the ground and laughed as it shattered. They approached her hiding place, still singing.

They opened the door.

The girls looked young enough to be in high school. They smiled sweetly when they saw her. The taller one reached down and grabbed her hand.

"Hello, piggy."

The heat of the summer had badly decomposed the three bodies by the time they were found by Pam's sister eleven days later. If it hadn't been for the divorce, a housemaid would have found them much sooner, but on the advice of her lawyer, Pam had laid off the maid during the divorce proceedings. That same attorney assumed she had simply gotten cold feet about the settlement, and put that down as the reason she didn't return calls. As for Milt, he had a habit of running off on "dirty vacations" with his girlfriends. That was what his co-workers assumed when he disappeared.

After an investigation in which they interviewed forty-four witnesses, including the divorce attorneys, co-workers, neighbors, and relatives of the victims, the homicide team assigned to the murder had a reasonable explanation for everything that had happened that night. Their decision was that an argument about the divorce had escalated, and Pam Carling killed her husband and his girlfriend, then herself.

The multiple stab wounds seemed to contradict this theory, but even the coroner admitted that in a rage, especially of the sort that often accompanies an ugly divorce, people can do remarkable things. On the walls were words written in Milt' Carling's blood, which only briefly puzzled the homicide detectives. It either said "Skeeter" or "Skelter" and then "Love Is Slavery." Two witnesses thought they remembered Pam calling Milt terrible names, and thought it was possible she might have called him "skeeter." "Love is Slavery," said the report, was an obvious reference to the divorce. No further inquiries were made.

2

THE EXQUISITE COMBINATION OF EARTHQUAKE-RELATED ROAD closures and torrential rains that spring created a windfall for Trumbo Walsh. His living consisted of arriving at car wrecks before anyone else and yanking the twisted metal out of traffic and to a police garage. Walsh usually drove his truck twelve hours a day or more, trolling the drug- and gang-infested eastern part of Hollywood for customers who had no choice but to pay the city-mandated tow fee. Like most other drivers, Walsh worked for himself, not the city. He profited from rules that allowed maverick trucks to keep the streets clear.

The six-foot-five-inch, muscular twenty-eight-year-old kept his thick, dark hair out of his eyes beneath a baseball cap. Although he didn't play poker, he had the perfect poker face: steady, unflinching brown eyes above an unsmiling mouth, and a square-shouldered posture that rarely betrayed his emotions. His stoicism was often mistaken for indifference, but was in fact a product of his deep concentration. Walsh was always one move ahead while driving. He read the traffic like a river guide, anticipating problems before they happened.

The trick was to get there first. Walsh was only one of hundreds of gypsy tow drivers, wild asses who would drive the wrong way up one-way streets, across sidewalks or backwards and up highway exits to get to a wreck first. The rules were simple and draconian: The first driver there, however the hell he got there, got ninety-four bucks. Numbers two, three, and four get zilch. Fortunately, most of the drivers preferred safer parts of town like yuppie West L.A. or the bedroom communities of the San Fernando Valley. However, those who worked in Rampart district were the most aggressive sons of bitches in the world. Like Trumbo.

On an ordinary day, Trumbo considered the other tow drivers his competition, almost the enemy. But the rains had created such a bumper harvest of wrecks that a tenuous camaraderie had developed among the drivers. Walsh was racking up four, five, six tows a day; he was well on his way to paying off the truck. No one in L.A. knew how to drive in the rain, and no one had decent windshield wipers. The oil on the streets turned soapy-smooth, and all the usual traffic rules of engagement became irrelevant. *Bang!* Chevy runs a red light, hits a Hyundai and a Toyota. Three wrecks, three tow gypsies make ninety-four bucks each. *Bang!* Guy comes off a ramp too fast, spins his Porsche into oncoming traffic. Maybe four, five tows. In short, it was the high season, the good life.

In spite of the traffic and gore, Trumbo found the life of a gypsy tow driver extremely satisfying. Before he arrived at any site, cars would be backed up for miles behind some accident or other. Afterwards, thanks to Trumbo's efforts, a tragedy was cleared away and life resumed its normal pace. There was secret honor in his work, nobler *because* it was never celebrated. Unlike firemen or policemen or ambulance drivers, no one ever gave awards to tow truck drivers, yet they kept the city from falling apart.

It was the first Friday of spring break when Walsh heard the news that started his life on its downward spiral. He wasn't on vacation himself—he'd been out of school for almost a decade. On this day, the usual heavy traffic of a Friday, plus rain, plus drunken college students leaving town, created an especially lucrative, accident-rich day.

He heard the news while standing in front of Tommy's Burgers, a favorite hangout for college students. The occasion was a three-car pileup nearby on Beverly. Walsh waited in the rain for the paramedics to drag a bloodied Mexican family from a station wagon that had encountered a BMW full of SC students head-on, so that he could tow the metal away and collect his fee. Lt. Petey Mazer, a Rampart division motorcycle cop, took him aside. Mazer was a cool guy, for a cop. Nearly the same age, Mazer and Trumbo worked the same neighborhood and often wound up at the same accidents. Sometimes after a long night they'd share a couple beers at the Smog Cutter on Hillhurst and talk about how the city was going to hell. The city was always going to hell.

Mazer wore a police-issue poncho and a special plastic wrapping for his helmet. Walsh just did the best he could with an old blue raincoat marked 1984 OLYMPICS and a Dodgers baseball hat, both of which were saturated through to his skin.

"Walsh, come here," said Mazer.

Walsh squinted suspiciously at the cop. "Petey, Huger's gonna try to jump the line and get *my* tow." He pointed to a competing tow driver hungrily eyeing the pileup. Trumbo didn't want to drift too far from the scene. Drivers sometimes got into fistfights over a twisted pile of steel.

"Cool out, Trumbo, it's going to be a few minutes. They have to pull eight people out of that car, and besides, I'll back you up that you were here first. Look, I heard someone talking to one of the dispatchers."

"Yeah?"

"Your dad's up in the state hospital in Pacoima, right?"

"Dispatchers tell you that? I told you about him months ago," said Walsh, slightly embarrassed to be reminded of his mentally ill father. He smirked and tried to make a joke out of it. "It's his biggest achievement, losing his mind. I try to tell as many people as I can."

In spite of his glibness, Walsh's heart sank when he thought of his father, who had once been tough, independent-minded, and above all, reliable. After the OD, Luther Walsh became a shadow of his former self. Trumbo felt the loss deeply. There were few people who understood the troubles Trumbo endured as well as his father did.

"You're cold, Walsh," said Mazer. "Listen: That hospital just asked downtown for some backup. There's been a riot out there."

"I was nowhere near the place."

"A couple patients got killed."

"There's five hundred something patients. You think my dad got hurt?" he asked rhetorically. "He knows how to take care of himself, let me tell you."

Mazer threw up his hands. "I just thought you might want

to know. I thought maybe you'd want to call and see if he's okay. I thought you might have human feelings."

"Tear my heart out, Petey." Walsh adjusted his hat to block the rain. "I'll call. I do care about the old fart. You keep an eye on Huger, right?"

"No problem."

Walsh found a pay phone outside the graffiti-covered men's room and dialed the California State Mental Hospital at Pacoima. He identified himself to the woman answering and gave his father's name, Luther Walsh. Eventually Trumbo was connected with the public relations director for the hospital, a shrill Brooklyn transplant who sounded like she was speaking through a kazoo. She waffled when Trumbo asked the direct question: Is my father okay?

After a long hesitation, she said, "We cannot give out that information right now."

"Look, either he's fine or he isn't."

"You might want to come in."

"It's raining and traffic is for shit. I'm working and don't want to drive to Pacoima just to see that my dad's zoned out on painkillers as usual. Why can't you tell me?"

"I'm not allowed to give further patient information via the telephone. Thank you very much."

"Hello? Hello!"

Trumbo stared at the receiver in disbelief.

He found Mazer by the side of the road, trying to measure skid marks that were rapidly disappearing in the rain.

"Petey . . ." Trumbo noticed other police around. "Uh, Lieutenant Mazer, may I ask you a question?"

The cop rolled up his tape measure and stepped onto the sidewalk.

"Petey, the assholes up at Pacoima won't tell me anything. Can you call in and find out the names of the people who got killed?"

"Yeah, come over here."

Mazer hooked a wire from his helmet into the police radio on the motorcycle and asked the questions, translated into cop-speak for the dispatcher. He held up his index finger.

"Just a sec. Dispatcher's gotta look it up." Then Mazer nodded a few times, listening to the reply. "It'll be a couple more minutes."

Trumbo glanced over his shoulder through the rain at the accident site. The paramedics were loading and rolling away. Trumbo whirled around just in time to see Huger from Echo Park Tow Co. backing his truck up to the station wagon. Walsh ran across the rainy street.

"Huger! You jerk! That's my steel!"

The driver leaned out the window. "You snooze, you lose, Trumbo! See you next time, sucker!"

Trumbo raised his middle finger at the driver, but didn't consider the loss of one tow fee worth holding a grudge over. He would have done the same to Huger, and had many times.

Petey waved at Trumbo from across the street, gesturing him over.

Trumbo soaked his left foot in a deceptively deep puddle, dodging traffic as he jaywalked across Beverly. He lifted his arms in the air when he was in earshot of Mazer. "Did you see what that asshole did? He got the Mexican's station wagon! *My* station wagon!"

"Forget about it, Trumbo." Mazer looked over his shoulder, as if for help, before turning to Walsh. "Your dad is Luther Walsh?"

"Yeah."

Mazer shifted his weight uncomfortably on his feet. "I don't know how to tell you this."

"Just say the words, Petey."

"Your father's dead."

"What do you mean? If you're bullshitting me, I'll kick your ass across the parking lot even if you are a cop."

Mazer just shook his head. "I'm not kidding. Some patients got out of hand. There was some kind of incident and three patients and one orderly are dead. Your dad was one of them."

"You're serious." Walsh backed away from the cop, letting the words sink in. He lowered his arms to his sides and stood perfectly still, the rain washing over the bill of his hat and dripping down his face. He stared at his feet. All the noise of the street faded away. He simply could not believe this. His father had gotten away from more dangerous situations dozens of times during Trumbo's peripatetic youth. Luther

Walsh was there during student riots in Berkeley. He had extricated himself safely from tangles with rednecks in the Midwest, gangs in Chicago, muggers everywhere, dealers in Atlanta, a psychotic landlord in Phoenix, and any number of fistfights. In spite of it all, Luther had never lost his dignity. Trumbo was saddened that his father should die in an uproar at some loony bin, rather than out in the world, fighting the good fight.

Mazer approached cautiously. "You okay, Trumbo? I thought you'd want to know. Look, you want me to go with you? Wanna talk?"

"Yeah, I'm okay. I just can't believe it."

"You want a ride in an LAPD car up to Pacoima?"

"No. I can manage. I'll deal with it. I'll deal with it!"

He spun the back wheels of his truck as he sped from the parking lot. It took almost two hours driving through a nasty thunderstorm and past panicky drivers to get out to Pacoima, a trip that on a good day might take twenty minutes. When he arrived, Walsh felt as if he were watching himself from outside. He walked past the police tape and riot cops outside the hospital, past the workers boarding up the broken windows at the reception area, into the waiting room, where he found a plump woman wearing a CRISIS INTERVENTION COUNSELOR ribbon attached to her hospital name tag, Dr. Deborah Thorne. She looked more like a banker than a psychiatrist and wore a pressed blue business suit with a bright red scarf instead of a necktie.

In a drab room with a couch and overstuffed chair, normally used for psychotherapy but today handed over to the more pressing needs of the inmate riot, Thorne explained what had happened to Trumbo's father. His throat had been slit by another patient. In measured, unemotional tones she told of the incidents leading up to his death. That afternoon an argument between a nut and a shrink (Thorne said "client" and "facility employee") over the shortage of coffee and cigarettes escalated into a violent melee over the general conditions of the hospital. Hostages were taken, and at one point the rebellious patients had controlled the entire fifth floor of the hospital.

Sometime in between the coffee shortage and the arrival

of the riot police, three people were killed. Thorne refused to elaborate because of an "ongoing investigation into the causes of the irregularities."

Trumbo cut her off. "So that's it? The lunatics take over the asylum and you throw up your hands and say, 'We don't know how your dad got killed'?"

His question barely registered on her face. "I can understand that you are very upset. Traumatic incidents like this can be hard to come to interpret even for the best-adjusted people."

"Knock off the shrink-speak, okay? I'm not one of your patients. You're right I'm pissed off, and it's you people who I'm pissed off at."

"You are being belligerent, Mr. Walsh."

Trumbo rolled his eyes. "No duh, sister. I don't need to be crisis-counseled or whatever you call it. Just show me where to sign and tell me how I can get my father and whatever stuff he had in his padded cell."

Thorne escorted him from the room.

Walsh spent several hours arguing with a long parade of hospital officials: his father's attending psychiatrist, the head of hospital security, the orderly who had gathered his father's possessions into a cardboard carton. There were several notebooks filled with drawings, eleven paperback books, a photo of Trumbo, a California ID card, five bags of Cheetos, and the portable CD player Trumbo had given him the previous Father's Day. He had only four CDs: the *Complete Led Zeppelin* set that Trumbo had given him. Not a lot to show for fifty-one years.

Trumbo didn't have a funeral for his father; Luther always called organized religion "the big scam," and even before the overdose that landed him in the hospital, Luther didn't have enough friends to warrant a big service. His co-workers at the commercial metal shop where he'd worked for three years—the longest he'd ever had a job—were assholes in Trumbo's opinion. Only one, the shift supervisor, ever came to visit him, once, the first week Luther checked in. There were no relatives to invite, at least none Trumbo knew about. All Trumbo knew about his own mother was what Luther told him: She was a very nice woman, and she died in a car crash when Trumbo was two. His parents never married. Luther never even showed him her photo.

The cremation cost more than eighteen hundred dollars; or, in Trumbo's accounting, five and a half payments on the truck. He picked up the ashes from Forest Lawn, packed into an urn and wrapped up in a fancy box as if it were a delivery of flowers or books. As he drove home he remembered a long-forgotten episode in his life.

Trumbo was in the third grade. He and his dad lived near Atlanta, Georgia. He had just come home from school to the rented house where they had lived almost a year. That night was the first baseball game in the Little League, the only time he'd been on a sports team. His father was packing up the station wagon once again. Trumbo went into the house. Things were scattered from one end to the other—drawers dumped out on the floor, coffee and flour spread all over the kitchen, the couch slashed with blades.

Trumbo went outside to the driveway and asked his father, "What happened?"

"They found us."

"Who found us?"

"Guys you don't want to know about. The bad guys." His father's tone was calm and casual, as if such a tumultuous event were an everyday occurrence.

"So what do we do?" little Trumbo asked.

"We have to move on. Just for a little while."

"Oh."

They had the station wagon almost ready to go when another car pulled into the driveway. It was his friend Steve's father, Trumbo's ride to Little League. Steve's father got out of the car, a puzzled look on his face. He was a potbellied guy with a big smile, and Trumbo and his teammates called him Coach Bear.

"Trumbo! You're supposed to be playing tonight. What's going on? Taking an early vacation?"

"Oh no, we're moving."

Luther cut in at that point, taking the Little League father aside. The two men argued. Trumbo went to the car and chatted with Steve, keeping an eye on his father. Then Steve and Coach Bear left.

Trumbo and his father finished packing up the station wagon. The route out of town took them past the park where the game was held. As the sun set over Atlanta and the park lights came on, Trumbo could see his team across the flat plateau of grass, playing the game. They wore brand-new team uniforms marked HOUSE OF PANCAKES TIGERS. *Steve was laughing and having a good time, or so Trumbo thought from the distance. As they drove away he turned his head and watched until the field lights disappeared over the horizon, then cried silently. That night the seven-year-old Trumbo realized he wasn't like other kids. He understood that he wasn't meant to be part of any team. He buried those longings deep within himself.*

Trumbo had no comparison by which to gauge his unusual childhood. In spite of the hardship, he had one advantage over children from more stable backgrounds: an especially deep bond with his father, something "regular" children didn't seem to enjoy. Other kids saw their fathers on evenings, or weekends, or for children of divorce, not at all. Through the darkest times, Trumbo always knew his dad would come through for him, look out for him, take care of him. And Luther taught Trumbo that nothing is a gift. You only get what you fight for.

A few weeks after he picked up the ashes, the urn still languished on the passenger seat of his truck. The rains had ended and business was again slow and cutthroat. It was only now Trumbo began to sense his loss. The old man had his problems, but he was the only family Trumbo had. Trumbo began to notice the families all around him. He felt like he couldn't turn on the television in his tiny apartment without seeing the Cosbys or the Brady Bunch or some other perfect happy family.

He was in a melancholy funk when he got the call from Hollywood National Bank. It was Ms. Barber, vice president of something or other, calling about a safety-deposit box at the bank.

"A woman identifying herself as your father's wife has contacted us and asked permission to claim the contents of the decedent's vault enclosure, but our records show only one next of kin listed. That would be you."

"My father didn't have a wife. Or at least if he did, I never knew about it."

"That is why the bank contacted you. The claimant was unable to produce positive identification.

"Why?"

"To recover the contents of the safety-deposit box belonging to the decedent."

"What's a decedent?"

"That would be your father, who, according to our records, passed away March twenty-fourth."

"Back up. My father, Luther Walsh, had a safety-deposit box?"

"That is correct, sir."

"What's in it?"

"The bank does not inspect the boxes."

"So whose box is it now?"

"His records list you as next of kin."

The bank was in an old building on Sunset Boulevard, in the heart of the city. Ms. Barber ushered him to an oak desk in the center of dozens of similar desks. Fatter in person than she sounded on the phone, she was tightly wrapped in a bright red business suit.

"Who was this woman?" he asked. "If my father really did have a wife, I would like to know who it is." He tried to sound cool about it.

"This happened more than a week ago. We sent out a form letter but didn't hear back from you."

"Do you think she was on the level?"

"We get this kind of thing all the time. People read the obituaries and try to claim the contents of the vault boxes. If they cannot produce identification, it's unlikely that they are aboveboard."

"So she was just some kind of scam artist, maybe."

"That would be my guess." Barber smiled pleasantly.

Trumbo stood up to leave. "Well, thanks."

"Mr. Walsh?"

"Yes?"

"Wouldn't you like to claim the contents?"

"Oh, right." In the disappointment of learning that he had no relative, he had forgotten about the box.

Trumbo filled out numerous forms and showed his driver's license and Social Security card. Then Barber, another bank official, and a security guard followed him into the vault. They removed a red wax seal from the drawer—Barber explained that was a code that indicated that the owner had died—inserted two keys, then slid out a box. The drawer reminded Trumbo of the morgue where he had claimed his father's body.

Inside a gunmetal-gray container was an ordinary cardboard shoe box, deteriorated with age, and several manila envelopes. Trumbo opened the shoe box, which contained dozens of sealed envelopes: some blank, others addressed but unmailed, others covered with doodles. Several large manila envelopes were stuffed to overflowing with other papers.

"If you'd like to examine the contents in privacy, I can take you to the viewing room," said Ms. Barber.

"I'm not gonna keep the safety-deposit box. I'll just take the contents with me."

At his apartment Trumbo spread the envelopes across the grizzled shag carpet and gingerly opened them one by one, curious to see what his father had stashed away.

One manila envelope contained dozens of flyers for music clubs, most in Los Angeles, but a few from San Francisco. The tattered mimeographed sheets were covered with psychedelic paisley patterns, crude knockoffs of the intricate embroidery found on any Grateful Dead or Jimi Hendrix album. Trumbo flipped through them carefully.

He lined up several flyers side by side. The headliners were all different, mostly bands he never heard of, except for a couple flyers that listed the Strawberry Alarm Clock and one that listed Atomic Rooster. Among the backup bands he noted that one name appeared on almost every flyer: "Horseman's Clan." A typical flyer read:

JUNE 22nd AT THE WHISKY-A-GO-GO
ALL-PSYCHEDELIC BE-IN FEATURING
Straight from San Francisco
LIQUID MARBLE performing their hit "MAD HATTER"

Also Appearing
PSYCHIC SUNRISE   FUR TEACUP
and
L.A.'s very own HORSEMAN'S CLAN
PLUS
GO-GO DANCERS

He gathered up the flyers and put them back into the envelope, then perused the remainder of the contents from the safe-deposit box. He chuckled when he discovered one envelope containing dozens of paid electric bills. Luther had always suffered a dread fear that the electricity would be cut off and so paid the bills in person in cash, the day they came in the mail, as long as Trumbo was growing up.

Another envelope contained legal records from every run-in Luther had with the law: vagrancy charges when father and son slept in their car in Phoenix; public drunkenness and brawling in Chicago; drug charges, tax evasion, public indecency. Trumbo read the public indecency charge. In the thick language of bureaucrats and police reports, it seemed that his father had been caught skinny-dipping on a golf course the year before Trumbo was born. The penalty had been an eighty-eight-dollar fine. Trumbo laughed.

He emptied out another manila folder. Inside were fifteen or twenty letters, postmarked between 1968 and 1975. They had never been opened. He picked one at random from the pile. It was a small envelope addressed to his father at a post office box in Hollywood and bearing a return address on Twenty-second Street in Santa Monica, with the name "J. Wilmot." The handwriting was careful, feminine calligraphy. The envelope had been sealed with a wax imprint, the kind one buys at Hallmark Cards.

He broke the seal and unfolded the old letter. Tiny handwriting crammed both sides of the page. The letter was dated in 1970.

"Dear Luther,

"Hope this letter finds you well. Since you have not returned my previous three notes, I don't even know if you are still alive."

The next several paragraphs concerned the comings and goings of people Trumbo had never heard of—who was in

37

college, who was in jail, who was sleeping with whom. It was signed "peace & love, Joi."

He opened up several more letters. Most of them concerned the same circle of friends—who seemed to have had repeated run-ins with the law. One letter mentioned that "Iceman" had died, shot by cops. Luther had always maintained that he was on the run from the draft board, but nothing in any of the letters even hinted at the war or the draft. The big surprise was contained in the eighth letter. Typically, the note was filled with cryptic gossip. Then came the bombshell:

"Regardless of what she may have done, or said, or thought, it is terribly cruel to Trumbo to prevent him from seeing his own mother. I beg you to reconsider keeping Baba-Boo's very existence a secret from Trumbo. One day he'll find out about her and he'll hold you to blame."

Trumbo was so astonished, he read it twice. His mother was alive? The letter was dated late 1973. He would have just turned six years old, and was probably enrolled in the first grade up in Marin County, the first school he ever attended. Luther always maintained that Trumbo's mother died when he was two. Was he lying? Who was "Baba-Boo"? He quickly scanned the other letters.

From 1970: "Baba-Boo still over in Kaui. A warrant for her hasn't yet reached her but probably will someday."

From early 1971: "They caught up with Baba in a convenience store in Honolulu. Doesn't look good."

From late 1971: "Baba's foot is in the Man's leg-hold trap—she won't get no justice. Will you be coming for trial?"

From 1972: "Baba very depressed about situation with you and her and the little one."

Trumbo felt as though he'd been kicked in the head. His mother might still be alive.

He dialed 411 on the off chance that the woman who signed the letters—Joi Wilmot—still lived in Santa Monica. There was no listing, but he knew that a majority of Angelenos preferred unlisted phone numbers. He neatly replaced most of the papers into their respective envelopes and headed for the seaside town twenty miles away, the "Baba" letters in his hand.

The building on Twenty-second in Santa Monica was an average sixties-style two-story apartment complex built around a pool. The faded pink exterior hadn't been painted in at least a decade.

The "security door" was unlocked. He let himself into the open foyer and scanned the mailboxes for the name "Wilmot." About half the boxes had names listed, the rest just had numbers. In the open tray below the mailboxes were magazines and flyers that did not fit into the mailboxes. He sorted through a stack of forgotten mass-mailed Home Depot flyers until he found one labeled J. WILMOT OR CURRENT RESIDENT, APT. 13.

He walked into the main courtyard, scanning the doors for number 13. An enormously fat woman in a bathing suit that resembled a Victorian dress bobbed in the pool. She was not swimming, just standing in the water.

"What are you looking for?" she asked, in a surprisingly high-pitched voice. "Can I help you?"

"I'm trying to find apartment thirteen."

"I'm the manager. There is no thirteen."

He sat down in a beach chair next to the pool. "Maybe you can help me. I'm looking for Joi Wilmot."

The woman reddened, turned her back on Trumbo, and pulled herself up the stairs of the shallow end of the pool, displacing torrents of water. She then stood next to Trumbo, dripping on his feet.

"Are you a friend of Joi's?" she asked.

"No, not exactly. But my father was her friend."

" 'Was'? It's always terrible to break up with a friend, don't you think?" she said in her singsong. "Isn't he still her friend?"

"He died."

She didn't blink an eye but carried on in her annoying whine. "Well, he's still her friend up in heaven. I like to think so. Friends are forever."

"Sure. He's still her friend in heaven, then." Trumbo moved his feet from the puddle under her and tried not to roll his eyes. "Where do you think I might find her?"

"Would you like to come in for some lemonade and I'll give you her address?"

"I'll pass on the lemonade, if you don't mind."

"I just made it, and there's nothing so refreshing as fresh lemonade on a hot day, don't you think?"

"All right. I'll have some."

"That makes me feel very happy. My name is Joanne."

Joanne waddled into the corner apartment, followed closely by Trumbo. She donned a vast terry cloth robe and poured two glasses of lemonade, setting one at a table in front of Trumbo.

"I always thought that Joi was a fascinating person. Don't you think so?"

Trumbo didn't want to repeat that he'd never met her. "Why did you think that?" he asked.

"She had so many interesting friends in the many years she lived here. I thought perhaps you were one of them."

"What kind of people?"

"Oh, all kinds. Musicians, poets, all sorts of very special people. Right up till when she moved out last year, then it started getting strange."

"What happened?"

"One very handsome man, oh, he was older than you are, perhaps forty, I'll never forget him. He was so tall and romantic with big blue eyes, I'm just sure he was a poet or an artist of some kind. He would always say hi to me. I like people who say hi to me."

"Do you know his name?"

She took a deep breath and continued, every phrase going up in pitch as if it were a question.

"His name was Joseph? I really liked him a lot? Before she moved out, Joi wasn't here much? And he would bang on my door and ask where she was? I always told him that I didn't know, but he would hang around the pool, waiting for her? He kept coming around even after she was gone, and I told him no one but tenants can stay in the pool area—insurance, you know?" She sipped her lemonade and continued in the same grating tone. "When he kept coming around I finally told him that although I liked him very much, he must leave? Because he was scaring the children away from the pool? I told him that even though I didn't want to call the police, I might have to? Do you know, he thanked me politely and I never saw him again? Isn't that funny?"

Trumbo quickly finished his lemonade. Her voice was as appealing as a dental drill. "Joanne, that's fascinating, but I have to get going, you know, traffic. Do you have Joi's address?"

"Oh, yes, I almost forgot." She scribbled out the address on a napkin: Cove Avenue in Echo Park.

"Thanks."

During the hour-long drive across town, he had to resist the impulse to chase after two wrecks reported on the police radio. He needed the money, but was more curious than ever about this woman who wrote secret letters to his father. It was easy enough to find Cove on the map, but he drove past it several times before he realized it had no road access. It was only a long stairway. He skipped down the cement steps two at a time until he came to the correct number.

The pea-green cottage was crammed onto a tiny lot and hidden behind a cheap wire fence overgrown with vines. The front door was one of those that split into upper half and lower half. He knocked. The top half opened just a crack, secured by a chain. He could barely see the face of the person speaking through the door.

"Who is it? Whadda you want?" a woman asked, her voice impatient and tired, the strung-out tone Trumbo associated with accident victims.

"I'm looking for Joi Wilmot."

"Who are you?"

"My name's Walsh." He pushed a business card against the screen that read WALSH 24-HOUR TOW SERVICE: ECHO PARK/SILVERLAKE/CHINATOWN.

"I don't have a car," she said, and began to close the door very slowly.

"Are you Joi Wilmot?"

"Eh, yes."

"You wrote some letters some years back."

"I write a lot of letters."

"They were to my father, Luther Walsh. Are you the same person?"

"Oh my God." She opened the door. Her hair was brunette with gray roots, tied back in a bun. She wore overalls and a black T-shirt, both splattered with paint. Lines in unexpected places marred her otherwise youthful-looking face, and she had full lips and sparkling gray eyes. He could tell she had once been attractive and desirable, perhaps even a great beauty.

She opened the entire door, stepped onto the porch, and placed her thin hands on his face. Her palms were cold and dry.

"Is it real? Are you Trumbo?"

"That's right."

"My God. You're a man now. Come in."

The tiny cottage was kept meticulously neat. An easel stood near the kitchen. On its canvas was a partially finished abstract design—somewhere between a Hopi Indian pictogram and a Salvador Dali painting, brilliant colors and shapes integrated with unusual primitive symbols. Two shelves were filled with a mix of self-help books and oversized art books. The room smelled of sandalwood incense, making Trumbo a bit dizzy.

"I feel strange just walking in on you like this, but I just found out you used to know my father, Luther Walsh."

She smiled broadly, hinting at a girlish delight over a long-past guilty pleasure.

"You could say I knew Luther very well."

"How well?"

She blushed. "Well, it was the late sixties, you know, and it meant something different then than it does now, but we were lovers."

Trumbo looked at her more closely. It was difficult to imagine her with his father.

"I found a bunch of your letters."

"How is he? What's he doing now?"

Trumbo sighed deeply, then looked at the floor as he spoke. "My dad died about a month ago."

"Oh God! I'm so sorry. Luther. Wow. What happened?"

"He was killed in a mental institution by another patient."

Trumbo related the circumstances surrounding his father's death, then backtracked and filled her in about his last job at the metal shop, and the years before that. Joi's girlish delight faded into a gray look of disbelief as she lowered herself onto the couch.

"It's so terrible. I always thought he'd get his act together someday."

"He did okay."

She stared up at the ceiling, uncomfortable with news of death being uttered in her house.

Trumbo spoke softly. "I came here because I saw in one of your letters that you knew who my mother was."

"I do."

"I've never met her. Dad always said she died in a car crash when I was two years old."

"She didn't die. We called her Baba-Boo, but to others she was Mimi Black."

"Really? Is she still alive?"

"I have no idea."

"You knew where she was in 1974."

"A lot of things have changed since then, a lot of water under the bridge."

"How come you stopped talking with her? How come you stopped talking to my dad?"

"You're so young. There is so much you couldn't possibly understand."

"Try me. I know a helluva lot about the sixties. I spent half my life trying to outrun 'em."

Joi's face reddened. "I don't want to think about it. There are some things that it's best to leave alone. I've been trying to live my life comfortably."

Trumbo stood up. "Don't you even have a picture? Some hint about where she might be? I'm not doing this as a hobby. My father just died, and now I find out that his story about the car crash is a big crock of crap. She's out there somewhere. I want to meet her and talk to her. I don't have any other family."

"Maybe he had a reason for hiding her from you."

"Like what?"

"Mimi was a wild card. Whoever she was with got into terrible trouble. Some of them went to jail. If someone made a rule, Mimi would be the first to break it."

"What was she like?"

Joi shook her head. "He really didn't tell you anything about her?"

"He said she was a good woman and left it at that."

"She was just a kid when you were born. Okay? Just trying out her wings. She and your father and several others met for the first time at a party up at a rock star's house in the Hollywood hills. I had just moved here from Bakersfield. Luther came from Idaho maybe six months earlier, but he seemed like an old hand. We're talking 1967, summer of love.

"That was the great summer. Your mother was always in the center of things. She grew up in L.A. and knew all the cool things to do. Backstage passes, secret parties, the beautiful people—all that stuff. She and your father were inseparable. I was kind of a fifth wheel, but they let me come along anyway."

She closed her big eyes, and Trumbo could see her straining to recapture the lost world of her youth. "Things were *different* then. There weren't the kind of gangs and things you have now. We hitchhiked everywhere. Three beautiful hippies, just standing by the side of the road with their thumbs out. Now nobody hitchhikes—you're always suspicious of strangers. Then, every new ride was a fabulous person, and you wanted to learn all about them. Part of it was that we were so young and naive—but part of it was the sense that things were changing and the world was full of possibility.

"That was the summer I'll remember forever. After that, things got complicated. Mimi got pregnant—and then things started getting bad for all of us."

"Bad how?"

"Just bad. We fell in with some dangerous types. We started doing more drugs than I suppose we should have. We got in some trouble with the law. Your mom got in more trouble than the rest of us."

"Drugs?"

"Among other things."

The telephone rang. Joi froze and stared at the phone, and the color drained from her face. It rang twice more, but Joi made no move toward it.

"Aren't you gonna answer it?" asked Trumbo.

She nodded and reached gingerly for the handset, as if it were a heated piece of iron.

"Yes?" she said meekly. She turned away from Trumbo, but he watched with interest as she spoke in hushed tones. She raised her voice. "I can't . . . Just a sec. Let me get it in the other room . . . No, nobody's here! I just want to . . . Just hold on for a second."

She pushed open the bedroom door a crack, slipped in, then leaned back out and hung up the phone, closing the door behind her. During the moments when the phone was lying on the table, Trumbo could hear a man's voice angrily ranting, but couldn't make out what was being said.

A few moments later she emerged, shaken and upset, but trying to put a good face on things.

"You okay?" asked Trumbo.

"Oh, fine. Just fine. It was an old friend calling. You know, personal stuff. I have to get going."

"Sure. What about my mother?"

"I can't really talk right now. You ought to get your stuff and go." She glanced frequently at the door, almost like a nervous tic. "We'll have to get back together soon."

Trumbo shook his head and stood up. "Right. Sure. When?"

"I'll call you."

"Can I have your phone number?"

She froze, as if considering the consequences of the simple act of sharing her phone number with Trumbo. "It'll be better if I call you."

"You're going to call?"

"Sure, I promise." She rushed around the apartment, straightening up the things that were already neatly in place.

Trumbo started toward the door, but paused. "Something happened on that phone call. Are you okay? Is someone hassling you?"

She gnawed on the knuckles on the back of her hand. "Trumbo, there's so much you don't understand." She shook her head furiously as if trying to deny what she knew was true. "You should go."

"I'm going, I'm going."

He opened the front door. A huge man, even taller than Trumbo, stomped through the garden toward the house. He wore blue jeans, a leather jacket, black leather biker boots, and had a ratty, thick beard.

The man rushed in the door and pushed Trumbo aside.

"You bitch! I called from the cellular! You lied to me! You said no one was with you!" he growled.

Joi shrank into the corner and lifted her hands protectively to her face as the man raised his arm to hit her. Trumbo leaped across the room and grabbed the man's upraised fist, spinning him around.

"Motherfucker, get your hands off of me!" yelled the biker. His breath smelled of whiskey and cigarettes.

Trumbo kept his grip. "Don't hit her."

"Who the hell are you? You know nothing about it."

"I don't care what I know or don't know. You're not going to hit her."

"Are you her piece-of-shit boyfriend? Joi, you're sure robbing the cradle these days."

Joi cowered in the corner.

Trumbo seethed with anger. "You're not going to hit her as long as I'm here. I don't know who you are, but I suggest you get the hell out."

Joi stepped between the two men. "Trumbo, it's okay. He's a friend. Just leave him alone."

"No one should treat you like that."

"Stop it!" Joi screamed.

The man jerked his hand away from Trumbo and turned to face her. Trumbo grabbed both of the man's arms from behind, locking them in his grip.

"Goddammit, let go of me, you stupid fuck!" yelled the biker.

Trumbo held tight. Without warning the man kicked furiously, like a burro on uppers. His cowboy boot smashed into the glass coffee table, knocking a ceramic cat onto the floor, where it shattered. He kicked again and knocked the table over, cracking the thick glass on top.

"Let me go or I'll kick the shit out of everything in this house!"

Trumbo lifted him and shoved him toward the door.

Joi rushed across the room, tears running down her face. "Stop it! Please, stop fighting!"

The biker flashed a few rotten teeth and mustered a grin. "Okay. I give up. All right? I give up, man."

"No. You're leaving, asshole," Trumbo said, and pushed.

"Name's Blue." He squirmed in place. "Come on, let go, let go of me, man!" He shuddered in place. Trumbo had the upper hand.

Blue stopped struggling. "You gonna hold me here all day? I said I give up."

"You going to leave?" asked Trumbo.

"Yeah. Come on. I was pissed. It's not your fault. I felt bad about Joi." He pleaded in a whiny voice. "Just let go."

Trumbo let loose his grip and backed away, watching Blue carefully. The man shook his head, as if to reset the circuitry, brushed himself off, and flashed an odd smile.

"Go on. Get out of here," said Trumbo, holding one hand up to staunch the flow of blood from his nose.

"I'm leaving," muttered Blue, then he left.

Trumbo paused a moment, then figured he'd leave, too. As he turned to shut the door, he felt a blunt blow to the back of his neck and fell to the floor. Blue towered above him, a garden hoe in his hand. Before Trumbo could react, Blue kicked him in the chest. Trumbo's breath blew out of him. Blue kicked again and again, and Trumbo tried to stop the kicks with his hands. The last thing he heard before blacking out was Joi screaming at the top of her lungs, "Stop it! He's not my boyfriend! Stop it . . ."

It was dark when he woke up in Joi's tiny front yard. The back of his head pulsed painfully. He didn't move for a long time after opening his eyes. Slowly he worked one hand out from under his stomach and felt his face. A thick sediment of dried blood covered its right side. He scratched off some of the brown muck and coughed, spitting out more blood. Then he supported himself on one arm and pushed himself up to his feet.

He leaned against an avocado tree and surveyed the area for signs of life. No sound came from the house. No one was around. He felt for his wallet. It was still there. As he pulled himself up the long stairway toward the road where his truck was parked, he chuckled perversely to himself as he thought: *No wonder Dad didn't want me to meet his old friends.* Then he spit out a mouthful of blood.

3

STRANGE SCRIBBLES OF GOBLINS AND GHOSTS CLUTTERED THE margins of lined notebook paper. Words were blotted out, and the entire missive seemed frenzied and out of control. Paul Winston scrutinized the document:

> *Love is all around us every day. I still want stamps and paper and didn't here from you did you get the last message? peace and love to everyone and keep the faith. the other need is for ever ready—aa need that cannot be gotten in the place where I have found myself.*
>
> *listen to yourself in your heart and feel my need. I have got to the fourth level for the first time in this past week and then have not been able to go further altho god knows I spend every waking hour trying to destroy the creepers which multiply infintly expecially those in the city—god how difficult it is to destroy that creature in the city but if I am ever to get to a higher place than just the fourth level I need your ever ready aa gift I cannot obtain easily. There are six good deemons and six bad ones but it is sometimes hard to tell them all apart. One other special child-creature has all the power to stop any one.*
>
> *Remember everything you do for others is always repayed tenfold so I need you to do what you can do to help resolve this situation and share your love with all who seek it and put your faith in your self and in your love*
> *Yrs*
> *Charly*

Winston asked his boss about the letter.

"Manson writes a lot of weird stuff, but this letter sounds more dangerous than usual. What do you make of it?"

The older guard took one look at the paper and then chuckled. "You don't have kids, do you, Paul?"

"No. Why?"

"Manson got a Nintendo Game Boy a couple weeks ago. If I'm not mistaken, the demons and monsters are all about a game called UrbAdventure."

"Yeah?"

"My daughter has the same game. It keeps him quiet, anyway. He wants batteries for the damned thing."

"Are you sure?"

"Pretty sure."

"Go ask him if he has this game. If he does, we'll let the letter go. If not, let's shitcan the letter."

Winston leisurely walked to the end of the passageway. He was accustomed to the irrational rants coming from the cell at the end. He thought of the prisoner as a dog: Don't let him see that you're scared and he won't bother you.

"Manson, what's this letter about? What video game are you playing?" Winston held the letter up to the window of the cell.

The prisoner kept his back turned and mumbled an answer. "UrbAdventure. Why?"

"Trying to decipher your letter."

Manson whirled around and flashed his crooked teeth, then squinted at Winston. "Hey, where's the nigger that's usually here?"

The word hit Winston's ears like a blow. He had grown up near Bakersfield, where, during his youth, he had suffered repeated racial taunts from white kids, and he was still quite sensitive to the word "nigger." He'd sworn never again to let anyone make racial slurs like that.

"I didn't hear what you said."

The bearded prisoner cackled. "I said, 'Where's the nigger that's usually here?' You're new to this wing, aren't you?"

"Manson, I don't know who you're used to dealing with, but you'll address me as Mr. Winston."

"I didn't call *you* a nigger, *Mr. Winston.* You pretty light-skinned, almost a high yellow. I was talking about that guy who was here before you—jungle black, thick lips, that kind of thing. He's the one I was talking about."

"Okay, that's it. You crossed the wrong man."

"What're you gonna do? I'm in here forever," said the prisoner, with a smirk.

"There's still solitary. There's still revocation of privileges."

"Yeah, but you gotta get those from your boss. He hates niggers, too. He might not tell you, but he does. I seen a tattoo on his ankle once. He's a Viking. White supremacist."

"That's enough!"

"He won't show it to you, of course, even if yer high yellow. But I seen it. He's not the only screw who's a Viking, either. Why do you think the low-level screws are all niggers, and the bosses and administration are all white at Corcoran? Ever think about that?"

"Manson, don't you forget who's boss."

"Okay, Mr. Winston, Mr. Boss, what do they pay you?"

"That's none of your business."

"You make eighteen thousand four hundred, plus benefits. It's public information. I made over a hundred grand this year."

"What?"

"Guns N' Roses recorded my song. I got the royalty check this week. A hundred five thousand plus change. What you make in the next six years. Hah!"

Winston was tempted to call the prisoner out for a fight, but he knew that's exactly what Manson wanted. He restrained himself and counted to ten.

"You're on my list, Manson," said Winston, banging the cell door. Without looking back, he rushed away from the cell and walked to the end of the hall, where he found Dick reading *Soldier of Fortune*.

He handed the letter to Pond, his boss. "He's writing about the video game. I asked him."

The older guard stared for a moment at Winston. "You look shaken. What got into you?"

"It's Manson trying to get to me."

"What'd he say?"

"You really want to know?"

"Sure. We'll write him up if he's screwing with you."

Winston drew a deep breath. "He said that a few of the white officers are in some sort of racist group."

Pond looked at the floor. "Yeah? You believe his crazy gibberish?"

"Any truth to this rumor of 'The Vikings' or 'The Order' or whatever they're called?"

"Come on, Paul, what do *you* think? That's an absurd idea." Pond patted Winston on the back and studiously avoided eye contact. His smile was forced. "Why don't you take your break now? You look like you need it."

"Thanks."

Winston slowly walked from the cellblock. *Dick didn't deny it, he just evaded the question.* Then he thought better of it. *Nahhh—start letting Charlie get to you and you're sure to go crazy. I knew what I was getting into when I transferred to this wing. Dealing with the most hardened, desperate, dangerous souls ever put behind bars, all for eighty cents more an hour.*

Six days later, after it passed muster at the hands of two more censors and a mail delay caused by an improper ZIP code, J'osüf Sunn retrieved the letter from his box at a company called Mail-n-More in a mini-mall in Highland Park.

Sunn took the letter home and retired to his private room atop the abandoned mansion. Before opening the missive, he dusted the floor, changed into the silk smoking jacket he kept for special occasions, then ate two hits of Ecstasy. Once the hallucinogen kicked in, he carefully opened the envelope and spent the rest of the afternoon scrutinizing the one-page note. So that he would not miss any subtle innuendo, Sunn used a Tarot deck, a Ouija board, and a mirror to extract every drop of meaning. By the time the sun cast its brilliant twilight magenta hue through the windows, Sunn was nearly certain that he knew what was required. He felt a thrill of anticipation as he realized that Manson wanted assistance in a momentous mission: an assignment that would change the world.

Sunn opened the door of his small chamber. The steamy smell of spices wafted up the narrow stairway. Sunn was pleased that the girls obeyed without his having to say anything. He cupped his hands over his mouth and yelled.

"Peace! Cleopatra!"

He heard a rustling sound in the kitchen. Peace appeared at the bottom of the stairs, her long black hair tied in a knot above her head. She smiled when she saw Sunn.

"Yes? We wondered where you were."

"Something wonderful has happened."

"What?" asked the girl.

"I'll tell you all tonight. Boil up some water and fill the bathtub for me. I need to cleanse myself. I have had an important breakthrough."

The girl bounced hopefully from foot to foot. "What is it? Can't you tell me?"

"Tonight we'll have a bonfire and I'll tell all."

Peace returned to the kitchen, where her sister Cleopatra was boiling rice and vegetables on a portable camp stove precariously balanced atop the disconnected kitchen range.

"What is it?" asked Cleopatra, wiping her hands on her dress.

"I don't know, but I've got to boil some water for J'osüf. I think we should all be cleaned up for tonight. Something big is happening."

"Where are you going to boil water?"

"I'll build a fire outside."

Sunn suddenly appeared in the room and kissed Cleopatra once on each cheek, then hugged her. She blushed, and an unfamiliar, delicious warmth surged through her body. As if understanding her awakening passion, Sunn slid his hand across her breast before ending the embrace. "Why don't you build that fire?" he whispered.

The sixteen-year-old girl walked softly out of the house and across the lot. Every nerve in her body seemed to tingle at once. She half closed her eyes, longing to hold on to the exquisite sensation surging through her. She felt herself becoming a woman, and credited Sunn. Only a few months before, she'd been Patricia Clemens, just another ninth grader from Seattle. That was before she and her older sister—once called Anne, now known as Peace—ran away from home.

Sunn had found the two girls asleep on the beach beneath the Santa Monica pier. He offered them a place to stay. Cleopatra didn't like him at first. She hung around simply because Peace told her to. Peace was always going on about the terrific things he did and how wonderful he was, but Cleopatra had never understood what she meant until now.

Cleopatra gathered tinder from the edges of the compound, all the while thinking of Sunn. There were no words to express her feelings for him. She liked the way he smelled. She liked his long, flowing hair and the blue dot on his forehead. He was exotic and exciting and dangerous, and he made her feel so electric.

She dropped her pile of tinder into the empty oil drum and lit it with a wooden match. Standing a few feet from the flickering flames, she closed her eyes as the flames grew larger, running her hands along the front of her dress, thinking about how good it might feel if Sunn's hands did the same. She would do anything for him.

As it grew darker, word passed around the house that J'osüf had important news. Each prepared herself for an important ritual.

By the time J'osüf finished his bath, all seven girls had prettied themselves up as much as possible in a house where the only running water came from a fire hydrant. Someone had discovered a handsome embroidered tablecloth, probably in a dumpster. Even though the dining table was set up on a gravel lot and had one broken leg, the girls had eked out a rough kind of elegance. Various plates and silverware, begged, borrowed, and stolen over a period of months, were neatly arranged on the table, and eight chairs placed around it.

At the south end of the compound, leaning against the chain-link fence, one girl watched in silence. Thursday had covered herself with a poncho and was curled up on the ground, overwhelmed by feelings of loneliness and horror. When she arrived three months earlier to join Sunn's "Rebirth Fellowship," it seemed as if she had gone to heaven. She liked the other girls. She worshiped Sunn. This was the fulfillment of her long-standing fantasy of escaping her parents and finding people who really understood her.

But she had misgivings about the violent turn the group had taken. She tried to comprehend what Sunn said—that the people they killed were pigs and deserved to die. Still, she became obsessed with a strange detail of their violent night in Pasadena. It wasn't the killing that bothered her. That seemed as if some other girl had done it, like she was watching it in a movie. Rather, it was a photo that she saw just before they left the huge house.

In the kitchen was a frame that contained several photos of the dentist and his wife: on vacation at Disneyland, skiing, prom photos, that kind of thing. One of the smallest images was a faded Polaroid of the wife, obviously taken several years earlier. The woman wore jeans and a halter top, and sat bareback atop a beautiful palomino. Thursday could not stop thinking about the horse. All her life Thursday had hoped someday to work on a horse farm, and she saw sadness in the horse's eyes. Now he had no owner. What had happened to him? Did the horse miss the woman?

She covered her head with a blanket and cried until she fell asleep on the hard gravel. Sometime later she was awakened with a gentle nudge.

"Thursday. What's the matter, honey?" J'osüf asked, gently holding her hand.

Tears welled up in her eyes. "I was just thinking about what happened to that family, where we, you know, where we went into the house."

"The Night Of Cleansing," said Sunn, correcting her.

"Yeah."

"We had to do it. Sometimes you have to do a painful thing now—"

She finished his sentence. "So you can have pleasure later. I know we had to. But I just can't shake it from my mind."

Sunn sat on the ground next to Thursday and let her lean against his shoulder. "There's a lot you don't understand. You're young. Sometimes you've got to trust me that I know what's best for you, for all of us."

Her voice cracked. "I guess so."

"Why don't you come back and eat with us? Peace has made a wonderful dinner."

"Okay."

He stood up, offered Thursday his hand, and helped her up. Then he kissed her quickly on the cheek. "You'll be okay, Thursday, just you see."

She smiled and followed him to the outside dinner table. It was nearly dark, and the only illumination came from burning scraps of wood in the trash can. They ate the rice and scavenged vegetables in silence. When the last girl finished, Sunn stood. Without a word, the girls did likewise.

He threw several more pieces of scrap into the fire. Sparks danced in the air, and the flames leaped higher from the barrel. Sunn extended his hands. Thursday took one hand, Cleopatra the other. Then the other five girls clasped hands in a circle around the bonfire.

Sunn stared ahead in silence, allowing the flames to grow until they spilled out from the top of the garbage can.

"Oh, you beautiful children. *We* know what love is and we want to share it with the world. Our little house here, abandoned by the Man, dumped on a gravel lot like so much refuse, holds as much love as any consensus-reality mansion. We're just the start. We're a microcosm of the whole world. You all know how consensus reality treats people— work and work and work and die. Slaves to the machine. I've heard all your stories about life before you got here, and wondered how it can be so harsh, wondered why others don't live as we do, taking every day at its fullest and loving one another more than any other beings have ever loved.

"I want to tell you tonight that our reality is going to change things. Each and every one of you is a goddess." He raised his arms above his head for emphasis. "Each one of you is a special, chosen one! Our love is going to manifest the second coming."

Cleopatra hoped he'd go on forever, talking about love and commitment and how they were "humanistic potential pioneers" testing out a new utopia, which they would then share with the rest of the world. She loved the tone of his voice and the way he alternated between long, quiet passages and loud, showy exclamations. The musical, lullaby quality of his speech pacified her tumultuous emotions. Twice she was moved to tears, and her powerful love for Sunn intensified with every word.

Thursday, on the other hand, remained confused. The others seemed to believe him, so how could it not be true? But his words rang false to her. She felt alienated from the group, as if the other girls were privy to secrets she could never understand. Nevertheless, she listened, hoping for the insight the others had.

As the sky darkened and the bonfire burned down to glowing embers, the tenor of Sunn's voice abruptly changed. Cleopatra sat up and listened carefully.

"There is in the world today a man who has done more for love and peace and freedom and the new utopia than anyone who ever lived. A man who is Mahatma Gandhi and Martin Luther King and John F. Kennedy rolled into one."

Sunn raised his hands above his head. "Sometimes consensus reality folds back on itself. They tried to kill the only teacher who knew more about peace than Gandhi, more about freedom than Kennedy, and more about love than King. They tried, but their system failed them. Now this martyr sits isolated in a cold steel cell, charged for crimes he did not commit, kept under lock and key because he holds the truth. He is the wisest man that ever walked the earth. His name is Charles Manson."

Thursday gasped. *Manson. Wasn't he a killer?* She struggled to remember the story. It had happened long before she was born. She was about to speak out, but looked around at the other girls, who gazed with unquestioning admiration.

Sunn walked twice around the circle, every girl watching him. Then he stopped in front of Thursday.

"My child, there is fear in your eyes. Why?"

Oh my God. He really does know what I'm thinking. She lost her breath for a moment, then spoke. "Nothing. Really."

Sunn moved close enough to bite her. She could smell the sweat and campfire smoke on his body. Then he yelled. "What is it? You have doubts. Address them here!"

"Wasn't Charles Manson . . . Didn't he . . . Isn't he a murderer?"

"No! That's a part of the *lie* that's perpetuated in *consensus reality* to make you *scared* of him!" He grabbed Thursday's wrist and pulled her to her feet. She felt dizzy as the blood rushed from her head. "Come with me."

He pulled her to the side of the trash barrel. She could see the white-hot embers inside.

"Trust, trust, you must trust." He wiped his hands on the dirt.

"I will put it to a test, a trial by fire. If I am wrong, my hands will burn. If I am right, they will not."

He plunged his hands inside the barrel and extracted a red-hot ember, then cupped it in his hands. He did not flinch. The eerie crimson glow reflected off his face. "Sometimes what you think is true is not. Cup your hands."

She put her hands in front of her. To her horror, Sunn rolled the ember into her hands. She screamed as her hands began to burn, and dropped the smoldering wood. "Jesus! What are you doing?"

"Submission is a gift you give to your lover," he said. He tightly gripped both her hands, then kissed her on the forehead. "The pain will go away . . . now." Thursday gasped, but the pain stopped as he promised. Tears flowed down her cheeks and she returned to her seat. She stared at her hands with wonder. She did not know how J'osüf handled the coal without getting burned.

Sunn resumed his spot in the center of the circle. "Charlie is love. Charlie is light. Charlie will protect us. And he has laid out a task for us. Someplace in the world right now are thirteen special children: Charlie's disciples. Six are evil. Six are good. And one is the leader for the next millennium. We must find the good ones and bring them into our fold. We must find the unclean ones and destroy them. And we must find the one true leader walking with the living and elevate him to his position of righteousness before Charlie is released."

He walked around the circle, and each girl kneeled before him. As if at Communion, he slipped a tab of Ecstasy onto each girl's tongue.

"We have a lot to do. Tomorrow at dawn we will find the first of the thirteen."

"Carriers get all the gravy. Carriers get all the gravy." Boyd Trevore repeated the phrase as if it were a hit song. The U.S. Post Office never put air conditioning in the repair trucks because the mail carriers didn't get air conditioning and the repair guys like Boyd never got *anything* that carriers didn't get. That was the only thing Boyd Trevore disliked about working for the post office. He loved everything else, especially the uniform. People everywhere respect uniforms. The work was easy: Boyd repaired rural mailboxes that had been vandalized, and installed new collection boxes in subdevelopments when needed. The supervisors—"soups"—rarely checked on him, and as long as he did something each day, however minimal, he could never be fired.

Scores of doctors had told Boyd the same thing: Take lithium tablets and your mood problems will be cured. He would occasionally take the drug for a few days, but inevitably he missed the thrill of the manic highs more than he feared the depressions. Boyd ignored the doctors whenever he could, preferring to ride his mood swings like a surfer, from the highest highs to the lowest lows.

The box maintenance gig was the last in a long string of offbeat jobs. He had driven a taxi until he got fired for berating a passenger who had a bad haircut. He worked as a stock clerk in a supermarket until the day when, because he wanted to order dozens of free cookbooks, he removed the labels from 1,440 cans of Campbell's soup. He worked in a photo lab for exactly one hour, until he put a new light in the darkroom. Those were only the tip of the iceberg. Before the post office, Trevore had been fired from fourteen jobs in four and a half years. His life changed the day he took the Post Office Civil Service Exam during a luxurious, glorious manic high. His score was just good enough to land the box maintenance position, and in his three years Boyd learned that no matter how many times the soups wrote him up for infractions, it was very, very difficult to actually get laid off.

Today he was *supposed* to be installing a PC-330 Mail Collection Box with Automobile Acceptance Slot in the suburb of Diamond Bar, but didn't much feel like doing it. He'd awakened that morning feeling a high come on. The sun looked brighter than it had for weeks, food tasted better than he'd ever tasted. His mind was hitting on all six cylinders and then some, and Boyd just wanted to drive around. So he did—pushing the maintenance vehicle over ninety miles an hour on the wide, flat, little-used roads of the desert.

But after he sped around for an hour chasing desert animals with his truck and playing chicken with oncoming vehicles, he began to feel a slight twinge of guilt and decided, "What the hell. Do a little work. I can put this box in in an hour and say it took all day."

He found the correct corner on his map and parked the truck. He'd done a lot of work in the desert, and all the communities looked the same: hundreds of carbon-copy single-family homes, one after another stretching to the foothills. Having grown up in foster homes and orphanages, he had a perverse contempt for middle-class neighborhoods.

He got out of the truck, thoughts racing through his mind at miraculous speeds. In an instant, he knew how he would install the box. The gas and electric lines were already marked with spray paint, and he figured he could install the box without measuring, a definite violation of the "USPS Installation Specifications" pamphlet. He stared at the spot where the box was to go, sizing up the installation like a matador assessing a bull.

Then he turned back to face his truck. Three girls and an older man were leaning against it. *Where the hell did they come from?*

None of the girls was older than twenty or twenty-two. There were flowers woven through their hair. Each looked to the man who accompanied them as if he were her closest boyfriend and grandfather rolled into one. He wore jeans and a leather vest, and had a blue spot in the center of his forehead.

The man approached Boyd. "We have to talk."

"Who the hell are you?"

"You should know who I am, Boyd," replied the man.

Boyd did a double take and his manic thoughts raced. *Could be someone from the soup's office, nah, why would he have that blue dot oh look at the girls they are cute but if they say they know me and they know my name it must be someone I met when I was zoned should I play along?*

"Oh, it's you." Boyd tapped his fingers on the un-installed box. Rat-a-tat-a-tat, rat-a-tat-a-tat. "Right. You're from— where are you from? I'm sorry but I've been terribly busy and you know I have a million things to do and sometimes people forget each other's names."

"My name is J'osüf. You should know that."

"Right, Joe, bud, what can I do for you, whatever I can do is okay by me what is it exactly that you need?"

"It's J'osüf. Why don't we go for a ride and talk about it?"

"I don't know if I can do that or not, you know I have a million things to do, on the clock, on the clock for my work you know, got a job to do—"

"Are you with us or against us, Boyd? You are one of the thirteen." The three girls were joined by four more, who formed a semicircle blocking Boyd's exit. A bead of sweat ran down his brow.

Boyd rapid-fired out a string of words. "Right, let's think about this a little, we know each other, right? You said we did. So I guess that would mean that I'm with you."

"Then you'll join us." The girls moved in closer, birds of prey sizing him up.

"Can't do that, nah, can't do that, would like to, but in the middle of things, busy busy busy, so I have to take a pass, Joe old bud, and we'll just have to take it up later." Boyd nervously scratched his scalp and backed away, toward his truck.

He stopped in his tracks when the man produced a large handgun. Boyd's eyes grew large.

"What's this, Wild West or something? I mean, what are you doing, you don't really need that or something, work is important, yes, work is important but you know sure, we can go for a ride, I'm sorry about what I said, yeah, let's go for a ride, right? My old friend, Joe."

"Your truck."

"Sure, not a problem, we'll take my truck, how about it, hop in. Let's go for a ride."

Boyd left his tools and the marking spray paint on the curb, thinking he would soon be back, and got into the United States Postal Service repair truck.

Thursday rode in the back of the windowless vehicle, keeping guard over the thin, chatty man in the uniform. The others rode in front of the orange van. Boyd's hands and feet were bound with electrical tape, but he didn't seem to mind. Thursday made small talk with him, and in a short time learned that he had a collection of beer cans, he liked the band U2, and that he had been raised in foster homes. She barely listened to his patter: The whole long ride through the desert she kept thinking as hard as she could, *Let him be a good one. Please don't let anything happen to him.*

When they began bumping up and down, she knew they had taken a dirt road somewhere. The truck stopped. She heard J'osüf's door open, then squinted her eyes as he opened the rear door of the truck.

"Out," said J'osüf. He had that strange glint in his eye, the same look he had that night in Pasadena. She knew what would happen.

"J'osüf, don't! Please, don't hurt him!"

"Are you with us or against us, Thursday?"

Tears streamed down her face. "Don't do it!"

J'osüf dragged the man from the truck and threw him on the ground. He sliced off the electrical tape on his ankles and pointed a gun at him.

"Let's go, Boyd."

Sweat poured down Boyd's face. "There's been some kind of mistake. You're looking for someone else and mistakenly found me, right out here in the middle of nowhere. So why don't we all go back and talk this over and I'll pretend it never happened."

Sunn pulled a long kitchen knife from his pocket and handed it to Thursday.

She trembled and crossed her hands across her body.

"Take it, Thursday!" said J'osüf.

"I don't want it."

"Take it."

She didn't move.

"Take it. I want you to take it."

She could not resist. She limply held out one hand, and Sunn put the knife in it.

"Put the knife at the back of his neck."

She tried to think of something else. She watched from outside herself as she put the point of the blade against the back of his neck.

"Now, walk."

Wooden pegs marked out spots where future roads and

houses would be built: square, geometrical lines separating desert from desert.

The other girls jumped out of the van. The group walked single file several yards into the desert, a macabre parade through the middle of nowhere.

Thursday began crying.

Boyd kept talking. "Now, what can I do for you? I can make some sort of deal. If you're going to rob me, the keys are in, well, you have the keys, right, so you do whatever you want, take the truck, I won't talk, trust me, why should I talk I don't care about what happens to that truck—"

Sunn smashed the back of his palm into Thursday's hand. The knife plunged into the postal employee's neck. He abruptly stopped talking and tried to reach for the wound, but his bound hands would not stretch that far. Blood sprayed from the severed artery onto the parched desert ground.

Thursday screamed. "No! *No! No!*" She fell to the ground, writhing, horrified.

Sunn spun around. "Who would like to finish off this pig?" he said, facing the other girls just behind him.

Cleopatra tentatively stepped forward. Sunn placed a knife in her hand.

"Good." He smiled. Cleopatra walked toward the suffering man bleeding to death on the ground.

"No," said Sunn. He pointed to Thursday.

"Her?" asked Cleopatra.

Sunn nodded.

Cleopatra tried not to look into her friend's face as she plunged the blade into Thursday's chest. She focused her gaze instead on J'osüf Sunn, who smiled at her. She was so happy to please him that she did not hear the screams. After it was over she received Sunn's look of approval. The strange, warm sensation poured through her body, hotter than ever before.

When Boyd Trevore failed to return that day, his supervisor didn't investigate immediately, mainly because the repairman did so many unpredictable things. When he didn't show up three days in a row, a "Stolen Property" report was put out on the truck, and the postal inspectors notified the highway patrol.

Two and a half weeks later, a survey engineer discovered the truck in a gully where a new development was to be built. Written on the side were the words SKELTER—DAY ONE. The truck had been towed away, washed, and repaired before they found Boyd's femur and a badly decomposed arm several hundred yards away. The girl's body was never found.

4

IN SPITE OF THE INJURIES FROM BLUE'S SAVAGE BEATING, TRUMBO didn't go to the hospital. He couldn't afford it. After crawling up the cement steps to his car, he somehow made it to his tiny apartment, swerving erratically on the four-mile drive home.

Once there, he searched the medicine cabinet and found two codeine-laced aspirin that were yellowed with age. He swigged them down with a bottle of Lucky beer, then collapsed on the single bed, dried blood flaking onto the sheets. He felt his chest and discerned a couple of broken ribs. If he had decided to shell out the big bucks and see a doctor, all they'd do was wrap him up and tell him to avoid heavy lifting. On his budget, that kind of service wasn't worth hundreds of dollars in doctor's fees.

The brush with violence brought into sharp relief the loneliness of his life: *What if I had died?* No one would have come to pick up his body. Sure, he had acquaintances like Officer Mazer, and the paramedics and the other truck drivers, but no actual friends.

He'd dated a few girls, but his relationships always slowly disintegrated. He never had big ugly breakup scenes, instead just drifting apart from whomever he was seeing. His last serious, sleep-together girlfriend had moved to Orange

County a few months before his father died. Her name was Sara and they'd had some good times. She worked at a camera store and liked foreign movies and long, slow weekends of red wine and pizza and sex. One weekend Sara took Trumbo home to meet her parents. Her polyester-clad folks kept asking upwardly mobile Orange County questions like "What does your father do?" and "Are you planning on expanding your tow truck business?" and "Don't you have any other family?" and "Are you planning to go to college?"

Trumbo answered some of their questions and avoided others, but never bullshitted them. He was pretty miserable already when, late in the day, Sara took him aside and told him he was making a bad impression. Something about the way she said it tore into him, as if he were a pet on display, and after she said it he just started spilling it all, good and bad, just to shock her parents: *Well, actually, I chase down car wrecks and try to tow the cars as soon as they pry the bodies out* and *to tell you the truth, my dad is in a state mental institution 'cause he took some kind of bad drugs, but before that he was a drifter.* Sara stopped returning his calls.

He had no connections to much of anyone save bill collectors. As the codeine kicked in and the throbbing receded, he made a vow to return to Joi's house and find out everything she knew about his mother, good or bad. *His mother was alive.* That one glimmer of hope was worth getting the shit kicked out of him.

Just as he began to drift into unconsciousness, the phone rang. He let the answering machine pick it up.

"Trumbo. It's Joi Wilmot." She spoke in a hushed voice.

He rolled off the couch onto the floor and started crawling toward the phone while she spoke.

"I'm sorry about what happened today, Blue's kind of crazy, I guess you figured that out. I want to talk to you some more, but you can't come to the house anymore—you might get, uh, in trouble. Meet me Saturday, eleven P.M., by the big hats. Call Moon Man for the address."

He grabbed for the phone, but it was too late. Joi had hung up. He hit replay on the machine and tried to figure out what she meant. *By the big hats? Call Moon Man?* He thought,

*Either she's bonkers or that codeine is stronger than I
remembered.*

By the next afternoon both the pain and his patience for
sitting around the house had receded, so Trumbo downed
his last codeine and went out foraging for work.

Within an hour he had a catch: two Japanese businessmen
had somehow spun their Acura around backwards in an
intersection clearly marked NO U TURN and were greeted by a
Ford pickup truck packed with Mexican day laborers.

While the paramedics packed and shipped the commut-
ers, sending the businessmen to upscale Cedars Sinai for
treatment and the laborers to County Hospital for triage,
Lieutenant Mazer wandered over to Trumbo's truck.

Trumbo stepped down from the driver's seat and leaned
against the door. Mazer gasped when he saw him. Trumbo's
eye was black and blue, and he hunched over in pain. His
nose was alternately blue and purple and looked like it
belonged on someone else's face.

"Didn't see you yesterday," said the cop. "What happened? You went some rounds with a two-by-four?"

"It's a long story, Mazer. You got a minute?"

The cop looked over his shoulder at the paramedics
before answering. "Yeah. So what was it?"

Trumbo filled him in about the letters, the woman who
might have known where his mother was, and the freak who
beat the hell out of him.

"His name was Blue."

"Just 'Blue'?"

"It was a fight, not an interview."

Mazer grinned. "Were you screwing the woman?"

"No!" Trumbo punched the cop in the arm and grinned.
"You got a lot of class to ask, though, Mazer. She's probably
fifty years old."

"Older women, some men like that. You can tell me."

"You dick—I was just asking her questions. The guy beat
me up for no reason."

"You going to press charges?"

"Mazer, you're a cop, you know how much good that'll
do. Besides, I want to talk to this woman again. She said not
to come back to her house."

MICHAEL R. PERRY

"Sounds like good advice."

"But I wanna see her again. She left me a batshit-weird message on my machine. She said 'Call Moon Man.' Like I know who Moon Man is."

Mazer shook his head. "I don't have a clue. Is it a shop or something?"

"Uh-uh. I looked it up in the phone book."

"Beats the hell out of me."

The ambulance slammed its door and pulled away from the wreck.

"I gotta get this tow. Call me if you find anything out."

"Trumbo—you want me to look up the woman?"

"What do you mean?"

"Run a check on her. Give me her name. I'll find out if she has a record or anything."

"That'd be cool. Her name's Wilmot. Joi Wilmot. There's one other name I want you to look up, but I don't want you to ask a bunch of questions. Mimi Black." He spelled it out for Mazer.

"Who's this other woman?"

"I'll tell you if you find out anything. Gotta go."

Trumbo ran across the road, jumped in his truck, and backed up toward the crumpled Acura.

As he towed the wreck toward the police yard, he read a bumper sticker on an old Toyota filled with teenagers. Yellow flowers and astrological symbols adorned the sticker, and at the bottom it read CALL MOON MAN. He pulled into the middle of the road, drove alongside the Toyota, and flashed his lights at them. A startled young girl rolled down the window.

"Hey—what's Moon Man?" he yelled.

"It's techno."

"What?"

"It's a party—a rave!" the girl yelled.

They approached a stretch where the three lanes narrowed into two. Several hundred yards ahead of him a Sparkletts water truck raced straight toward him.

Trumbo yelled over the roar of traffic at the driver, "Yeah, but what does Moon Man mean?"

The girl laughed. "It's a phone number!"

Trumbo screeched on the brakes just before he met the Sparkletts truck head-on, then drove toward the wrecking yard and dropped off the crushed Acura.

When he got home, the first thing he did was dial M-O-O-N-M-A-N. After three rings, loud, syncopated electronic tones filled his ear, and a male, British voice yelled cryptic messages:

"Landing on the dusty surface this Saturday is Moon Man Three! For your blasting psycho-tonic pleasure! Twelve hours of extraterrestrial binging, featuring the hottest acts from around the planet, including: from London, Deejay Dachau; from Belgium, Marathon Man and Chat Okay; from France, Dacron Enema; and from New York, the Wavy Navy! Sixteen-color smart rays provided by Intelligent Weaponry; cranial coverage by Numbskull and Trojan Boner Hats, plus the full force of one hundred thousand searing watts of sonic abuse brought to you by the Ripper! Keep alert and call this number for updates on the day of the show."

He was so bewildered by the gibberish that he called back twice, to make sure he'd heard it correctly. Then he dialed Lieutenant Mazer at the LAPD. He was lucky. Mazer was in.

"Mazer, what did you find on those names?"

"Nothing on Mimi Black."

Trumbo felt a surge of disappointment.

"I found some dope on Joi Wilmot. She had some unspecified convictions prior to 1975, but the record has been purged."

"What's that mean?"

"Means she served some time, then paid some serious lawyer fees. Purging happens mostly when a perp has an embarrassing item on their record but convinces some pinko liberal judge to hide it. It's usually done for rich kids who get caught smoking pot, or have drunk driving convictions. If your lawyer can convince a court, you can get anything purged. Since it happened in the early seventies, my guess would be drugs. Probably pot, before it was decriminalized."

"Anything else?"

"Some recent traffic tickets. A few bad checks in 1978; she

paid them off a couple years later. And here's some weird recent convictions: This chick has a bunch of fines and court appearances for violating fire regulations."

"Come again?"

"Fire regulations. That usually happens to slumlords or restaurant owners. She paid a thousand-dollar fine last summer for violating fire rules—the code in the report was so obscure, I hadda look it up. Either your girlfriend Wilmot runs a restaurant, or she's a firebug and plea-bargained down to a lesser offense."

"Mazer, she's not my girlfriend."

"Well, whatever she is, don't go near her when she's playing with oily rags and a lighter."

Trumbo dialed the Moon Man phone number for the next two days, always hearing the same loud, cryptic message. Then on Saturday morning, there was a new recorded announcement. Gone were the noisy synthesizers and the hype-filled pomp of the original recording. In its place was a man with a faint Jamaican accent.

"Okay. All acts are secured and paid, and this is a no hassle, go event. Let's be peaceful, everybody, and have a good time. The Moon Man ticket point is going to open at two P.M. this afternoon at *Double-X Magazine* on Washington Boulevard two blocks west of La Brea. Peace, love, and see you there."

He checked his watch. It was a little after 10:00 A.M.; he figured he could get at least one tow on the way over. He wolfed down some stale doughnuts pilfered from the police wrecking yard the night before, then drove toward *Double-X Magazine,* wondering what he'd find.

The morning was sunny and warm, and L.A. drivers were, unfortunately for Trumbo, not crashing their cars. During his three hours of trolling for wrecks, there were only two accidents within driving distance reported on his radio. Other trucks beat him both times. At around two P.M. he drove south on La Brea toward the address in the message.

Echo Park, where he lived, was no great neighborhood and had its share of gangs and mayhem, but the stretch of Washington he drove down was far worse. Burned-out buildings had never been repaired, and most of the remaining buildings were either boarded up or shielded behind thick metal bars.

He saw a long line of teenagers, mostly white and Hispanic, unusual for the predominantly black neighborhood. Dressed in oversized hats and colorful clothes, the hundred or so kids waited patiently in a line that wound around the block, in front of a partially demolished building covered with graffiti. He drove around the block again, to make sure he was in the right place, then parked and walked toward the line.

The first thing he noticed on reaching the group was how *young* they all looked. He didn't feel that he'd aged so much since sixteen, and yet these were children. His blue work shirt and jeans were definitely out of place. Most of the girls wore baggy overalls over tube tops; the boys, either overalls without a shirt, or bright tie-dyed shirts and shorts.

At the end of the line he stood next to a girl with cotton candy hair pushing out under a gigantic orange hat. She looked about fifteen and swigged Evian water from a bottle.

Trumbo ran his hand through his hair and approached her. "Uh, is this the line for Moon Man?"

"Yeah. They stopped with the tickets for a few minutes 'cause the cops came around," she said nonchalantly. "The cops will be gone in a few minutes, though."

As they waited, a young man walked up and down the line, quietly muttering under his breath, "X . . . X . . . X." The boy was a little older than most of the others, but dressed similarly, in overalls and a blue hat emblazoned with the letter *X*. The kids in line shook their heads as he passed, until, fifteen yards away or so, one girl nodded. She left the line with the boy in the X hat, moved into a doorway near Trumbo, and handed him some money. *A drug deal,* thought Trumbo.

Soon the kids were admitted into a building in groups of four, and came out with slips of paper. They headed off to their late-model BMWs, Volvos, and Acuras. *Rich-kid cars,* thought Trumbo. The ticket buyers obviously lived in the affluent neighborhoods of the San Fernando Valley or in Orange County, not here in South Central.

When Trumbo was admitted to the tiny offices of *Double-X Magazine,* he approached a counter. "Twenty dollars, cash," said a young woman with pink hair. The other three kids, including the girl who stood in front of him in line, anted up crisp twenties without asking a question. He pulled a ten, a five, and four ones from his wallet, then dug into his pocket for change and came up with just over twenty dollars, pocketing the remaining forty cents.

For this he was given a sticker and a crudely printed map to another part of Los Angeles.

"Is that it?" he asked.

"Party starts at ten. No weapons or alcohol. That's all."

Back outside, he stood on the sidewalk staring at the map, wondering if he'd been duped. In any other circumstance he would have kicked up a fuss, but there was an air of secrecy and he didn't want to blow his chance to see Joi again. As he walked back to his truck, he noticed that in the last half hour or so the line had quadrupled in length, extending far off of Washington Boulevard onto a residential street. He estimated that there were five hundred in line, with more arriving every minute. A quick calculation showed that the ticket sellers would get more than ten thousand dollars in *cash*, received in exchange for a few cents worth of maps and stickers. He drove home and slept the rest of the afternoon, then left the house at ten P.M.

The map, photocopied onto pink paper, led to a warehouse in a commercial area of Culver City, a business district that was home to MGM studios. Not exactly a safe neighborhood, it wasn't South Central, either. You didn't fear getting out of your car, but you still watched your back.

He parked on a side street and walked back toward the building, an abandoned furniture warehouse. A line of one thousand or more kids snaked around the block behind the huge building. Three teenaged boys shared a bottle of watermelon juice at the end of the line.

"This is for Moon Man, right?" asked Trumbo.

"Yeah," said a boy in a bright purple T-shirt.

"It was supposed to start an hour ago."

"Yeah."

"What's taking so long?"

"Don't know. They're always late."

"So you can't complain or anything?"

"It's not the promoters. They're just waiting for the fire marshal to leave before they can get in."

"What're they gonna do, burn the place down?"

"What?" The boy stared at Trumbo, uncomprehending. Trumbo spoke exaggeratedly slow. "Why a fire marshal?"

"You know, overcrowding. This your first party?"

"I guess so."

"Peace, man."

"Thanks."

The boy handed Trumbo a slip of red paper folded origami-style into the shape of a flower. Trumbo unfolded it. Printed inside were the words "Try world peace. It's the ultimate." A Tootsie Roll fell out.

"What's this?"

"A gift."

"Is it drugs?"

The boy smirked. "No, it's a Tootsie Roll. A nutty kind of thing, but maybe it will bring some happiness to the world." The boy giggled.

"Right."

Trumbo pocketed the candy without eating it and avoided eye contact with the boy. But as he looked around him, he noticed that plenty other kids had the same happy, empty look like toddlers with ice cream cones. It didn't entirely make sense to him. When he was their age, the teenagers who went to nightclubs smoked, drank, swore, and went out of their way to scowl and appear dangerous. These kids seemed like they'd be rejected from Disneyland for being too goddamn happy.

Soon a powerful thumping sound emanated from the warehouse. A cheer ran through the crowd, and the line began to move.

Trumbo was searched twice—once by bouncers who took his ticket, and once at the door. When he got into the foyer, he realized that the jackhammer sound was simply electronic music, amplified to just below the threshold of pain. *Duh duh duh duh duh duh duh,* repetitive, loud, and driving. A shrill synthesizer riff provided the only counterpoint. It was music unlike any he'd ever heard; not punk, not disco, not rock, not heavy metal. Just endless fast, repetitive riffs.

He entered the main room of the warehouse and was

instantly assaulted by the smell of dry ice. The center area of the old warehouse was filled shoulder to shoulder with gyrating kids dancing rhythmically. No one danced *with* anyone. They just reveled as one mass moving in synch to the electronic rhythms.

Dozens of laser beam projectors sprayed the floor with an ever-changing pattern of light. They mutated from loops to pictures to a galaxy of dots, red, green, and blue littering the walls and floors with pure color.

Hats. Meet me by the hats, said Joi. He worked his way across the floor, staring at the blissed-out faces of the revelers. The music penetrated his body as the *duh duh duh* pulse grew louder. Songs had no beginning or ending or even recognizable lyrics. The closest thing to singing that he heard was an announcer's deep voice which repeated, "Fire in the heart. Fire on the art. Fire in the heart. Fire on the art." The words had no relation to the music, as if the speaker were giving instructions on how to park at the airport. Although he wasn't trying to dance, Trumbo unconsciously walked in time with the music.

He ascended a stairway to the platform overlooking the gigantic dance floor. The bodies below seethed and pulsated as one enormous, organic whole. At the top of the stairs was a series of tables where various goods were sold. A man with silver hair—not gray, but shiny, metallic silver—had a pitcher filled with colored liquid and a hand-painted sign announcing SMART DRINKS: BIO-ENERGETIC PROTEIN AND BRAIN-ENHANCING FORMULA—$2.50. Several booths sold T-shirts and jewelry. Then, at the end of the long passageway above the dance floor, he saw what he was looking for: hats.

Most of the oversized hats seemed to have been inspired by Dr. Seuss. He pushed his way through the crowd to the table. Joi Wilmot wore a silver lamé shirt, gold lamé pants, sparkling earrings, and a necklace. The left side of her face had been painted with metallic blue paint. Her hat towered three feet above her forehead and was decorated with flashing red and blue lights.

"Joi—Joi—hello!" He yelled above the earsplitting music.

"Would you like to try on a hat?" she asked.

He leaned in to her ear. "It's me! Trumbo. You said to meet you down here. Talk about my mom!"

"Oh, God."

She walked out of the booth and grabbed his arm. "You can't be seen here! Come with me!"

"Hey, what the hell?"

"Blue is here. He's armed."

Behind the balcony was a row of doors, leading to the former offices of the furniture company. She pulled him into a room and slammed the door behind them. Inside the office one girl stood on a chair while another used finger paint and makeup to draw intricate designs on her body; she wore only a bikini bottom.

Joi turned to the girls. "Are we bothering you? Is it okay to be in here?"

"Whatever," said the girl on the chair, and her friend continued painting the intricate sun and moon design on her back.

"What on earth is going on?" asked Trumbo.

"This is a rave, Trumbo," said Joi. "Get used to it. It's the future of the planet."

"And is a lobotomy mandatory for entrance? There must be thousands of kids downstairs, and none of them look like the fastest puppies in the litter."

"They're just happy. Give it a rest."

"Why can't I call you?"

"You can't call or contact me. Blue will blow a valve."

"What is his problem, shorts too tight?"

"It's a long story. He may be demanding, but he gives me a lot in return." She cracked the door open and glanced out. "I only can stay away from the booth for a few minutes."

"Right. What were you going to tell me?"

"Your mother is alive. I made some calls."

"Where?"

"She's hiding out. I don't know where. But someone I talked to has seen her recently, and wouldn't tell me more."

"Who? This is my mother we're talking about."

"Friends of Blue."

"Why can't you tell me who they are? I just want to find my mother. I'm not a narc or something."

"Trumbo, there's a lot you don't know about your parents. I shouldn't even be talking to you, but I like you, and I liked your father. I can't tell you more because . . ." She looked around behind her. The girls doing the body painting were eavesdropping on their conversation. Joi leaned in to Trumbo and whispered.

"Your mother was involved in some pretty heavy shit. Drug dealing. Robbery. Maybe even murder. You don't mess with these folks. Your father may have been murdered. And the people who did it may be after your mother."

"This is nonsense. My dad was knocked off by a lunatic."

"That's not what I heard."

He grabbed her by the sleeve of her shirt. "Don't dick around with me. Why can't you give me names?"

"Because those same people may be after me."

"Who are they? That's all I want to know."

She tore herself from his grip. "I can't tell you. They'd know it was me who leaked. Your mother is alive. Isn't that enough?"

"Who the hell would want to kill my parents?"

"When I met you, you believed she was dead. Maybe it's better to leave it at that. You'll be happier in the long run. I risked my life finding out this much."

She ran out the door, back to her hat booth. Trumbo chased after her.

"Leave!" she yelled. "If Blue sees me talking to you, he'll hurt both of us!"

"I'm staying where I am until you tell me where she is. I can take whatever Blue can dish out."

"Here he comes." Joi tried to behave nonchalantly, as if she'd been there all night. She leaned in to Trumbo's ear and yelled.

"Get the hell away from me. Don't call me. Don't bother me. I've done everything I can."

"Jesus Christ!"

Trumbo looked down the long walkway. Blue rapidly approached. His threatening appearance—leather jacket, boots, and black T-shirt—was wildly out of place at the rave.

"Please!" Joi implored.

Trumbo stood his ground as Blue strode toward him.

"Shit, Joi, I thought I told you to avoid this trouble-maker," said Blue.

"Maybe I just showed up. Got a problem with that?" said Trumbo, bracing himself.

"You little fuck." Blue punched Trumbo in the shoulder, sending him into the stand. Two racks of hats tumbled to the ground.

Trumbo jumped back and pounded Blue in the stomach. Blue doubled over, then grabbed Trumbo, and both men fell to the floor.

A circle of teens watched in fear and disgust as the two men grappled.

Trumbo pinned Blue to the ground. "What's the problem, fuckwad?" he asked.

Blue spit in Trumbo's face, catching him off guard.

"You dick!" Trumbo let fly another punch, knocking Blue's head back to the ground.

Two massive guards in yellow security jackets hauled Trumbo to his feet. One was black, one was white, and they held Trumbo's arms behind his back.

"Come on, you're out of here."

Trumbo resisted. "He started the fight."

"Didn't look like that to us." With a grin, the white guard lifted Trumbo off his feet. "We gonna carry you or you wanna walk?"

Blue got to his feet. As Trumbo was dragged out, Blue yelled after him, "Keep bugging me, kid. I'm not done with you, ya little prick."

Trumbo wrenched one arm away from the bodyguard and flipped his middle finger up at Blue before he was carried down the stairs and thrown out into the parking lot.

5

Marilyn McLeod, slightly drunk from lunch with a friend (charged to the production company), staggered into the Clandestine Productions New York office. The receptionist's desk, which for the previous two weeks had been covered with cookies and doughnuts, was now immaculately clean. A strange deathly silence hung in the office. Gone was the rock music that had been blaring through the room when she left. Marilyn leaned across the simulated-marble reception desk and barked at Mark-Jon, the slender receptionist.

"Where the hell is everybody?" asked Marilyn.

"They're all here, Marilyn." He pursed his lips. "You better check your messages."

She grabbed a fistful of pink message slips from the rack.

"The boss called four times? Since I've been gone? He calls that a goddamn vacation?"

"Look where he's calling from."

"Airplane, airport, cellular phone." Marilyn slapped her forehead. "Fuck me! What the hell is the dwarf doing? He's supposed to be in Paris for another week!"

Mark-Jon spoke softer than usual, in marked contrast to Marilyn's bellowing tirade. "He got the idea to come back early. It's his company, Marilyn. He can do whatever he wants."

Marilyn quickly saw her job—as a well-paid television producer—flash before her eyes. She had promised the boss that when he came back, she'd have three alternative proposals for the next Clandestine television special. If he demanded one of his "pop quiz" meetings, she was dead meat. Her plan had been to throw them together in the few days before he got back, like she always did.

She stuffed the message slips into her tattered Filofax and marched back to her cubicle, muttering aloud.

"That mutant midget! That isn't fair! How does he expect us to play by the rules when we don't know what the fucking rules are!"

The company produced true-crime television specials, one per month, and the system by which the subject was chosen ensured maximum stress. The company required each of the four producers to come up with three ideas for shows. Each idea had to be a full-blown proposal, ready to shoot. Then, on what they called "Decimation Day," one of the twelve ideas was picked, and the other eleven were shitcanned. If a producer didn't get an idea through the ranks at least once in a while, it was "best of luck in your future endeavors" time. The system set employee against employee in a particularly vicious way.

A cheery male voice greeted her from behind a cubicle.

"Hi, Marilyn! You must have heard the good news!"

"Blow me, Wytowski."

"I love it when you talk dirty, Marilyn."

She leaned into the junior producer's cubicle. He had straightened out all his papers and was diligently typing something into a computer. Wytowski had a strange habit of acting calm when he was panicked, though he shrieked like any other producer when things were under control. Today he was suspiciously calm.

"How're your proposals going?" she asked.

"Reasonably well," he said cheerily. "I'll probably have two complete shows for the boss. One on satanic cults within the Catholic church—I got this great ex-Jesuit who agreed to appear, and if we can get it past the network, I feel pretty good about it. The other is baby-sitters who murder their charges. I have two weepy mothers who will show up. How about you?"

"Nothing, zero, zippo, crapola. The best thing I've come up with is a trailer park in Arizona. Everyone who lives there—fifty-eight people—thinks they're aliens, and to get in, you have to say you are one, too. But the brainless wonder who runs it doesn't believe in television or some such bullshit. When the boss gets back, he's going to cut off my head and go bowling with my eye sockets. That little shit! I can't believe he'd come back early!"

She felt a tap on her shoulder. She looked down, all the

way down, to five feet one, the height of James St. James, owner of Clandestine Productions and star of all the *Clandestine Report* specials. Marilyn bit her lip and dug her sixty-dollar fingernails into her palms. She turned a deep shade of red that was heightened by the contrast with her green business suit.

"Ray! Gosh—you're back early! What a surprise." She brushed back her hair in an effort to appear nonchalant.

St. James bounced on his elevator heels and chuckled deviously. "Bowl with your eye sockets—I like that, Marilyn. On any other day of the year you'd be right." He licked his broad handlebar mustache and smoothed it out with his finger, a habit that had been the subject of as many nasty jokes as his lack of height. "Come with me. Right now. I figured out our next special while I was in Paris, and it's a ratings home run. We've got to get to work."

Wytowski looked on in envy. The boss had not even made eye contact with him. "Hey, Ray—what is it? What's the great idea?"

"You'll find out soon enough, Wytowski. That's why you're a junior producer."

St. James started to walk away, and Wytowski leaped up from his seat. "Hey, Ray—I dug up a great piece on some satanist Jesuits—"

St. James turned on his heel. "Can it, Wytowski. It sounds great, but we can't do it. Send it to your mother or something." He started to walk away, then stopped. "Another thing." He inhaled deeply. *"Don't call me Ray! And don't call me Garvey! I changed my fucking name eight years ago!* Goddamn it, if there's anyone else in earshot, it's St. James—*James* St. James! Get the memo! Read it! Learn it! Do it!" St. James lowered his voice, turned toward Marilyn, and was suddenly all sweetness. "Shall we?"

Marilyn burped and tasted cheap Manhattans. She urgently wanted breath mints. "Shouldn't I get some notes or something?"

"No."

In his magnificent cherry-paneled corner office, St. James positioned himself behind the enormous desk and threw his jacket across the room. One of the rumors about the massive desk was that it had been specially designed so that a woman could hide underneath it and perform oral sex on St. James during meetings. Marilyn happened to know that the rumor was true. The office itself had been specially designed, at a cost of eighty two thousand dollars, so that it ramped slightly down, making St. James about six inches higher than anyone on the other side of his desk—just about eye level, for a person of average height. The studio set was designed the same way. St. James pressed a button on the intercom.

"Mark-Jon, hold all calls. And don't tell anyone I'm back from Paris."

"But, sir, you've already told everyone in town," came the reply through the squawk box.

"I'm not here! Got it? Learn it. Do it."

Marilyn squirmed uncomfortably, uncertain whether she should sit down. "So what's the great breakthrough?"

"Look at this, Marilyn. I got these in Paris."

He threw two newspapers down on the inclined desk so they faced Marilyn. She picked one up.

"It's in French, Ray." He shot her a dirty look. "Uh, I mean James."

"Yes, of course it's in French, I bought it in France." He licked his mustache again, then quickly checked his jet-black toupee to see that it was in position. "Marilyn, what were our biggest hits?"

"I don't know—'Inside Hitler's Bunker'?"

St. James shook his head slightly.

"Maybe the thing about the government storing alien bodies—what was that called?"

"'Inside Hangar Eighteen.' It did well, but wasn't the best." St. James shook his head and grinned. "Think harder. You're just naming things from this season."

"If you mean all-time greatest-ratings hits, they'd have to be the two Manson shows. 'Inside Charles Manson's Mind' and 'Inside Charles Manson's Jail Cell.'"

St. James thrust his arms over his head. "Bingo! Those would be the ones."

"So you found a new Manson?"

"No—I found a new hook. These newspapers are French. They're crap, of course—Frog tabloids—but no one in America knows that. Look at this story."

Marilyn stared at the text without comprehending. "What's it say, James?"

"It's a little piece by a self-proclaimed expert claiming that Charlie's going to get his parole this time around."

"Is there any reason to believe that?"

St. James threw down the paper. "No, of course not, Marilyn—it's total bullshit. But what does *that* matter? We've got enough problems without worrying about *accuracy*. We start plugging it a month in advance. I've been writing the *TV Guide* teasers in my head—*Experts Say Manson's Getting Out*. We drag in this French dodohead and get someone stateside who agrees. We do two-minute interviews with them and plaster it morning, noon, night. Everything we do suggests he's going to get out this time, without promising too much. Then we go live on the day of the parole hearing—call it *Manson Unleashed!*"

Marilyn tried to appear enthusiastic, but was secretly appalled. *The midget cuts short a trip because he says he has a breakthrough show, and it's another bogus Manson piece.* "It's brilliant, Ray! When do we start?"

"That's 'James—*James* St. James'!" He pulled off a shoe and threw it across the room. It missed her by a yard. "We start yesterday—I'm pulling you because you're the only one who can get this kind of thing together fast enough. His hearing is in six weeks. Where's your notes?"

"You told me not to bring any."

"You should always have notes. Here, take my legal pad—and don't ever say I never gave you anything." He threw the legal pad across the room, down the incline toward her. "Start writing."

He detailed the master plan to her. In Marilyn's view it was less than brilliant, but St. James considered himself an "idea man," and anyone who pointed out the holes in his schemes often wound up unemployed. His instructions to her were to find the most credible people possible who would support the contention that Charles Manson was about to be unloosed—"Cops are good, judges are better, I'd really like to have a Nobel Prize winner make the claim." Marilyn pointed out that Nobel Prize winners don't ordinarily comment on the parole system, but St. James was unfazed. "Just remember two things," he said. "Get the most reliable people who believe this bullshit, and get them on tape. Get it? Learn it. Do it."

The next part of his scheme was to hire "every two-bit freelance crew in Central California" so that they could have the coverage be as exclusive as possible. Then he lowered his voice.

"Marilyn, this is the hard part. This is why I've got you for the job. You are willing to do anything"—he paused—*"anything* to make this come off because this is the linchpin. I need you to accomplish two things, and I won't ask how you do it. First, the parole hearing has to be somewhere we can broadcast it. Not tape, it's going to be live."

"But, James, the hearings won't be on at a good time for viewer numbers."

"That's the second thing," he said, grinning. "This is why you make the big bucks. They've got to do the hearing at five o'clock California time. Eight P.M. on the East Coast. Prime-oh time-oh. We're going to kick 'Seinfeld' right in the balls."

Marilyn bit straight through a fingernail. "Uh, Ray, they don't move parole hearings around for TV shows."

He shot up from his desk. "Don't tell me what can't be done." He threw his remaining elevator shoe across the room, knocking over a tall Art Deco lamp. "It's got to be at fucking five o'clock."

"I just think you should know it's unlikely."

"I'm putting this show on live and they're going to do the goddamn hearing at five o'clock. Think of the numbers, Marilyn. We drew a thirty-two share for the 'Inside Hitler's Bunker' show just because it was live! If it had been on tape, everybody would have known in advance that his secret diaries weren't down there! Manson ain't getting out! If this is on tape, it may as well be the local news—which, I might remind you, is where you came from. Clandestine Productions does not report news! Clandestine makes news! Get it! Learn it! Do it!"

She nodded her head. "I'll look into it."

"What do you need? Money? The bank vault is open. Get a fistful of credit cards from Mark-Jon or whatever that kid's name is. I'll approve every expense, and cash is no problem. Do you understand? You will make it happen! Unless you miss doing the local news, that is."

After Marilyn left, St. James bolted the door to his office, straightened up the Art Deco lamp, and removed his itchy toupee. If anyone could make the show happen, it was Marilyn. She had slept with him to get the job at Clandestine Productions. He liked that—although not for the sex. It was because he respected the Machiavellian directness with which she attacked every problem. Ends always justify the means.

Even though he was never attracted to her sexually, he was in awe of her because she possessed the same kind of "succeed at all costs" talent he did. When she had joined the team two years earlier, he took her out to dinner, just to see what made her tick. She came on to him so slyly, so subtly, he took it for a sincere crush and was flattered. They did the big nasty. It was nothing spectacular, although she tied him up, which was enjoyable.

The next day when she insisted on becoming a full-fledged producer, bucking the usual system, St. James balked, until she showed him the photos of himself naked, tied up, and obviously enjoying himself. Lots of women had fallen for the promise of promotion and given in to his favorite kink, but only Marilyn had the wits to blackmail him. And he recognized talent when he saw it.

He flipped open another "Frog tabloid"—this one a real estate circular. During his trip, he visited a beautiful estate for sale on the outskirts of Paris. Four and a half million bucks, at the current exchange rate. St. James made better than nine million a year, but he realized to his dismay that he couldn't afford the estate. He already was paying mortgages on a beach house in Tahiti, two New York apartments —the residence he shared with his wife and the "secret" apartment he kept for affairs—his ski lodge in Utah and the one in Aspen, and a leaky flat in London he rarely visited.

His desire for the Parisian villa had increased because he couldn't presently afford it. There was room for horses, and even though he had never ridden in his life, the notion of fox hunting with the French appealed to him. The deal with the network for Clandestine Productions was up for renewal in three months. It had been two years since his last ratings blockbuster, and he knew that in conjunction with the general downturn in ratings, the network would try to pay him less money.

He needed a hit. The Frog tabloid in fact had nothing about Manson, but he knew that Marilyn didn't read French. He'd been carrying the idea for another angle on the Manson story in his head for months, but it only became crystal-clear when he was touring the beautiful villa.

Even while raving about the show to Marilyn, he had fantasized himself wearing a handsome riding outfit, surrounded by leggy French girls, returning from a long day's ride in the country to savor expensive champagne in the hot tub. In America, everyone knew who he was. And while his shows got high ratings, he couldn't get respect, even from the people who watched them. Overseas, he *bought* respect and told everyone he was an award-winning American newscaster. St. James didn't just *want* the villa: he needed it.

6

No fanfare greeted Denise Jennings's arrival in Hollywood, U.S.A. Even the Greyhound station on Vine was disappointing. The building was smaller than the McDonald's next door. The station contained only eleven hard plastic chairs, some lockers, and a counter staffed by a phlegmatic gray-haired woman in a stained blue polyester uniform. The girl carefully sized her up. She needed to win her approval to earn her freedom.

The bus driver walked behind the glassed-in counter and handed a letter and duffel bag to the ticket lady, who spoke into a creaky public-announcement microphone. "Barbie

Parker, please report to the ticket counter." Denise Jennings screwed up all the courage of her twelve years and approached, repeating to herself, "Barbie Parker, Barbie Parker. My name is Barbie Parker." She patted down her unkempt hair in an effort to appear as mature and responsible as possible.

"Yes, ma'am?" said Denise, extra politely.

"Says here your aunt is suppose to pick you up."

"Yes, that's correct. But she's very old, and when I called she asked me to walk to her apartment."

The ticket lady stared plaintively and rustled some papers. "Says *here* she's *supposed* to pick you up."

A knot grew in Denise's stomach. "I can walk over, I don't really mind . . ."

"Know where she lives?"

"Sure. It's over on Cahuenga." Denise pronounced it *cow-hunga*. She'd seen the sign when the bus pulled into town.

"That's *cah-wainga*. You sure you know where you going?"

"Yes, ma'am."

The ticket lady glared at Denise through bifocals, then pushed a piece of paper through the slot in the window. "Sign here."

Denise stood on tiptoe to reach the counter. She had signed all the custody forms required for children under sixteen years of age. She had typed the forms herself back in the St. Joseph, Missouri, library, using the name Barbie Parker. She knew enough not to use her real name like the first two times she ran away, first to Chicago and then to Denver. Her stepfather tracked her down in a matter of days on both trips. This time she wanted to do it right.

"That's it, Barbie," said the ticket lady.

"Can I get my bag?"

"Sure."

Denise hefted the enormous duffel bag and began walking toward Hollywood Boulevard, five blocks away. The town was dirty and she saw no sign of beaches anywhere near. If not for the plaques with stars' names on the sidewalk, it might have been any large city. But no matter how decrepit, at least Hollywood wasn't St. Joseph, and she didn't have to lie awake at night wondering when Ned, her stepfather, would get stoned and wake her up to play one of his "games." She didn't have to hear her mother crying through the thin walls of their apartment when Ned beat her up. Denise was determined to stay away this time.

She hadn't taken the Greyhound from the St. Joseph terminal—she knew they would be looking for her there. Instead, she took the airport van to Kansas City, using Ned's credit card, which as a bonus saved her twenty-two dollars. That way scummy old Ned would be knocking himself out looking for her in Kansas City instead of trying to find out where she really went.

Then she got a regular city bus from the Kansas City airport to the bus station. Her original plan was to go to Texas, but it was an eleven-hour wait for the bus to Austin, whereas the bus to Los Angeles was leaving almost as soon as she arrived. The ticket cost her sixty-nine dollars. As she rode through the mountains and desert, Los Angeles loomed large in her imagination. When she learned from the printed schedule that the bus stopped in Hollywood before it went downtown, her mind was made up. *Hollywood.* She imagined a chance meeting with someone from the movies or television. She was sure if she met the boy from "Beverly Hills 90210" or Bill Cosby that they'd like her and take care of her. She wouldn't tell them she was from St. Joseph, which was too small, preferring instead to be from someplace *important* like Kansas City or Chicago.

Her cobalt-blue eyes pinned wide open, Denise walked north, eager to broaden herself. The heavy duffel bag was buoyed by her enthusiasm for a new beginning and the exhilarating spectacle of the city. She was fascinated by the signs written in foreign languages, the stores that unabashedly displayed sex videotapes right in the front window where everyone could see them, and most of all by the people: black, white, Oriental, punks, businessmen, and beggars all sharing the sidewalks as equals. She stopped at a little stand run by a brown-skinned man, and ordered a meal without knowing what it was. *Falafel,* the man called it, and it tasted pretty good. She hadn't eaten since leaving

St. Joseph, primarily to conserve money. The meal cost her three dollars and sixty-five cents, leaving forty-two dollars and change in her blue plastic billfold.

After many hours walking around the streets, she realized what thousands of other runaways learn. There is nothing in Hollywood but discount stores, fast-food restaurants, and movie theaters. She searched in vain for the big houses where movie stars live, but found only run-down apartment buildings with burglar bars. The cheapest hotel cost more than fifty dollars a night. She stood on the sidewalk in front of a rancid all-night movie theater.

Her duffel bag felt so heavy, and she was on the verge of tears. The fleabag theater was showing two of those stupid *Ernest* movies, but she didn't care. She paid the three bucks and took a seat near the front. She watched part of *Ernest for President* and scoped out the room to see if there were ushers watching her. When she noticed two men sleeping several seats over, she leaned back and fell asleep herself.

Some hours later—she didn't know how long she'd been sleeping—Denise awoke with a jolt. Her duffel bag was open! It was almost as if she'd been hit. She dug through the bag, searching for her wallet, pulling out her clothes, maps of Texas, her Walkman—but she found no wallet.

"Oh no."

She looked up and saw a middle-aged white man smiling at her with nicotine-stained teeth. "Lose something?"

"My wallet is gone."

"I saw the thief, but you know what? I stopped him." The *s* sounds whistled through his teeth like a cartoon character. He held up a wallet. "Is this it?"

"Yes!"

When she reached for it, he quickly pulled it away. "Not so quick. Is there a reward?"

She frowned. The wallet contained all her money in the world. Without it, she didn't know what she would do. "I'll give you, I don't know, I'll give you five dollars. Is that enough of a reward?"

"I was thinking of another kind of reward. I'd even be willing to pitch in some more money, like another twenty dollars as well as the thirty-five bucks you have. If you can give me the right kind of reward."

Denise felt a leaden sensation in her stomach. "What kind of reward?"

"Maybe come out to my car, and you know, a little half and half . . ." His voice dwindled to a whisper.

"What?" Denise shook her head, not comprehending.

"You know." He cleared his voice. "Okay then. I'll pay you forty bucks. I know you need the money."

"What is half and half?"

He whispered. "A blow job."

Denise's jaw dropped in disbelief. "Fuck you, you old horndog. Give me my wallet!" She tried to pull the wallet out of the man's hand, but he was too quick for her. She grabbed on to his arm and dug in her teeth.

"Give it back!"

"Little bitch!" he yelled.

One of the patrons a few rows back cupped his hands and yelled, "I'm trying to watch a goddamn movie!"

Denise sunk her teeth into his arm. "Ouch! You cunt!" he yelled, then yanked his arm away and jumped over two rows of seats. He raised his middle finger toward Denise. "Little bitch!"

Scared, Denise picked up her bag and ran to the lobby. The manager was in the ticket booth, listening to a radio news show.

"Sir? Sir? Someone robbed me in there."

"Just a minute."

"Sir—he's in there right now, watching the movie."

"Hold on, I'm coming."

The manager, a young Hispanic kid, walked with her into the theater. The man who took her wallet was gone.

"Where is he?"

Denise sighed. "Never mind."

She glumly trekked back out to the boulevard, where the morning sun made all the buildings look shiny and new. The street was almost deserted. It was nearly seven A.M.

A powerful hunger came over her. She had nothing to eat, and no money. She entered a Woolworth's drugstore.

"Leave that bag here."

"Okay."

She wandered around the store, pretending to look at stationery and shampoo but really watching the store employees. When she thought she wasn't being watched, she stuffed three cans of Vienna sausage into her jacket pocket. Then she returned to the counter.

"Could I get my bag back?"

The man behind the counter ignored her. He yelled back into the store. "Security. Security."

A uniformed guard strode to the front of the store.

The cashier glared at Denise. "Show him what you stole."

"I didn't steal anything!"

"Show him!"

The guard stood between her and the front door. "I swear, I didn't take anything!" she yelled.

"We'll call the police right now or you can show us."

"No! You can't! You can't call the police!" she yelled. "I didn't mean to take anything!"

Just then a man who had been milling about in the store walked up and pulled the security guard's arm off of Denise's shoulder. She looked at the stranger—he wore jeans and a leather vest that was inscribed with intricate patterns. His hair was long, and a blue dot graced his forehead. Something about him looked very friendly, accessible, as if she'd known him before.

"What's the trouble here?"

"Sir, it's none of your business," said the rent-a-cop.

The man in the vest spoke softly. "I know this girl. I told her to get some things and I'd pay for them. She's not from here and doesn't know you have to use a basket."

He spoke with authority. The store manager and the security guard were intimidated. He smiled at Denise. "Put those things on the counter. Let's pay for them and be on our way."

"Sir, she was stealing," said the cashier.

The man puffed himself up and spoke brusquely. "She did not steal anything. Did she leave the store? No, she didn't. I was planning to pay for those things. Do you want a lawsuit for picking on this little girl? I think you don't. So get off your high horse."

The cashier sighed. "Fine."

"Put the things on the counter, dear."

Denise put the Vienna sausages on the counter. The man spoke again. "We'll also get a candy bar, a Coke, and some of those peanuts."

They rang up the order, and Denise and the man stepped out to the boulevard.

"Thanks, man," she said. "How come you did that?"

"The favors we do are always returned tenfold."

"Well, thanks tenfold."

"You shouldn't be eating Vienna sausage. Come on, I'll buy you breakfast."

"You're not a horndog, are you?"

"What?"

"I mean, you're not going to buy me breakfast and then ask me to give you a blow job or something?"

"We are wise beyond our years. No, I'm just going to buy you breakfast. That's it. No deals, no favors. And no blow—I won't say it. You're too young. My name's J'osüf. J'osüf Sunn."

"I'm Denise. You saved my fucking life in there."

He hesitated. "You saved your own life. You are always in command of yourself. Don't forget that, Denise."

"Yeah, right."

He took her to Roscoe's House of Chicken & Waffles, and Denise scarfed down three waffles and four hot chocolates. J'osüf talked kind of funny—in poems or something—but she liked him. He seemed like a decent guy. Pretty soon she was telling him her whole life story, starting out with her father dying and right up to her pervert stepfather and how she ran away. He understood when she said she couldn't go back.

When the check came, he put down a twenty-dollar bill. Then he looked her in the eye. "You don't have any place to stay, do you, Denise?"

"Yeah, and I'm dead-squat busted broke."

"Would you like a place to stay? Or would you think I'm just what you call a horndog?"

"You're no horndog, J'osüf. I can tell."

"Good. Well, I can offer you a place to stay. It's a house with lots of kids, some almost as young as you."

"Shit. You're one of those Bible-beaters with a shelter,

aren't you? Thanks but no thanks." She donned a pair of sunglasses, then stood up. "It's been nice, man."

He pressed on her shoulder, and she sat back down. "I'm not from a runaway shelter. It's a place to live and breathe and do what you want to do. No Bible meetings, no obligations. You can leave whenever you want. Come out and look at the place. If you don't like it, I promise I'll drive you back to this very corner."

Denise sized up her options. It was either go with Mr. Blue Dot, or panhandling and shoplifting. She used her best poker face. "I gotta be level with you. If it sucks, I'm outta there. But I'll give it a look. No problemo."

He paid the check and they walked out to his orange van. She watched him like a hawk the whole time they were driving, and he didn't try to lay a hand on her once. Maybe, just maybe, he was on the level. She hoped so.

Sunn was pleased. The new girl fit in just fine. She had already met some of the other girls and had taken the room formerly occupied by the traitorous Thursday. He liked having seven girls. Six was a bad-luck number.

That evening he drove into town to sell some Ecstasy, and saw something so intriguing that he stopped the van to stare. On a billboard high above the Sunset Strip was a picture of the Man Himself, Jesus, his Spiritual Leader, known to consensus reality people as Charles Manson. Beneath the enormous billboard were the words "Countdown till Charles Manson is UNLEASHED." Next to that was a lighted digital counter that read "[5] Weeks [2] days [6] Hours and [22] minutes. WATCH JAMES ST. JAMES, ONLY ON L.A.'S CHANNEL 8." While Sunn stared, the "22" changed to "21." It was a countdown clock.

On the four-mile drive south on La Brea toward his dealer, Sunn saw three more billboards and six park benches that promoted the same notion. "This Time He's Getting Out!" said one. "Would You Want Charles Manson In YOUR Neighborhood?" asked another.

Sunn was delighted that the consensus-reality types had finally realized it was time for Jesus to be freed. But at the same time, he was panicked. There was so much to do. He still had to locate the thirteen, as instructed in his letter, and he had a little over a month to do it. What if Charlie got free and Sunn hadn't accomplished the mission? He drove on, eager to make his sale and get home.

Sunn parked the van in front of Boardner's, a restaurant/bar whose vinyl booths proudly wore every cigarette hole that had been burned on them in the previous twenty-five years.

Sunn nodded to the bartender, then moved to the back. A forty-year-old man occupied the booth and stared at a golf game playing on the television set. The man wore khaki slacks and a pink shirt. He looked like Dan Quayle with a massive hangover. Chris Mayhall always looked that way.

"Chris."

"Hey, Sunn. Sit down, man."

"I gotta unload some dope."

"I'll buy whatever dope you got. I'm back into the circuit again and could use the cash. What say, I sell it inside of a week, we split whatever I make fifty-fifty?"

"Eighty-twenty," said Sunn.

"Sixty-forty," offered Chris.

"Deal. Sixty for me." Sunn handed over a paper bag.

"Sunn, something weird is happening. You know Joi Wilmot?"

"Yes."

"She's been asking a lot of questions lately. Blue told me so. She also called me up."

"And what'd she say?"

"I think she figured out what happened to our friend Luther. She's also looking for Mimi."

"Why's she looking for her?"

"Said a kid who says he's Luther's son showed up on her doorstep one day. Wanted to find his mother."

"She knows where this kid is?"

"I think so."

"Thanks, man."

Sunn walked out slowly, engrossed in thought.

Joi Wilmot double-bolted the door on her small bungalow. She hadn't seen Blue, her sometime boyfriend, since the previous week's Moon Man rave, when he dressed her down for not selling enough hats. That night, as they were packing up his van, their argument grew intense and Blue started to hit Joi again. She kicked him in the groin. Her last words to him were *Nobody hits me anymore. Not you, not anybody. Go fuck yourself.*

Blue had turned vicious soon after Joi tried to track down Mimi Black. Trumbo, the kid who stopped by, seemed sweet enough, but Blue beat the hell out of him for no apparent reason. Joi forgave him, on the assumption that it was the *crank* talking. Blue had periods when he took lots of cheap speed—crank—and it gave him a short fuse. She wanted to find Mimi Black, maybe hook her up with Trumbo Walsh, her long-lost son.

The previous night Joi's psychic had told her that the relationship with Blue was over, which made Joi terribly sad.

She tried to lose herself working in one of her experimental paintings. Just when she dabbed the first few swatches of color on the canvas, Blue walked in. He was cranked up. Behind him appeared J'osüf Sunn. Behind Sunn were half a dozen girls.

She threw down the brushes in anger.

"I did not say you could come in, Blue," growled Joi. "I'm working."

Ignoring her, Blue sat down. Sunn put a hand on Joi's shoulder. "We have to talk, Joi. About your daughter. And about that kid who visited you."

"I told you before that that's all behind me."

"That may be so. But we have all night to talk."

Joi looked around. She was surrounded. The girls blocked the front door.

"Blue, get them out of here."

"Sorry, Joi, no can do."

Joi saw that one of the girls held a knife. Then she noticed they *all* had knives.

"Is this it?" asked Joi, resigned.

"I'm afraid so. Unless you want to talk."

A tear rolled down her cheek. "I will NOT screw up another young life."

"You makes your choice," said Sunn.

Slowly the girls moved closer to Joi.

Joi quietly started chanting her mantra, *om,* and tried to block what was about to happen from her mind. *Every death is a new beginning,* she thought. Joi closed her eyes and waited for the inevitable.

7

TRUMBO WALSH WAS CRUISING DOWN ALVARADO STREET look-ing for a car wreck, any car wreck, when he heard the strange dispatch. The police radio that he illegally carried belched out the report in the arcane codes of police radio talk: The Rampart Division canceled a "domestic disturbance" call at 1997 Cove Avenue. In a nasal LAPD monotone the dispatcher elaborated on the brief message: "Neighbor called back and said the yelling stopped."

1997 Cove Avenue was Joi Wilmot's bungalow. Trumbo pounded a U-turn on the crowded street, burning some rubber and earning the enmity of drivers in the facing traffic, then pulled over a curb into a liquor store parking lot. He extracted his lanky frame from the truck, left the engine running, and dialed Joi's number from a pay phone. The line was busy. He tried twice more before he gave up and sped north on Alvarado toward Echo Park. The mercury-vapor lamps bathed the decrepit neighborhood an other-worldly mustard color. Since it was past midnight, most of the immigrant-owned shops and businesses were closed, burglar bars drawn tight.

He ran the red light at Glendale Boulevard and gunned into the hills toward Joi's bungalow. On the clapboard houses, gang graffiti and burglar bars were juxtaposed with old Christmas decorations and carefully tended gardens.

Trumbo parked in a gravel lot atop a hill next to a house burnt out years earlier. He jumped from the truck and grabbed the rail atop the concrete steps that led to Joi's bungalow.

The streetlights along the steps were off. Trumbo waited for his eyes to adjust, then took the stairs slowly, one at a time, wary of a stray palm frond that might trip him up. The cold steel rail was moist with evening dew. The air was a strange mixture of cut grass and freeway exhaust.

Halfway down the steps, he stopped and peered over the pine fence in front of Joi's home. The tiny pea-green bungalow was dark. He reached over the gate and pulled the latch, letting himself into the yard.

He pushed the buzzer twice. It made no sound.

He yelled, "Joi? Are you home?"

He rapped on the front door. It swung open, creaking on its hinges.

"Joi? It's Trumbo."

All he heard in response was the roar of the nearby freeway and his own furious breathing.

He groped around on the wall, then flipped the switch next to the door. The power was out. He squinted, vainly attempting to see into the murky front room. He considered fetching the flashlight from his truck but didn't want to hike back up the steps. He felt his way across the room to a little stand where he remembered seeing Joi's votive candles. He knocked over a photo before he found some matches and lit a candle. Its dim light flickered across the tiny room.

The room was as tidy as it had been during his first visit. The shelf filled with dusty books and kachina dolls was undisturbed. The small table next to the plaid couch held the latest copies of *TV Guide* and *New Age Magazine* arranged atop a hand-knit doily. He walked toward the dining table on the other side of the room, but hesitated when his hiking boot clacked on the hardwood floor.

Holding the candle in front of him, Trumbo made his way to Joi's bedroom. The room was minuscule and smelled of sandalwood incense. A window looked out on the freeway. Native American artifacts decorated one wall. The double bed was neatly made. Above the bed was crude graffiti, jarringly out of place in her meticulous abode. He kneeled on the bed and held the candle near to the wall. Smeared in characters that appeared black in the candlelight were the words:

Day One
Joi Hates Jesus.

As he moved back and the candle illuminated a larger patch of wall, he could make out another word, huge letters scrawled at a deviant angle across the wall: *Skelter*. Drips trickled down from the penultimate *e*, which was much larger than the rest of the word.

Trumbo touched the lettering. It was sticky and damp. His hand left a dark streak on the wall. Blood, he thought: Joi's blood. His heart pounded furiously and his lungs worked furiously. Survival instincts, honed through a life on the run, quickly kicked in. *Can't make noise, what if they're here?* He silently counted to ten: remain calm, remain calm. He darted through the living room, into the kitchen to call the police. The phone line was dead. The ancient fuse box near the back door was open; the fuses had been crushed into a pile of green glass shreds on the floor. *Think quick, think quick.* He pulled a penny from his pocket and jammed it into the fuse box. In the living room a light and the television abruptly came to life.

He blew out the candle, then grabbed a knife from the kitchen drawer and walked toward the front door, squinting in the sudden light. Joi's Oriental carpet was rolled up along the wall. A deep burgundy stain had soaked through. *Oh my God.* He unrolled the carpet, knocking over the table next to the couch. He beheld Joi's lifeless body, one arm contorted unnaturally behind her head. Her baggy blue dress was stiff with dried blood. Her head was twisted strangely to one side.

"Joi, oh Jesus, who did this to you, who did this to you!" Trumbo felt for a pulse on her wrist; found none. Her eyes stared off into space. Trumbo pulled her eyelids closed and stumbled out the door, still clutching the knife.

He ran up the steps two at a time, at one point slipping on an unseen pile of leaves. He narrowly avoided stabbing his knee and dropped the knife, which tumbled down the incline into thick grass. At the top of the stairs he leaped in his truck and raced down the hill, out of breath, his vision blurred with fear. In the AM PM Mini Mart at the bottom of the hill he had to argue with the Indian owner before he could use the phone to call the police.

He raced back to Joi's house, waiting for the police. The twenty-five minutes before they arrived felt like an eternity. In his mind he saw Joi's lifeless body staring sadly up at him, seemingly resigned to her fate. The things she said began to take on ominous new meanings. When she had talked about the search for his mother, she said, *The truth can be dangerous. Sometimes it's better not to know.*

A droning, repetitive roar heralded the arrival of a police chopper, which circled overhead and shined a powerful spotlight on the cottage, making it appear like a toy in a train set. Trumbo felt like a bug under glass. "Move away from the house," said a deep voice amplified by a powerful speaker system. "Put your hands in the air!"

He did as instructed. The helicopter maintained a low circular flight path above him, the powerful spotlight isolating Trumbo. His figure cast long, sharply defined shadows on the brilliantly overexposed lawn. The chopper's blades blew dust and pollen into the air. When Trumbo lowered a hand to scratch his eye, the voice boomed out, "Keep your hands up!"

Embarrassed and infuriated, he glanced up and down the stairs and saw neighbors peering out of windows in the cottages along the stairway, scrutinizing the invader of their sanctuary. After a couple minutes eight officers in full riot gear approached him slowly, four from the bottom of the stairway, four from the top.

"Lie down on the ground, and keep your hands visible."

Trumbo slowly lowered himself to the walkway in front of Joi's home. Moments later his hands were cuffed behind his back and a nightstick pinned his head to the ground. Someone removed the wallet from his back pocket.

Trumbo tried in vain to plead with the police, explaining that it was he who called them, but they weren't listening. He was marched at gunpoint to a waiting patrol car, had his rights read to him, and after a long wait, was driven to the Rampart station, where he was booked on suspicion of murder. They exchanged his clothes for prison blues, performed an embarrassing body cavity search, and kept him overnight in a tiny cell that he shared with a drunk who repeatedly vomited into the sink.

He had just drifted off to sleep when he was awakened by a guard banging on the steel bars of his cell.

"Walsh?"

He sat up on the bunk. His drunken roommate still snored, oblivious to the noise.

"Yeah?"

"A city-appointed attorney is here to see you."

He was led through three steel doors and taken to a small room with a telephone, table, and several folding chairs. Already seated was a shaggy-looking man with long gray hair, in an ill-fitting tweed suit a decade out of style. He stood when Trumbo entered.

"Trumbo Walsh?" he said, extending a hand.

"Yeah."

"Kevin Saunderson. I'll be your attorney."

Trumbo shook his head. "This is a bunch of crap. I didn't do anything. I was the one who called the police, goddammit!"

Saunderson nodded politely. "Yes, I understand. You think you'll enter a plea of not guilty?"

"A plea? They're going ahead with it?"

"Although, as your attorney, I'm supposed to do whatever you tell me to do, the case looks pretty damning. Your fingerprints are all over the murder scene. A knife that you handled was discovered on the walkway. They're going to have ten or twelve pieces of evidence that connect you to the murder. What's more, you have a police radio in your truck—it shouldn't be there."

"I use it to find out about wrecks!" he yelled. "All the tow trucks have 'em."

"I'll listen to what you have to say. But if this goes to trial, I'm probably going to recommend a plea bargain."

"That's bullshit. I didn't do anything."

Saunders looked over the top of his glasses and spoke in quiet, firm tones. "Well, then, you better have a damn good story to tell the judge. Why were you hanging around an ex-con like Joi Wilmot?"

"Joi was an ex-con?"

"Armed robbery, seventy-one. Bunch of other charges, mostly drug possession and parole violations, up till eighty-six."

"Jesus."

"Why did you go to her house last night? Do you have an alibi of any kind?"

Trumbo bit his lower lip. "Is this all confidential? I mean, you say you're my lawyer, but I never heard of you before."

"Everything is held in attorney-client confidence." A smile briefly manifested itself on the attorney's face. Trumbo took it to mean that the attorney thought he was going to hear a confession.

Trumbo slapped his hand against the wall, fire in his deep brown eyes. "Look—I'm not going to confess to the murder, if that's what you're thinking, because I didn't kill anybody, okay? It's just that some of what I've got to tell you is deeply personal. It's embarrassing to me. I had a fucked-up child-hood, I had a fucked-up family, and I don't like telling everybody who comes along all about the skeletons in my closet. Okay?"

Saunderson nodded. "Right. Whatever you want to tell me is fine. Let me in on as much as you want."

Trumbo sat down, his mind reeling. He'd have to tell everything. He ran his fingers through his hair and started at the beginning.

8

AFTER THE LAWYER LEFT, TRUMBO WAS PLACED INTO A SIX-BY-eight-foot felony holding tank, which he shared with three other men. One claimed he had been "set up by his wife and her boyfriend" on a felony abuse charge. One had been arrested breaking into a pharmacy and was pretty strung out. The third said nothing but "They got nothing on me, nothing!" and then he'd smack his fist against the cement wall. Track marks crawling up his arms suggested to Trumbo that the man was in on drug charges.

After about an hour the guard opened the door and escorted Trumbo out to see Saunderson. The lawyer smiled when Trumbo entered the lawyer-client briefing room.

"What's up, Kevin?"

Saunderson laid his palms flat on the table. "Let me level with you. At first I was pretty skeptical of what you told me. You know, everybody ever arrested on a serious charge will always insist he's innocent. But I've located an NOK who confirms your story."

Trumbo racked his brain trying to think of anyone who knew what he had been doing. "What the hell is that?"

"The next of kin. The cops tracked down the victim's daughter, living in Columbus, Ohio."

"She didn't say she had a daughter."

"I talked to the woman. Her name's Alison Wilmot. She left home about ten years ago and only recently reestablished communication with her mother."

"What'd she say?"

"She said she knows who you are. She's flying out here on some sort of red-eye special. Ought to get here tomorrow sometime before noon."

"So what happens now?"

Saunderson bit his lip. "You were supposed to be transferred down to the Glass House—the downtown city jail—and go before a magistrate tomorrow. Apparently the investigating officer was impressed enough with what the girl told him that he's gonna keep you here overnight and see her in person before pressing charges."

"Think they will charge me with anything?"

"Depends on what the girl says and whatever physical evidence they unearth."

"So I'm stuck here?"

Saunderson smiled. "Beats the hell out of the Glass House, let me tell you. If they book you down there, the paperwork alone means you could be stuck there for two, three days, even if they don't bring charges. Don't fight it."

"Thanks, I guess."

"You're welcome, I guess." The lawyer gathered his papers and left.

It was past six o'clock the next evening before anyone came to speak to him. Finally he was escorted out to see Saunderson again.

"Well, buddy, the girl produced a letter from her mom. Sounds like you were on the level about what you were doing there. Seems to *me*, that is. LAPD is not going to press charges right away, but you should watch your step."

"What do you mean, watch my step?"

"Beware of the little things. If they decide they don't like you, they'll bust you on something else."

"Like my police radio?"

"They already confiscated that. I don't think they'll bring charges for it, though."

"That cost me two hundred fifty bucks!"

Saunderson shrugged, then shook Trumbo's hand and gave him a business card. After signing some papers, Trumbo walked back into the station to recover his wallet and keys. Saunderson was in the hallway, drinking a cup of coffee. He put a hand on Trumbo's shoulder.

"Look in there," said the lawyer.

Through a one-way glass, Trumbo could see the DA talking to a young girl.

"Who's that?"

"It's the daughter."

"Whose daughter?"

"Joi's. Hasn't seen her mother in about ten years."

"She looks awfully young."

"Twenty-five. Ran away at age fifteen."

"Huh."

Through the one-way glass, Trumbo sized her up. Unglamorous, she wore no makeup. Her thick, brown hair fell over one eye and down onto her shoulder. She wore jeans and a large blue sweater. There was something fascinating about her, not traditionally beautiful, but compelling. Trumbo couldn't take his eyes off her. Anger illuminated her brilliant green eyes, and her full lips were pressed into a determined line. Trumbo got his keys and waited for her in the front of the station. Some time later, she returned to the waiting room and immediately began yelling at the receptionist.

"When you searched me, you took my Walkman and a

sandwich I was eating," she yelled. "In the Walkman was an L-Seven tape. And now it's gone. That's ten bucks. My sandwich is gone, too, and I'm hungry."

"Ma'am, I don't know what happened to your sandwich."

"Could you please look? I'm starving. You made me give it up. I want it back."

A moment later the man reappeared with a plastic tray containing the missing tape and sandwich.

"I'm sorry about the inconvenience," said the officer.

"I hope you have better things to worry about."

She tore into what remained of the sandwich as if she were famished. Then she straightened her hair and walked toward the door. Trumbo followed her.

"Hey—hey—excuse me!" yelled Trumbo, trying to catch up with the young woman.

She spun around and glared at him. "Yeah?" Her cheeks were flushed with color.

"I knew your mother. Joi Wilmot was your mother, right?"

"Yeah. So what're you doing here?"

"Cops wanted to ask me some questions. By the way, what's your name?"

"What's *your* name?" she asked. "You chased after me."

"Trumbo Walsh."

"Alison Wilmot." She threw one hand on her hip and sized him up. "I've heard about you. You're the one she wrote me about." She folded her arms across her chest and spoke in a mocking voice. " 'I feel like I've found a long-lost son' and all that crap. I hope you know you're the reason she started poking around with her scumbag drug fiend friends again."

"I'm sorry about what happened."

She raised her hands. "Please, please. I don't want to talk about it again. I just need to get a cab and get out of here."

"I can give you a ride."

"I'd rather be alone if you don't mind. I've been up more than twenty-four hours straight and I'm not happy."

She quickly walked to a bank of pay phones in front of the police station.

Trumbo recovered his truck from the impound. He knew the guy who ran the lot, having dropped off dozens of wrecks there, and got the towing and storage fee waived. When he drove back around the building he saw Alison Wilmot counting the cash in her wallet. He stopped in a red zone and walked over to her. She appeared exhausted.

"Need something?" he asked.

"It costs twenty-eight bucks to get to the airport. That's where they have a car I can afford to rent."

"I'll still give you a ride."

She hesitated. He was obviously not her first choice. "Would that be okay?"

"Sure."

He threw her bag in the space behind the seat and drove toward the airport.

"I owe you one," said Trumbo. "You did me a big favor. If it weren't for whatever you told the cops, I'd still be in the lockup."

"I know."

"What'd you tell them?"

"I just showed them the letters my mom wrote about you where she said what a great guy you were and all that."

"Did she tell you why I looked her up? I found out that my mother is alive—I always thought she died when I was a baby. Joi was helping me to track her down, and then this all happens."

"I heard the whole story. She wrote me about it. About your father and the mental institution and all that."

"I only met her twice, but she seemed like a good woman."

"I wouldn't know."

"Come again?" said Trumbo.

"I haven't seen her in years. When I was a kid she was 'into' everything—you know, transcendental meditation, primal screams, all that kind of stuff. I just wanted a regular mom who was, like, in the PTA and baked cookies. I ran away when I was fifteen."

"And did what?"

"I got a job. I didn't want to be like most flaky runaways. I went to Chicago and started working in a bakery. Then I got a fake ID and got a job in a bar in Columbus, Ohio. I chose Ohio because it seemed like such a 'regular' place. Lemme tell you, it's not."

"Then what?"

"Like, I don't want to go through my whole life history, okay? I came out here to settle up my mother's affairs. I was planning to come see her as soon as I got some time off anyway. We started writing each other about six months ago. I just wish I'd visited sooner." She gazed out the window. Trumbo began to see a vulnerability that earlier had been carefully concealed.

As they pulled up to Rent-A-Wreck near the airport, the lighted sign went out. The chain-link fence to the front of the lot was closed.

Trumbo and Alison jumped out. They yelled to get the attention of a man in coveralls who was locking up the main building.

"Sorry, we closed at eight," he replied.

"I just called out here," said Alison. "They said come right out."

"Sorry. All the sales reps left about ten minutes ago." The mechanic smiled. "We'll be open tomorrow morning."

Alison kicked the gate.

"We're closed," repeated the man, and then he disappeared into the offices.

"I'm totally screwed now," said Alison. "I need to get a car."

"I'll give you a ride back wherever you're staying, okay?"

"Yeah. Thanks." She stared glumly out the window. "Ugly city."

"Welcome to L.A.," said Trumbo.

They drove for several minutes before Trumbo broke the silence.

"Do you need anything else while you're in town?"

"I just got here."

"Yeah. But if you want something, just give me a call." He handed her a card. She stuffed it in her purse without looking at it.

"Don't wait by the phone, okay?"

"Suit yourself. Where am I taking you?"

"Hollywood and Western. Some kind of cheap hotel."

"That's a bad part of town," said Trumbo.

"I can take care of myself."

"I mean, a *really* bad part of town."

"I can *really* take care of myself, thank you."

Trumbo gave up and drove to an address Alison had clipped from a newspaper advertisement for weekly rentals.

He parked his truck near the intersection, wondering if it would still be there when he came back. No sooner was he out of the truck than he was asked three times if he had any spare change. A boy no older than twelve offered him "ten dollars worth a' crack for five buck."

The apartment was in an old brick building. Half of the once luxurious windows had been boarded up in the name of earthquake safety. A huge canvas sign hung between two windows offering ROOMS FOR RENT—DAILY/WEEKLY/MONTHLY. Alison pulled her suitcase out of the truck.

"Are you sure you don't want to go somewhere safer?" asked Trumbo.

"No, thank you. I'll be fine from here. I don't want to talk all night, so thank you for the ride." She dug in her purse and pulled out a ten-dollar bill. "Maybe this will cover the gas."

Trumbo grimaced. "You don't have to pay me."

"I want to. We're not friends and I don't want you getting the idea that we are." She tried to hand him the money. When he refused it, she threw it on the seat of his truck.

"Good night."

She disappeared into the building, dragging the suitcase behind her. Trumbo waited a moment, then got in the truck. He left the ten-dollar bill on the seat.

9

"MARK-JON, THIS IS MARILYN. GET A PENCIL. GET THIS APproved now. Go straight to the dwarf. He'll approve it. I need, by the Fed Ex deadline, the following: a cashier's check to the California Correctional Officers Fraternal Organization for fifty thousand."

The receptionist gasped. "Fifty thousand dollars?"

"I don't mean fifty thousand pesos, you twit—yes! Fifty thousand dollars! And it better not fucking be a regular business check. Has to be a cashier's check, and the issuer has to be someone besides Clandestine Productions. Also: Get the credit limit on the business Visa pumped up to a hundred grand. Also: Get to that deli a couple blocks up from the office—you know the one, on Sixth—and I need ten pounds of their expensive lox and ten pounds of their expensive pastrami and as much whitefish salad as they've got. Pack it on dry ice and get it in the same package. Send it to the Bakersfield Hilton care of me."

"Marilyn, it's twenty-five after four. The cutoff for Federal Express is six o'clock."

"That means you'll have to haul ass. Good-bye."

She tapped down the receiver and dialed James St. James's personal direct line.

"St. James."

"Take off the speaker phone. This is Marilyn."

She heard her boss pick up the receiver.

"I found someone who has the authority to move the parole hearing. It's gonna cost us fifty grand plus every bit of deli food you can dig up."

"What?"

"It's all below the table. It ain't gonna happen any other way. Trust me. We need the fifty grand to be an anonymous check. I told Mark-Jon. Now I'm telling you. If you want this thing to come off, we have to move now."

"But fifty grand?"

"Fine. Don't do it."

She slammed down the phone. Then she leisurely poured herself a glass of Gilbey's. The phone rang forty seconds later.

"McLeod."

"You don't fucking hang up on me."

"Must have been a bad connection." She smiled. St. James *wanted* this show pretty bad, because he didn't challenge her obvious fabrication. "You want it moved, it'll cost us fifty grand plus plus plus."

"Done. I told Mark-Jon to set it up. The check'll be there in the morning. If we miss the cutoff, I'll send a courier."

"Good."

"Now, Marilyn, what about visuals? What're we going to use for the teasers?"

"It's a courthouse, Ray. That's what you wanted." She hesitated to see if he hassled her for calling him "Ray." He didn't.

"We need something for a buildup. I'm thinking, armed guards all around the exterior of the building."

"I'm already making miracles happen here. I don't know if I can get them to accept that, too."

"There's ten grand in it for you if you can get them to allow, say, fifty armed guards."

"It's difficult."

"There's ten grand plus a one-year pay-or-play deal to do your own pilot," said St. James.

Marilyn smiled. "Do they have to be real guards?"

"Nah, who gives a damn as long as the old lady in Peoria thinks they're real guards. Get extras or something, I don't care."

"Old lady in Peoria" was shorthand for St. James's target audience: couch potatoes across America who watched his show, taking at face value anything they saw, whether it was UFOs fabricated by the prop department, Hitler's bunker on a German soundstage, or in this case, "guards" who were out-of-work actors earning pin money.

"I'll work on it."

"One more thing."

"Yeah?"

"Don't call me Ray. It's St. James—*James* St. James!"

"Sorry, Ray."

She hung up. She had just three weeks. Bribing someone was easy. What was hard was helping the director of the parole board figure out how to pull the strings that needed to be pulled. The previous night she sat with him for three hours in a darkened restaurant working out the details of his lie, which had to convince a judge, a prison warden, some guy in the governor's special task force on violent crime who had an interest in Manson, and various other petty officials.

The phone rang again.

"McLeod."

"We have a problem." It was Lenski from the parole board.

"We have a problem? I've got my end sorted out. The check—"

"Don't mention that on a phone. Meet me at the same place in an hour."

He hung up.

Her stomach churned at the thought of going back to the cheap seafood joint where she'd met Lenski the previous night. But business was business. She changed out of her conspicuous power suit into a plain blue dress, touched up her makeup, slugged down another shot of gin, and headed for Lobstermat.

Lenski was already seated when she arrived. The parole board scheduler was pale and nervous. Lenski was forty-five or fifty and had that haunted look men get when they realize that they're never going to be as rich or as powerful as they once hoped. Marilyn hoped to play that to her advantage.

"I ordered you the same as you got last night, soft-shelled crabs."

"Oh, joy," said McLeod, flatly, thinking of the grease-soaked flash-frozen heaps of salt that passed for seafood. "So what's the problem?"

Lenski leaned close to McLeod and spoke softly. "The attorney general is worried about publicity. He was the one who, back in 1976, passed the current regulations that require parole hearings for lifers like Manson. He used to be a liberal, but he changed his tune some time ago, became 'tough on crime,' and now is contemplating a run for governor. He's throwing a lot of weight around to see that Manson's hearing is low-key."

"Because it would embarrass him," said McLeod, cutting to the chase.

"You got it."

Marilyn shook a little salt from the shaker into her hand, licked a finger, and tasted the salt. She exhaled deeply.

"Yesterday you said it was very doable."

"Yesterday I thought it was."

"You told me you have the authority, with limitations, to schedule hearings wherever you want."

"Ninety-nine percent of 'em are in the prison complex. Once in a while there's a reason to do one outside. And yes, I can do it. But if I piss off the AG, I'm out of a job."

Marilyn massaged her forehead, deep in thought. "I've got it."

"Got what?"

"What we'll do. You say the attorney general—What's his name?"

"Lockwood."

"Lockwood is scared of bad publicity, and rightly so. What we can do is change the attitude so that he'll look bad if he *doesn't* have a public hearing for Manson."

"How do you mean?"

"Clandestine Productions does the 'Inside' TV specials, like this one on Manson, but we also have our hooks into two network TV departments, and do three daily, syndicated reality programs. Of course, you've heard of 'Suspect at Large' and 'Exposé!' We can do an hour on both of those shows about how the California attorney general is hiding the truth about the corrupt, rotten-to-the-core parole system by prohibiting publicity at parole hearings."

Lenski flinched. "But that's not true!"

"You wanted to buy a boat, right? Or maybe put in a pool in the old backyard?" said Marilyn.

"But the parole system is my bread and butter."

"It won't make you look bad. We'll say that Lockwood is embarrassed about the piss-poor quality of the current parole hearings because of, I don't know, funding or something. There's always something. We'll suggest he's letting maniac killers loose and buying them bus tickets to nice neighborhoods. It's not that hard to gin up a story. Clandestine Productions does it every day of the week. You shoulda seen our piece on the Texas parole system. Made a governor almost resign."

"And then what?"

"And then we let the editorial pages of all the newspapers around here fill up with righteous indignation about whatever we expose. I can already envision what they'll write— something about, oh . . ." She held her fingers in the air as quotation marks. "'Sunshine being the best disinfectant, let's open up the parole hearings to the public, let's not let Lockwood keep them secret. You get the idea."

"What do I do?"

"You steer us to people we can interview. That's all. Your name won't come up if you play ball."

The food arrived. Lenski tried to hide his face from the waitress. McLeod frowned at the soft-shell crab.

Lenski picked at his swordfish. "I don't know. When you asked me to move the hearing, I thought that was okay. But now I feel I'm on a slippery slope. When will you stop asking me to make little compromises?"

"The day after the parole hearing."

"I'm not sure I can do it. I've got to look at myself in the mirror every morning." Lenski sighed.

"I guess you'll never see yourself in a mirror on a *yacht.*" Marilyn smiled and finally began to enjoy the taste of her food. She had discovered Lenski's weak point: He was worried about appearances. The negotiation had taken a sudden turn in her direction, and she moved in for the kill with all the self-assurance of a vulture. "Fine," she said, smacking her lips. "We'll just do a show on the parole board, instead of the attorney general. I don't mind. End result is the same for me."

"You'd blackmail me?"

"Blackmail is a pretty strong word, Mr. Lenski. We only tell the truth on 'Exposé!' Of course I'm not blackmailing you. I'm just thinking out loud."

"You'd do it, wouldn't you?"

She cut off the head of the crab and popped it in her mouth. "Why? Is there something in your department you wouldn't want to be seen on national television?"

"Shit." Lenski pushed his food away. He realized he had been cornered. "Do you have a notebook?"

"Yes."

"If you're going to make a show anyway."

Marilyn pulled out her Filofax.

Lenski looked at the tablecloth and muttered, "Take down these names. They're hardened cons who slipped through the cracks, thanks to that parole law."

"For my show?"

"For your goddamn show. Better the AG than me, I guess. And you better have that check tomorrow."

"It'll be here."

Marilyn smiled. California was an easy place to do business. The people were friendly, flexible, and willing to compromise. An attorney general would have to take some heat, maybe lose his bid for governor, a parole official might bend a few rules, but Clandestine Productions would have its show.

That night she faxed the premise of the 'Exposé!' show that would be researched, written, and produced within a week, and embarrass an attorney general for several months. St. James called back, understood immediately the necessity for blowing up the AG, and shipped Marilyn a bouquet of prickly pear cactuses.

There was one more immediate objective to satisfy. She flipped through the *San Francisco TV and Film Production Directory* until she came to a listing for extras casting services. She purposely chose one with a cheap, one-line listing, rather than someone with a full-page ad in the directory: someone who was hard up for cash. The company was called Upper Atmosphere, and the woman who answered the phone was the owner. Her name was Greta Kirby, and she had the slightly desperate tone of an out-of-work actor trying to make a living on the fringes of the business.

"Ms. Kirby, three weeks from Thursday I'm going to need about fifty extras. All men, all over six feet tall."

McLeod could hear Kirby calculating her percentage. "Sounds great. I can do the job for you."

"What are your usual rates?"

"My people get, uh, seventy-five a day, plus extra if they have to bring any kind of particular costume."

"What's your cut?"

"It comes out of their pay."

"Ms. Kirby, this is a very sensitive assignment. I'm not going to tell you where they're going until the day before. The men must all be between twenty-five and forty, and in good shape—no potbellies. We're going to supply them with uniforms, and they've got to carry rifles. Do you still think you can do it?"

"What kind of TV show is this?"

"If we paid you a hundred per—twenty-five over your usual rates—in cash, and then a bonus of one thousand

110

dollars to you on the day of the show if everything comes off without a hitch, do you have to keep asking questions?"

"I've been in the business fourteen years. The old hurry-up-and-wait routine. That means I have to call them all on the day before to tell them where they're going."

"If you don't think you can handle it, I understand. I'll just call my usual . . ." Marilyn flipped through the production guide until she found the extras casting service with the biggest ad. "You know, Extra Special. I just thought you might like the work instead."

"I think I can do it. Can you make a deposit?"

"How much?"

"I don't know, fifty percent? Would that be okay?" The out-of-work actress was playing her role perfectly: terrified of negotiation and desperate to please.

"We'll put down forty percent."

"Sure. Okay. Here's my address."

Marilyn opened up a bank bag containing the production slush fund, extracted twenty one-hundred-dollar bills, and stuffed them into an envelope. She called a runner and sent the money directly to Upper Atmosphere, satisfied that the woman could cough up at least thirty decent extras. Extras who would pretend to guard Charles Manson at his parole hearing, for the express benefit of some old bitch in Peoria.

10

EXHAUSTED, TRUMBO LET THE HOT WATER IN HIS TINY SHOWER wash over him as the events of the previous two days solidified into reality. He kept half remembering *gotta talk to Joi* and then was stopped by the realization that she was dead, gone, erased forever.

Her daughter, Alison, so angry, but pretty, too. What was her story? Why hadn't Joi mentioned Alison once, even in passing? Why were there no photos of her in the apartment?

He immersed himself in the hot stream, grimacing at the sting of the water on his bruised, cut face. Then he heard something. He leaned out of the shower and listened. Three sharp, martial raps. A hesitation. Then the same rapping noise.

He threw a towel around his waist, picked up an aluminum baseball bat, and held it over his head as he approached the door. It was past ten o'clock at night.

"Who is it?"

"Guttierrez."

"Who?"

"Los Angeles Police."

"Right." He threw down the baseball bat, which rang when it hit the floor, and opened the door a crack. Two men in business suits were on his porch. One of them was the homicide detective he'd spoken with the previous day.

"Come on in," he said.

"Thank you. Mr. Walsh, this is Detective Roddam."

"Have a seat," said Trumbo, pushing a stack of record albums off the couch. "Be right with you."

He ran into the bathroom, dried himself off, and threw on a tattered bathrobe. When he returned to the living room, both men were wandering around, casually picking up books, records, bills, and examining them. When they saw Trumbo they returned to the couch.

"What's up?" asked Trumbo.

"We wanted to ask you a few more questions."

"Fire away. I'm not doing anything."

For the next hour, Trumbo repeated everything he'd told them at the station: why he knew Joi, why he was at her house, how he got there, the whole nine yards. Every so often they'd quote statements he'd made earlier, but change one detail, such as:

"So what else do you know about this guy named 'Red'?"

"His name was 'Blue.'"

"Right. Blue. You really don't know his name?"

"How long is this going to take? We're not covering any new ground. I told you everything already."

Guttierrez stood. "We can leave any time you say." The detective exchanged knowing glances with his partner.

"It's almost midnight. This is not my idea of a good time. Is there any point to this?" demanded Trumbo.

"Would you like us to leave?" asked Roddam.

"Yeah, something like that. It's been real fun, gentlemen." Trumbo stood and opened the door.

"Stay in touch," said Guttierrez. The cops picked up their notebooks and left.

Trumbo watched through the venetian blinds as they walked to their car, drove up the hill, made a U-turn, and left the way they came.

Trumbo knew little or nothing about criminal law and nothing about how police handled an investigation. If they wanted to nail him, he would be at the mercy of the system, whether it worked or not. He checked the clock: just past midnight, shift change for cops. On a chance, he drove down to the Smog Cutter.

Mazer was stationed at his usual table back behind the pool table, sipping the beer that he got at half price because the owner liked having off-duty cops around. Trumbo navigated past a man playing solo pool and sat down across from Mazer, still in uniform.

"Trumbo, you in deep shit," said the cop, smiling.

"Nice to see you, too, Mazer."

"The homicide boys already asked me everything about you. Does he have a girlfriend? Any unusual hobbies or interests? A bad temper?"

"What'd you tell them?"

"That you like to trip little old ladies and torture small animals on your days off. What do you think? I told them you were a reliable tow driver. I said you'd had a rough couple of months."

"So they haven't ruled me out."

"They can't rule you out. That's the nature of homicide investigation. Pretty soon they'll get tired or bored or maybe just move on to a livelier case."

Trumbo rolled his eyes. "Great."

"You got a lawyer?"

"Just a guy appointed by the courts."

"You ought to have a real lawyer."

"Even if I didn't do anything?"

"Especially if you didn't do anything. Legal Aid and the court-appointed guys are overloaded and just want to get home. You need one of these true believer mouthpieces who works on charity cases. There's one who's a friend of my brother. He looks a little hippy-dippy, but he's been working for years. I know he's good because the DA's office hates his guts."

"I don't have any money to pay a lawyer."

"You'll have to convince him to represent you, then. Tell him a good story. His name's Dennis Clemenson, and he's in the book. And for Christ's sake, Trumbo, get some sleep."

"I have more important problems than a good night's sleep. I was *this close*"—he held his thumb and forefinger together—"to finding my mother. Then this bullshit happens."

"Shit, Trumbo, put that on the back burner. You ought to just do your job—tow cars, and do whatever you regularly do. If you start off on some weird quest now, those detectives will be all over you like a cheap suit."

"If I don't find her, she could end up like Joi."

"It's your life, man. If she never saw you in twenty-something years, I don't know why you're so eager to save her ass now."

Trumbo stood up. "Yeah. I know it sounds crazy."

He left the bar and drove home. When he got in the door he could hear the shower running. He picked up the baseball bat and kicked open his bathroom door. Through the filmy curtain he could see the figure of a woman, rinsing her hair off under the water. A pile of clothes lay by the edge of the shower stall.

"Who's there?" he demanded.

Alison Wilmot jumped in surprise, then leaned her head out of the shower curtain, covering her breasts with her arm. "You scared me! Am I glad I found the right place. The HollyWest Apartment manager is only there during the day. Can you believe that? I had a reservation and everything. So I came up here to take you up on your offer. When I saw you weren't home I let myself in."

Trumbo threw up his hands. "Right."

"Will you stop staring at me and close the door?" she demanded.

"I wanna talk to you when you get out."

"Shut the bathroom door!"

Trumbo lay down on the couch, trying the best he could to keep from drifting off to sleep. Finally she emerged, wrapped in *his* bathrobe and with *his* towel over her shoulder. She smelled soft and her dark hair was shiny and slicked down. She leaned over him, and a few drops of scented water landed on his forehead.

"So is it okay?" she asked, toweling off her hair.

"Yeah, I guess. I said I owed you one."

"I'll be out of your way first thing in the morning. Promise. I can even pay you if you want."

"Stop it with the 'paying me' business. If you wanna stay, be my guest, but be gracious about it, okay?"

"Sorry."

"And don't leave first thing in the morning. I want to talk to you. I'm just too beat to talk right now."

"I have a lot of things to do tomorrow," she said.

"Then you can just find another place to stay. Is it too much to ask?"

"You got me where you want me."

"Stay in my room. The sheets are relatively clean. I'll sleep on the couch."

"No, I should sleep on the couch."

"Stop arguing with me. Just enjoy it."

He flipped himself around on the couch so he could see back toward the bedroom and watched her through half-slit eyes, careful that she didn't see him watching. He heard her run his hair dryer. On the way to the bedroom she hesitated in the hall for just a moment to look at him. Gone was the fiery, argumentative girl he had seen during the day. Instead she appeared lonely and lost. There was a sadness in her eyes, as if things had gone wrong but she couldn't say where or how. He drifted off to sleep wondering about her past, why she had a falling out with her mother, what he'd say over breakfast.

In the morning Trumbo awoke with a crick in his neck. An unfamiliar but pleasant smell permeated his apartment: coffee. Groggily he straightened up.

Alison sat at the kitchen table, dressed in jeans and a blue cotton shirt.

"Morning," said Trumbo.

She looked over her shoulder at him. The vulnerability he had briefly witnessed before was gone. "G'morning. I didn't want to wake you up. I was getting ready to leave."

Trumbo stood up, wrapping the blanket around himself. "That's not part of our deal. I wanted to talk to you."

"Then talk." She stared at him impatiently.

"What are you going to do in Los Angeles?" he said.

"I told you, I'm going to wind up my mother's affairs and then get the hell out of El Lay."

He twisted so that he was seated backwards on the couch facing her. "Humor me for a minute. Let's pretend you care. Let's pretend that you want to find out what happened to your mother. Last night you said she was hanging around with old friends because of me, and that's why she got killed. Who are these people?"

"Biker trash. Dealers. Fucked-up hippies." She pushed the hair out of her eyes. "God, how I hate hippies. They come on like they're going to save the world, and then when you get near them, all they can think about is themselves. I grew up with it."

"Where'd you live growing up?"

"L.A. mostly, but we moved around. Spent some time in Texas, spent some time on a commune in North Carolina, here, there, everywhere."

"Sounds familiar to me. Don't you think we should track some of her old friends down?"

"We?"

"Yes, we. Joi knew who my mother was. That's why I contacted her. Maybe we can find out what happened to your mom."

"That's what the police are for."

Trumbo straightened up. "The police just want to close the easiest case they can. If it's too much work, they might give up and move on to the next one. There's fifteen hundred murders a year in L.A."

"That's it? Nobody cares?"

"You don't care. Why should they?" said Trumbo.

Alison's face flushed. "I care!"

Trumbo smiled. "Oh. I thought you said you didn't."

Alison stared at the table. "So many times when I was growing up, I just wished she'd die. I'd close my eyes and think about it and wish it would happen. One time I was in Chicago, I had twenty bucks in my pocket and wandered around for hours, trying to find someplace to eat, someplace to work, someplace to stay. I knew I couldn't go back. I just concentrated long and hard and wished she'd die." She sighed deeply. "And now it's happened." She fixed her gaze out the window and touched her hand to her eye.

Trumbo wrapped the blanket around himself and went to her side. "I'm sorry. We all think all kinds of things." He reached out and touched her shoulder. She let his hand rest there for a moment, then squirmed and shook it off.

"Go get dressed. Give me a minute by myself." She blew her nose and he left the room.

When Trumbo returned, Alison had composed herself. She looked him straight in the eye and spoke softly. "What can we do? I don't know where to look. I don't know how to find people. I haven't lived here in ten years. But I want to do something."

"Let's start out by looking at those letters."

She fished three letters from her backpack. The envelopes and the lettering were similar to the ones from Joi that Trumbo discovered in his father's safety-deposit box. Trumbo read through them.

The first letter, dated some months earlier, was a pretty typical mom-to-daughter note, considering the circumstances: so glad you decided to write me, when are you coming out to visit, do you have a boyfriend, what do you do for a living now, and so on. The second was more of the same for the most part, but concluded with a passage about Trumbo.

I had a visitor today. I foresaw his coming. My psychic said that a dream I had last week was about him. He's a young man named Trumbo Walsh, and his father was a close friend. In many ways he reminds me of you and makes me wish you were near. His father was Luther Walsh, who introduced me to many things, good and bad. The son seems lost in life—his father dead, he is now searching for his mother, a woman I knew. At least he cares enough to make the effort, which is something I think is important, don't you? If you need a plane ticket or travel money, I can help you with that.

His visit got me to thinking. There are some things I've never told you which I should make clear. People sometimes do things they regret. I have done many sad and terrible things in my past, but that past is someone else, someone different from me. I make a new life every day when I wake up. It helps if other people can forgive. Perhaps someday you will forgive me.

Trumbo's mother is a woman we called "Mimi," a woman who I once knew. Mimi was a beautiful young girl, full of life and love, and then she fell in with some people who led her to do things she regretted. I broke off with her many years ago but have found room in my heart to forgive. Remember, my lovely daughter, no matter what happens to someone, they should always get a second chance.

I will be seeing faces and hearing voices I haven't encountered in a long time, but now is the time to settle up old accounts. Nothing comes without risks or danger.

The letter concluded with a list of New Age spiritual books for Alison to read.

The third letter was much like the second except for one passage that hinted that she may have known what was about to happen.

I say leave the door open to love and take the chance that someone has turned over a new leaf rather than continue to live in fear. There may be people who do not want to hear from me, but I have contacted them nonetheless and am willing to give them one more chance. If it helps Trumbo find his mother, if it helps me move to new and better grounds, then so be it. If it turns out bad, no one can say I didn't try.

Trumbo put the letter down. "She knew she was in danger?"

"I got that letter the day before the police called."

"The cops have these letters, right?"

"Copies of them. They were disappointed—said she didn't name names in them."

"What's all this stuff about what she did in the past?"

"I don't know. It could be the biker guys. She let them deal drugs from our house when I was little, but we moved. She didn't like to talk about it."

"When can you get into her house?"

"Probably Monday, the cops said. They're tearing the place apart."

"We ought to go through her notebooks and stuff and see if there are any names, addresses, that kind of thing. She ever write you about a guy named Blue?"

"Nope."

"That's the name of a gorilla who was her boyfriend."

"The police asked me about him."

"I know where he might be. I think I can track him down before Monday."

"Did you tell the cops?"

"Everything I knew. He beat the crap out of me once. The last time I saw him was at a rave, Saturday before last. He might be at the same rave this weekend."

"I don't know if I want to get mixed up with him."

"I'm going," said Trumbo.

Alison stared long and hard at Trumbo. She glanced at the letters, folded them, and replaced them into their envelopes. "I'll go with you." Alison suddenly stood and picked up her backpack. "I guess I should leave."

"Why? You can't do anything until Monday, can you?"

"I can call a cab if you don't want to give me a ride," she said.

"What's your rush?"

"I just feel completely helpless, useless. It's weird waiting around for other people to do things for you. I hate it."

"What's the first thing you're going to do?"

"I was going to go eat breakfast."

"Alone?"

"Yeah."

"I'll go with you."

She clutched the backpack to her chest as if for protection. After a long pause, she nodded. "Okay. But don't expect me to be cheery about it."

When Trumbo drove out he noticed a dull green Oldsmobile start up at the same time he did. He pulled to the side of the road; so did they.

When he started up his car again, they continued following. He came to a stop sign before a major road and waited for them to catch up. In his rearview mirror he saw who it was: Guttierrez and Roddam, waiting for him to make a mistake.

11

DURING THE SHORT RIDE TO BREAKFAST, ALISON STARED OUT THE window and said nothing. She didn't know what to make of Trumbo: His offers of assistance made her suspicious. Too many times in the past she had put her trust in others, just to see them take advantage of her. It had begun with her mother. She had grown up in a hot-and-cold environment where the rules were always changing. If she got in trouble at school, sometimes her mother would discipline her severely. Other times she'd say, *Screw the authorities, you can't let the bastards push you around.* Alison never could figure out the rules, and one day decided to live by her own rules. She left.

After, she'd had a series of relationships at least as bad as those her mother endured. The first was an older guy in Chicago who took her into his apartment when she had nothing, fed her and took care of her. It was a good setup until he started beating her up.

After she moved to Columbus, her meager income as a cocktail waitress always fell short of her expenses. The woman who ran the bar had picked Alison as a favorite, gave her the best tables, best shifts. She even invited Alison over for dinner from time to time and took her into her trust. Then one day the barmaid hinted that Alison could make some extra cash by going on the occasional "date" with a visiting businessman. Alison laughingly refused her boss's offer. Then one day she came home to find an eviction notice on her apartment and her belongings on the street.

That night she had a "date" with a chemistry professor visiting the Ohio State campus. The fat fuck sweated all over her body and tried to bite her. As a final insult, the geezer left her with a nasty infection. After that, she vowed never to be dependent on anyone ever again—not her mother, not a boyfriend, not an employer. *Never trust anyone.*

She took out a government loan and attended cosmetology school for the mandated one thousand hours, securing her license with the best test score in her class. She rented a space and wheeled and dealed to get two chairs, the necessary equipment, insurance, supplies.

Hair by Alison quickly earned a reputation as the place to get the trendy, fashionable hairdos not available at Supercuts or the local barber, and as a bonus was open odd hours—until midnight on Fridays and Saturdays. Within several months she had hired a second stylist, then a third. By working herself to the bone, she was able to make a go of it. The best part was, no one could fire her, no one could compromise her. She occasionally even kicked out a customer she disliked, just to reinforce the fact that the shop was hers alone.

It remained profitable because she trusted no one. She fired two stylists the first year for stealing, a third for setting up appointments at home and stealing customers. She routinely hassled the bank when they made even a tiny error on her statement. The officers got to know her, and took special care to see that her accounts were double- and triple-checked.

In the two and a half years that she'd been running the business, her personal life had been put on the back burner. Once in a great while she'd go for a drink with a customer, but that was it: *a drink.* She was generous with her employees, but demanded loyalty. When she had to fire someone, or stop working with a supplier, no emotional entanglements prevented her from doing so. Friends were just enemies with a smile. Sex held no sway over her—sleep with someone and they think they own you. She had only two affairs. One was utterly forgetable, more a function of the beer than the boy. The other was quite delicious—a nice boy from Akron she had met in her shop, attending OSU, funny, smart, a good listener—but fundamentally she distrusted her heart. When he called the next day, and then sent flowers, she suddenly took an intense dislike to him. All the things that seemed so charming before suddenly seemed precious, obsequious, repellent. He came into the shop a few more times, but she treated him like any customer. To her relief, he stopped dropping by.

Trumbo made all the warning bells go off: He was trying to help and didn't ask for anything. As they pulled into the parking lot of Astro Coffee Shop, she regretted staying in his house and regretted agreeing to let him join her for breakfast.

"This is Astro," said Trumbo as they climbed out of his truck. "The food isn't that great, but they make up for it by overcharging."

Alison ignored the sorry joke.

They sat at a window booth. Before she was even seated, Alison cornered the middle-aged Greek waitress. "Two checks, please."

"That makes it difficult for me, honey. Can't you split it up on your own?"

Trumbo pitched in. "Yeah, no problem."

Alison shook her head, then scowled at the waitress, whose name tag said DONNA. "Okay. One check," she said, then tossed two menus onto the table. They quickly ordered —Trumbo a big farmer's breakfast, Alison a bowl of oatmeal.

Trumbo cracked his knuckles.

Alison avoided direct eye contact with him. "Why are you so interested in what happens to me? What's the *real* reason?"

"You still playing that game? Let's say I'm lying. Let's say I don't give a damn about you or your mom, and I'm just in this for whatever I can get."

"That's what I wanted to hear."

"Look at it this way. Whoever the hell Joi was talking about in the letters—all the people she wanted to forgive, and settle up with, and all that crap—those people are links to my mother. They also might be the people who killed Joi. So I want to find them as badly as you want to find them."

"Fine, agreed. But why have me tag along?"

"Continuing your wrong idea that I'm in this for myself only, right?"

"Yes."

"Okay then. You have her letters. You have all the stuff that was in her house, her Rolodex or daybook or whatever. One of those names is probably my mom."

For the first time since he'd met her, Alison smiled. "That, I can understand. I can do business with you."

Trumbo grimaced. "What do you wanna do, shake hands or something?"

Alison extended her hand. Trumbo shook it.

"If you still want to stay at my place, the invitation is open."

"I'd rather not."

"I'll give you a ride wherever you're going."

"No, I can't impose on you like that. I'll just call a cab."

"It's no bother, really."

"I'll pay you, if that's okay."

Trumbo laughed. "Still on that kick? Okay. Fare to Hollywood is one American dollar. Paid in cash, up front, before the taxi leaves."

She pulled out a dollar bill and handed it to him. With great ceremony he placed it in his wallet. Their breakfast arrived.

During the drive into Hollywood, Alison arranged and rearranged the papers in her handbag, pondering her situation. She had no friends or contacts in Los Angeles, and her business was two thousand miles away. She felt the panicky feeling that had set in when she first ran away a decade earlier.

The apartment building looked even worse in daylight than it did at night.

"This is it," said Trumbo. He pulled in front of the building, stopped the truck, and hopped around to open her door. "Don't worry, I'm not opening your door to be nice nice. You can't open it from the inside."

"Thanks," she said. Before she was fully out of the car,

Trumbo reached into the space behind the seats and yanked out her duffel bag. Alison pulled it out of his hand as soon as she got out of the car.

"Here you go," said Trumbo, releasing the bag. "Remember, that rave is tomorrow night. How am I going to contact you? You can't get a phone that fast."

"I'll call you."

"I can't call you?"

"No. What time will it start?"

"Sometime after ten."

"Then pick me up at ten P.M. tomorrow."

"What apartment will you be in?"

"That's my business. I'll be at the curb."

"Fine." Trumbo stood uncomfortably next to her on the curb for a moment, then got back in his truck and drove away.

As soon as she got in the door, Alison noticed that in the clear plastic pocket on the duffel bag where a name tag would go was a one-dollar bill, and Trumbo's card. She pulled it out and stuffed it in her wallet, then went in to arrange for her lodging. Something about Trumbo made her anxious. She didn't like it.

12

TRUMBO PULLED THE SLIP OF PAPER FROM HIS POCKET AND double-checked the address before going in. He had the right street address, all right, but the building just didn't look like a lawyer's office. Lawyers usually were on ritzy Wilshire. This was a decrepit warehouse in an industrial park.

He climbed three steps and banged loudly on a metal loading door. He heard rustling, then the rolling garage door lifted. A hefty, dark-complected man with a goatee stared at him.

"Jess? May I help you?" The man had a thick accent.

"I'm looking for Dennis Clemenson."

"Come in, please."

Trumbo followed the man across a massive loft with forty-foot ceilings. In the center of the room was a gigantic pile of twisted, distorted metal, partially covered with colorful graffiti. Trumbo could pick out bits of tractors, mobile homes, and pieces of telephone poles in the heap.

"Excuse me, I think I'm in the wrong place," said Trumbo, halfway across the room.

"Dennis is back here," said the man, bouncing on his heels impatiently.

"What's all this?"

"I call it *The Magi Reincarnated as Tornadoes.*"

"It's, like, sculpture?"

The man laughed heartily. "I can't explain all of art history to you right now, young man. Yes, it's 'like sculpture.' Maybe I'll call my work that from now on, 'like sculpture.'" He laughed again to himself. "Come on."

The sculptor escorted Trumbo to a door at the rear of the studio, and rapped loudly three times.

"Come in!"

Trumbo pushed the door open and was immediately overwhelmed at the astonishing clutter. Rickety metal bookshelves stretched twenty feet up the wall. Post-it notes hanging off the shelves carried legends such as CA TORT LAW, RIGGS V. CA, BOYLE HEIGHTS SEVEN V. COUNTY OF LOS ANGELES, and RADICAL DEFENSES. On the floor were various other stacks of papers, annotated in much the same way. The narrow room had a metal desk, several folding chairs, and two filing cabinets. All the drawers in both filing cabinets hung open.

Seated at the desk was a gray-haired man who, though balding on top, wore a ponytail that extended halfway down his back. His suit was Salvation Army, his glasses vintage Teddy Roosevelt. The man leapt to his feet as soon as Trumbo came in. He was a few inches taller even than Trumbo yet was so thin, it seemed like a miracle of physics that he could stand.

"Dennis Clemenson," he said, extending his hand.

"Trumbo Walsh."

"Take a seat."

Trumbo carefully positioned one of the folding chairs so it wouldn't tear any books or papers.

"You're the lawyer, right?" asked Trumbo.

"You got it."

"Um, why is your office here, if you don't mind my asking?"

"Jorge Artero is one of my clients," he said, pointing out to the studio. "He couldn't pay me in cash when I handled an obscenity case for him a couple years back, so he gave me the office space in trade."

"Sure. It just wasn't what I expected."

"When you do a lot of pro bono work, you make whatever accommodations are necessary." Clemenson nodded his head sharply, as if declaring the end of the discussion of his office. "Pete Mazer told me about you. You're up on a murder rap."

"Yeah. I didn't do it."

"Cops questioned you, right? You were at the scene of the murder? Knew the victim?"

"Yeah."

"Then you're a suspect. Cops hanging around your house?" Clemenson asked the question the same way a doctor might ask, 'Do you have any itching or burning sensations?'—flat and without inflection.

"Yeah, how did you know?"

"That's what they do. Do you answer all their questions?"

"Sure, of course."

"You have to stop. Be nice and polite, and tell them this. Write it down." He threw a scrap of paper across the desk and handed Trumbo a pencil. "On advice of counsel, I cannot answer any further questions."

Trumbo started to write it down. "Won't that make me look guilty?"

"Kid, you're talking to one of the best criminal trial lawyers in the country. I may not look the part, but I know what I'm talking about. Either take my advice or don't, but if you don't, I won't be much good to you."

"Just don't reply?"

"Read it back to me."

"On advice of counsel, I cannot answer any further questions," said Trumbo, somewhat mechanically. "Just like that?"

"Very good. You'll reply, just not necessarily answer. If they had something on you, they'd have your ass in jail by now. They're fishing." Clemenson stood and raised a pot of coffee that looked as if it had been there a week, poured some into a paper cup, and continued his lecture. "Don't talk to them, don't let 'em in your house unless they have a warrant. If they do have a warrant, give me a call, and only *then* let them in. Tell me, what were you doing going into this woman's house, anyway?"

"Door was open. I wanted to see if she was home. I had some questions for her."

"What's her name?"

"Joi Wilmot."

Clemenson paced, avoiding the stacks of papers and books and staring up at the high ceiling. "Joi Wilmot, Joi Wilmot, Joi Wilmot. That name's damned familiar, but hell if I can place it. Thanks for coming to talk to me."

"That's all?"

"That's what a fancy-pants lawyer might have charged you several hundred bucks for."

"You don't want a statement or anything?"

"Why would I?"

"You're my lawyer, right?"

"Yes. Now, you're not under arrest, you're not in hot water. If something further happens, then I'll want a statement. In the meantime, just keep your nose clean and don't talk to the cops." Clemenson jumped up on his desk, started to pull a book down, thought better of it, then climbed off the desk and sat down. "One more thing."

"Yes?"

"Don't associate with the people associated with Wilmot if at all possible."

"No can do. Her daughter, Alison, needs me. She's all alone in this town. I can't just dump her."

Clemenson laughed. "I direct you to the sign above my door: 'God takes care of fools and drunkards. We do not.' Don't see that daughter!"

"Will you still represent me if I do?"

"Talk to me then. I'm not making any promises. You have to do what you have to do."

Clemenson stood and opened the door. In seconds Trumbo was back in the artist's loft, wondering if he'd completely screwed the pooch. He couldn't stop seeing Alison.

13

SATURDAY, TRUMBO AWOKE BEFORE DAWN, HOPING TO EARN some quick cash towing the wrecked cars of late night partyers slamming into each other on the way home, or of hapless vacationers crashing off unfamiliar roads on their way into Los Angeles. Most gypsy tow drivers knocked off around three A.M., an hour after the bars closed and the drunk drivers tried to get home, but Trumbo preferred working in the early morning.

He had some quick luck: An ancient Dodge van full of nuns on their way to a spiritual retreat had a close encounter with a bread truck backing out of a grocery market. Less than an hour later a Mercury-driving widow on her annual visit to Forest Lawn Cemetery stalled out on a narrow, high-speed road. A four-by-four pickup truck full of fishermen slammed into her, forcing her to take a detour through the morgue on the way to her husband's grave. That one tickled the paramedics, who made plenty of bleak jokes as they pried her body from the twisted wreckage.

Around noon people started driving more safely and other tow drivers began their shifts. Trumbo drove into Hollywood to see if Alison was home. The manager of the weekly-rental apartments gave Trumbo Alison's room number, and he headed up three flights of stairs to get there. The entire building smelled musty and rotten, like a locker room. On her hallway were two eviction notices, and some poor sap's belongings had been hurled into the hall. He quickly found her door. It was open. He tapped on the doorframe.

"Hello?"

"Come in," said Alison.

He walked into the tiny apartment. Alison's moth-eaten couch was filled to capacity by Guttierrez and Roddam, the homicide detectives.

"Hi, guys," said Trumbo to the two men. He turned to Alison. "Hey, if you have visitors, I can come back."

The detectives stood up. Trumbo shook their hands.

"You know each other?" asked Alison.

Trumbo tried to appear flippant. "Sure, they dropped by the other night. We had some laughs."

"We were just discussing you," said Alison. Roddam shot a glance at Trumbo.

"I thought my ears were burning. Go right ahead. I won't be any trouble," said Trumbo.

"We were just wrapping things up," said Guttierrez. "Trumbo, we'd like to clear up some discrepancies. Can we drop by again?"

Trumbo bounced on his heels. His lawyer had told him not to talk to the detectives. And yet if he refused, Alison might not understand. He took a deep breath. "What about later?"

"Tonight?" asked Guttierrez.

"Nah, I'm booked tonight. Tomorrow's the Sabbath, and I think you and I both ought to have a day off. What about Monday?"

"It won't take long. How about now?"

Alison looked at Trumbo expectantly. He bit his lip. The catchy little phrase the lawyer had given him would sound awfully suspect right now, but he didn't want to screw himself up. "No, I can't. I only have a couple minutes. I want to talk to Alison in private. But give me a call Monday."

"Clemenson's repping you, isn't he?" asked Guttierrez.

"Yeah."

"Thought so. How about Monday, three P.M., at your house?" asked Guttierrez.

"Sure."

Alison's face flushed with anger.

The detectives folded their notebooks, thanked Alison, and left. As soon as the door closed, Alison blurted out, "What was that all about?"

"I went and got myself a lawyer."

"Why?"

"Because a cop friend told me I should. The lawyer told me not to answer any questions."

"I thought you wanted to help find out who killed my mom."

"I do. Of course I do. But I have to make sure that I don't get railroaded."

Alison kicked the door. "That's bullshit, Trumbo."

"I will talk to them with my lawyer present."

"They asked me a hell of a lot of questions about you."

"That's what cops do."

"That means they think you did it."

"No it doesn't. It's just that they have to do something, and they don't have anything better to do but hassle me. They're no closer to finding out who did it than they were the night they arrested me. Or they wouldn't be hanging around like this."

"That's what they said you'd say if you were guilty."

"What?"

"They said that you'd put on a big show of being innocent, that you'd talk all about how bad a job they were doing, that kind of thing. Said you are very clever, and might be good at spinning stories that make yourself look good, but that doesn't mean you didn't do it."

"That's the biggest line I've ever heard in my life. What else should I do? Go on with my life as if nothing happened? I *liked* your mom. She was helping me out."

Alison walked backwards until she was in a corner. "I don't know. It all sort of makes sense."

"Jesus Christ. I came down here to see if you were okay, if you needed anything, and if you were still going with me tonight."

"I can't tell anymore whether you're who you say you are. The stuff the cops said made a lot of sense. They told me you could be dangerous."

"If it's any consolation, my lawyer told me not to hang

around with *you*. If I'm so goddamn clever, I would have just listened to him and we wouldn't be talking right now."

"Did you listen to him?" said Alison.

"I'm here, aren't I?"

Alison slumped down on the couch.

"If it's any comfort, Crocket and Tubbs will probably follow me tonight," said Trumbo.

"Crocket and Tubbs?"

"Roddam and Guttierrez. The cops. They've been following me sometimes. Makes me feel kind of safe, actually. If anything happened to me, I know two of L.A.'s Finest aren't far behind."

"God, everything's all so fucked up." She stuck a finger into her mouth, nervously chewing on a fingernail. "I'd feel better if it wasn't just the two of us. Can I bring one other person with me?"

"Bring the Mormon Tabernacle Choir. I don't care."

"I put up a notice for a roommate to split the rent."

"Bring your roommate, fine. Whatever."

"I don't know whether to believe the cops," she said.

"Think what you're gonna think. I can't change your mind. I'm going to Moon Man tonight, and you're welcome to come. If you don't want to come, that's fine. It's your decision." He stood and walked toward the door.

She sighed deeply. "I'm going to back out. I hope you're not upset."

"No. Take care."

He stepped out into the hall and slammed the door. Footsteps echoed down the staircase. *Crocket and Tubbs,* he thought. He walked to the end of the hall and peered out the grimy window above the fire escape. There, across Western Boulevard, was their car.

Trumbo stopped and picked up a greasy hamburger and ate it on the way home, downed two cheap beers, and took a shower. Wrapped in a towel, he peered out the window. Either Crocket and Tubbs had given up on him or they were getting better at concealing themselves. He set the alarm for ten P.M. and lay down to take a nap. He had a long night ahead of him.

* * *

Before his alarm went off, he was awakened by persistent tapping on his front door. He pulled on a pair of shorts, walked to the front room, and cracked open the door. Alison stood before him, decked out in a short black cocktail dress, her hair styled into a fashionable wave, wearing makeup that radically changed her face.

"C'mon in."

"Thanks."

"Why the change of heart?"

"I want to meet this man. I have to know what happened to my mother. You're the only lead I have."

"Why the, uh . . . ?" He gestured to her clothing.

"Is something wrong? I dressed for a nightclub."

"You look great, I mean, *really* great."

"So?"

"I was hoping to blend in. Most of these kids wear a T-shirt or maybe a button down-shirt."

"Oh hell."

"I'll loan you some of my clothes—you'll have to roll up the pants, but the baggy look is okay." Trumbo sat down. "So did you get a roommate?"

"Yeah. Some girl from East Los Angeles, first time she moved away from home. She seems nice enough—a partyer, wants to act in movies."

"Good. Help yourself to what's in my closet. Everything hanging is clean."

Alison wore Trumbo's blue jeans, gathered tight around the waist with one of his wide leather belts, and a button-down short-sleeved shirt. They headed out in search of the rave.

The ticket line was pretty much the same drill as before—four people admitted at a time, cash only, and twenty bucks bought a map and a ticket. Standing next to Alison, surrounded by several dozen kids, Trumbo scrutinized the map, then walked back into the record store to have a word with the man who sold him the tickets.

"Hey, this is in a different place than it was last week."

The emaciated, balding employee with a tiny ponytail wrapped in a rubber band leaned back his head and tittered nervously. "Izzat so?"

"This is Moon Man, right? I thought it was going to be in Culver City."

"Not this week. It's different every week."

"Shit."

Trumbo joined Alison back in his truck. "It's at a different place."

"Think Blue will be there?"

"Who knows? May as well go—we're out forty bucks anyway."

They followed the map thirty-seven miles into the desert north of Los Angeles. The final instruction on the paper said "Right at the water tower." Trumbo spotted the landmark, illuminated in the moonlight, but saw no road.

"Alison, I think we may have been ripped off."

"You're kidding."

"It says 'Right at the water tower.' Do you see a road?"

As they drew closer, several cars ahead of them turned. Trumbo saw that they were taking a gravel service road.

They followed a long caravan of cars down the gravel road, around a slag pile, and across a wide, flat plane. "This must be the place."

Ahead of them, outlined against the night desert sky like an ocean liner on the sea, was a huge cooling tower. As they drew closer, he remembered reading newspaper articles about the tower. It was a half-constructed nuclear plant, abandoned due to cost overruns. He parked on the grass, among the hundreds of cars already there.

Alison balked. "Where are we?"

"The Norville Nuclear Reactor."

They got out of the truck. Trumbo looked around the parking lot until he saw something that made him smile. He whispered. "Alison, look over there."

"Where?"

He stood behind her, held her arm, and pointed until she saw what he was indicating. "Over there. It's Crocket and Tubbs. The cops. They've decided to join us."

"Those geeks."

"My thoughts exactly."

They laughed, then walked toward the imposing structure. As they drew nearer, the steady drub of amplified electronic bass could be heard. A door in the side of the enormous black tower opened, and brilliantly colored lasers flickered inside.

"This is the weirdest thing I've ever seen," said Alison.

"Welcome to El Lay."

They got in line and soon were admitted to the structure. The interior of the perfectly round building was almost as wide as a football field. It was divided into areas with tarps and parachute fabric. The music echoed oddly up the tall cement tower; patterns of lasers played on banks of fog, creating ephemeral pictures and patterns in a multitude of colors that dissolved almost as soon as they appeared. Thousands of teenagers danced in the center of the room.

Alison shouted in Trumbo's ear to be heard over the din. "This is where Blue is?"

"I think so!" yelled Trumbo. "We have to look around!"

Trumbo spotted a counter where two men sold cotton candy. "Excuse me!" he yelled. "Where's the concessions? I'm looking for the hats!"

One of the cotton candy salesmen pointed across the dance floor. "Other side. By the deejay. Peace."

Trumbo grimaced. "War." The cotton candy seller ignored the dig.

Trumbo gripped Alison's arm and steered her through the crowded dance floor. They were briefly separated when they had to go through an especially crowded area, but on the other side Alison took his arm.

Two different booths sold hats. The first was occupied by a boy of about seventeen whose face was painted with fluorescent stars and moons. Trumbo got the boy's attention.

"'Scuse me!" he shouted. "I'm looking for a guy named Blue. Have you seen him?"

"What?"

"Blue! I'm looking for Blue!"

"That some kind of drug? I don't do drugs."

"Never mind."

Trumbo shook his head for Alison's benefit and mouthed the words *not here*. She nodded. Then they worked their way to the other booth, jostling around a stage where two go-go dancers in metallic bikinis swayed to the music.

Several teenaged girls worked at the other hat booth, all

dressed in long, flowing, flowery dresses, which contrasted sharply with the jeans, T-shirts, overalls, and giant hats of most of the kids dancing. Trumbo leaned into the booth and caught the attention of one of the girls.

"I'm looking for Blue!"

"A hat?"

"A person!"

She nodded and stepped behind a covered partition. A moment later a man emerged who stood out from the crowd more obviously than even the girls. It wasn't exactly his clothes: jeans, boots, and brightly colored vest. His hair was long, but that wasn't uncommon. The thing that caught Trumbo's attention was the man's deep, gray eyes, sharp and dangerous. There was a large blue spot in the center of his forehead. Trumbo was on guard.

The man yelled over the music. "What is it?"

"I'm looking for Blue. Guy who sells hats."

"Why?"

"Long story. Do you know him?"

"Maybe I do. Come where we can talk."

"Where?"

He pointed to the back wall of the cooling tower, where several temporary rooms had been set up. Alison, Trumbo, and the man pushed through the crowd. Halfway across the room the musical tempo suddenly sped up. A hundred dancers linked together snaked between Trumbo and Alison, separating them. When the dancers passed, Alison and the man were nowhere near Trumbo.

Trumbo raced to the back of the dance hall, but saw only more dazed teenagers. Five doors to small private rooms lined the wall. He opened them one after another but found no sign of Alison.

A lighted EXIT sign nearby caught his attention. The door outside was closing. He raced for the door and pushed it open. Outside, half a dozen kids stood in the cold night air, passing a joint.

"Did a man and a woman just come by here?" asked Trumbo.

A young girl nodded. "Lot of people been passing through."

"Damn!" shouted Trumbo.

Trumbo jogged around the perimeter of the building toward the parking lot. When he arrived at the front of the building, he saw a line of three dozen cops in riot gear, standing near the entrance to the building, preparing to go in.

Trumbo tried to maneuver around them but was stopped by a uniformed deputy.

"Proceed directly to your car. We are closing down this illegal gathering in just a few minutes."

"I need to get back in! My friend's in there!"

"No one is going back in."

Trumbo started for the door, but the cop grabbed his collar. "To your car, son."

"Shit."

Trumbo made one more search of the perimeter, then ran to his car, on the chance that Alison and the dotted guy had run into the same cops. When he finally made it to the car, he was greeted by Guttierrez and Roddam. "Hello, Trumbo."

"Hi, guys. I was just going."

"Probably not." Guttierrez held a pair of handcuffs.

"Shit! You're not going to arrest me?"

"Unlawful gathering. It's only a misdemeanor charge, but you could stay with us for a couple days nonetheless. If you want to talk with us, we could make a deal."

"There's thousands of people here! That's not fair."

"We're not fair. We're homicide detectives."

"I already told you everything!"

"Well, that's not what we think. Put out your hands and let Detective Roddam handcuff you."

"I came here with Alison. She's going to expect me to give her a ride home. You can't just arrest me on a whim!"

"Oh, yes we can."

He felt the cold steel handcuffs fasten around his wrists and once more heard the warning that he'd almost committed to memory. "You have the right to remain silent. . . ."

14

ALISON WILMOT HAD JUST STEPPED INTO A TINY MAKESHIFT office, accompanied by the weird long-haired hat seller, when the music abruptly ceased. She stopped in her tracks.

"Cops," the man said. "Place has been busted. We ought to get the hell out of here. Name's J'osüf."

"I'm Alison."

He led her through the back door of the office onto the main dance floor. Through bullhorns, cops instructed the revelers to clear the floor. At once, the mob of thousands pushed toward the entrance.

"This way," said J'osüf. "There's a back door."

They maneuvered against the crowd, ducking behind several barriers that had been erected to keep dancers off of the electrical cords and generators that crisscrossed the floor. J'osüf led her to a canvas barricade covered with psychedelic pictures, suspended on metal scaffolding. They stepped beneath the scaffold to an exit door. He pushed it open and they both skipped outside, to the gravel lot.

"Good shortcut—thanks!" said Alison as they stepped into the cool night air. "We have to find my friend who gave me a ride."

"The guy you came with?"

"Yeah."

"With everybody leaving at once, you're probably out of luck. You going back to L.A.? I'll give you a lift." He inched closer.

Alison backed away. "Thanks, but no thanks. Let's go look where he's parked."

"Don't you want to know about Blue? I can tell you a lot of things about him."

"Let's find my friend first and then we'll talk." She walked quickly around the perimeter of the building, hoping to find safety in the crowd. J'osüf kept her pace.

"I understand why you want to ride with your friend," he said. "People just can't be trusted anymore."

"That's right," she answered curtly.

They turned a corner and were confronted by thousands of kids rushing out of the building. A police helicopter hovered over the parking lot, announcing through a loudspeaker system, "Go directly to your car. Do not linger. Go directly to your car."

"Hammer came down," said J'osüf.

"I can't believe the cops in this town," said Alison, exasperated. "I got a jaywalking ticket the first hour I was here. Now they send a battalion out to close down a peaceful party."

J'osüf smiled warmly. "Right on. Wait till you start getting parking tickets. Then see the real soul of Los Angeles."

"Sure," said Alison.

She ran toward the area where she thought Trumbo's tow truck was parked, Sunn at her side. After searching for several minutes, she finally spotted it. As she approached, a police car was pulling away from the truck.

"This is it," she said. "He ought to be out here any minute."

"Right." Sunn saw the sign painted on the driver's-side door of the truck and made a mental note: *Walsh 24-Hour Tow Service: Echo Park/Silverlake/Chinatown.* The name had a familiar ring to it.

"You wanted to know about Blue."

"Yeah."

"How come? You want to buy some speed?"

"Oh, no, not that!" said Alison.

"Good," replied Sunn earnestly. "I like it when people just say no to drugs."

"Yeah, right," said Alison, rolling her eyes. "My friend's trying to find his mother and thought Blue might know where she is."

"Blue's been hiding."

"Why?"

"His girlfriend was murdered. I don't know whether he did it, but he doesn't want to tangle with the law anyway."

"Did you know the victim?" she said.

"Yeah. Her name was Joi Wilmot." Sunn took a deep breath. "God, it's so hard to believe she's gone. Joi was a real angel. If anyone ever needed a place to crash, or had to borrow money, or whatever, Joi was there for them. A couple years ago I had a dog that ran away—a cute little terrier named Bekins. Anyway, Joi heard what happened. She came over and made these great posters with a drawing of Bekins on it, and in the middle of the night went out and Xeroxed hundreds of copies. We stayed up all night plastering the neighborhood with posters." He bit his lip. "Joi had worked the whole day, and had to work the next day, too. Even so, she stayed up all night helping me. I kept saying she didn't have to do it, but Joi told me that's what friends are for."

"Did you find the dog?" asked Alison.

"Nope. Bekins never came back. Everyone else said, well, you can get another dog. Joi understood how much I missed him. She even wrote him a little memorial poem and made a painting of him when I was so sad. She really came through. I'll miss her."

"Wow," said Alison. "I probably ought to tell you something. She was my mother."

Sunn's eyes lit up. "You're the famous Alison?"

Alison chuckled. "I don't know about famous . . ."

"She talked about you all the time! She was so proud of you. You had some sort of business, back in—where was it?—Iowa?"

"Ohio."

"Yeah!" said Sunn. "She really loved you. I wish you could have seen her. Joi grew so much in the last couple years. You even look a little bit like her. I'm so sorry about what happened." He hugged her.

"Thanks," said Alison. "I guess I can tell you. It's not just my friend looking for Blue. I want to find him, too, so I can find out what happened to my mom."

"Whew. If your mom had one fault, it was that she was too kind to people. Blue was a jerk—took advantage of her. She deserved better."

"Where does he hang out?"

Sunn let out a low, long whistle. "Nowhere you want to go. Biker bars, strip joints—he's that kind of guy."

"Know any specific spots he might go?"

"Not off the top of my head, but I think I could find them if I drove into Hollywood."

"That's not much help."

"I'll take you to one of Blue's favorite bars if you want."

"How about just telling me where it is?"

"I can only get there. I don't know the name."

"How about the street? The town?"

"It's in Hollywood. It's a side street in the movie district. I don't know the address."

"When my friend gets back, we'll follow you there."

"I'll go get my van. Will you be okay by yourself?"

"Sure—as long as the cops don't get to me!"

They both laughed.

"It's an honor to meet you. See you in a minute," said Sunn, before he disappeared into the crowd.

Alison waited by the side of the tow truck while the parking lot emptied out. The truck, once surrounded by hundreds of cars, was now one of only a handful of vehicles left. Twice, cops urged her to move along, and twice she explained that she was waiting for her ride. Finally a bright orange van pulled up and parked next to her. J'osüf hopped out, accompanied by two young girls.

"Still waiting, huh?" he asked.

"Yeah. I don't know where he might have gone."

"If he doesn't show up, I can give you a ride," said J'osüf. "By the way, these are my friends—Peace, Cleopatra, this is Alison."

"Good to meet you," said Alison. Both girls smiled and said nothing. There was something *whacked out* about the girls. Maybe it was drugs, maybe they were retarded, but whatever it was, Alison distrusted them.

J'osüf ushered them back into the van and closed the door.

"They're old enough to be here?"

"Sure. Of course," said J'osüf. "The offer for a ride is still open."

Alison considered her options. If Trumbo didn't return, she could be stuck fifty miles out in the desert. Yet she didn't want to accept another ride until she was sure Trumbo wasn't coming back. She took a deep breath.

"Can you wait here a few minutes?" she asked. "I want to go look for my friend."

"No problem."

Alison hurriedly walked the hundred yards back to the entrance of the building. She was greeted at the door by several cops in riot gear on either side of a strip of yellow police tape. She tried to wriggle by but was stopped by a young black cop.

"Miss, this area has been secured."

"I'm looking for the guy I rode in with."

"His name?"

"Trumbo Walsh."

The cop walked a few steps away, spoke to another, who in turn picked up a megaphone. "Trumpet Wash, please come to the front door. Trumpet Wash, please come to the entrance."

After several minutes, the cop shrugged. "Must not be here."

"Thanks."

She wandered to the back of the building, but found only more police. She searched the remaining parking lot: no sign of Trumbo. Eventually she worked her way back to his truck. J'osüf hopped out of the orange van parked next to it.

"Not in there?" he asked.

"Nope."

"Just ducked out on you."

"I don't know where he's gone."

"Come with us, then."

Alison groaned. "I don't know."

J'osüf smiled. "If you're worried—and I understand what women go through these days—let me assure you that there are other women in the car. Besides, I was a friend of your mom."

"Thanks. I guess it'll be okay." Alison reached into her purse and rested her hand on a small can of Mace she carried for protection, just in case.

J'osüf swung open the side door on the van. On the backseat were the two girls she'd already met. By the door sat a younger girl, obviously no older than twelve.

"Just sit anywhere," he said.

Alison sat next to the younger girl.

"Hi, my name's Alison."

"I'm Denise."

J'osüf turned around and stared at the young girl significantly.

The girl grimaced. "I meant to say my name is Diva."

J'osüf smiled, then started the van and drove out of the parking lot. As soon as he turned his back, the girl—Denise or Diva—rolled her eyes so that only Alison could see.

The young girl sat silently during the remainder of the ride into Hollywood.

As they drove, Alison pumped J'osüf for information about his relationship to Joi. He seemed genuinely interested in talking about Joi, but somehow never divulged much, despite his nonstop chatter. He eventually got around to saying that he'd known her since the late sixties, when they both were in a band. He told the tale as an episode of carefree youth, but Alison detected something darker. She couldn't discern what. He offered few specific details.

Throughout the trip the three girls in the back of the van were peculiarly silent. At a couple points Alison looked to see if they were asleep. In fact, Denise, the young girl, was dozing soundly, but the other two stared straight ahead, listening to every word of the conversation without ever contributing.

The black sky of the desert turned rusty orange as they drove over the mountains between the desert and Los Angeles. Alison reminded J'osüf of his promise to take her to the bar where Blue might be.

"We're not taking any detours, are we?"

"We're going straight there," he said.

"Just reminding you."

On Sunset Boulevard low riders and teenagers from the valley cruised aimlessly up and down the street, stereos blaring. It was nearly one A.M., a long time since rush hour, and yet they were stuck in solid bumper-to-bumper traffic.

"It's just up here," said J'osüf.

A few blocks past the Cinerama Dome, Sunn turned in to a narrow alley, then stopped the car. One doorway had a neon sign marked COCKTAILS. Four of the letters had burned out, so that the sign read TAILS.

"This is it," he said. "See why I couldn't tell you its name? I don't even think the place *has* a name."

"Let's go see if Blue is in there."

"I can't go with you," said J'osüf.

"How can I find him by myself if I've never seen him?"

"We can't leave the girls alone in this part of town. Tell you what. I'll go in by myself. You stay here with them," he said.

Before she could reply, he jumped out of the van. Alison looked back and saw that the two not-quite-right girls stared vacantly, not quite comprehending what was going on. However, Denise was groggily sitting up.

"Where are we?" asked the little girl.

Alison crawled to the back of the van and sat next to her. "Sign says 'tails.' I guess that's where we are."

"Oh. I thought we were home."

Alison leaned toward the girl and whispered, "What's the deal with your name? Are you Denise or Diva?"

Denise whispered back, "Denise. The 'Diva' junk is some queerball thing Sunn's trying to do, give me a new name."

"Why?"

"'Cause everybody needs to have one, he says. I think it's the stupidest thing I ever heard." The girl peered over the bench seat and looked at the other girls.

"They're not listening. Tell me more," said Alison.

"I been living with him and the other girls for about a week. He's not, like, a horndog or anything, and he takes okay care of us. But he has some weird ideas. He goes 'you gotta have your true name' and I'm like 'well what's wrong with Denise' and he's like 'we'll call you Diva from now on' and so I go 'okay, you know, whatever floats your boat,' and if he's going to feed us and stuff, I guess it's all right." She caught her breath. "But he is weird."

"What's this place you all live?"

"It's just a place where you can hang out, do your own thing, at least that's what he says so far. Some of the girls are, like, crazy, you know?"

"How many girls live there?"

"Like seven. Plus Joe. Don't tell him I called him 'Joe' 'cause he always goes 'my name is J'osüf' if you say that to his face and so I only call him 'Joe' behind his back."

Alison couldn't repress a chortle. "Tell me more about *Joe*," she said.

"I don't know what his gig is, but he gave me someplace to stay that isn't home, and that's enough for me," Denise whispered back.

"Huh. Sounds strange," said Alison.

Denise continued. "They're always going on these late night expeditions, and I always ask if I can come, but this was the first time they allowed me to go. If you ask me, I'd rather stay at home. It's boring as all get-out."

Sunn ran out of the bar and rapped on the passenger window. Alison crawled over the seat and rolled it down.

"Yeah?"

"He's not in there. None of his buddies are, either."

"But he hangs out here."

"Yeah."

"Any other guesses?"

"Not tonight. I have to get the girls home," said Sunn.

"If it's okay with you, I'll just get out here. I'd like to have a look around in that bar myself."

Sunn bit his lip. "Where are you staying?"

"Close enough." Alison wasn't about to let Sunn know where she lived.

"Can I come visit you again?"

"Nah, I'd rather not."

"I think I can find Blue. I have to be able to contact you if I do."

Alison opened the passenger door before replying. "What if we meet here?" she said. "Say, tomorrow afternoon?"

"Here?" asked Sunn. "In front of this bar?"

"Yeah."

Sunn shook his head. "What about breakfast? I'll buy."

Alison smiled. "Bring Denise and it's a deal."

"Deal. Roscoe's House of Chicken and Waffles. It's on Gower. Ten A.M. Okay?"

"Sure. Thanks, Joe."

"It's J'osüf!"

Alison winked at Denise. "Right," said Alison. See you tomorrow, J'osüf."

Alison climbed out of the van and went into the bar.

There were only two customers, middle-aged men who

wore the leather and blue jeans of a long-ago rebellious youth. Alison walked to the bar and interrupted the bar-maid's game of Donkey Kong.

"Do you know a guy named Blue who drinks here?"

"Nah. Never heard of him."

"Got a phone?"

"In the ladies' room. Go back, last door on the right."

"Thanks."

Alison dialed Trumbo's phone number twice, but received no answer. Sighing, she started the long walk home.

Guttierrez and Roddam took Trumbo directly to the county jail. In minutes they'd swapped his street clothes for a cheap cotton shirt and baggy pants resembling surgeon's scrubs. He used his phone time to call Clemenson, who, to his amazement, came straight to the station even though it was two o'clock in the morning. Clemenson arranged for them to meet in one of the semiprivate booths in the attorney room: a glass enclosure about twice as big as a telephone booth. The lawyer looked as if he'd dressed in a hurry. He wore no socks, and his hair was out of its rubber band.

Clemenson chuckled wickedly when he heard Trumbo's story. "What were the things I told you to do? One, don't talk to the cops. Two, don't talk to Alison Wilmot. Three, keep your nose clean. It's been, what, a day since we talked?"

"So sue me. You're a lawyer."

Clemenson smiled. "I probably would have done the same thing at your age. It just makes my job difficult. Especially seeing as how I'm not getting paid."

"Sorry, but i've got things I have to do, man."

"What the detectives are doing, Trumbo, is trying to wear you down. If you are Joi's killer, they figure you'll crack if they keep busting your chops for minor infractions. I woke up a judge and told him you were unfairly singled out at the rave. You can get your things and go."

"Thanks."

"What were you doing at Moon Man anyway?"

"I was looking for a guy named Blue, Joi's boyfriend. How do you know about Moon Man?"

"I may look old, but most of the folks I defend are younger than you. It's a rave, right?"

"Yeah."

"Most of these big underground parties are pretty harmless. But not Moon Man. Cops tell me there's some ugly people running Moon Man. One time the owners asked me to defend them. I turned 'em down."

"What kind of charges?"

"Drug charges, overcrowding, fire violations—routine problems for any nightclub. Let me tell you. I don't turn down political cases, I don't turn down cases where I won't get paid, I don't turn down unpopular cases. I've represented Klansmen and Black Panthers. But I do turn down vindictive, vicious assholes. I may be a true believer, but I'm not a schmuck."

"Why are you telling me about this?"

"Because you should stay away from these people. They're dangerous and they'll do you more harm than good."

"Dangerous how?"

"I'll send you a few clippings I've got on them. It'll give you some idea. They are *not* nice people."

"All right. I'd like to read up on them. This guy Blue used to be Joi Wilmot's boyfriend."

Clemenson sighed. "The more I find out about Joi Wilmot, the more questions I have about her. She hung with some rough characters besides Blue. That might be why she was murdered. Who knows about Blue or Alison Wilmot? If you keep hanging around them, a lawyer might not be able to help you, even a handsome, smart, free lawyer like myself." Clemenson chuckled.

"Alison didn't see Joi for ten years. Whatever Joi was into, Alison isn't part of."

"That's what she told you."

"I believe her."

"That's your choice. I have an obligation as your attorney to give you my opinion."

"You don't even know why I was hanging around with Joi Wilmot, do you?"

"Enlighten me, Mr. Walsh, if you must, but only if it won't tend to incriminate you."

"Joi was the only contact I had to my mother."

"What does *that* mean?"

"Until recently I believed that my mother died when I was a baby. I found out that's not the case, and Joi was one of the few people who knew where I might find her," said Trumbo.

"You might want to put off your search until things cool down."

"I don't know if I can, my mother might be in danger."

"Like I said, God protects fools and drunkards," said Clemenson. "Trumbo, I came down here to get you out, and now I want to go home. Take my advice seriously: Don't see Alison unless you have to."

Trumbo stood up. "I have to know what happened to Joi. I'm in too deep to quit. It's not just to save my own ass, either."

"Why else do you care?"

"'Cause I'm not gonna be pushed around—not by the cops, not by the people who killed Joi, not by anybody. If they don't want me to find out, then the hell with 'em. I'm going to track down my mother."

Clemenson laughed. "Watch your ass, Trumbo. I'll find out what I can about Moon Man if you think it'll help."

"That'd be cool. One more thing: I gotta know what happened to Alison. Was she arrested?"

"Nope. Total arrests tonight: two. You and some guy who was dancing naked on top of a cop car. That's why the judge agreed you were unfairly singled out."

"So she's out there someplace?"

"Your guess is as good as mine."

On the drive home, Sunn grilled Denise.

"What did you two say while I was gone?"

"Nothing."

"I saw you talking."

"I dunno. She asked 'who is this guy J'osüf' and I told her that you let me stay at your place. That's about it."

"Did she say where she lives?"

"No."

"Did she like you?"

"I dunno."

"We have to persuade her to visit us," said Sunn.

"Not my problem."

"You have to contribute, Diva. You can't just take and take and take."

"I dunno. If you want her to do something for you, why not do something for her?"

"Interesting idea."

Sunn pondered Denise's words while he drove back to the Rebirth Fellowship complex. *Give her something she wants.* She's looking for Blue. Sunn knew exactly where Blue was. The problem was figuring out how to use that information to his advantage.

There are thirteen: six bad and six good. Alison Wilmot was one of the thirteen. She was not one of the bad ones. She was either one of the good ones or the leader. Jesus said that the good ones must be assembled, must be part of the team. Dealing with the bad ones was simple and direct. It takes no imagination to kill. Luring someone to join his cause was a trickier problem. And he had less than a week.

Blue was not one of the chosen ones. He had served his purpose. It was time to cut him loose.

15

ALISON WALKED FOURTEEN BLOCKS TO HER APARTMENT IN FEAR for her life. Prostitutes hissed at her. Gang members circulated through the streets in groups of five and ten. Homeless people slept in doorways filled with piss. A car trailed her for half a block before speeding away. She picked up her pace. She was almost home when four drunken youths stumbled out of the pool hall in front of her building.

"Hey, girl, looking for some action?"

She ignored the young man, who wore a Raiders jacket and backwards black cap. Gang insignia. Two of his companions blocked her path.

"My *friend* asked you a *question.* You too good for him? Or you just deaf?"

She froze in place. "I'm walking home."

"We'll walk with you, then. Somebody could get hurt out here."

"No, thanks."

She tried to dart past them, but another of his friends grabbed her arm.

"We wanna walk you home. What's wrong with that?"

She shook free and made a dash for her apartment, just a few yards away. Two more blocked her path. "Stuck-up bitch," said a two-hundred-pound thug.

Alison trembled with fear. "What do you want? Do you want my purse? Do you want money?"

"We didn't say we wanted something. Gimme the purse, though."

As he reached for her purse, the man was suddenly knocked to the ground. His companions whipped around to see what had happened. Trumbo Walsh stood on the sidewalk, wielding a baseball bat.

"Teach you to fight with a girl, dickhead!" said Trumbo, gripping the bat. The boys backed away. "Come on, Alison."

They ran, while the gangbangers swore at them. Quickly turning in to her apartment building, they raced up three flights of stairs to her apartment. She bolted the door behind them.

"What were you doing there, Trumbo?"

"Waiting for you!"

"Jesus. What happened to you at Moon Man?"

"I got busted."

"Again?"

"Yeah. My lawyer got me out. He told me that the folks who run this Moon Man thing are trouble."

"What do you mean?"

"He's going to send me some articles. I think they're bikers and dope dealers. Blue is one of them. And I'll bet the same's true for that guy we talked to tonight. What happened to *you* out there? How'd you get home?"

"I caught a ride with that hat guy. Name is Joe Sunn, and he's truly bizarre. He kept saying he knew Blue, knew my mother, but then was tight-lipped about them. Didn't tell me anything I don't already know."

"Does he know where you're staying?"

"No."

"Good."

"But what if he does know where Blue is?"

"Then he would have told you tonight. Blow him off. If he has something to say, he should have said it."

"He lives with a bunch of underage girls in an abandoned house."

"Really? He told you that?"

"There were three girls with him tonight. Two of 'em didn't say a word. The third told me that Sunn has seven girls that live with him and he supposedly doesn't ask anything from them, but I don't believe that for a minute."

"Sounds like a real winner."

"A *wiener* if you ask me."

The bedroom door cracked open and a small Hispanic woman with dark hair leaned out. She squinted as if she'd just gotten up.

"Hey, keep it down, okay? I'm trying to sleep."

"No problem."

The door closed. Trumbo moved closer to Alison and they spoke in whispers.

"Got the roomie, I guess."

"Yeah, name's Elena. Paid a week's worth in cash, so in my book that makes her a good roommate."

They sat in the dim apartment, exhausted from the long and complicated night.

"Why'd you come here instead of going home?" asked Alison.

"Three reasons. My truck is still out in the desert. The late night bus stops at this corner. I would have had to walk two or three miles to get to my place. But mostly I wanted to see if you were okay."

"Thanks. I guess I owe you one stay-over. Elena's in my room . . ."

"You take the couch. I don't mind sleeping on the floor," said Trumbo.

Alison crept into the bedroom and returned with two sheets. "This is all I have. You can have one sheet, I'll take the other."

Alison went to the kitchen to wash up. Trumbo wriggled out of his pants and slipped under the sheet at the foot of the couch. He watched Alison's shadow get ready for bed: washing her face in the kitchen sink, wriggling out of her pants, removing her bra from beneath her shirt and pulling it out through her sleeve. She turned off the overhead light and tiptoed toward the couch. Light from the street washed into the room, casting long shadows. She hopped up on the couch and pulled the other sheet over herself. Her head was only inches from Trumbo, who was on the floor. After a long pause, Alison spoke.

"Trumbo? You asleep?"

"No." She let her hand dangle down and touch his hair.

"What if you find out something you don't like?"

"Like what?"

"The more I hear, the more I wonder if I should just stop. The weird folks at that party tonight. I don't know, I just might want to remember my mother the way I do now, and let the details blur." There was a tremor of sadness in her voice. Trumbo caressed her hand. It was warm and soft. "Have you thought of that?" she asked.

Trumbo whispered. "Sure I have. My dad always fed me what he jokingly called the 'party line' about my mom— that she was pretty, that she tried hard, and that she died young. I didn't believe it entirely, but it was a nice fantasy. I sort of thought of her like a Brady Bunch mom, making cookies, PTA, that sort of stuff. But as I got older I began to wonder . . . what was she *really* like? And when I found out that she was alive, I had to know. I imagine it's not pretty. But I don't have any family, I don't have anyplace I call home. What have I got to lose? She's out there somewhere. I'd like to meet her."

Alison sighed. "But what's better? Believing in something that's sweet and lovely that doesn't exist or finding out the harsh reality?"

"Give me the reality any day. See, I pick up wrecked cars, right? Old people, young kids, families, whatever, get into car accidents and I go clear the way. I clean up the road for the people who are scared of the truth. There's something about all the folks who show up at the crashes—the

Highway Patrol, the local cops, ambulance drivers, sometimes the coroner—that I like. We're always standing around chatting about what movie we saw or how the game was on TV last night, and inches away might be a bloody corpse. Knowing the reality makes you appreciate the small things.

"I remember one guy, works for the coroner's office, basically comes out and picks up the bodies whenever there's a 'fatal.' One day we were at this wreck where a guy and a girl on a motorcycle were decapitated. It was ugly. But the guy from the coroner's office, y'see, his wife had just had a baby. We all congratulated him, wished him well; he passed out cigars. All this while he's wrapping up these bodies. Somehow the moment was sweeter because death was nearby, and we were still alive.

"Maybe my mom's a shit, maybe your mother was in with some bad crowd, but I'd rather know the truth."

Alison squeezed his hand and whispered, "That's me, hiding my head in the sand, hoping the bad things will go away. I could never do your job. I always say 'leave well enough alone' and keep it at that."

"Twenty years from now, won't you wish you tried to find out what became of your mother?"

"Twenty years. Hah. I live every year like I'm going to shoot myself in the head on New Year's Eve."

"What, and leave me alone?"

"What do you mean?"

"There's just hardly any no-bullshit people around like you. You come trucking into L.A. telling everybody what to do, the cops, the detectives, me. It's great. If you kill yourself, then the namby-pambys win another victory. I would hate for the namby-pambys to defeat you."

"I wasn't seriously considering suicide. It's just something people say, you know, live fast, die young, leave a pretty corpse."

"I wish you wouldn't."

She let go of his hand and they lay silent for a while, Trumbo on the floor, Alison above him on the couch. Then she quietly slipped off the couch and lay next to him on the floor.

"No fooling around, okay? I just wanted to see your face," said Alison.

"Why?"

"So I can see if you're bullshitting me."

"I'm not." Trumbo grinned. "See?"

They lay silently for a few moments. Alison's eyelids grew heavy. "Okay, just a sec," she said, "and I'll get back up." She closed her eyes and reached out, putting an arm around Trumbo. Under her breath she mumbled, "No fooling around, right?"

Trumbo embraced her. They held each other, her hot breath against Trumbo's ear. He brushed his hands gently through her hair, until her breathing grew heavy and she was sound asleep. After several minutes she turned, so that she was even closer to him. Trumbo drifted off, holding her tight.

It seemed like an instant after he'd drifted off that Trumbo was awakened by sunlight glaring into the apartment and the insistent beat of a Spanish language radio station. He glanced around as if he'd been whacked on the head. Alison was by his side, her legs entangled with his. Her shirt was further unbuttoned, and when he started to move, she groaned and pressed her breasts against his side, murmuring, "Don't leave." He glanced across the apartment towards the kitchen. Elena, who had leaned her head out of the door the night before, was in the kitchen making an omelette. Every few seconds she glanced over at Trumbo to see if he was awake. When he fluttered his eyes, she walked over.

"Hey, man, you guys can't sleep all day. My friends are coming over."

"What time is it?"

"It's almost eleven. You little lovers been snoring away there on the ground. My name's Elena." She pronounced it ay-LANE-ah.

"Can you turn that radio down?" asked Trumbo.

"No way, man. This apartment is half mine now."

Alison began to wake up. Suddenly self-conscious, she buttoned up her shirt. "Give us a break, Elena," she growled.

"My friends is coming at lunchtime and I don't want youse crashed out on the floor like winos. They're already ascared of me being here."

Alison looked at Trumbo. They both smiled. "Sorry about this," she said.

"I wanted to get up anyway. I gotta get my truck." Trumbo wriggled into his pants and stood.

Alison stayed on the floor, nestled in the sheets. "I have a lot to do myself."

"Should we go to breakfast?"

"No. I'm meeting Sunn," said Alison.

"What?"

"I'll be okay. It's at a public place."

"Be careful."

Trumbo kissed her on the cheek. He let it linger, and she didn't push him away.

"How'm I gonna reach you?" he asked.

"I'll call you."

"Promise?"

"Hell no. I don't do promises." Her eyes showed that she was kidding.

"Right."

Roscoe's House of Chicken & Waffles was a surprisingly stylish restaurant, with darkened, stained wood walls. She spotted Sunn at a circular booth in back, accompanied by two girls: Denise and one other she didn't recognize.

"Hello, Alison," said Sunn. In the morning light he seemed like a normal, middle-aged guy. "This is my friend Silhouette."

"Nice to meet you." Silhouette nodded silently. Alison sat down at the table. "Hi, Denise."

Denise nodded.

They ordered breakfast. The girls asked for exactly the same thing Sunn got, pancakes and apple juice. Alison indulged in Carol's Special: a waffle and a chicken breast.

"Did you find out anything else about Blue?" she asked.

"Wow. Straight to business," said Sunn. "Sure. I made a couple of calls. It seems that he skipped town or just isn't going to his regular places. I'd say that looks pretty damning. He might have been the murderer."

"Oh, God. What do you know about him?"

"Usually quiet, but he had a hell of a temper when he got angry."

"Was he the kind of guy to kill his girlfriend?"

"Who can say?"

"I'm asking *you*. I never met him."

"Maybe. He was always in and out of jail."

"On what kinds of things?"

"Fights, mostly. One time he stole a car."

Alison laughed. "You sound like a politician. You keep saying just enough to get by. It sounds like you're holding out on me. What's the real story, Joe?"

Denise stifled a giggle at hearing Alison call him "Joe." Alison winked at the girl.

"I met him like twenty years ago because he works on motorcycles," said Sunn. "I had a piece-of-crap Honda and he would come over whenever it broke down, fixing it in exchange for dinner and a beer. We became friends, sort of, but never that close. We went to the same parties, but he wasn't a friend I saw all the time."

"How come you were at his booth selling hats?"

"You've got it backwards. He was at *my* booth selling hats one night when I couldn't go."

"You just called him?"

"I called Joi."

Alison nodded.

The food came. Alison ate in silence. The three girls picked at their food. Finally Sunn spoke.

"Alison, I know you're going through a hard time. You don't know who to trust, who to listen to, where to go."

"Bingo," she said, scowling.

"And you don't even have a car."

"Which in Los Angeles is like being buried in cement."

Sunn laughed. "I'm going to make you an offer. If you have errands to run or something, we can help you out. Get groceries, see people, or whatever. Maybe together we can track him down."

"Why would you do this? You barely know me."

"I knew your mom. What happened to her shouldn't happen to anybody. I want to find Blue as badly as you do."

She decided to accept. "That'd be great."

"Good." Sunn smiled.

16

IT TOOK TRUMBO THREE AND A HALF HOURS BY BUS TO GET TO HIS truck. When he arrived at the power plant, the chain-link fence had been locked and the weird fantasy of the previous night was now just another abandoned building. He found a guard and, with some bullshit about being a friend of the cops and a twenty-dollar bribe, persuaded the man to let him get his truck.

When he got home, a packet of papers from Clemenson's office was leaning against his front door. Inside was a collection of photocopied newspaper articles, some dating back to the 1970s. A Post-it note from Clemenson attached to the front of the packet read "Trumbo: Thought you should know why I told you to stay away from the Moon Man folks. Best, Dennis."

DRUG DEALER IMPLICATED IN MURDER PROBE was the headline of a story from one year earlier. It detailed the investigation of an amphetamine dealer named Skylar Desmond, who was suspected in the torture-murder of a woman and her two children, over a drug deal gone sour.

The next article detailed Desmond's release on a technicality relating to a search warrant. Trumbo did not understand the connection to Moon Man until he read the third article.

In a series of articles on raves from the "View" section of the newspaper, the owners of underground nightclubs were interviewed. Buried deep in the third of five articles was an interview with the Moon Man operators: Skylar Desmond and a few others, whose names he did not recognize.

The next stapled packet of articles was much older, dating from the mid-seventies. It concerned the trial of a group of drug dealers, convicted of selling a lethal batch of synthetic heroin, which took the lives of fourteen users. Trumbo's attention was drawn to an accompanying photo of the group, taken at a party some months before they were arrested.

Although a dozen people were in the dark photocopied picture, the caption identified only seven of them. The remaining five were listed as "unknown." He squinted to read the photo caption; Skylar Desmond was identified, then several names he didn't recognize, then a woman listed as Joi X. Null. J-O-I: He'd only ever seen that name spelled that way once before. He squinted at the blurry photo. It was indeed Joi Wilmot.

The next several articles were recent obituaries.

Of the seven people identified in the old photo, five, including Joi Wilmot, had died in the previous year. One had been in a car accident, one overdosed on heroin, one was stabbed to death in a federal penitentiary, and one was found with her throat slit in a Glendale alley, "assailant unknown."

Other than Skylar Desmond, the only person in the photograph still alive was a convict named Barbara Thompson, currently serving time for the attempted assassination of a Supreme Court justice.

Who were these people? Trumbo stared hard at the photo. Suddenly, as if seeing a ghost, he recognized one more face. Standing directly behind Joi Wilmot was Trumbo's father. Luther Walsh's hair was longer, and he was younger than the image Trumbo carried in his mind, but it was definitely him. He felt light-headed as he looked at the photo. What was his father doing with murderous drug dealers?

He stepped onto his porch to get some fresh air.

Guttierrez and Roddam were parked across the street, doing crossword puzzles in a nondescript Ford. Trumbo was initially angry that the detectives were still following him, then decided to put the cops to some use.

He grabbed the articles and jumped down the front stairs two at a time. He rapped on the detectives' car window.

Guttierrez didn't flinch. "Afternoon, Walsh."

Trumbo leaned into the window. "You've been with me all day?"

"More or less."

"You ought to come in and say hi sometimes. I have some articles that might interest you."

"What are they?"

"I'll share, but I want to ask you a favor in return."

"Show us what you have and we'll talk."

"We're still negotiating. I want you to get me a meeting with a woman—Barbara Thompson—who is in prison now."

"That's possible," said Guttierrez. Roddam, as was his wont, nodded silently. "Depending on what you have."

"Look at this." Trumbo pulled out the photograph.

Guttierrez handled it and nodded. "Pretty picture, Trumbo."

"Let me show you something. That's my father there. Next to him is Joi Wilmot, but then she went by the name Joi Null."

"Yeah."

"Both died in the last year."

"Right. Your dad died in a mental home, right?"

"Or he was killed. Look at these other folks—this guy here, Reggie Foxx, got in a fatal car crash last February. The woman next to him—see, part of her face is blocked—she's named Mercedes Huston. Heroin overdose in June. This other guy, Markum Fowler, stabbed to death just over a year ago at a federal penitentiary. This woman here was found in a Glendale alley during the summer, dead, her throat slit. This one here, Barbara Thompson, seems so far to have escaped the curse."

Guttierrez let out a long, low whistle. "Sheesh. Roddam, look at this." Roddam handled the picture delicately, as if it might break. Guttierrez redirected his attention to Trumbo. "How'd you know to look for this stuff?"

"That rave where you busted my chops is run by these same people. Including this guy—his face is partially blocked in the picture. Name's Skylar Desmond."

Guttierrez raised his eyebrows.

Roddam finally spoke. "Skylar Desmond is—"

Guttierrez scowled at his partner, cutting him off in midsentence.

"What is it?" asked Trumbo.

"Nothing. Nothing at all."

"You're not telling me something. Come on, fair's fair. What is it?"

"Nothing I can tell you."

"Fine, then, can I have my picture back?" asked Trumbo.

"We'd like to make a copy," said Guttierrez.

"Can you set up the meeting with Thompson?" asked Trumbo.

"I'll look into it."

"I want your word."

"Bureau of Prisons is a whole different ball of wax. I don't necessarily have the pull."

"Come on, Guttierrez. You said you could do it. I wasn't born yesterday."

Guttierrez threw up his hands. "Why are you so hot to meet her?"

"My dad is in this photo. It was probably taken when I was one or two years old, judging from the clothes and haircuts. Barbara Thompson may be the only one in the photo who is still alive. She might know where my mother is."

"That's the only reason?"

"Yeah."

"I'll set it up."

"Word?"

"I give you my word. I don't take a commitment lightly, either."

"Okay. Give me the photo back after you make a copy."

"Thanks," said Guttierrez.

"You gonna keep following me?"

"You shouldn't ask that."

" 'Shouldn't,' huh? I shouldn't be talking to you if I did what my lawyer said. So what is it?"

"We probably will."

"Why?"

"You're our best lead. And it's producing results." The detective shook the photo at Trumbo.

"Be cool about it, then. My downstairs neighbor is starting to get suspicious."

Guttierrez smiled.

"You talked to her?"

"Yeah. She's kind of cute."

"She's a lesbian, Guttierrez."

"All the good ones are taken," said the detective.

"What'd you tell her?"

"Walsh, do I have to remind you that you're a suspect?"

"I have to live upstairs from her."

"We didn't tell her anything."

"I know you have a job to do and all that, but trust me, you're going to find out that I didn't do anything. After this blows over you'll completely forget about me, but I have to live there."

"We'll do our best."

They shook hands. Guttierrez rolled up the window.

Trumbo went inside and made a quick dinner, then checked his message machine for the third time in an hour. Alison had not called.

Tailed by the cops, he drove to her apartment in Hollywood and joked around with her new roommate, Elena, for an hour in hopes that Alison might return. Elena was all right, Trumbo decided. Just starting out in life, this was her first apartment. She wanted to be an actress, and had already had two auditions. She was pretty and bilingual. Trumbo thought she had a better than average chance at her chosen career.

Long after dark, Alison still hadn't returned. Trumbo wrote a note asking Alison to call when she returned, and left. He was relieved that the cops were no longer following him. Just as he got home, his phone rang.

"Alison?" he answered.

Click. The caller hung up.

Moments later the phone rang again.

"Hello?"

Click.

At two in the morning he moved into the bedroom and finally slipped into a troubled sleep. In the morning the phone answering machine was blinking. He pressed play, angry that he'd missed the call. Background noise made it sound like Alison was calling from a pay phone.

"Trumbo, this is Alison. I'm staying with some friends but

wanted to call and let you know I'm okay. There's no number here, but I'll call you tomorrow. Take care!"

He heard laughter in the background, as if there were a party going on. He wondered who these friends were, and if Alison was safe.

17

AT FIVE-THIRTY IN THE MORNING, THE SMOG BEGAN TO GLOW WITH what passed for a sunrise in L.A. Eleven-year veteran Officer Bob Tower and his inexperienced partner, Virginia Cooper, were at the tail end of the graveyard shift and had one more stop to make before heading home. The call came in almost three hours earlier, and was given a low priority by the dispatcher. Someone had heard a gunshot at the Isaacson, a seedy single-room occupancy hotel downtown. Tower and Cooper, as usual, had too many things to do that night, and the gunshot report kept getting bounced by more urgent matters: a prowler inside an apartment complex who got away before they arrived; a gang dustup outside a bar, which dissipated before they arrived; and two domestic violence calls that unfortunately required that they actually do something. A drunken father was in jail, his wife in the emergency room, as a result of their intervention. A Hispanic couple promised in broken English to kiss, make up, and above all, keep the noise down. A good night's work.

"So, Ginny, do we do the Isaacson call or do we leave it for the morning shift?" he asked, flexing his left hand, which had gotten crunched during one of the domestic disputes. "I bet dollars to doughnuts it's long over by now."

Cooper was an overambitious third-year officer who took her duties a little too seriously. "They nailed a crack dealer in the Isaacson last week. We ought to check it out."

Tower nodded, silently cursing his partner, and steered the police car toward Sixth Street. Twenty minutes to go. He wanted to clock out promptly so he could make a seven A.M. tee time at the Roosevelt Public Golf Course.

They parked in the red zone and entered the tall, narrow building, which had once been a businessmen's hotel. The front of the building was covered with metal bars and multilingual gang graffiti. Tower went on so many calls to the Isaacson, they ought to give him a room. The cops went straight to the manager's apartment on the first floor and rapped on the door. Moments later a Japanese-American woman, well past sixty years in age, leaned out of the door. Her hair was in a nighttime net and she wore a terry cloth robe.

"Hello, Officers."

"Hi, Lisa. You called us after hearing a gunshot?" asked Tower.

"Right, oh, right, I remember. It was a new fella—moved in last week. I knew there was something about him that didn't seem right. Both his neighbors called me."

"Could you take us to his room?"

"Come this way." She tightened her robe and escorted them to an ancient elevator, which took them to the eighth floor, top of the hotel. Lisa was very animated and gossiped about the comings and goings of various tenants. She tried to run a clean building, but it was impossible to attract classy tenants to the run-down SRO, so she instead kept close track of everyone who moved in, maintaining a close relationship with the cops. Most of them knew her on a first-name basis.

She took them out of the elevator and down a dimly lit hallway to the second to last room. Freeway noise rumbled in through the open window at the end of the hall.

"This is where they heard it—803. Frances in 805 heard it, and so did Jenny in 801."

"Thank you, Lisa."

Cooper knocked on the door. No answer. She pulled out her baton and knocked louder. Nothing.

"I can let you in," volunteered the manager.

"Maybe you should stand back."

"Right, Bob. Here's my master key." She handed Tower the key, then retreated back toward the elevator, watching them closely but without undue alarm. She yawned. Police activity was not unusual enough to be exciting.

The two cops drew their service revolvers and stood clear of the doorway. Tower put the key in the lock and pushed the door open. "Los Angeles Police. Is anyone in there?"

Cooper reached around the doorframe and flipped on a light, then quickly withdrew her hand. She pulled a telescoping mirror from her belt, extended it, and pushed it in the room so that she could look inside without exposing herself to danger.

"Man down!" she yelled.

The two walked into the room. Devoid of any decoration, it had only the standard-issue couch, single bed, and table that was in every room of the Isaacson. Face down on the floor was a man in a leather jacket and blue jeans. Completely ignoring him, they did a quick search of the rest of the two-room apartment to make sure no one else was there, then Cooper went to the man's side. She lifted his wrist. "I'm getting a faint pulse! Call the paramedics!"

Tower saw his golf game receding into the distance as he called the ambulance. *Motherfucker,* he thought. *If you're going to get shot, why'd you have to do it on my shift?* While Cooper tried to stanch the flow of blood, Tower did a quick scan of the room: First impressions are important. On the stove was a note written on legal paper.

"Suicide note," said Tower. He left it where it was, where it could be photographed and then transported downtown for analysis. He didn't read much more than the first few lines. He was pissed off.

The bleeding man was shipped to County Medical's emergency room, where he was sewn up, given blood, fluids, and antibiotics, and dumped into the overcrowded intensive care unit, either to die or to recover.

The letter, on the other hand, had a long journey through the police bureaucracy before it became useful. Questioned Documents Department confirmed it as Desmond's writing. Fingerprints confirmed. Records made an official copy and filed it. It would be another thirty-six hours before someone decided to read the damn thing.

An inexperienced young woman in the police laboratory was trying to decide where to ship the official photo of the note labeled DESMOND, SKYLAR, SUICIDE ATTEMPT, and rather than bother her superior for a sixth time that morning, she decided to read the note. Within minutes she knew to contact Guttierrez, who had been searching for a man named Blue.

> TO THE POLICE:
> I AM FILED WITH GUILT AND SHAME.
> I DONE SOMETHING WRONG AND IT IS TIME TO COME CLEAN OF IT. I CANNOT CARRY THIS ROUND SO I'M WRITING THIS NOTE TO MAKE CLEAR WHAT HAPPENED.
> MY GIRLFRIEND, MY BEST FRIEND, THE WOMAN CLOSEST TO ME IN MY LIFE WAS JOI WILMOT.
> SHIT HAPPENS AND I WAS DOING SOME CRANK MAYBE SOME X AND DRUNK A LITTLE TOO MANY BEERS. THAT NIGHT WE HAD A ARGUMENT LIKE WE SOMETIMES DID LIKE ALL PEOPLE IN LOVE SOMETIMES DO. AND THEN I GOT OUT OF CONTROL AND I DIDN'T KNOW QUITE HOW IT HAPPENED BUT IT HAPPENED.
> I KILLED HER. IT PAINS ME TO WRITE IT BUT THATS THE TRUTH AND I HAVE TO FACE UP TO THE MUSIC.
> I BEEN BUSTED OVER THE YEARS A NUMBER OF TIMES AND LOTS OF COPS WILL KNOW MY NAME BUT NONE OF THEM WILL SAY I WAS A KILLER AND THAT WAS RIGHT UNTIL NOW.
> IN THE HEAT OF THE MOMENT I THOUGHT I WOULD COVERED IT UP AND MAKE IT LOOK LIKE SOMEONE ELSE DID IT MAYBE A RELIGIOUS FANATICK.
> IF YOU WANT PROOF I DID IT—I WROTE THOSE WORDS ON THE WALL I DO NOT KNOW WHAT I WAS THINKING IT SAID JOI HATES JESUS.
> EVER SINCE I HAVE ONLY BEEN THINKING OF HER AND FILLED WITH GUILT AND EMPTYNESS AT THE HORROR OF IT.

BY THE TIME YOU READ THIS YOU WILL KNOW THAT I AM ALREADY DEAD.
(signed)
Skylar "Blue" Desmond

After Guttierrez chewed out Cooper, Tower, the documents and fingerprints technicians, and anyone else in hailing distance, he tried to contact Alison Wilmot. She was not at the phone number he had. Later that day she called them to check on the case, from someplace in South Pasadena. Guttierrez sent a black-and-white to escort Alison Wilmot down to the station. She arrived about an hour later. As in previous encounters, she was impatient and testy.

"This happened, what, *yesterday?*" was her greeting.

"We didn't want to bring you down here on a false alarm, ma'am," said Guttierrez.

"It's a note saying the guy did it. What kind of false alarm is that?"

"Who told you about the note?" he asked.

"The cop who drove me in."

Guttierrez made a mental note of one more person who needed to be chewed out, then put on his polite "public" face and questioned Alison quietly.

Alison told him everything she knew: about Trumbo, about the rave, about meeting Sunn, about driving around with Sunn and the three girls looking for Blue. The cop wrote it down as if it were all news, which worried Alison.

"We told you about Blue a couple days ago," she said.

"We, who?"

"Trumbo Walsh and me."

"I mean who did you tell?"

"You. I don't know if it was you personally, but it definitely was a cop."

"Yes, we knew that." He didn't know that. "You're sure this man lived with your mother?"

"Trumbo said so. I don't think she mentioned him in any letters, but she kept her love life pretty much to herself." Alison pushed a lock of hair out of her eyes and leaned forward. "Why did he do it?"

"We're not one hundred percent sure."

"Not sure of what? That he killed my mom? Or why he did?"

"We have to talk to him. Doctors say he'll probably regain consciousness within a week. We have some questions to ask him."

"So you're not closing the case."

"I can't say."

"And you'll keep following Trumbo around."

"I can't say."

"You don't seem to say much, Detective. How likely do you think it is that this guy killed my mother?"

"Everything looks right. He knew her, he lived with her, he left a confession."

"That sounds pretty closed to me. Now, can I finally get into my mother's house? Are you people done with whatever you were doing?"

Guttierrez drummed his fingers on the desk. "Sure. You could have gone in any time you wanted."

"That's *definitely* not what I was told."

"I don't know of any reason why you can't. It's your place now, I suppose, since you're next of kin. I think we've gotten all from it that we can get. You want to go there now?"

"Just give me a ride to my apartment. I'll go to my mother's later."

Alison would always regret this hasty decision.

Monday morning, before he even drank a cup of coffee, Trumbo drove to Alison's apartment. Again, she wasn't home. Then he called Guttierrez, who wasn't in. He spoke to Guttierrez's partner, Roddam.

The detective lied, said he hadn't seen Alison, but he had set up a meeting for Trumbo with Barbara Thompson. Roddam made one provision: Trumbo had to share whatever he learned with the police. Trumbo agreed. He didn't know that the conversation would be taped and complete transcripts were to be made available to Guttierrez after vetting by prison legal counsel.

The women's pen was located on the far side of Riverside County. As Trumbo drove the seventy-seven miles to Riverside, the smog intensified until it was an acidic, yellow haze that lay over the city, filtering the color from the sun and giving the city a monochromatic, dulled appearance. He drove through several miles of foul-smelling cattle ranches before reaching the long road that led from the highway to the correctional facility.

Two guard gates and three metal inspections later, he was seated in a medium-sized room set aside for inmates to meet with lawyers, the press, and family members. A guard at the entrance to the room stood on an elevated stand that gave him full view of the thirty small tables. Trumbo waited for about fifteen minutes. He felt overwhelmed by the institutional feel of the prison. It reminded him, strangely, of kindergarten.

He didn't notice the woman he'd come to visit until she tapped on his shoulder. Startled, he turned around. She was accompanied by a female correctional officer.

"Mr. Walsh? This is Barbara Thompson. You have sixty minutes. I'll come back in when you have ten minutes left to remind you to wrap it up." The guard directed her attention to the woman. "Thompson, sit on the opposite side of the table. Do not accept objects of any sort from your guest—you know the drill."

"Yeah."

The woman sat down in front of Trumbo. She looked substantially similar to the twenty-year-old picture: trim, with bright, brown eyes and a thin, regal mouth that smiled at him now. She wore no makeup, and only the lines around her eyes betrayed her true age. Above her nose was a scar, partially healed, in the shape of a swastika. Her brown hair was clipped short, and a few wisps of gray appeared near the temples.

"You wanted to see me," she said. "Why did you come?" There was defiance in her voice.

"I found this picture in a newspaper. My father is in it, and you are, too."

"Let me see."

Trumbo started to hand it across the table when the public-address system blurted out, "Thompson, you may not accept anything from visitors."

"Give it to the screw," she said. Trumbo walked over to the door and handed the picture to a correctional officer standing by the exit. The guard rubbed her fingers across the picture, then walked over to the table and handed it to Thompson.

"You gonna give her anything else?" asked the officer.

"Probably not."

"If you do wish to, you must give it to me first."

"Right."

The guard left them. Thompson bit her lip, staring at the photo.

"So what?" she asked.

"You knew my dad? Luther Walsh?"

"Yeah, I knew him. He was a beautiful man."

Trumbo nodded. "You knew Joi Wilmot, too?"

"Joi X. Null?"

"I guess."

"Yeah, I did. I knew all these people. It was an amazing time."

"That's why I came. I'm trying to find my mother. My father always said she died, but then I found some letters that indicated she might still be alive. Her name is Mimi Black."

Thompson stared at the ceiling for a moment, then began giggling. "There is no such person. You just don't get it, do you? You don't even know what this picture really is."

"Tell me."

She snorted. "How can I tell you about a whole generation, all about a time when we had a chance to do it right?"

"What are you talking about?"

"The sixties. The whole world was ready to change overnight. Then the Man rejected it, the Man knew what would happen, put his foot down and stopped it. So much love, so much happiness."

"We were talking about a picture. Where was this picture taken, and why are you holding guns?"

"We're in another world. That's what I'm telling you. This is a picture of another world."

Trumbo frowned. *She's a major flake.* He spoke slowly and deliberately, as if to a child. "Let's say I agree with you, it's another world. But someone took this photo. You were *somewhere*. Look, I can see a railroad in the background. They don't have railroads in 'other worlds,' do they?"

"I was speaking figuratively. I mean the picture isn't the whole picture."

"Cut it out. Where were you?"

"At the Ranch."

"What kind of ranch?"

"Not a real ranch. Used for shooting movies, once, until Jesus came."

"Jesus."

"Yes, Jesus. The smartest man in the world. A leader sent from God. Luther loved him once. I love him still."

"My father was not religious."

She laughed heartily. "You don't get it. Call him Jesus, call him the Devil, it doesn't matter. He had a name given him by the Man, too. You never heard of Charles Manson? He's only the most important person to walk the earth in two thousand years."

Trumbo did a double take. "Charles Manson? Like, the psycho-killer?"

"No!" she yelled. "He never killed anybody. Those're *lies* perpetrated by the Man, trying to keep him down. Jesus was only about love and peace and everything that was good."

Trumbo stood up. "You're trying to make me believe that my father hung out with Charles Manson?"

"I'm not trying to make you believe anything. I'm telling you the truth. T-R-U-T-H. It's as simple as that."

"The Manson Family?"

She hissed, furious. "That 'Family' label is a lie made up by that prosecutor Bugliosi. We never called ourselves anything. We just *were.*"

"But you mean it was the same people who are in that movie *Helter Skelter.* Sneaking around at night, killing people."

"That movie is another lie. If Charlie was like they showed him in that movie, nobody would have loved him the way they did. And still do."

"Was my mother one of them?"

"One of who?" she asked.

"The Family."

"You just don't get it, do you! There ain't no family. Never was."

"Whatever you wanna call it, was my mother one of them? A follower?"

"Did she love Charlie? Yes, she did."

"And where is she now?"

"Maybe I know. But why should I tell you?"

"I want to meet her. I want to know who the hell she is before I die."

"I don't think you're ready to meet her."

"Do you know her name?"

"Maybe I do."

"Why are you doing this? Why not just tell me?" Trumbo realized he had lost control of his temper and was ranting. The guard at the door approached.

"Sir, you must remain seated during all conversations."

"Sorry."

He sat down. Thompson chuckled.

"Boy, you have a lot of learning to do. You have to find out what really happened. It's not your fault, but you've been force-fed the Man's lies about Jesus, about everything. Before I can tell you anything, you have to know about the sixties and Jesus. There were gods with guitars and poets and people sharing love in the streets, in their houses, opening up their hearts. All of the world was balanced for a short instant, all there for the changing. The new day would have come, too, and it still might."

Trumbo had had enough. "I just want a simple answer about where my mother is. You can babble on about the wonderful sixties, but I'm not buying. I was on the other side of that equation. I saw the downside. The flower children and all that other bullshit—bullshit!—was the biggest lie ever perpetrated. A bunch of self-centered egomaniacs who didn't give a good goddamn for anyone but themselves."

She laughed. "I touched a nerve, Trumbo-man. You can keep yelling, but I don't have to tell you nothing."

Trumbo didn't know what he *could* say; what can you offer a woman who was in prison for the rest of her life? How can you make her do what you want? He gritted his teeth. He had to find out where his mother was.

"Do you know all the people in that picture?"

She glanced at the photo again. "Yeah."

"Do you know where they are now?"

"Some yes, some no. I don't know."

"Think about this: My father died—maybe he was killed —in a mental home last year. Joi Wilmot—the woman you called Joi X. Null—was killed in her home last week. Four of the others were either killed or died in 'accidents'—that's what they're calling them, anyway—in the last year alone. You and one other in this picture are the only ones still alive."

Thompson closed her eyes and rocked back and forth in her chair, a delirious grin on her face. "It's happening, isn't it? Can't you feel it? Isn't it delicious?"

"What's happening?"

"Charlie's going free!"

"What the hell has that got to do with anything?"

In a singsong tone she continued. "Charlie's going free, Jesus is coming back, he's going to save us all. He's going to show the world real love again. Charlie's going free. It's going to be Day One. The new era. The Rebirth. The fellowship."

"What are you getting at?"

"It's all clear now, I knew he'd send a sign, I knew it, and you are the sign, Trumbo-boy. Nothing happens without a purpose. Charlie wouldn't let the traitors get away with it, oh no he wouldn't, he's too smart for that, he's smarter than anyone you ever met."

"Are you saying these people were all killed by him?"

"Oh no, he'd never do that, Charlie is light and Jesus and he's pure love. The people were freed by themselves. Everyone has a time to die, and some die sooner than others. It's happening in preparation for his return, Day One, the time of enlightenment and happiness. I know it, I see the truth in it."

"Nobody 'freed' my father. He was stabbed with a shiv in a public mental hospital."

"That's one way of looking at it, but it happens to be wrong."

"Aren't you scared of the same happening to you? I know I would be if I was in this photo."

"I'm not afraid of anything because I have true peace in myself. No, you can't worry about anything. 'Just do it.' That's what Jesus says."

"That's a tennis shoe ad."

"Wisdom comes from unexpected sources."

Trumbo, exasperated, tried the direct route. "What's it going to take you to get you to tell me my mother's name?"

"You'll know her name when you're ready to learn it."

"If things keep going like they've been going, she might be dead before I get the chance."

"She'll survive. She's a survivor. She'll be there on Day One, I guarantee it, and she'll make herself known."

"Day one, you keep babbling about day one."

"You'll know it when you see it. Trumbo, you're a special messenger, perhaps even a leader. You must stop searching for your mother, for answers, and realize that the answer is in yourself. Things will come to *you*. You've had the answer all along."

"You've been a lot of help." He stood and summoned the officer in charge, who nodded.

"You're leaving?" she asked.

"I have a life. I don't need this."

The color drained from her face. "Be careful, Trumbo. Keep your head low. There are those who want to twist you and use you for their own purposes."

"Yeah, right."

"The new era is just around the corner. Watch what you say. Watch what you do."

She suddenly stood, reached across the table and grabbed Trumbo's head in her hands, and delivered a big, wet kiss on his forehead. The guard reached the table just as she did it.

"Knock it off," said the guard, pulling Thompson from Trumbo.

"Take care of yourself," she said.

"Thanks for your time," said Trumbo, his voice thick with sarcasm. He turned to the guard. "I want my picture back."

Thompson handed the newspaper photo to the officer, who in turn handed it to Trumbo.

"Your mother will make herself known on Day One!"

shouted Thompson as Trumbo left the room. He did not look back.

At Alison's apartment, Elena told him she had gone to her mother's house. Trumbo sped from Hollywood to Joi's house, a place he hadn't visited since the night of the murder.

As he neared the house, he smelled a harsh odor like burning rubber. As he rounded the final curve, he spotted two fire engines and an ambulance. Trumbo leaped out of his truck and ran to the top of the stairway. Several firemen were spaced evenly along the stairs, supporting a hose that ran from a hydrant to Joi's cottage. Trumbo started down the stairs. A fireman blocked his path.

"You can't go down there."

Trumbo stood stock-still until the fireman wasn't paying attention, and then he darted down the steps. Joi's house was a heap of charred timbers, steaming under the torrent of water coming from the fire hose. Then he saw Alison standing in a neighbor's yard, tears streaming down her cheeks.

"Alison!" he ran to her side.

"God, am I glad you're here." She hugged him. She crushed her face into his chest, sobbing. He ran his hands through her hair, comforting her, consoling her.

She pulled away from him and wiped her eyes on a smoke-stained shirtsleeve.

"What happened?"

"No one knows," she said. "I came over here about an hour ago and there was all this smoke coming from the window. Oh God. I don't know if I can take it anymore. I wanted to get in there and get her things. She's gone, and now everything she had is gone as well."

Trumbo held her tight. "Come on. Let's get out of here."

Trumbo led Alison to his truck and had her sit down.

"I'll be right back. Okay?"

"Don't leave, Trumbo."

"Just one minute."

Atop the stairs Trumbo saw a cop he recognized. He walked up to the tall, gray-haired man and read the name on his shirt.

"Officer Vanzetti. I'm Trumbo Walsh; I think we've met before."

"Right, sure, you're a buddy of Mazer's. Tow guy."

"That's my rig over there. I'm a friend of the owner. What do you think happened?"

"I talked to the arson investigator. This is all off the record, right?"

"Yeah."

"He hasn't gone through the place yet, but he's ninety percent sure it's arson because of the way it burned. We're gonna go in there in a little while."

Trumbo returned to his truck, where Alison watched the last wisps of smoke climb into the air. He hopped into the driver's seat and held her hand.

"Can I get you something?"

"I just want to leave this shitty town."

"Let's go to my house. You need some rest and something to eat."

At his home Trumbo warmed up two cans of Spaghettios —the only food readily available—and he and Alison compared notes. He wanted to tell her about the Manson family, and her mother, and his father; but she wasn't ready to hear it yet. Alison was exhausted by the day's traumatic events. He made her some tea, wrapped her in a blanket, and sat quietly as she told him about "Blue" Desmond and the attempted suicide and the note. He listened patiently. Then she told him about Sunn.

She'd spent the previous day with the man, mainly hearing stories about her mother and searching for Blue. She knew there was something strange about the guy, but at the same time, he was her only lead. As she rambled on, several things she told him sounded familiar: His home for runaways was called the "Rebirth Fellowship."

Trumbo sighed. Thompson at the women's pen had talked about a "New Rebirth" and a "New Fellowship." Maybe this *Rebirth Fellowship* and the Manson Family were one and the same. Thompson did warn him to be careful. He didn't want to tell Alison too much because she was still on the verge of shock. He did not think she should go back to her apartment; Sunn knew where she lived.

"Alison, it's okay, it's over now. You should get some rest."

"I just want to leave."

"I understand. You need to rest now." Trumbo was firm in his resolve. He stroked Alison's hair.

"I do feel beat."

"You can sleep over here. I'll get your things."

"Why are you so nice to me?"

"Because I care about you. Because I—"

Alison cut him off. "Don't say the L word. Every time someone says that, they always fuck me up."

Trumbo bit his lip and wiped the tears from her face. "I'm sorry it scares you. Maybe I should have said I want to use you."

She choked out a laugh. "You jerk." She didn't mean it. "I just don't want you to leave, that's all."

He led her back to his room. He didn't need to pull back the covers because he'd never made the bed. Alison kicked off her shoes and crawled in, fully dressed. Trumbo kissed her on the forehead.

"I'll go get your stuff. You probably shouldn't go back to your apartment. Whoever burned the house probably knows where you live."

"The key is in my purse."

Trumbo fetched the key. "I'm going to be right back. Whatever you do, don't let anyone in. If Sunn or anyone else calls, let the answering machine pick it up. If it's anyone but me, don't answer, okay?"

She sat up. "Why shouldn't I talk to Sunn?"

"Trust me. Don't talk to him."

"Hurry back."

"Okay."

Trumbo double-bolted the front door and, for extra protection, leaned a metal chair against it, then he ran to his car and drove off toward Hollywood.

A police surveillance car tailed Trumbo at a distance of several hundred feet.

A young girl hiding in the trees by the side of the road noted that the police car had left, and hiked down to a pay phone so that she could report the news.

* * *

As he approached Alison's apartment on Hollywood Boulevard, Trumbo could see the flashing red and blue lights of police cars. As he grew nearer, he saw that they were gathered outside her building. He parked illegally in front of Le Sex Shoppe across the street and ran toward the crowd.

A crowd of onlookers pressed against the yellow police tape, despite the repeated warnings broadcast through a megaphone for them to disperse. Trumbo approached three onlookers before finding one who spoke English.

"What happened? A fire?"

"No, man, someone got murdered," replied a young black man wrapped in a bathrobe.

"You live here?"

"Yep. The cops went door to door and ordered us all out on the street. They're searching every apartment."

"Which apartment was it?"

"I don't know, man, it was on the third floor."

Alison lived on the third floor. "Any idea what happened?"

"Some sort of gang chit. I hate those fogging gangs. They nailed a cute Mexican girl I seen around who jess moved in."

"How do you know it was a gang?"

"I heard from the superintendent that they left graffiti all over the walls. Just like gangbanger assholes always do."

"Did you know her?"

"Yeah. Elena something or other. She was new."

He ran to a pay phone and dialed his home number. It rang three times before his answering machine picked up.

"Alison! Alison! Pick up the phone. It's me, Trumbo. Come on, Alison, pick up the phone!"

No answer. He hung up and redialed, hopeful that the ringer would awaken her.

"Alison! Pick up the phone. It's an emergency!"

He jumped into his truck and used every shortcut and back alley he knew to reach his apartment in record time. As he raced up the street, he could see that all the lights in his apartment were on. He had left them turned off. He parked and ran up the two flights of stairs that led to his porch.

The doorframe was shredded. Someone had used a crowbar to defeat the deadbolt. The window next to the front door was shattered.

He pushed the door open and ran to his bedroom. It had only been a half hour since he'd left.

"Alison!"

She wasn't in the bed.

He opened the bathroom door. The room was dark and empty.

He opened every closet and cupboard in the house, yelling, "Alison! Alison!"

18

TRUMBO PICKED UP THE TELEPHONE TO CALL THE COPS. THE LINE was dead. He ran out the front door and jumped down the steps two at a time. He rang the doorbell on his downstairs neighbor's apartment. Nothing. *Must be asleep.* He pounded on the door. Still nothing. He darted to the back of the house, thinking, *Wake her up, get her to call the cops.* Her rear window was smashed. Shards of shattered glass glinted in the moonlight. Trumbo squinted and stared into his neighbor's bedroom. When his eyes adjusted he saw her twisted body leaning against the bed, head down, a pool of dark liquid around her head.

"Lois! Lois!" She didn't respond. She was dead.

Trumbo raced to his truck parked in the street below. *If only they hadn't confiscated the damned police radio,* he thought, *I could contact the cops.* He sped down the hill toward the AM/PM Mini Mart.

On the way he flipped on the radio and tuned in KXNB, the local news radio station, to see if there was a story about the murder in Hollywood. He heard only an advertisement for big-screen television.

At the gas station a burly Hispanic man was using the telephone. Trumbo scowled at him. The man held up a finger—*one minute*. Trumbo leaned into his truck and turned up the radio. The news station played only the local traffic and weather conditions.

The man hung up the phone, and Trumbo thanked him. Then he dialed 911; he was put on hold and heard a recorded message. "You have reached Los Angeles Police Department Emergency Line. All circuits are temporarily busy. If your call is not an emergency, please dial 555-6245. If this is an emergency, please stay on the line and someone will be with you as soon as possible."

Finally a human being answered. "Los Angeles Police; how may I direct your call?"

"I'm calling to report a murder and a kidnapping. There's been a—"

He was cut off midsentence by the monotonic operator. "Please wait while I connect you to the police emergency line."

There was a moment of dead silence while his call was transferred, during which he heard a story on the radio. He leaned back and listened. The sound of staccato typing at the station provided background for the earnest newscaster.

". . . have already identified a suspect in the murder of a nineteen-year-old Hollywood woman. Police are searching for Trumbo Walsh, twenty-eight, of Echo Park, last seen driving a blue and white pickup truck. Walsh is a male Caucasian, six foot five inches tall, with dark hair. If you see this man, please call the KXNB Crime Tipster hot line. Last week's Tipster of the Week won one hundred dollars for—"

A male voice barked in the phone, "Los Angeles Police."

Trumbo held the phone to his mouth for a moment, wondering whether to say anything.

"This is the Los Angeles Police. Hello?"

"I'm sorry. I dialed the wrong number."

Trumbo hung up the phone. If they suspected him in Joi's murder, when he wasn't even around, they'd throw him in jail for Alison's roommate and his own landlord.

He jumped into his pickup truck and sped up Glendale Boulevard toward the Hollywood Freeway. Two police cars approached him in the opposite direction, lights flashing, sirens blaring. He didn't have a plan beyond *Just drive normally. Just be cool.*

He heard the pounding of his heart as loud as a hammer on an anvil. The cops passed. He was only a few blocks from the freeway, where he could lose himself in traffic. *Stay straight, stay cool.* Then, in his rearview mirror, he saw one of the police black-and-whites execute a U-turn and come toward him.

This is it, he thought. Two impulses fought for dominance in his mind. If he gave himself up, they might realize that he had nothing to do with the murders. But if he ran away from them and was caught, they'd book him on evading arrest and he'd be locked up where even Clemenson couldn't spring him. Which chance to take? He thought of Alison and stepped on the gas.

Head is throbbing. Alison used all the concentration she could muster to open her eyes. She slowly realized that she was in a moving vehicle. Her wrists were handcuffed around the bench seat in the rear of a van.

Last thing she remembered, she was in Trumbo's apartment.

Trumbo had left a few minutes earlier. Alison had been reading the instructions on a packet of microwave popcorn when the door crashed open.

Before she knew what was happening, someone shoved her to the floor.

She recognized one of the girls.

Someone pushed a damp sponge in her face. It had a sharp smell like cleaning fluid—ether? Chloroform? She didn't know. It burned her throat. She struggled for a moment and then the world clicked off, like pulling the plug on a television set. And now she was here.

She tried to gather her thoughts. *Where are they taking me?* Her temples throbbed. The faint smell of exhaust dried her throat. She retched.

A girl with long, dark hair leaned over the seat and gazed at her for a few moments before speaking.

"Alison?"

It strained her throat to speak. "What are you doing with me?"

"Alison, it's okay. We saved you."

The girl didn't seem to make sense. Alison wondered if

she was losing her mind. She cleared her throat. "Where are you taking me?"

"We're taking you to the happy place, where Day One will happen. You're lucky. Everything's going to be all right. You're one of the chosen."

Alison wasn't going crazy. "Unlock my hands," she said, trying to straighten herself out.

"I can't do that. You might not know what's best for you yet, but it will all work out in the end."

Alison took a deep breath and screamed. The girl just smiled vacantly. "Here, have some water. You might be thirsty."

The girl put a glass to Alison's lips. She drank. "Who are you people?"

"We're the Rebirth Fellowship. And so are you."

The water revived her. Alison yelled as loud as she could. "Stop the car! Let me out!"

The girl smiled and spoke in a measured tone, like a teacher. "There, there, you're upset. Discovery is always a painful process, but submission is a gift we give to our lover. I don't want to use the sponge again, but I will if I have to. Please try to understand."

Alison screamed louder. The girl lifted a white bottle, poured some clear liquid onto a sponge, and held it in front of Alison's nose. The burning odor filled her with nausea. She resisted.

"No! Not that!" said Alison.

"Then be quiet, silly!" said the girl, grinning. "You don't have to scream. We saved you from yourself, Alison Wonderland. You'll thank us on Day One." The girl ran her fingers through Alison's hair.

The girl left Alison alone. Tears ran down her cheeks. She sank to the van floor, feeling every bump in the road amplified through her aching skull.

Cautiously she groped around on the floor of the van, lifting pieces of carpet, looking for anything she could use to escape, or to communicate with the cars outside whose light reflected through the van. Soon she discovered a coil of wires nestled along the edge of the van beneath the molding. *Maybe it'll make the car stop. Maybe I can run out.* She gripped them in her hand, waiting for the right moment. On a downhill slope, a noisy truck overtook them, obscuring any sound she might make. Quickly Alison yanked the wires until they broke. Nothing happened. Her heart sank.

She cried for what seemed like an eternity as they drove down the highway. The passengers in the front of the van, whom she could not see, were silent.

Then her prayers were answered.

Blue and red flashing lights reflected in the rear window of the van. The van slowed down. She heard Sunn's voice: "Remember what I said."

One of the girls, someplace farther up, said, "Okay."

Alison heard gravel under the wheels of the van as it moved into the breakdown lane. The van stopped. The flashing blue and red lights were right behind it. *It's the cops. Thank God.* She leaned up from her reclining position but still could not see over the car seat in front of her.

An electric window rolled down. *Wait, wait, wait for the right moment.* A voice, obviously that of the cop: "May I see your driver's license and registration please?"

Alison closed her eyes and took a deep breath, ready to scream.

Burning in nasal passages. Burning in my head. That same chemical smell.

She coughed. Her mind seemed disconnected from her body, as if she were looking at the world from the bottom of a deep well. Everything was far away and distorted.

She realized what had happened: They'd put the sponge in her face again.

She tried to yell. All that came out was the word "no," as soft as a whisper. Then she receded down the well, away from the world, still barely awake, yet unable to move, unable to open her eyes. In spite of the ether, she still could hear things, and could think just clearly enough to understand the horror of her situation.

The cop chatted with Sunn. Their words made no sense. In her stupor Alison tried to direct thoughts at the policeman: *I'm here, I'm here, I'm here, don't you see me, I'm here!*

The cop did nothing.

The van door closed.

The engine started and her world began to move.
The chemical in the back of her throat intensified.
Alison blacked out.

As Trumbo drove through Echo Park, the police lights grew closer. He considered the winding, narrow streets to his left, in the hills of Echo Park. He knew them backwards and forwards, probably better than the cops. He had home-court advantage. Trumbo turned onto a small winding street and gunned up the hill. Then he killed the lights and turned into an alley that looked like a dead end but that actually led to another street, after a slight detour around an auto repair shop.

The cop flew past the alley without even slowing down. *Momentarily safe.* Trumbo drove around the repair shop, back to the street, driving half a block in the wrong direction on a one-way street and then across a curved driveway onto a wider road.

Then he saw more flashing blue lights coming up the hill. They had split up. One came his direction. He could either try and outrun the cop or outsmart him. The narrow road was a one-way street for about a quarter mile. There wasn't room to turn a cop car around. Trumbo waited in the driveway until the cop passed, then roared out of the driveway and headed back down the hill. Trumbo counted five police vehicles—two motorcycles and three cars—and knew by experience that they didn't have any more cars easily available in the neighborhood. It would be at least five minutes until another car came.

He barreled down the hill and suddenly was blinded by the glaring light of a police helicopter. The light passed over him without stopping. *Shit. Can't outrun a helicopter, even if I get to the freeway.* There was only one slim opportunity to escape.

At the bottom of the hill he jerked the car up over the curb into Echo Park, sped around the perimeter of the park, spraying dirt and grass behind him, and entered a broad boulevard heavy with traffic. The helicopter searchlight was still on the other side of the park. He had about a minute before someone saw him.

He charged down the street and drove under the freeway

overpass, which had been converted into a storage area for old freeway signs. He drove to the narrow end of the freeway overpass, parked the truck, and looked over his shoulder into the park. Like a tornado of pure light the helicopter search beam swept across the ground in irregular swirls, poking, probing, looking for its prey. Trumbo jumped out of his truck and ran as fast as he could away from the damning beacon. First he darted along the edge of the freeway, down an alley, and finally up a hill on a residential street. When he was completely out of breath, he stopped at a break in the hill where he could see down into the park. He stood behind a large palm tree and watched the helicopter flit about for a few more minutes, probing the ground with its searchlight before disappearing over the horizon.

Trumbo hung his head down for a few moments to regain his composure. His situation was dire and he was completely without resources. He couldn't go back to his apartment, which was no doubt crawling with cops. He couldn't recover his truck, which would probably soon be towed. He had no one to call, no place of refuge. He pulled out his wallet and assessed his fortune, which consisted of eighty-six dollars cash plus three credit cards: Sears and Discover, both in default, plus the Chevron card, which wasn't. If they were broadcasting his name on the radio, he could safely bet that his picture would soon be on television. He had to get some wheels before everyone in town knew who he was. He was completely useless without a car. He briefly considered stealing one, but quickly realized that a hot ride would make it that much more likely he'd be caught. Then, as he walked down the main road out of Echo Park, he hit on an idea.

It took him two and a half hours on the late night bus lines down Vermont to get to the wrecking yard in South Central Los Angeles, the only privately owned wrecking lot open twenty-four hours.

When he got off the bus in a slum industrial district, it was a short walk to Fryer's. Their sign was a '65 Mustang on a twenty-foot-pole; razor wire surrounded twenty-five-foot heaps of crushed automobiles. Trumbo crossed the lot to the tiny office booth where a night watchman worked.

"Hello?" yelled Trumbo. "Anyone home?"

A dark-skinned black man in stained blue coveralls

pushed open a plywood window. When he opened his mouth, two gold teeth were visible: one on top, one on the bottom.

"Can I help you?" Trumbo could see the glint of a .45 in the watchman's hand.

"Paxton. It's Trumbo Walsh."

The man leisurely returned the handgun to a cigar box at the back of the booth, then turned and faced Trumbo. "I didn't recognize you, Trumbo. Where's your truck? Usually you tell us you're coming on the CB."

"I took a bus. Pax, I got trouble."

Paxton scowled. "If you got trouble, why did you come to me?"

"I need a car."

Paxton lit a menthol cigarette, took a puff, and exhaled before answering. His eyes squinted in anger. "What *kind* of trouble are you in, Trumbo?"

"Cops are looking for me."

Paxton threw up his hands. "I can't help you. Cops think just because a business is in South Central, it must be crooked. Twice a month at least, auto car theft unit scopes my lot. In fifteen years they haven't found a thing, but they're still convinced I'm some sort of fence."

"Man, I really need your help."

"No way. Trumbo, you're on your own."

Trumbo looked up at the rust-colored night sky as if for help, then locked eyes with Paxton. "How many cars have I brought down here for you?"

"I don't know. I don't count."

"Probably fifty over the last couple years."

"Okay, fifty cars. What's the dif?" asked Paxton.

"I just need one."

"None of these cars are *my* cars. We just store 'em and wreck 'em and salvage 'em."

"You store 'em for a year, right? Then you auction the ones that are never claimed? That's the law."

"Yeah, so what?"

"You gotta have one that's running that you know nobody's gonna claim. One of those so-called total losses that's just an insurance scam, or one of those dope-dealer cars. I wasn't born yesterday. You know the cops are just gonna take it away from you and send you a hundred bucks."

"Give me a reason," said Paxton.

"I bought you a beer once—no, twice!"

Paxton laughed so loud, it echoed. "Oh, that's a good swap. Two beers for a car."

Trumbo stared at the ground, despondent. He *had* to get a car. If he stayed on the streets much longer without one, it was almost certain that he'd be picked up by the cops.

Trumbo paced in front of the booth, spinning bullshit as fast as he could. "How often do you do inventory?"

"Once a month we count the lot."

"When do you do it next?"

"Two and a half weeks."

"Here's a deal. Give me a car that runs and has reasonably legal tags. I'll have it back in two weeks. If it's not here, you call and report it stolen when you do inventory. I'll take all the risk."

Paxton laughed again. "Walsh, you're a piece of work, you really are."

Paxton threw something. Trumbo caught it reflexively. It was a pair of keys.

"Back against the fence is an eighty-six Mazda three-two-three, bright red, big dent in the passenger door. It's been here for almost a year. We're gonna auction it in about six weeks if the owner doesn't claim it. And I feel damned sure he won't."

"Someone just left it?"

"It was abandoned on Crenshaw. A grocery owner towed it off his lot. Some drug thing, no doubt. If we're lucky, the owners are dead or in the joint."

"Thanks, Paxton."

"Don't thank me. Just get the car and get out. God be with you. And don't mention my name to a soul. I'll deny I ever even knew you."

Trumbo winked. "Don't worry. You're still the meanest man in the junk business in all of Los Angeles."

"That, sir, is a privilege I've earned over the years by not doing stupid favors for punk ass gypsy tow drivers, and I hate breaking my perfect record. Now, skedaddle."

* * *

When he hit the highway, he headed south for Long Beach, twenty miles away. His first stop was an all-night convenience store, where he bought a soggy turkey sandwich, a candy bar, a bottle of beer, a pair of scissors, and some disposable razor blades. Then he searched the city for a place to park.

He wanted to catch some sleep while it was dark, but didn't have many choices: The beach or city parks would be patrolled at least once a night for transients. In one of the suburban bedroom communities, some nosy neighbor would notice a guy in a car and call the cops. He decided to chance it in one of the heavy industrial sections of town. He drove down a long stretch of road where dozens of oil rigs endlessly moved up and down like monks doing penance, turned onto a dirt road, parked his car behind a small hill, and killed the engine.

He got out and inspected the hill. No one could see him from the road, and if he got up early enough—when the sun woke him up—he probably wouldn't be discovered.

Trumbo leaned in the car and pulled out the scissors. He peered into the rear view mirror for one last look at his thick, dark hair which hung almost to his collar. He'd worn his hair that way since he was twelve years old and now he'd have to kiss it goodbye. He stepped away from the car and grasped a few strands. After some hesitation, he snipped them off and watched them drop to the ground. Soon he was clipping off big hunks of hair, working quickly, before he changed his mind. When he was done he ran his hand across the short bristles of hair remaining; it felt alien, like someone else's head. He brushed off the loose strands from his neck and shoulders and then climbed back into the Mazda.

He lay on the hill for an hour, planning his next move. As far as he could tell, there were only two people who could help him locate Alison. Neither would be easy to contact. Blue was in a hospital under guard of police, and Barbara Thompson was in a maximum security prison.

Two hundred miles north of Trumbo, as dawn broke over central California, a bright orange van lumbered across a sunbaked field, leaving behind it a wake of dust swirling high into the air. The tract once used for growing cotton now lay fallow. Parked dead center in the thousand-acre wasteland was a stolen mobile home. Lean-tos of scrap metal and surplus army canvas stretched out from both sides, providing the only shade for hundreds of yards.

The abandoned farm was in an unincorporated section of Kern County, in the enormous California Central Valley, where twenty percent of the nation's food is grown. The hardworking people of Kern clung to old-fashioned virtues like working hard, paying their bills in cash, and above all, minding their own business. J'osüf had found the site a month earlier, and it had numerous advantages: far enough away from Los Angeles to keep it above suspicion, yet close enough to get back for the few remaining errands. It was also conveniently close to Corcoran, where Jesus lived.

The orange van stopped in front of the abandoned mobile home. Its side door slid open and J'osüf Sunn stepped out, followed by four young girls. The others were asleep in the van, as was Alison Wilmot.

J'osüf squinted into the bright morning sun and danced a little jig around the perimeter of the van as the bleary-eyed girls looked on. He stretched his arms over his head in a wide V and clasped his hands together, as if in celebration.

"We are in the final days of purgatory," he said.

Silhouette, bleary-eyed, repeated without enthusiasm some of what he said. "In the final days . . ."

"Yes, in the final days. Soon our leader will be back with us. If the Man lets him go, all will be forgiven. But the Man is a wily trickster who can't be trusted."

"Man is wily, man is a trickster," mumbled Silhouette.

"Shut up!" snapped Sunn. Silhouette bowed and stepped backwards a few steps to join the other girls in a semicircle around Sunn.

"What will we do if the Man refuses to deal?"

None of the girls had the will to answer.

"We will do whatever is necessary," said Sunn. "We prefer to operate on the ethereal plane, but Jesus is entrapped in a cage of the Man's making, so we have to accumulate some of the Man's devices."

Sunn paced back and forth, hunched over deep in thought, one hand clapped to his forehead, the other behind his back, clenched in a fist, drubbing the base of his spine.

"We can win against them if we apply our own spirituality to the Man's strategies and if we have the Man's weapons. The mind is the greatest weapon, but in the world of the Man we need the Man's tools."

Sunn counted the girls and scowled. "Who is still asleep? Who is still in the van?"

Silhouette tentatively raised a hand. Sunn pointed at her. "Um, J'osüf, um, Diva is still asleep."

"Wake her up! This is the beginning of the beginning!"

Silhouette disappeared into the van and shook little Denise awake, then pulled her out of the van. The girl rubbed her eyes. Her stockinged feet quickly were covered with dirt. The two rejoined the line. Sunn's team was in the ready.

Sunn walked toward them. "Which of you is under eighteen?"

None of the girls moved. "What's the problem?" Sunn demanded.

Red-haired Panda stepped forward meekly. "We're thousands of years old. All of us. You told us that."

Sunn smiled. "Very good, Panda. I should have said"—he waved his arms above his head—"which of you is under eighteen on the Man's clock? In *consensus reality?*"

One by one, all of them raised their hands.

"All of you?"

They nodded. Peace stepped forward. "I know we're not supposed to keep track of these things, but my birthday will be in two weeks and I'll turn eighteen then."

"That's no good." Sunn sat on the ground. "We need weapons. None of you can buy them. I can't buy them because . . ." He didn't want to mention his legal difficulties. "Because I can't. Leave it at that. Y'see, the system is set up to throw away people like us, people who have society's best interests at heart. We're trash people. You are, I am, most people are. They've set it up so we can't defend ourselves. We're going to have to get them some other way. And we need money to get them. This Wednesday we can get the money. And if things go well, on Thursday we can get the iron, and on Friday we begin training."

Sunn drew a diagram in the dirt—a box representing a building, a thin line representing an alley, and a thick line representing a road. He labeled each of them, then gathered the girls around him.

"What's that?" asked Diva.

"This is the Side Arm Gun Shop in Altadena. We'll be visiting them soon." He continued to detail his plan.

The girls listened carefully.

Meanwhile, inside the van, Alison Wilmot tried without success to pull her thin wrists free of the handcuffs that bound her to the car seat. Her throat was parched; the van grew hotter by the moment. She leaned up and saw through the window that Sunn and his brood were kneeling in the dirt beside the van, paying no attention to her.

She examined the car seat in detail. It was made of chrome-plated metal, but when she peeled up the carpet, she saw that only two bolts fastened it to the floor. She tried to turn one of the bolts with her finger; it wouldn't budge. She would need some sort of tool. In hopes there might be a crowbar, Alison tried in vain to loosen the spare tire with her toes, stretching her body across the van. It was futile. Tired and angry, she stared at the bolts for a long time before arriving at a plan. She lay on her stomach, her hands stretched in front of her. Carefully she wrapped the chain around the bolt. She pulled her wrists in opposite directions and the chain dug into the bolt; she groaned as she increased the tension. Her hands turned blue as the circulation was cut off, but she kept pulling. Then the bolt creaked a fraction of an inch to the right. It was working. She exhaled, let the feeling return to her hands, and tried again. This time the bolt moved a bit farther. The tiny victory gave her renewed energy and she continued to loosen the bolt a little at a time until she could unfasten it with her fingers.

Only one more bolt to go. This one was significantly tighter than the first, or perhaps she was losing her strength. After many attempts, it finally budged an imperceptible amount. On each successive attempt it moved a little farther. *Come on, little bolt,* she thought, her energies focused entirely on loosening it. Finally it gave way and she unscrewed it by hand. She skidded the chain of the handcuffs against the ground, pulling it slowly, inch by inch, underneath the bar of the bench seat. Halfway through, it caught on something and she pulled as hard as she could. Beads of blood formed around her wrist where the handcuffs cut into her skin, but she persevered, and with a loud *pop,* the cuffs slid the rest of the way under the bar.

She was free. Or at least, freer than she had been. She stretched out for the first time in at least eight hours. Her back was sore, her shoulders were stiff, and she felt needles and pins in her cramped calf, which had been underneath her weight without relief for the entire night. She peeked out of the window. Sunn and the girls were still staring at some diagram in the dirt.

Quickly she grabbed a bottle of water from the front part of the van, and drank it so fast, it spilled across her chest. She splashed some cold water on her face and on her aching wrists. Then she crawled up to the passenger seat of the van. Slowly she pulled the handle to open the door. It hardly made a sound. She carefully, steadily, pushed open the van door and crawled out. She peeked underneath the vehicle; they hadn't noticed her. Quietly she crawled away from the van. After she was fifty feet or so away, she jumped up and ran as fast as her legs would carry her.

It was probably a thousand yards to the road. She heard the van start up. She glanced back. They were bumping across the farm toward her. In a panic she dashed to the narrow farm road.

A beat-up Chevy truck rose over the horizon. She looked over her shoulder. The orange van would reach her in a matter of seconds. The Chevy hurtled toward her. She stood in the middle of the road and waved her handcuffed hands over her head. The Chevy swerved and screeched to a stop.

She raced toward the truck as Sunn's van approached from the opposite direction. She reached it just as Sunn's van did, and rapped on the window.

"Help! Open your door! Goddammit!" She pelted the driver's window with punches. Sunn's van parked on the opposite curb. Finally the Chevy's door opened. A woman in her forties with long, gray hair, dressed in a biker's leather jacket, stepped out.

"What's the problem here?" asked the woman.

Alison yelled. "I've been kidnapped!"

The woman looked past Alison as if she weren't there and walked to the van. "Hello, J'osüf," said the woman.

Sunn grinned. "Hello, Adelaide. Good to see you."

"One of the chickens got out of the roost, eh?" asked the woman. "You gotta be more careful."

"We are careful."

Alison fell to the ground in exhaustion. Sunn seemed not to notice. "Adelaide Naomi, meet Alison Wonderland. She's one of the chosen ones."

"Not quite up to the task, I'd say."

"Oh, she will be by next week. How was the trip?" asked Sunn.

"I got lost finding the place."

Alison stood and dusted herself off. The woman from the truck grabbed the handcuffs and yanked Alison near. "Alison, I knew you when you were just *this* high. You might not know it yet, but great things are in store for you. But you've *got* to stop running away like that."

Tears poured down Alison's face as the woman dragged her back to the van.

19

ONCE A MONTH, WHETHER HE LIKED OR NOT, MARK WHITE-field, the warden at the California Women's Penitentiary, Riverside, endured an inspection from the Inmate Rights Project. He liked to refer to the watchdog group by their acronym IRP, pronouncing it *urrrp!* as if he were belching. He considered IRP naive do-gooders who didn't know the first thing about running a penal institution, but because of a court order, he had no choice but to welcome them to his institution.

He prepared thoroughly for their visit. Any leaks were patched. All the plumbing problems had to be covered up, if only cosmetically. Everyone was given a fresh set of sheets even if they'd only gotten some the day before. The group also checked on things like "roof time"—whether the inmates were getting enough exercise—so Whitefield liked to schedule as many inmates as possible for basketball and handball games on the days IRP visited.

At eleven-thirty sharp, six representatives from IRP arrived—five women and one man. Whitefield maintained a contentious but cordial relationship with IRP's leader, an older woman named Dr. Turan who nailed him on every shortcoming, but granted him enough leeway to correct the problem. Before the tour began, Whitefield answered their penny-ante questions about whether he'd corrected the problems they found on his previous visit. Whitefield sweated out an hour of questions, and then took them on the walking tour. He silently cursed the judge who ordered these inspections.

Their first stop was lunch with the inmates. He noticed one woman scowl and make notes on a clipboard.

"What's the problem?"

"It's all high-cholesterol food. You've got hot dogs, corn dogs, cheeseburgers, macaroni with cheese, cakes and cookies, but almost no low-fat food."

Whitefield's secret desire was to yell, "Shut the hell up," but previous encounters with IRP had taught him that the best thing was to agree with everything they said, and then ignore them.

He gritted his teeth and spoke ever so cordially. "You are correct. You'll notice we have salads as well, but I'll talk with the cook and see if the menu can't be improved somewhat on the, er, cholesterol front.

"I'll have a printed copy of the menu for you next month. Shall we move on?"

The improbable parade of do-gooders followed him through the facility, scrutinizing bunk space, music levels on the PA system, cleanliness of hallways, and every other detail of the prison. Throughout the day they were passed by groups of women prisoners being shuttled from their cells to the dining room, from the dining room to the exercise facility, from the exercise facility back to their cells. The business of running a penitentiary consisted in large part of safely moving groups from one area to another. Whitefield was pleased that everyone had on clean, ironed shirts and pants—something he always arranged for on inspection days.

Repeatedly during the two-hour tour, one IRP inspector fell far behind the pack. She was fortyish with long brown hair, wore wraparound sunglasses even in the dim corridors of the prison, and rarely opened her mouth. Early on, when she failed to keep up with the tour, Whitefield reminded her that it was essential that she stay with the group. He was immediately barraged with snide comments suggesting that he had something to hide. Whitefield stopped keeping such close tabs on her, until they reached the medical facility of the prison, when he did a quick head count.

"Three, four, five . . . We seem to be missing one of our group. Where is that woman with the sunglasses?"

It was the third time she'd disappeared.

Dr. Turan, leader of IRP, momentarily stopped scribbling on her clipboard and shook her head. "I'm sorry," said Dr. Turan. "She's new with our group. She's been a terrific volunteer back at the Inmate Rights Project offices and puts in more than forty hours a week without pay. I thought she would be more responsible on the prison inspection than she has been."

Whitefield winked at Turan. "Dr. Turan—you're suggesting I might have a point? A red-letter day."

"Don't get too excited, Whitefield." Turan rummaged through the wastebasket and found a syringe. "Improper disposal of medical waste, Warden. We asked you about this last month, and you said you'd get right on it."

"Duly noted. I'll have yet another talk with the head of the infirmary. Thank you for pointing it out."

After a brief delay, they were again joined by the woman with the long hair. Turan reprimanded her for falling behind. She apologized. For the rest of the tour she hung on the heels of the group and maintained her characteristic silence. No one paid her much attention after that.

The tour ran until nearly four o'clock, an hour earlier than usual. Whitefield promised to take care of the problems they'd thoughtfully pointed out, escorted them to their cars, and bid them good-bye. Another month, another inspection. All of them made nice-nice and thanked him, except for the weird chick with the sunglasses. Twelve hours later he learned the real reason she'd lagged behind. By then the inmate she swapped places with was long gone.

Trumbo started the Mazda and cruised through Long Beach until he found a street burgeoning with tattoo parlors, car repair shops, and topless bars. He figured that the "bad part of town" would be the best place to pick up a fake ID.

At a little past seven A.M. all of the establishments were closed, and Trumbo wandered the streets without interference until he found a shop that might do the trick. He found two likely candidates: one, a shop that advertised in Spanish and English, ALL IMMIGRATION PROBLEMS SOLVED QUICKLY AND EFFICIENTLY NO QUESTIONS ASKED, and another that had subtler clues—a photo shop with a handwritten notice in the window offering IDENTIFICATION—ALL TYPES. Neither business opened until ten o'clock.

Trumbo killed time until they opened, lingering over a pecan waffle and a bottomless cup of coffee. He bought two newspapers, but found no mention of himself in either. In fact, the only crime story was a background piece concerning a recent upswing in armed bank robberies. In a metropolis with seven million citizens and three murders a day, a crime had to be exceptionally bizarre, kinky, or political to become news.

Slightly after ten A.M. he walked to the photo shop, owned by a Filipino gentleman. After some small talk with the owner, Trumbo was able to get him to admit that, yes, he could make a driver's license, but it would cost one hundred fifty bucks. Trumbo haggled the price down to forty dollars and then posed for his picture. A half hour later, the driver's license was ready. The fake ID with Trumbo's picture and the name William Wachtler was remarkably convincing, especially after the photographer crushed it under his foot and wore down the edges with some fine sandpaper. "If it's old, they'll scrutinize it less," he told Trumbo. Before he let Trumbo out of the shop, he took great pains to emphasize that the ID was "for amusement purposes only," a tactic to cover his ass in the event that Trumbo was an undercover cop.

At a video parlor he changed ten dollars to quarters, then drove seventy miles to Riverside County, where he could make a local call to the women's pen. He dialed the main number of the prison.

"California Women's Penitentiary, Riverside."

"I'd like to know how I can contact Barbara Thompson," asked Trumbo.

"Let me transfer you to the press relations officer. One moment."

A female voice came on the line, gruff but respectful. "Press relations, Quimby speaking. What newspaper do you represent?"

"I was calling about Barbara Thompson," said Trumbo.

"Yeah, right, but what paper do you represent?"

His eye caught the Pacific Bell logo on the pay phone and he spun a fib. *Pacific Coast Reporter.* I need to speak to Barbara Thompson."

"We're going to have to fax you the press release. I've had two dozen calls in the last fifteen minutes. Can you give me the fax number at your paper?"

"We don't have a fax machine. I'm . . . um . . . I'm a field reporter. Should I come in? I just want to speak to Barbara Thompson."

"You want to talk to her? So do we, let me tell you, so do we! I guess you haven't heard. Thompson went AWOL."

"AWOL?"

"Away without leave—she escaped. You'll have to pick up the press release if you want more details. Jesus Christ! I've got to go. You won't believe this, but Dan Rather and James St. James both just walked through my door. Good-bye."

Trumbo hung up, then drove back to Los Angeles. On the radio he heard a brief update concerning Thompson. Her escape sounded original if unspectacular. During a routine prison inspection an accomplice switched places with her. Before the accomplice could be interrogated, she had eaten a cyanide tablet concealed in a headband. Trumbo's ears perked up when he heard that the dead woman had ties to the Rebirth Fellowship, and the escapee was a former member of the Manson Family. Something big was going down, and Alison was in the middle of it.

Trumbo remembered Alison mentioning the abandoned houses near Pasadena where the Rebirth Fellowship crowd lived. From a pay phone he called the Pasadena chamber of commerce to see if they knew of some abandoned Victorian homes. They didn't. He spent the next two hours driving back and forth through Pasadena, but saw nothing that remotely resembled the spot Alison had described.

He stopped at a coffee shop in South Pasadena and struck up a conversation with the waitress behind the counter. She was a pretty brown-haired teenager whose name tag said PEG.

"Peg, maybe you can help me out. I'm completely lost in this burg."

"What are you looking for?"

"Friend of mine told me there were some abandoned Victorian houses around here somewhere."

"I don't know what that is," she said, perfectly at ease with her ignorance.

Trumbo spoke slowly. "Victorians? They're big, pretty houses with lots of fancy windows, that kind of thing."

"New houses?"

"Nah, old ones. They're supposed to be in Pasadena, but hell if I can find them."

"Nahh. I don't know much about architecture."

"Tell you the truth, Peg, neither do I, but you're supposed to be able to see these from the highway."

"I don't know."

"Someone lives in them, or so I've heard, but they're all kind of abandoned."

She smiled, dimly recognizing his description. "Ohhhh! It's those haunted houses."

"Haunted?"

"That's what we thought when I was a kid. They're not really, I suppose. But there are weird homeless people living there. A friend of mine went there one night about two months ago. Those houses, like they used to be the place where couples went for, you know . . ."

Trumbo slapped a hand to his face in a faked display of shock.

The girl blushed, slightly embarrassed. "Anyway, my friend Anna and her boyfriend drove out there the other night, and it's like they're moving out; these people who we thought were bums all of a sudden have a new van and tons of stuff. So Anna's boyfriend goes, 'Let's watch and see what happens,' but she's scared as hell. They watched for a while, but even her boyfriend got freaked when she thought they had guns, so they split."

Trumbo nodded. "Sounds like the place I'm looking for."

"Why?"

"I'm supposed to meet someone there. Where is it?"

"It's real easy to get there from here." She drew him a map on the paper place mat. He tipped her a dollar for the cup of coffee.

He drove past twice before realizing where it was—the freeway underpass blocked a direct view of the houses from the street. He parked his car illegally and hiked around the perimeter of the compound, reconnoitering it through the chain-link fence. There were five colorful houses on the lot.

Satisfied that no one was there, Trumbo bent open a space under the fence and crawled through. The metal sprang back and scratched his calf when he released it.

He found evidence that campfires had burned in trash cans around the gravel lot, then walked into one of the houses. It was just a shell of a building. Trash and cardboard containers were strewn across the once majestic living room, but there was no indication that anyone had been there recently. He looked inside two more houses, finding little besides junk. Then he approached the biggest of the homes on the lot. Its front door had been nailed shut with orange crates. He circled it looking for a way to get inside and found a bay window in the back. He pulled off a couple of boards and crawled through.

He immediately sneezed from the thick accumulation of dust and mold inside. Paper plates had food stuck to them, but no mold. With each step he took, the floorboards squeaked and rattled. He turned a corner and encountered an enormous painted mural covering the entire wall of a stairway. The faint odor of latex indicated it had been painted recently.

Trumbo lit a match and leaned against the rail to get a better look at the painting. At first glance it appeared to be a map of the solar system. At its center was a garish, fiery cartoon of the sun, with a grinning face and tentacles of light shooting out from all sides. Thirteen concentric circles radiated from the face at the center like a shooting target. The innermost circle was tight around the sun cartoon; the last one took up the entire wall. At some point on each circle was a cartoonish drawing of a face—some angry, some silly, some serene. Trumbo burned his finger as the match burned down to a stub.

He lit another and examined the wall more closely. Next to some of the "planet" faces was strange writing. He stood on tiptoe and examined the words next to the highest planet-face on the wall. Written in arabesque psychedelic letters was WORLD WITHOUT JOI, AMEN, DAY ONE MINUS 18. There were three other names he didn't recognize, each with a cryptic slogan and the "Day One" inscription. Then he saw LITTLE BOY BLUE WE'RE DONE WITH YOU, DAY ONE MINUS 11 written next to a masculine-looking face. He lit another match and found a picture of a happy woman's face. It read LSNSND HOUSE! DAY ONE MINUS FIVE. He rubbed his finger on the paint; it was still tacky to the touch. It had been painted in the last couple of days. What did it mean? He assumed it must be a reference to the drug LSD. He lit another match and found a final picture. As soon as he read it, he dropped the match in shock. It was his own name. LSNLBD QUEEN! TRUMBO SD TRUE SUN! JESUS N DAY ONE!

He read it again, slowly, and suddenly realized what the messages said.

"LSN" was "Alison." The first said, "Alison is in the house." The second, "Alison will be the queen, Trumbo is the son."

He did some quick calculations. Blue shot himself seven days after Joi was killed; the words next to her name said "Day one minus 18." Blue's drawing read "Day one minus

11." They were counting backwards toward something a little more than a week away.

He crept around the empty house but found little else of note: empty cans of fruit cocktail and condensed milk, tattered bits of clothing, paper plates, and miscellaneous junk that looked like it had been left by vagrants.

It was growing dark by the time he stepped outside. After scanning the streets for cops, he drove to a pay phone. He had one more lead to follow up.

"County General Hospital."

"Do you have a patient named Blue Desmond?"

"One moment please."

"Nursing station."

"I'm looking for Blue Desmond."

"He's asleep right now and can't take any calls."

"Is he out of the coma?" asked Trumbo.

"Oh yes, he was moved out of intensive care yesterday."

"So he's awake? Talking?"

"Yes, sir. Visiting hours are from six to seven-thirty if you'd like to talk to him."

"Is he still in that same room he was yesterday?"

"Yes, room 1021."

"Thanks."

Trumbo sped down to the hospital near USC, a place he'd been many times before trying to collect overdue tow bills from patients. He parked a block away, walked around to the back of the hospital, and went up the service elevator.

On the fifth floor he was joined by a maid bearing a horrific-smelling hamper of soiled sheets. He got off at the tenth floor, scanned the hallway for cops, found none, and made his way to room 1021.

The door was open. It had beds for four patients, two against each wall, separated only by thin curtains. Blue was in the back corner, asleep, as was the patient in the adjacent bed. One patient across the room was barely awake but had a tube in his throat, unable to speak.

Trumbo was amazed Blue was left unguarded, but as he got closer, he realized Blue was going nowhere.

Trumbo grabbed a nurse's stool, pulled the curtain back to conceal Blue's bed from the other patients, then sat down next to him. A thick plaster and bandage contraption covered most of Blue's head and a feeding tube went through his nose, but he seemed to be well on his way to recovery.

Trumbo leaned over and shook the man gently, steadily, for several seconds. "Wake up, wake uhh-up!"

Blue's eyes flipped up briefly, then opened wide. He looked at Trumbo, dazed.

"Hello, Blue," whispered Trumbo.

Blue forced out a grunt.

"You can talk. I know you can talk, can't you?"

"What's going on?" gurgled Blue, with great difficulty. It sounded like *Whuns ganon.* "Who're you?" came out indistinctly as *Whouna you?* But Blue was awake and aware.

"Good. Remember me? The guy you stomped outside of Joi Wilmot's house?"

"Shit." Blue's bloodshot eyes darted nervously back and forth.

"They said you tried to off yourself."

"Urggh."

"Yeah, I figure someone else did it."

"Uh-huh."

"I thought so. Who did it?"

"No."

"No, you won't tell me? Or no, you don't know?"

Blue grunted indistinctly.

"It was J'osüf Sunn, right?"

"Uh-huh."

"Where is he now?"

"Can't say." *Con suh ay.*

"Sure you can, Blue. Just give it a try. Where is Sunn now? Where did he go?"

Blue moved his lip a fraction of an inch into a scowl and forced out the words "Fuck you." *Funk yuh.*

Trumbo heard the distinctive click of sensible shoes walking across the linoleum floor. The curtain swung back to reveal a severe-looking Filipino-American nurse.

"What are you doing here?" she asked.

He had to think fast. "I was visiting my friend. Uh, my brother."

"Visiting hours are over."

He tried out his sappiest smile and thought fast. "Blue's

my older brother. I'm on leave from Camp Pendleton and have to be back to the base in another couple of hours."

Blue grunted, trying to get the attention of the nurse. Trumbo stood so that he was directly between the nurse and the patient, blocking her view.

The nurse stepped back and studied Trumbo. "We didn't hear about a brother. There's a policeman who wanted to know who the next of kin is."

Trumbo took a deep breath and lied as fast as he could. "Yes, ma'am. I've already spoken to the police, just yesterday."

"Can you list yourself as next of kin for our records?"

"Sure. I'll stop by the nursing station on my way out."

"No need to do that. I'll just have the nurse practitioner come down and talk to you. We need to find out about family medical conditions."

"Yeah, sure, right." He thought, *Supposed to be a marine.* "I mean, yes, ma'am. I'll be here."

She turned to leave. "Please don't close the curtain. It's against regulation."

"Sure." Just for good measure he saluted her, although he wasn't sure whether a real marine would salute a nurse.

Trumbo closed the curtain again.

"Let's get to it, Blue—where is Sunn now?"

"Forget it." *Fung gedded.*

"Maybe I can help you remember." Trumbo pinched Blue's nose and put his hand across Blue's mouth for a moment until the man twitched with pain.

"Unnh. Doan do that."

"You greaseball, you killed Joi Wilmot."

"Uh-uh."

"So did Sunn do that, too?"

"Uh-huh."

"And he has Alison Wilmot, right? Is she okay?"

"Uh-huh."

"Where are they?"

Blue emitted an eerie bleating sound, like a goat being drowned. His breathing became heavy and irregular.

"Why do you want to protect Sunn? He tried to kill you like a goddamn dog. He almost succeeded."

"I'm not talking." *Um nut tuck kig.*

Trumbo stared at Blue. He remembered that the biker had once sucker punched him, had kicked him in the head when he was down. He may have had a hand in killing Joi. Trumbo kicked the bed, angry and frustrated. "Let's see if we can refresh your memory."

Trumbo peered out of the curtains. The coast was clear. He sat down next to Blue and put his hand on his head and shook it a little bit.

"Bad head wound, eh?"

Blue emitted an inarticulate whine.

Trumbo grabbed the electric control adjacent to the bed and pushed a button. "Look at this! You can tilt the back of the bed!" The bed moved up, slowly. Blue's head slipped an inch to the right and he grimaced in pain. Trumbo released the button.

"You'll tell me."

Blue groaned, "Cut it out." *cun uh uht!*

Trumbo looked away from the bed and pushed the up button for several seconds. Blue shrieked in pain. When Trumbo turned, tears were running down Blue's face.

"Thuh neah mud-sid."

Trumbo couldn't make it out. "They're near what?"

"Mud-sid! Chars Mud-Sid! Puh me doan!"

"Charles Manson?"

Blue nodded. His face was contorted with pain.

The Charles Manson? The killer?"

"Uh-huh." Blue groaned. "Mud-sid guddig ote. They be there. Puh me doan!"

Trumbo wasn't sure he had heard correctly. "Manson? Getting out? Bullshit! Where is Alison?"

"Puh me doan!" yelled Blue with feral intensity.

Trumbo lowered the bed a notch. Blue took a deep breath and then talked more clearly. "With Sunn. Near Mud-sig . . . Mudsig . . . Manson."

"Where? Where are they?"

An alarm sounded. Another patient had pushed the nurse call switch.

Trumbo ran to the locker in the corner of the room and yanked it open. Inside was Blue's leather jacket. He rifled through the pockets and pulled out a wallet. He stuffed the wallet into his own pocket and darted out the door. He passed the nurse running towards Blue's room and nodded hello, then jumped onto the service elevator and took it to the lobby.

When the doors opened, he started to step out, but saw three policemen standing by the door outside. He let the elevator take him down to the basement. He walked past the morgue, then the employees' smoking lounge, and finally found an emergency exit. An alarm sounded when he opened the door. He raced up the fire escape, across a field to Figueroa Street, where he was parked. Nobody had followed him.

He drove slowly out of downtown—where the police had a reputation for pulling over anybody for no reason. In midtown, he pulled into a K-Mart and parked.

In Blue's wallet were nine twenty-dollar bills, desperately needed. There were business cards for several automotive repair shops, some rolling papers, and a California driver's license. Trumbo chuckled upon learning that Blue's real name was Skylar Desmond, the co-owner of Moon Man, the man who killed fourteen addicts with a bad batch of synthetic heroin.

The address on the license was in North Hollywood. He easily found the place in an industrial section. Several disassembled cars lay scattered about the pavement in front. Upstairs was a window obscured by lacy curtains.

He drove around the building several times to make sure there were no police, parked a block away, then walked across the parking lot. He quietly climbed an out-door stairway jutting up the side of the cinder block building.

Not knowing what to expect, he knocked on the door of the apartment. There was no answer.

He knocked again. The door opened a crack.

"Who is it?"

He tried, "It's me."

The door closed completely. A chain was removed, then the door opened all the way.

A woman's voice, friendly and vaguely familiar, called out, "Come on in!"

Trumbo squinted into the dim room and stepped forward. With a loud crack, a broom handle slammed into the crown of his head, and Trumbo crumpled to the ground, unconscious.

20

ALISON WILMOT'S ARMS WERE NUMB WITH PAIN. SUNN'S GIRLS had chained them behind her back with a metal dog leash. Her mouth was dry as dust and her jaw ached from the beating. Black paper and bed sheets covered the windows of the van. It was hot and she did not know what time of day it was. She heard the front door open up, and sunlight and fresh air blew into her cramped prison. She tried to pull herself up to see who had entered, but could not raise her head above the backseat.

Soft, tentative footsteps approached. A young girl peered over the bench seat and stared at her.

"Alison?" she said in her tiny voice. It was Denise. "Alison, are you okay?"

Alison shook her head.

"You look bad. Let me get you some water."

Denise scurried up to the front of the van and returned with a bottle of Evian water and poured some into a paper cup. "It's a little warm, but it's something." Denise held the cup to Alison's mouth. Alison emptied the first cup, then drank two more before uttering her first word. "Thanks."

"Sure. All of them are gone for a while. I sneaked away. It's totally fucked that they're keeping you cooped up like this." The girl pouted. "I'd unlock you, but I can't. Here, let me wipe off your face. There's some dried blood on you."

Denise poured some water onto a paper towel and wiped off Alison's face.

The water was cool and soothing. Alison spoke slowly. "Why am I here? What does Sunn want with me?"

"I asked him the same thing and he's all like 'you'd never understand' and then he laughs and he goes into this whole weird rap about special powers and shit. Sunn thinks you're especially witchy. Says you have magic in you."

Alison couldn't believe her ears. She would understand if she were kidnapped for ransom or extortion, or even for sex. But to be held because she was *magic?* How would they react when they discovered that she was just a regular person? She worried about the sanity of her captors; if they were that far gone, they might do anything.

"Do you believe all that stuff, Denise?"

"Hell, no. But I pretend. I just go, 'Oh, J'osüf, that's brilliant, oh, J'osüf, that's the best idea I ever heard,' and he doesn't bug me. I swear if you do the same, you can get along real easily."

"But *you* know it's not true, right?"

"Mostly. Some of it maybe not. But he's not like the world's greatest genius or anything."

"Can't you unlock me?"

"Sunn has all keys. He carries 'em around all the time. Look, I'm not even s'pose to be giving you water or even talking to you. Sunn's all like 'Alison needs to com, um, contemplate her actions and make the right decision to be with us.'"

"I didn't make a decision to be with you!"

"Duh! You think I don't know that? But what do you want me to do?"

"Go to the police."

"Not! I ran away from home. Like, I go to the cops, and then in like a New York minute my horndog stepdad finds me, right? And then they truck me back to his house of pain. End of story."

"If you get me out, I'll see to it that you don't have to go back to your stepfather. I swear I will."

"Shee-yeah, right. You're just saying that 'cause you're all chained up. Like, I have an okay deal going. Free food. Someplace to stay, even if it is a smelly mobile home. You'll just go back wherever you came from and then, like everybody else in my life, you'll forget about Denise. You'll say, 'Oh, her? Just some little kid.'"

"I can't stay here forever!"

"Do like I do! Just pretend like J'osüf Sunn is the greatest brilliant genius the world ever saw, nod when he tells his boring stories, and when he horns in on you, just tell him you're not ready."

"He tried to have sex with you?" Alison asked. She was shocked. Denise was barely in the first stages of puberty.

"He knows better than to try that stuff with me. The other girls, they're all suckers. They think they have to put out. They're all like 'mmm, it's so good, ooohh.' I seen 'em do it. Look, I gotta go 'cause they're gonna be back sometime. Drink another cup of water, okay?"

Alison tilted back her head to take the water.

"I sneaked you a sandwich. It's like cucumbers and stuff, kinda slimy, but it's something to eat."

"Thank you."

"Look, if he comes in here, just play along. He thinks you're like totally witchy, so if you make it sound like you'll put a curse or something on him, he'll freak. I swear. Just tell him directly. Maybe it'll work."

"Don't leave!"

"I gotta. I'll sneak back in. I can't do a helluva lot for you in here, but if you get out, maybe the two of us can get away." The girl blew some hair out of her face. "If you're serious about taking care of me."

The girl left. Alison twisted her hand around so that she could eat the sandwich.

That morning in the small farm town of Corcoran, Sunn and six girls played a game they like to call either "passing" or "normaling." The object was to hide themselves among outsiders—"the normals"—and "pass" as ordinary people. They had done it many times before. Today they were supposed to observe the townspeople without revealing that they were watching.

Before going out among the normals, they practiced at the mobile home in the cornfield. First they stole a "new" wardrobe from Goodwill boxes consisting of what Sunn deemed regular clothing. Sunn himself wore a slightly stained, ill-fitting business suit and a porkpie hat. Panda and Princess wore matching gray jumpsuits discarded from Sears Automotive Center. Sunn insisted that they be called "Rodrigo" and "Pete" so that none of the normals would become suspicious about the name patches. The other four girls wore a hodgepodge of polyester and denim, and were supposed to pretend to be tourists.

While Adelaide and Denise guarded Alison, the rest walked the three miles into town, full of excitement, practicing their "normal" behavior. Sunn stopped on the eastern edge of Corcoran, next to a swap meet that was housed in an abandoned movie theater, and gave a little pep talk to the girls. The swap meet was closed. No one else was around. He spoke in his "passing" voice, a little too loud with his mouth opened a little too wide.

"We have four main goals this morning in town. First, we want to get all the maps we can. I hope you can get them for free from the chamber of commerce, but if you can't, I'd say that any means by which you can secure them is okay by me. Second, we need to get the train schedule. The Amtrak schedule will be easy but getting a schedule for freight trains, which is what we really want, will require some ingenuity. Panda and Princess, you handle that. Third, we want to know the personnel schedule for the prison. About half the people in town work over at the pen, so chances are you'll run into someone who knows when they change shifts. You all understand?"

"Yes, sir!" responded Silhouette, with all the enthusiastic normality she could muster. The other girls nodded.

"Fine. That's all good. The fourth thing we need to do today, as important as any of the other things, is to get ourselves recognized around town. As normal people. We want them to think we aren't strangers. I'm not saying you should strike up conversations with everybody you see, but if they're used to seeing you in Corcoran, it'll be easier to be invisible next week when there's real work to be done."

They divided into three groups. Far from appearing "normal," they attracted undue attention everywhere they went. The business section of Corcoran consisted of a strip of road four blocks long punctuated by two traffic lights. There were three restaurants, a gas station, a bank, three bars, three farm equipment dealerships, and a professional building with one doctor and one dentist upstairs, a beauty shop and pharmacy downstairs. The only north-south street of note had the Correctional Workers Union Hall, a court-house, a police station, the city hall, a chamber of commerce, and several business offices.

Panda and Princess split off for the Amtrak station, ditching the others. The small, freestanding redbrick building was not much bigger than a two-car garage, and consisted of a ticket window, five chairs, and a soda machine. As they entered the building, Panda whispered to Princess: "Okay, *Rodrigo,* I'll ask for the tickets."

Princess replied, "Fine, *Pete.*"

Panda looked through the bulletproof Plexiglas ticket window but saw no one. "Hello?" she yelled, in her "passing" voice. "Is anyone here?" She rapped on the window. She heard a toilet flush, then a thin young man wearing aviator-style glasses and a sport coat with an Amtrak logo on the pocket walked from the back of the office. His smile, accented with a gold tooth, was slightly indecent.

"Well, what have we here?" He looked her up and down.

"Hello there," said Panda. "I'm trying to get some train schedules."

"Got the Amtrak sked' right here." He slid a long, thin printed schedule through the glass. "Where are you going? I know the trains pretty well."

"Um, I was going to . . ." She looked to her friend for help and found none, as Princess threw up her hands. "We're going to go to Kentucky."

"Lemme see. You probably would take the two-fifteen out of here down to San Luis Obispo, then switch to the Amtrak Commuter, put you into L.A." He flipped through a printed schedule. "There's the Coast to Coast that'll put you through Cincinnati. From there you can catch some sort of local to get to Kentucky."

"Oh." Panda stared forward, blank. "Thanks."

The ticket guy leaned on his elbows. "That all you want?"

"Could I take up some more of your time?" she asked.

"Honey, you can take up all afternoon. I don't have a train coming in until the four fifty-five out of Reno, and I'm caught up on the paperwork."

"I want to know all the trains that come and go from here. If that's okay."

"What for?"

Panda began spinning desperately. "My, uh, father, he likes to watch trains. Sometimes he'll stand all day and watch 'em go by and just count the cars." Even as the words were coming out, they sounded phony to her. She looked to her sister, who rolled her eyes.

To their surprise, the man was charmed. "Is that so? I used to like to do that, too. My grandfather and I watched them. I always wondered where all that stuff was going— cars, trucks, coal, big tanks full of something or other. I learned how to read the signs on the side of the tanks that told you what was in 'em. I figured out when the Japanese cars was going north, and when the Detroit cars was going south. Come on back into the office and I'll give you the schedules. How 'bout your sister?"

"Can she come back, too?"

"Sure. Name's Casey Jones."

"Really?"

He hung his head down. "Not technically, if you got to ask. It's really Rupert, but I always hated the name Rupert, so I started asking people to call me Casey."

"Cool."

"And your names?"

"I'm Pete and she's Rodrigo."

"Very funny! Like your patches. No, I mean really."

"Um, I'm Panda and she's Princess."

"Nice to meet ya, Panda, Princess."

They followed him into the office and to gather the information that Sunn had requested.

All over the town, similar encounters were occurring. Silhouette hung around the chamber of commerce building, listening patiently to an older woman who described her hopes to build the town into a real, modern highway stop. Silhouette considered the ambition a bit pathetic, but her reward for hours of listening was a complete set of maps of the town and surrounding area, including a few aerial photos.

Sunn, who was the most confident at the beginning of the day, had the most trouble. He wandered into Red & Black, the local bar, and tried to strike up conversations with a number of customers, hoping to find someone who knew the schedule of operations at the prison. He was shunned several times. One patron even scooted several chairs away from Sunn before he even had a chance to introduce himself. He became almost paranoid, convinced that they knew who he was, or somehow recognized him as an ex-convict. Finally, around three o'clock, the bar was almost empty. Sunn ordered his fifth soda water of the day and asked the bartender what the problem was.

"I've tried to talk to four or five people, just to make conversation, and every one of them reacts as if I'm some sort of pariah."

The barkeep, a hefty woman in her fifties with a gigantic bright red Toni home permanent, listened to his question but did not reply.

"You, too?" said Sunn. "What is it? What'd I do?"

"Mister, don't pretend you don't know what the problem is. My customers mostly work over at Corcoran Correctional. They don't want to be written up for drinking."

"Come again?" said Sunn.

"I said, you're making me go broke. This ain't the first time one of you Bureau of Corrections guys just about chased out every one of my customers. Working at the pen's a stressful job. Most of the guys don't have a drink until after work—and if a few have one *before* work, so be it. You internal affairs types shouldn't pick on a struggling entrepreneur like me."

"Internal affairs?"

She wiped off the counter and stuffed the towel into the pocket of her apron, defiantly. "Why do you pretend you ain't? It's written all over you. I don't know where you learned your undercover, but it ain't the best school in the world."

"I'm not internal affairs!"

"Uh-huh. You drink *soda waters*. You pretend you're from somewhere out of town. You're hanging around my bar all day as if you don't have anyplace better to go, asking all kinds of questions about who works at the prison." She leaned in closer to Sunn and whispered, "And that hat." Nobody who would come into *this* bar would wear *that* hat."

"What could I do to convince you I'm not from Internal Affairs?"

"Don't try. Forget I said it. I won't mention it again. You asked why you were getting a chilly reception. I told you. Okay?"

"Thanks." Sunn left five dollars on the bar and walked out. As soon as he was outside, he threw the hat into a trash can.

Walking up and down the streets of Corcoran, Sunn gathered the girls together and they walked back to the farm that was home. On the way they stole dinner from some of the fields that they passed, gathering lettuce, carrots, cabbage, and as many potatoes as they could carry. No one chased them away. Most of the farms were corporate endeavors covering hundreds of acres, with no one tending the fields. Sunn claimed that the lack of supervision was license to steal.

On the way they passed a bridge where the railroad tracks crossed beneath the eight-lane freeway, the main traffic artery to and from Corcoran. They jumped over a chain-link fence and walked up the gravel incline adjacent to the railroad track. Sunn stood on the tracks and spoke.

"In four days the Man will decide whether to release Jesus. I think they will. But if they don't . . . we have to be prepared to go in and get him."

The girls, in a semicircle around him, listened carefully.

"The kangaroo court will probably announce its decision by five o'clock on that day. What's the first big freight train that comes through here after that?"

Panda spoke up, proud to show off her new knowledge of train schedules. She flipped through the notes she had taken while visiting the Amtrak station. "There's none that stops here until a passenger train comes through just after midnight."

"I don't care if it stops here."

"Well, okay," said Panda. "At about quarter after six, depending on weather and schedules, a freight train will go right under this highway."

"What's it going to carry?" asked Sunn.

She squinted at her notes. The sun was low in the sky, and

in the dim light beneath the bridge, it was hard to read. "He said some container cargo, and then fifteen cars full of purt-oh chemical." She tilted her head back. "What's purt-oh chemicals, J'osüf?" she asked.

"Petrochemicals," he said, correcting her. "Gasoline. Oil. Just what we want."

Panda stepped closer to Sunn. "Why do you want *petro*-chemicals? What're you going to do, jump the train and steal gasoline?"

"No. What's our goal?"

"To get Jesus out, right?"

"Right. And we need something to distract the police from the parole hearing."

Silhouette stepped forward. "And this train going by is going to do the trick?"

"No. This train derailing, blowing up, and stopping the main freeway will take them away from there."

Panda frowned. "The guy at the train station was really nice. He told us all about train cars, and routing, and why trains are so neat. You're not going to blow up his train, are you?"

"Listen to me, children, and listen carefully!" His voice reverberated in the cavernous underpass. *"We* don't want to do this. But *we* didn't imprison the most important man on earth. *They* did. *They* might make the wrong decision. *They* might keep Jesus for another three years, or six years, or for the rest of his life. The world needs *him* now. The world can live with one less freight train." The words echoed away until all they could hear was the roar of traffic over their heads.

"Am I understood?"

Silhouette quietly said, "Yes," and the others remained silent.

Sunn yelled louder. "I said *am I understood?*"

All of the girls yelled, "Yes!" in unison.

"Good! We have an important mission. Derailing a train is hard work. I need two experts to handle those duties *if it becomes necessary.*"

Silhouette and Princess raised their hands enthusiastically. Sunn ignored them.

"I don't need volunteers. I need experts. Panda. Princess. You know more about trains than the rest of us. I want you to be ready to derail this train if the Man decides to keep Charlie behind bars."

Panda stepped forward, but Princess hesitated.

"What's the problem, Princess?" demanded Sunn.

"I'm just not sure I want to."

"You'll be doing all of us a big favor. It's something that might seem ugly at first, but it's a job that has to be done. It's never easy to do the right thing."

Princess frowned.

Sunn put his arm around her shoulder. "We'll all be glad if you don't have to do this. But if push comes to shove, you'll be a hero. You'll be helping all the world."

"I guess," she said.

Sunn addressed the group. "Come on. Let's get home. We have a lot to do. Tonight we're going to learn what C-4 is and how to use it."

Sunn led the girls silently down the railroad tracks toward the mobile home as the twilight faded into night. When the first stars appeared, someone began singing a slow, dirgelike version of "Amazing Grace."

Sunn had no concerns over what might go wrong. He was too excited at the prospect of finally reuniting the Family.

21

HE HAD THE DREAM AGAIN. AS ALWAYS, IT BEGAN HAPPILY.

Hush, little baby, don't you cry,
Mama's gonna sing you a lullaby,

Trumbo was an infant. He sat on his mother's lap, too young to walk, the scent of flowers and incense heavy in the air. He was the center of attention, everybody's favorite baby at the ranch. Everyone wanted to play with him, hold him, cuddle him. His mother smiled . . .

Hush, little baby, don't you weep,
Mama's gonna rock you right to sleep

He crawled across the floor as the adults laughed and played around him. Someone strummed on an acoustic guitar, and the sweet refrains of folk songs reverberated through the drafty, dusty shack. Mommy picked him up . . .

Hush, little baby, don't you blab
Mama'll feed you an acid tab

The world around him turned into one giant picture book of purples and greens and colors that he had never before seen. He didn't crawl. He floated like a bird. The big kids floated, too, just like him. Mommy caught him, like catching a balloon, and lifted him high up in the air.

He strained to see her face. He desperately wanted to know what she looked like. *Mommy.* He reached out, but as always, in the dream she was just a tiny bit too far away.

He was on the verge of recognizing her when the dream turned sinister: a palpable sensation that he had lost control, that the people who were once so playful and loving wanted to use him for . . . something horrible, and there was nothing at all he could do about it . . .

Trumbo awoke in a cold sweat, yelling and grinding his teeth so hard, his gums bled.

Barbara Thompson sat on the floor next to the couch, with a pan of water and some washcloths. Silent, she soaked a cloth in the water and draped it across his aching head.

"There, there," she said. "I hit you pretty hard. I thought you were a cop. Here, this'll make you feel better."

Trumbo tried to make sense of what was happening. He had walked into Blue's apartment, but before him kneeled Barbara Thompson. Prison escapee. The woman who might lead him to his mother. He rubbed the cloth on his forehead.

"Barbara?" he said.

"Yes, Trumbo."

"You escaped."

"I chose to leave the prison. Then you found me. I knew you would find me."

She rubbed the cool cloth across his forehead and neck. She unbuttoned his shirt and gently placed another cloth on his chest. It felt good. He took a deep breath.

"You whacked me pretty good."

"I heard you screaming," she said.

"A bad dream."

"There, there. You'll be all right. Would you like some soup? I found some chicken-and-rice in Blue's cupboard."

Trumbo groggily accepted her offer. She disappeared into the tiny kitchen, the only other room besides the grungy, dimly lit studio where Trumbo lay on a couch. While she was gone he tried to organize his thoughts. He sat up on the couch, trying to decide what to do next.

From the next room he heard the sound of a can opener, then water running, then singing. Thompson riffed some recent Top 40 hit, vaguely familiar. The voice crept into Trumbo's mind and insinuated itself into his deepest consciousness.

He propped himself up and stumbled toward the kitchen. His temples throbbed. Thompson didn't turn around. She continued to sing while stirring the soup heating on an electric plate.

It *was* the same voice from his dream. The warm trance of sleep was shaken with the icy revelation as a chill ran through his veins.

Trumbo leaned against the table. "Barbara."

"Yes, Trumbo?" She wiped her hands on an apron and turned around.

"We've met before."

"Sure, when you came to see me in prison."

"Before that."

She smiled cryptically and sat down. "Yes. A long time ago. I'm surprised you remember."

"Are you . . . ?"

"Yes."

"My mother?"

"Yes."

Trumbo's head reeled. He sat down across from her at the rickety kitchen table.

"You sang for me when I was very young. I recognized your voice."

"I told you your mother would make herself known when you were ready. And now you're ready."

"Oh, God."

Trumbo felt nauseated. He laid his head down on the table. He felt like he had been sucker punched.

"What's the matter?" she asked.

"Nothing. It's just not what I expected."

"Trumbo, this should be a happy time. We're together again. Mother and son."

"Look, Barbara. It's going to take me some time to get used to it."

"You don't believe me." She leaned back her head and closed her eyes. "On the back of your shoulder is a little scar. It's a brand that I made so you would always be known. It's a perfect circle—the whole world untainted, the truth, perfection, the beginning and the end, yin and yang."

Trumbo knew the mark well. His father had always told him that the strange circle was from shots for childhood flu that had created a rash.

Of course she was his mother. It was the answer that explained why his father didn't tell him about her and why they were always on the run while he grew up. It also fit in with his bleak life philosophy: Just when you think things can't get any worse, they get worse. "It all makes sense," said Trumbo.

"Because it's the truth."

Trumbo laid his hands flat down on the table. "What happened?"

"I was on my way out the door when you came to me. It was just a place to catch my breath."

"No. I mean, why did my dad ditch you? Why were you in jail?"

Barbara blushed. A tear formed in her eye. "I'm different now. I'm forty-four years old. I have been in prison the last 16. When I was young, I was furious with Luther for taking you. Now I see he was right to keep you away from me. I was bad, very bad. I did things I shouldn't have. I screwed up, Trumbo, I screwed up big-time, and I paid the price. The prison wasn't the worst punishment. Being denied my son was far, far worse." She wiped her eye and caught her breath.

"I could catalog the many errors of my youth, but the

specifics aren't important. I took too many drugs. I hung around with people a wiser girl would have avoided. Why was I in prison? I take full responsibility. I tried to kill a Supreme Court justice. At the time I thought it was the right thing to do. Thank God I was caught before I carried it out. Sixteen years in prison let me sort out my life, put things in perspective. There is a better way. Trumbo, the things I did were wrong. I learned my lesson. I don't want you to turn out that way."

"You're telling me all this, but you just broke out of prison," said Trumbo.

She shook her head. "I know, I know. I probably shouldn't have. Seeing you, visiting me there, it just alerted me to the fast pace of the world out there. They were going to keep me there until I died. Life imprisonment is just a death sentence carried out slowly. They don't believe that people can change. I'll turn myself in, I promise. I just want a few days in the free air, to see you, to see my friends. Is that so much to ask?"

A tear rolled down her cheek. She reached out and grasped his hands in hers. "Trumbo, try to understand. Imagine waking up every day behind steel, in a cold concrete building. You fall asleep there knowing this is the routine every day for the rest of your life. There's no hope. But then I was given a taste of hope—seeing you visiting— and almost any risk is worth taking. I've changed. I swear I've changed. I'm not Magick Mimi anymore."

"Mimi Black?"

"Black Magick Mimi. That's what they used to call me. Or that's who I once was. Magick Mimi is the one who did all those things, and I've exorcised her."

She stood, poured soup into a bowl, set it in front of Trumbo, and then pulled a brown-paper-wrapped batch of photographs from the counter.

"Eat, Trumbo. I want to take care of you. Here, I'll show you some pictures."

He fidgeted with the soup while she laid out faded photographs in front of him, narrating them as she spoke. Several photographs showed a young Luther and Barbara posing in front of various Scenic Picture Spots: a cliff overlooking the Pacific Ocean, Disneyland, a rose garden in Los Angeles. They looked fresh and naive in the snapshots.

A large truck passed nearby, rumbling the building. Barbara tore to the window and peeled back the curtain, peering out into the parking lot.

"What is it?" asked Trumbo.

"Just a garbage truck. We have to be careful. I just want a few days, Trumbo, just a few days. I don't want to go back yet. The cops will probably show up sooner or later. You found me here without trying."

"I wasn't trying to find you."

"What were you doing?"

"I'm trying to find a girl. Alison Wilmot."

"Joi Wilmot's daughter?"

"Yes."

"I know where she is. That's where I am going."

"Where is she?"

"With my friends. They're protecting her."

"Protecting her? Oh, no, I don't think so. They killed Joi! They're not doing her any good."

"Trumbo, you don't understand. They're trying to keep from happening to Alison what happened to her mother. Believe me, I know. I was Joi's friend for years."

"Where is Alison?"

"Up north. At a ranch."

Another truck roared by. Barbara ran to the window again and waited for it to pass. "We should leave," she said, worried. "The cops will be here any time."

"You really know where she is?"

"Yes."

"Okay. We'll take my car."

She gathered her meager belongings, stored in a trash bag, and they left in Trumbo's car.

As they drove north, the sky faded from a shrill unnatural pink to a dull yellow. Upon leaving the megalopolis entirely, they drove beneath the moonless, perfectly black sky. The darkness was soothing. If it weren't for the occasional highway sign, the car could have been a ship on a dark ocean. They shared an unspoken sense of intimacy. As they proceeded, Barbara began talking. Trumbo wasn't quite sure how much to believe, but he listened carefully. She told him about life in prison, how she had been transferred from facility to facility with no hope of getting out.

After much coaxing, he persuaded her to share the details of the crime for which she was arrested. She took a deep breath and began.

"April eleven, 1978. Your eleventh birthday. I remember it all quite clearly. It was downtown at the Ambassador Hotel. Have you ever been there?"

"They tore it down not too long ago."

She sighed. "What a shame. It was a beautiful place. I got out of my macramé class around three and caught the 241 bus down Vermont and walked a mile or so on Wilshire. It was a crisp spring day. Rains had washed out the smog, and the sun was shining crystal-clear, as if even the weather wanted to help me do what I had to do. I took a Smith & Wesson model 27 .357 Magnum. I remember the name because they repeated it over and over at the trial."

Trumbo tapped her on the shoulder. "Back up. Why were you going to kill someone?"

"Justice Frears was the swing vote when they reinstated the death penalty in America. I was a pacifist, but I was prepared to take one life to save many others. Or at least Magick Mimi was ready to do so."

"Okay," said Trumbo.

"I regret what I did, okay? I'm just telling you because you asked."

"Fine," said Trumbo.

"Frears came to the Ambassador to give a talk to a group of lawyers. I took a copy of *People* magazine and sat on the lawn near the entrance to wait for him. He was late for his four-o'clock speech. At four-thirty I still hadn't seen him and I was about to give up. Suddenly a limousine arrived, followed by several cars. It stopped near the door, and you know what?"

"No, what?"

"He was going to go in a different door. I folded my magazine, slung my purse over my shoulder, and followed him. There were lots of men in blue suits around him like a flock of deadly birds. I pushed my way through the crowd, but he was walking fast. Just before he went inside, I got the gun and carefully took aim. As I squeezed the trigger, I felt someone hit my arm. It went off—boom!—and I fell to the ground. My bullet completely missed and hit a young legal assistant standing near him. I squeezed off another shot, but by then someone stomped on my arm." She caught her breath. "They broke my arm and two fingers. I gave myself up peacefully. The trial was short."

"And that's why they arrested you?" asked Trumbo.

"Yes, and left me in jail to rot. *I didn't even kill anybody!*" she yelled. "There's murderers and gangsters and child molesters who got in and out of prison during my term, but they kept me in because they said it wasn't murder, it was an assassination and I was a danger to society. It upsets me just to think about it."

"I see."

Trumbo remained silent while she talked for hours about when she and his father were together. The more she talked, the more her story sounded suspect. He was fascinated by the strange tone of her denials and the gap between her perceptions of right and wrong and his own. She said she "hardly ever" used LSD—"probably only once or twice a week for about five years—maybe a couple hundred times." She said she didn't commit any other crimes, "just stole a few cars when money was tight."

Her craziest assertion was that she had indeed been a good mother. "I meditated for you every day." He refrained from contradicting her. After a long spell of silence, they began to approach Bakersfield, the first town of any size since leaving Los Angeles.

"We getting close?" asked Trumbo.

"Maybe we are," she said.

"'Maybe' meaning you don't know yourself, or 'maybe' as in you're just not going to tell me?"

"Little bit of both," she said. "I'll get us there. Don't you worry."

"We have to get some gas if it's going to be a long time."

"Pull off at the next exit," she said. "It might be forty or fifty miles more."

"Okay," said Trumbo. "I have to use the john anyway."

They drove into a twenty-four-hour Shell station, which had an adjoining minimart stocking soda pop, plastic-wrapped sandwiches, candy, gum, newspapers, magazines, almost anything a traveler might want. Trumbo parked next to a pump and took the keys.

"I'll fill it up," said Barbara. "You use the bathroom, son."

"Do you have cash?" asked Trumbo.

"Enough."

He nodded and walked around to the back of the building, to the men's room. Inside, he splashed cold water on his face and tried to wash up with the desiccated bar of soap resting on the greasy sink. Through the walls he heard a loud argument. Trumbo turned off the water and listened. The yelling continued. He could make out Barbara's voice above the fray.

He pulled several scratchy paper towels from the dispenser and dried off his face; then he heard two sharp pops. He dropped the towel and ran to the front of the gas station. A man's voice yelled in Arabic.

As he cleared the side of the building, he saw Barbara standing over the prone bodies of two cops, lying in pools of blood next to the gas pumps. She held a pistol over her head. Gone was the angelic, slightly stoned demeanor she had shown during their drive. In its place was a fierce, animalistic rage, eyes squinting, cheeks flushed, mouth pulled back in a scowl.

"Trumbo, you lied to me! You lied to me!" she screamed, waving the gun. "You called the fucking pigs, that's what you did!"

Trumbo raced into the main building of the gas station. Through the window, Barbara leveled the gun at him. Trumbo dove to the ground behind a rack of beef jerky. He heard a gunshot followed by the sound of the glass window at the front of the shop shattering into a thousand pieces. Shards covered the floor of the room.

Trumbo crawled up an aisle, away from the door, past NoDoz and Ding Dongs and pine tree fresheners until he could hide himself behind a pyramid of Diet Pepsi. When he glanced back toward the counter, he saw the clerk yank a sawed-off shotgun from beneath the counter. Trumbo watched with astonishment as the clerk, rather than pointing it at Barbara, aimed the two-barrel twelve-gauge at *him*. Two loud explosions stunned his ears, and a flash of light blinded him. He expected to see his life flash before his eyes, or at least his own blood spilling out, but instead saw the clerk crumple to the floor. Barbara had shot him.

During the commotion another customer, an older man in a cowboy hat, sprinted from the store toward a pickup truck parked in front. Barbara carefully took aim and spent the three bullets on the cowboy. He fell face-forward onto the ground next to his truck.

Barbara, still outside, yelled into the shop, "Trumbo, get the hell out here!"

He peered over a pyramid of Pepsi and saw that she was no longer aiming at him. "What the *fuck* was that? What are you doing?" he yelled.

"I'm going—you can come or you can stay." She popped out a seven-round magazine from the gun, rummaged in her purse and pulled out some Kleenex and a paperback book before finding another magazine of ammunition, and then reloaded. "Are you coming? I'd hate for my only son to die in a robbery," she asked, cocking the gun.

Trumbo was frozen with fear. Barbara casually closed the latch on her purse and slung it over her arm, then lifted the gun with both hands and drew a bead on Trumbo. "I'm not going to ask you again, son! Are you coming?" She cocked the gun. "I can leave you here, but not alive."

He scanned the gas station for an escape route. There was none. Whichever way he ran, she had a clear shot. And the four people dead were proof she would not hesitate to shoot.

"I'm there." Trumbo raised his hands.

He reluctantly walked out the door of the gas station and resumed his seat behind the wheel of the Mazda. Barbara sat in the passenger seat, fumbling with the gun. All he could think about was getting away from the gas station. He sped down the connector road and rejoined the freeway, able only to stare directly ahead, as if he had tunnel vision.

For the first time in his life, he remembered the rest of the song from the dream. It came to him in a flash, and the thought was complete.

Hush, little baby, don't you sob,
Mama's going to give you a blow job . . .

He remembered quite clearly, the times when he was still an infant, being lifted into the air, high on the LSD they put

*into his baby bottle, the many big kids passing him from one
to another, stripping him of his clothes, raising his baby
crotch before their hungry mouths and . . .*

Something snapped. It was something that really happened, not a dream, not some figment of his imagination,
and the memory had been suppressed for years, decades. It
was horrifying. He didn't care any longer whether Barbara
had a gun or not, let her shoot him. The bitch.

"You killed them! They didn't do *anything* to you. You
don't give a damn about anyone!" he shouted.

"I thought you called the cops on me."

"Why would you think that?"

"They were there. It wasn't until the cashier pointed the
gun at you—he thought you were trying to rob him,
too—that I realized you hadn't called anyone."

He gripped the steering wheel to stop his hands from
shaking. "Those cops . . . they probably came in to get
coffee. Now they're dead! Why the hell did you have to do
that?"

"It's just a couple of dead pigs."

"One of those guys was younger than me."

"Don't sweat it, Trumbo. There's plenty more where they
came from. The revolution is at hand. There will be
casualties."

Trumbo remained unimpressed, and stared at her in
disbelief. Then, slowly, her face changed: Her squinting eyes
relaxed, and her mouth slowly opened as her bottom lip
began to quiver.

She sighed deeply. "No, you're right, Trumbo. You're
such a good boy, and you are absolutely correct." Tears
welled up in her eyes. "I had no right to do what I did . . . I
should have let them kill me." She sobbed. "Please forgive
me. I now know better. I really didn't mean to do what I
did."

Trumbo gritted his teeth as he fully understood that
Barbara Thompson, the woman holding a gun on him—his
mother!—was completely unhinged. He was furious and
scared.

"Stop it," said Trumbo. "Don't waste your breath. You
can cry all day. I don't believe you." He turned to face her,
watching the road from the corner of his eye. "Why did you

even bother pretending you'd changed? You said that Black Magick Mimi was dead, and only a nice girl lived on. Why did you lie to me?"

She dried her eyes and spoke plainly. "I had to get you to go with me. It's too important."

"Fuck you," he said.

She fidgeted with the gun. "You just don't understand, do you? It's for Charlie. The end is near. He's getting out. He's going to help you and me and everybody. It's the most important thing in the world."

"Who?" growled Trumbo.

"Charles Manson, Trumbo. Jesus. And you're going to be a disciple, maybe even the new leader."

This is my goddamn mother, he thought. *Once we find Alison, I'm heading to the cops and turn her in. Let 'em arrest me.* He wished he could wrestle the gun away from her.

As if able to read his thoughts, Barbara spoke up. "You're probably thinking about how you could get away, son. Forget it. The video cameras at that place caught you on tape. Now you're a fugitive just like me, and you'll feel what it's like to be hunted like an animal. You were the driver, remember? You transported a fugitive."

He stared ahead, silent, considering his options. He wanted to find Alison, make sure she was safe, and then go to the police. But he had to get the gun from Barbara. He glanced down. The gas gauge was pinned to Empty. That gave him a plan.

Barbara leaned back in her seat, eyes half-open, one hand on the gun. When Trumbo looked at her, she met his glance, then resumed staring straight ahead. She wasn't paying close attention to his driving. *Good.* He turned on the radio.

"News okay?" he asked her.

"Nah, let's hear some music."

He turned to a country station, the only signal they could clearly receive. He didn't care what they heard. He just wanted a little bit of background noise as a cover.

He slipped his right hand down on the steering wheel, until it was next to the ignition key. Very slowly he gripped the key and flipped it a half click backwards. The engine suddenly died and red warning lights GENERATOR and ENGINE lit up on the dashboard. The power steering and brakes went out. He steered the car toward the breakdown lane.

"What happened?" demanded Barbara.

"Out of gas."

She leaned across his lap and stared at the gas gauge. "Damn," she said.

Trumbo maintained the facade. "We can't stop on the curb. The Highway Patrol will find us within an hour."

"How'd you let this happen?"

"If you hadn't gone batshit back there, we'd have a full tank of gas and four people would still be alive. I'll try to coast to the curb, and then we can push it off at the next exit. Look, it's only about a hundred yards."

The car silently came to a full stop, the gravel of the road shoulder crackling beneath its tires. Trumbo flipped off the lights and, unnoticed by Barbara, set the emergency brake. They sat in silence for a moment as a truck roared by, wake of air rattling the car.

"Now what?" asked Barbara.

"Now we get out and push."

As they got out of the car, Trumbo watched Barbara carefully. She stuffed the pistol into her purse and then threw the purse onto the passenger seat. They both walked to the rear of the Mazda.

"Who's going to steer?" she asked.

"It ought to go straight enough. If we need to, we can run up front and turn the steering wheel."

He leaned against the left rear of the car and began to push. Barbara did likewise on the right side. They both grunted and groaned, but the car would not budge.

"Something's screwed up," said Trumbo, scratching his head. "Oh jeez. I forgot to put it in neutral."

He ran to the passenger door, opened it, grabbed Barbara's purse, and extracted the pistol. He leaned against the car and pointed the gun at her.

"Trumbo! Put that down."

"Get in the car, Barbara."

"I thought we were out of gas."

"Get in."

She hesitated, standing behind the bumper. Trumbo got

into the driver's seat and yelled back to her, "Okay, don't get in. I don't give a damn. I'm not going to stay on the side of the road all night." He started the engine. Barbara quickly resumed her spot on the passenger side. They drove off.

"Now that I have the gun, why don't you tell me where Alison is?"

"I'll know when we get there."

Trumbo sighed. "You really don't know."

"I'll tell you. We want to go past that restaurant with a windmill about fifty miles north of Bakersfield and take the second exit after that, east. It should be Colonel Somebody State Park. Go about a mile east of there and I'll have to look around and see where we're going."

"When was the last time you laid eyes on this windmill restaurant?"

"Never. I got instructions from someone. I've never been up this way before. Charlie wasn't in Corcoran when I got sent up."

"We might be able to make it. Depending, of course, on where the damn windmill is."

Within fifteen minutes they passed the Dutch Treat Restaurant with its fifty-foot-tall neon windmill. Trumbo took the second exit after that. Within a few minutes they hit Colonel Jackson Martin State Park, unlike any park Trumbo had ever seen. It consisted of a few Depression-era houses, a library, and a general store, all abandoned. The Disneyland-style Middle America town square looked woefully out of place in the middle of empty cornfields, like an abandoned movie set. Martinville was a failed Utopian community, built as a "planned town" in which every need could be taken care of by its citizens. It had survived a brief twenty years before going bankrupt. Trumbo didn't want to point out the ironic parallel to the Manson Family, or Horseman's Clan, or whatever the hell Barbara wanted to call it.

"So we're here. You say go a couple miles east?"

"Yeah."

"Which road?"

"I don't know. There'll be a railroad track and a water tower before we get to the mobile home."

"Right."

The road ran north and south, parallel with the freeway. When he got to an east-west road, he took it and drove for seven miles. There were no railroad tracks, no water tower, and no mobile home.

The country road was perfectly black, without streetlights or houses. Darkened fields extended in every direction. As they came over the peak of a small rise in the road, an enormous oasis of light was visible a mile ahead.

Trumbo tried to determine what he was looking at. The lights were high above the ground, leading him to believe it might be a football field. But that didn't make sense. No one played football at two in the morning. Then he saw what looked like a control tower and decided it must be an airfield, but the rural community had no need for such an enormous airport. As he looked closer, he saw a second tower, and a third, and a fourth, and could make out the broad outlines of a series of gray brick buildings. He put on his high beams.

A moment later he saw a sign: YOU ARE APPROACHING CORCORAN STATE CORRECTIONAL FACILITY. DO NOT PICK UP HITCHHIKERS.

He was shocked by the size of the facility. It was as big as ten city blocks and was dumped in the middle of a vast cornfield, as if left behind by a UFO. When he looked closer he saw chain-link fences and razor wire and discerned the broad outlines of guards in the forty-foot-high towers. No doubt they were looking back at him, as well, with high-powered binoculars.

"Barbara!"

She was asleep.

"Barbara, wake up. We're nowhere near any of the landmarks you pointed out."

Groggily she sat up in the car. Her gaze turned to the right and she saw the facility.

"Stop the car!" she yelled excitedly. "He's in there. That's where they're keeping him. I can feel his presence. It's so strong, it's almost like he's sitting right next to me. I feel like I'm talking to him."

"Manson?"

"Yes. Charlie's in there."

"I'm not going to stop the goddamn car."

She pressed her face against the window for a moment and gazed out. Pressing her right palm against the glass, she spoke softly. "Hello, Charlie . . . I've come home . . . Yes, I'm fine. This is my son . . . Yes, he's come home, too." She laughed. "Yes, he has grown quite a bit! . . . He's not called that anymore. It's Trumbo now."

Trumbo heard her weird ramblings and tried to ignore them. She tapped him on the shoulder. "Charlie says hi."

Trumbo rolled his eyes. Barbara had lost her mind decades ago. "Great. Tell him I say hello back."

"I don't have to. He can hear you."

Trumbo raised his voice. "Look, Barbara, we can't keep driving around aimlessly. I don't know this car—we might have five miles worth of gas, we might have fifty miles worth, and I don't have a clue where we're going. Why don't you wind it up with your invisible friend? I don't like circling this prison."

She paid no attention to him and continued her conversation with herself. "What's that?" she said, staring out the window. "Okay . . . near the highway, of course . . . I got the directions from Blue, and you know how reliable he is . . . Right." She laughed. "I'll be seeing you."

"Cut this shit out!"

"It's okay. Charlie will take care of us. If we go past the prison and turn right, there's a twenty-four-hour convenience store that will have gasoline."

"What?"

"We need gas. It's probably fifteen miles back the other direction to get to the Horseman's Clan. Stupid Blue told me to go east and he meant west."

"Your invisible friend told you, right?"

"You don't have to believe me."

"I don't."

In spite of himself, Trumbo took the next road that went back to the highway. As soon as they saw the lights of the road, he noticed that on the other side of the overpass was a Pay-N-Pump gas station.

"See?" said Barbara. "There's the gas station."

"Barbara, there's a gas station at almost every single freeway junction."

"You don't have to believe me."

Trumbo stopped and filled up the car. On the floor by the counter was a stack of newspapers with Barbara's photo on the front page, reporting her prison escape.

When he got back in the car, Barbara was upbeat, placid, and in control of herself. "Okay. Go south about eleven miles or so, past the exit where we got off, and then turn left."

"Are these your psychic directions?"

"Do you have any better way to get where we're going?"

"No, I really don't. But if we're driving around aimlessly at daybreak, someone is likely to see us."

"Trust me."

With no faith in her ability to lead but without a better plan, Trumbo followed Barbara's route; they turned where she said to turn, and then about a mile farther they crossed a double set of railroad tracks. Straight ahead was an old-fashioned rural water tower.

Just beyond that, he saw lights emanating from a mobile home in the middle of a large cornfield. He was astonished that she had gotten them to the right place. His guess was that she had just lied about where they were going, made up the conversation, and then did this just to impress him.

As they passed the water tower, she yelled out, "Turn here! Turn on this dirt road!"

Trumbo jammed on the brakes and scrutinized her face, to see if she was lying. "Is this where Alison is?"

"Yes."

"How do I know you're telling the truth?"

"This is it. I said I'd take you to her."

"Okay. You get out of the car first. Now."

"What're you going to do?" she asked.

"You walk about fifteen feet in front of me and knock on the door. Walk slowly. I've still got the gun."

"You wouldn't kill your mother, would you?"

"Probably not, but I might shoot her in the knees if she pissed me off. You never know. When you get to the door, knock. Don't go inside the mobile home until I tell you."

"I don't have to do what you say."

"Just try me."

They got out of the car. Trumbo followed her into the field. The ground was muddy and wet from the evening dew.

Trumbo kept the gun in front of him; Barbara walked briskly, as if she'd been to this spot before. As they got closer, he flipped off the safety on the gun.

He lowered himself to a prone position on the ground, fifteen or twenty paces away from Barbara.

She walked to the front door of the trailer, energetically wiped her feet on a doormat, and then knocked. Trumbo watched her closely. After a brief pause, he saw the door open. A figure came to the door, partly obscured inside the mobile home. Trumbo was scared, but exhilarated at the prospect of finding Alison. *Only a few moments more; she's got to be here somewhere.* From the ground he surveyed the area in an attempt to guess where she might be. He hoped she was safe. He began to think about how he might get her away from here.

Barbara talked to whoever answered and then gestured toward Trumbo, talked some more, and then bolted directly away from the road, toward train tracks half a mile across the field. *Where is she going?* he wondered. He leaped up from the ground and ran after her.

When he passed the mobile home, he heard a deep voice.

"Stop *rye chair,* boy, or I'll shoot."

Trumbo spun around. A man in his thirties, balding and so plump, his bathrobe barely covered him, pointed a twelve-gauge shotgun at Trumbo's head.

"Drop the gun. Drop it, boy!" he yelled.

Trumbo did as instructed.

"You trying to rape that woman?"

"Say what?"

"I asked you a question. You try to rape her?"

"Don't bullshit me. You're one of the Horseman's Clan people, aren't you? Where is Alison?"

"I ain't no Klan and I don't know who Alison is. All I know is that you were chasing that woman, you had a gun on her, and she told me you were trying to rape her."

"Jesus Christ." Trumbo groaned. "Who are you?"

"My name's Howard Martin. This here's my home. What's it to you?"

"You really don't know Barbara?"

"Never saw her before in my life."

Trumbo started to walk forward. Martin delivered a blow

to Trumbo's shoulder with the butt of the gun. "Stay right where you are!"

"There's been a terrible misunderstanding. I wasn't trying anything on that woman—she's my mother!"

"Yeah, right. You called her Barbara a minute ago."

Trumbo shook his head. "You don't understand."

"Yeah, well, tell it to the cops." He switched the shotgun around so that it was in one hand, and flipped up a cellular phone in the other. While the man dialed, Trumbo inched forward.

"Yeah, I'd like to report a prowler," he said into the phone. "Maybe an attempted rape . . . No, no one tried to rape me . . . No, you don't understand at all . . . Transfer my call? Thank you, I'll wait."

Trumbo worked himself closer until he was within a few feet of the man. He turned his attention back to the phone, no longer on hold. "Yeah, I'm out on the old Market Road. You know the Martin Farms? . . . Yeah, that's me."

Trumbo dove forward and tackled Martin. It was a bit like felling a tree. The shotgun flew up and went off with a mighty blast, ripping a Frisbee-sized hole in the awning of the mobile home. Debris and gunshot rained down into Trumbo's face. He grappled with Martin for a moment, then got the phone away from him and hung it up. They both reached for the shotgun. Trumbo kicked the man's arm and grabbed the weapon, then stood up, pointing the gun at him.

"I haven't done anything wrong!" shouted Trumbo. "You just stay where you are. Don't follow me."

He backed away, stopping only to pick up Barbara's .45. When he was a good fifty yards away from the man, he turned and ran to the road, got into the Mazda, and sped away. When he had gone about two miles, a police cruiser passed him going the opposite direction, sirens blaring. He watched in the rearview mirror until it disappeared and then turned off on another road. He looked at himself in the rearview mirror. There were several new scratches on his face. His shoulder was sore from the blow of the shotgun butt. He had thought he was so close to Alison, only to fail once more.

He was tired.

He didn't know where to go.
The cops were after him.
The Manson Family was after him.
This had been a very bad day.

22

EVERY ITEM ON THE FRONT PAGE OF THE WELL-BOUND FILOFAX
had a check mark next to it indicating completion, but
cleverly lacked the explanation of precisely *how* and *why*
they were so important. Marilyn McLeod pondered her
hidden agenda as she scanned her list:

Five video crews lined up—check. *That is, every video
crew within a hundred miles of this backwoods hick town.
We'll bring in our own pros later, but the hell if some
local-yokel station's going to scoop us.*

Satellite uplink truck plus two backup trucks—check.
Again, the only three trucks in a hundred-mile radius.

Parole hearing moved to courthouse—check. *Where the
lighting is better, where the backdrops are more dramatic,
and where the administrators are more amenable to bending
rules for TV crews than the uptight by-the-rules prison
officials are.*

Extra security guards—check. *Actually, extras dressed up
as security guards—it's the look that counts for the broadcast.*

McLeod had gotten only five hours of sleep in the
previous three days. Her voice was reduced to a raspy
whisper from yelling at peons, a rash had appeared on her
ear from constant phone use, and she hadn't eaten a meal
since leaving New York that wasn't interrupted by a phone
call. Regardless, she felt a glow of deep animal satisfaction,
the kind a shark might feel after devouring a tasty young
swimmer. She had all but prevailed in a seemingly impossible task by solving every logistical problem, to facilitate the
live television broadcast of the show now called "James St.

James Presents Charles Manson's Final Parole Hearing: This Time He Could Go Free." Although the parole hearing and the show wouldn't occur for another four days, she finally felt she could relax for an hour or two and get a good night's sleep.

She had paid five hundred bucks cash to bring a professional Shiatsu masseuse up from L.A., and considered it worth every penny. After the massage, she took a scented bath, powdered herself, and now lay in bed, taking advantage of her hours of solitude to continue the Judith McNaught novel she'd started three weeks earlier. Hotel management knew to hold all calls. In case they didn't get the message, she disconnected the phone from the wall.

After she'd read just three pages, a sharp rap on her door disturbed her concentration. She sat silent on the bed, hoping to ignore the intruder. Whoever it was could not read the DO NOT DISTURB sign. The knocking continued. She looked up from her book.

"Who is it?"

"It's the hotel manager, ma'am." A man's voice. He sounded panicked.

"Didn't I tell you not to fucking disturb me?"

"Ma'am, it's an emergency. Truly."

She pulled the terry cloth robe tight around her and stomped to the door, angry beyond words. She slid the door open, making sure the chain kept the intruder out. The manager was a small man with soft, almost feminine features and deep lines in his face, about forty years old, the kind of guy who looks like he's been through the washer and dryer one too many times. Marilyn was furious that he had the temerity to disturb her.

"I believe I talked to you twice, and to your desk clerk, and to the maids. What did I say?"

He sputtered out, "I know you said not to be disturbed, ma'am, but—"

"What did I say?"

"You said that unless the hotel was on fire and your room was next to burn, you didn't want to be bothered."

"I'm pleased you remembered. You get an A for listening ability, F for follow-through."

She slammed the door. The manager immediately began knocking on it. "Please, ma'am, open the door."

She slid it open again. "The place is on fire?"

"No. But your boss, a Mr. St. James, has called us every five minutes for the past hour. First his secretary, then he himself called, demanding to speak to you and threatening unspeakable consequences unless we found you."

"What'd he say?"

"He said unless we got you on the phone immediately, he would buy the hotel and fire all of us. He sounded quite serious."

"That's my boss. I'll take the call." She trudged back to the bed and connected the telephone. As soon as plug made contact with cord, the phone rang. Before answering, she mumbled, "The son of a bitch," then counted to ten, took a deep breath, picked up the telephone, and in the sweetest voice she could muster, said, "Hello-oh!"

Immediately she was deluged with St. James's trademarked ranting. "Goddamn Marilyn I've been trying to get hold of you for four hours have we got problems let me tell you what kind of problems we have!"

"Calm down, Ray, everything's taken care of. We have a virtual stranglehold on an exclusive prime-time coverage this Thursday."

St. James spoke breathlessly, without pauses. "I know you handled everything I already asked you to do that's why I hired you that's not why I called. Something else came up and goddamn it it's being rammed right up our asses as we speak."

"Come again?"

"Manson got a jailhouse mouthpiece who's asked that the whole thing be called off."

"No parole hearing?"

"No video coverage! We're out half a million for promotion and we won't have the cooperation of the goddamned featured performer! Manson's so-called lawyer said he wants to ban all cameras this time around. Says the last hearing was a media circus."

"Can he do that? Can he call off the video?"

"Maybe he can, maybe he can't, but that same jailhouse

lawyer kept us from getting coverage on the sanity hearing for that kid last spring—you remember his name—the one who killed all the little gook children and caused such an uproar."

"Phillip Wilson, yeah, right. So what? That was a sanity hearing, this is a parole hearing. Why don't you throw some high-priced lawyers at the problem?" asked Marilyn.

"I talked to my fool high-priced lawyers, and they're of absolutely no use whatsoever."

"Why not?"

"Those twits in suits tell me Manson may actually have the *legal right* to ban us. Even if he doesn't, he only has to find *one* pinko liberal judge in the whole Ninth District who agrees with him, and video can be immediately withdrawn. The appeal process will take much longer than next Thursday, which is, of course, our deadline."

"So we're screwed."

"Maybe maybe not," screamed St. James.

"What do you mean?"

He lowered his voice to a theatrical whisper, the great general laying out a strategy. "We've got to persuade Manson that he *wants* video. More specifically, that he wants *us*. If we get his go-ahead, all lawsuits are off."

"We've got to persuade Manson?"

"You've got to do it for me. Manson hates *me,"* said St. James.

"I can't do it alone. He's obviously doing this to take revenge on you for making him look like a blithering idiot the last time you had him on your show."

"He is a blithering idiot," said St. James.

"But, Ray, dear, *you* must not be the sharpest tool in the shed if you still took out half a mil in promo for a show that depends on his cooperation. That doesn't sound too bright." Marilyn could hear the sound of a shoe flying across the room and breaking something, followed by a lengthy silence, followed by a loud crash, as if St. James had thrown the phone itself across the room. The line went dead. After a few moments St. James's voice came back, presumedly from another phone.

"I'm absolutely dead in the water unless we get this

show!" yelled St. James. "Useless! Done! Wasted! My picture will be in the dictionary under washout and has-been! You've got to cover my ass."

In the midst of the yelling Marilyn recognized a rare and unrepeatable opportunity for political advancement. All the ingredients were in place: *St. James needs something only I can get him.* She sighed before continuing. "It's too risky. I think we ought to call off the show."

St. James responded as she'd hoped. She had learned to play him like a trombone. "What? I know it's risky. What'll it take to get you to do it? Money? You already make more than anyone on the staff. Even though I pay you obscenely, well, I'll throw in a bonus."

"I'm flattered," she said, "but I just don't believe it can be done."

"It has to be done," yelled St. James. "What do you want? Look, if you can get Manson to agree to video coverage, I'll—I'll—uh, I'll give you the money and backing to make your *own* television pilot next year."

This was precisely what she was angling for. St. James really *was* desperate. Marilyn was delighted. "My own pilot? What a kind offer!" she said. "I'll see what I can do about getting him to cooperate."

"See what you can do! You have to come through for me on this. I'm counting on you!"

"You can—but not until I get the signed contracts."

St. James sighed. "It'll take weeks for your lawyer to work it out, and my lawyer to approve it."

"I'm one step ahead of you. My lawyer already has it."

"What do you mean?"

"Hold one minute, boss." She dumped the phone into the middle of the bed. Without missing a beat, she flipped open her briefcase. Inside were documents drawn up by her lawyer just in case this once-in-a-lifetime opportunity arose. St. James was famous for making promises and infamous for breaking them. He'd promised her a pilot once before— during a show about alligators in the sewers of New York— then conveniently forgot afterward, once Marilyn paid off a zookeeper to plant the gators in a drainage canal. As soon as that nightmare show was over, Marilyn paid three grand to have the pilot contract drawn up, with only the dates left blank. She got a black pen and filled in the correct dates; the deal specified a raise in pay, a minimum of five episodes to be produced, and even gave the name of the show: "Marilyn McLeod Investigates!" She picked up the phone again.

"Still there?"

"Only you, Marilyn, would have the gall to put James St. James on hold. Jesus Katy-Rist."

"Calm down. You'll get your show. I'm faxing you some contracts. I want you to sign them, fax back a copy for me, and send a copy on the next flight out with a courier. *Then* I'll straighten out the Manson thing, and not a minute before."

"I can't believe you had them waiting!"

"Well, I did. You always say 'be prepared.'"

"I'll have to read them over first."

"The show is in four days. Or isn't in four days, if I don't get busting right now."

"I'll sign them," said St. James. He added, "You, Marilyn, are ruthless, inhuman, and not ashamed to take advantage of a man when he's down."

"You say the sweetest things, Ray. You really know how to make a girl feel special."

She thought she heard something in his office break, and maybe even a scream before he slammed down the phone: music to her ears. Marilyn pulled out a portable fax machine from her suitcase and plugged it into the hotel phone, set the pages of the contract into the feeder slot, and dialed St. James's private fax number.

She had her private victory. Now she had to figure out how to get Manson on the air. But it was nearly midnight; she couldn't contact him until the morning at the earliest, and would have to pull lots of strings to do that. Happily she turned back to her novel and listened to the sweet purr of a pay-or-play contract grinding through the fax machine, no doubt raising the blood pressure of her boss.

As was her habit while in production, Marilyn awoke at dawn and ordered room service. While eating the blob of dough that passed for a continental breakfast in Corcoran, she watched the digital clock. The instant it turned to seven o'clock, she put down the cinnamon roll and dialed the telephone. A woman answered.

"Mr. Lenski, please."

"This is Mrs. Lenski. Mr. Lenski's in the shower. Who may I say is calling?"

"I'm putting through a call from the attorney general of California," Marilyn lied.

"Oh yes, one moment, I'll get him."

She wolfed down the rest of the roll while he came to the phone. She hoped he was dripping wet and terrified.

"This is Lenski."

"Lenski, babe, it's Marilyn McLeod."

"I thought it was the attorney general's office! I told you not to call me here!"

"I know you did, but I need a favor."

"I've already done you all the favors I'm going to do!"

"Maybe, maybe not. I've got a receipt here, from my company, for fifty thousand that I think—"

"All right, I get the picture. What is it?"

"Manson won't let us film him. I think it's your fault."

"What?"

"I think you set us up. Promised all kinds of things that you couldn't deliver."

"I never did that! I simply said I'd move the venue to the courthouse!"

"But you knew what we wanted."

"Manson won't let you film him, eh? That's not really my problem at all. I think he has—"

"Yeah, he has the *right;* don't bore me with rights. I've heard about prisoners' rights until I'm blue in the face. What about the people's right to know?"

There was a long, tense silence.

"Lenski?" she asked.

"I'm still here," he said. "There's nothing that I can do," he pleaded. "It's out of my hands. I should never have taken that money. When I get off the phone, I'm going to make a full confession to my wife, and then I'll resign my post."

"What? You schmuck! Don't do that!" Marilyn panicked as she thought of what might happen if her entire plot was blown up by one bureaucrat who suddenly came down with a case of conscience. "Keep the money! You can use it to put your kids through college or something. Think of all the good you can do with that money."

"I really don't know . . ." he said.

She hated dealing with guilt-ridden people. They were too hard to manipulate. She thought quickly. "If you confess, you'll only bring shame on your wife and family. You don't want to ruin *their* lives because of *your* mistake."

Again, a long silence. "You know, you're right? I did make a mistake, but there's no reason to compound it."

"Good. Nice talking to you. See you at the courthouse on Tuesday."

"Good-bye."

She slammed down the phone. When she bought someone, she preferred it if they *stayed* bought. She tapped her foot nervously and tried to think of another plan. The parole board had no authority. The judicial system wouldn't help her. She had no choice but to talk to the man himself. She made quick work of burning a few favors doled out previously to various political heavyweights in California. She contacted a state representative who owed them his career because of a show they opted not to run—"The Lolita Legislator"—that concerned his fondness for little girls. He happily took her call, then promised to bring immediate pressure to bear on the state prison to set up a face-to-face meeting with Manson that afternoon, in direct contradiction of the usual procedures. She had five hours to think of what she might say.

The correctional officers had to obey a strict regimen of preparations before they could escort any inmate confined in the B-3 (Recalcitrant Offender) Sectional Housing Unit. Inmate Number B33920 got no special treatment. However, owing to his notoriety, a third correctional officer was always sent along during any move to prevent possible attacks from other inmates. In his years at Corcoran, there had been four attempted attacks. In his twenty-two years with the California penal system, there had been more than sixty attempted attacks. The prison officials were proud that he was still alive under the circumstances, because they understood that even the most decrepit inmate in the system knew that he could make a name for himself within and beyond the walls if he became "the guy who killed Charles Manson."

The officer with most seniority drilled the other guards before they were even admitted to the SHU.

"Pierce-proof vest?"

"Check!" replied the two junior officers.

"PR-twenty-four at the ready?"

"Check." The two guards held out their batons.

"Pens, pencils, and other sharp objects removed from your own clothing?"

"Check."

"Pressurized aerosol cayenne charged, tested, ready?"

They tapped the containers of Mace-like spray that they carried on their belts. "Check."

"Gentlemen, let's go."

They took the shortcut across the prison yard before they arrived at prisoner block B-3. They passed the regular correctional officers stationed there, who exchanged greetings with them as they burrowed their way back into the deepest recesses of the most carefully guarded section of the highest-security penitentiary in the state. They aligned themselves across from his cell and the senior officer rapped on the door with his PR-24.

"Manson, Charles W. This is Officer Levant. We're ready to transport you." The prisoner sat with his back to the steel-mesh door of his cell, unresponsive. The only sound that came through was a series of odd beeps, clicks, and whirs.

"Manson!" Levant rapped louder on the door. "Let's get on it! We're moving you!"

The beeps and clicks were replaced by a slow crescendo and two sour musical notes. Then Manson's voice came through loud and clear. "Jeez, you guys, I was on the fifth level and you threw me off."

"Stand and show yourself."

He twisted his arms into strange, vaguely ritualistic shapes and slowly turned around, making eye contact with the officers one after the other. His grin was twisted and demonic.

"Drop the video game, prisoner."

Manson set the Nintendo Game Boy down on the stainless steel bunk.

"We're coming in. Drop your pants."

The officers had drawn lots earlier to see who would have to do the body search. The lucky winner slipped on a rubber glove and performed the search quickly, while looking away. After dressing him again, they fastened a hardened carbon steel band across his midsection. Chains went from there to his hands, and from his hands to his feet. Even if he escaped their escort, he wouldn't be going anywhere very fast.

"Who's our visitor today, boys?" asked Manson. "I hope it's one of your mothers, 'cause they keep sending me these nude photos of themselves."

"Knock it off, Manson."

"Oooh, touchy."

The guards ignored his rantings the rest of the short journey. Along the way every prisoner who saw the procession stopped what he was doing and took a few seconds to stare at the most feared man in America.

He was delivered to the attorney room, accompanied by two of the three officers. The third stood outside the room wielding a riot gun loaded with rubber bullets. Manson could either stand or sit on a metal bench. Bulletproof Plexiglas, three times thicker than that used in banks, separated the prisoner from his visitor. Although other prisoners tried to minimize the embarrassment of chains during attorney interviews by sitting still, Manson reveled in the equipment, often rattling them to emphasize a point.

He pressed his face against the glass and watched as Marilyn was led in. At once he recognized her.

"Hello, bitch."

Before she could even respond, a guard's voice came over the intercom. "The prisoner will please refrain from using profanity."

"Oh, sorry," said Manson, rolling his head around, looking for the source of the sound. "Hello, Mrs. Happy Face. Heard you had to dole out some favors to get this little visit."

On the visitor's side of the glass, Marilyn peered at his distorted features. "Hello, Charles. Long time no see."

"Why don't you just call me Satan like you did on that

stinkin' lyin' no-good TV show of yours? You want something from me, so may as well get to the point. Nobody ever comes to see me that don't want something. I gotta tell you about *my* rules. They're pretty simple—you screw with me, I screw with you. You hit me, I hit you back. You cut me, I cut you. That's the rules, man, and that's the way I survived forty years behind bars!"

Marilyn nodded. "Sure, Charles, I understand."

Manson lifted his left foot. The chains clinked noisily through the speaker system. Manson scowled at her. "Last year when your boss, Ray Garvey—let's call him by his real name—hit me with that pack of lies, I couldn't let it go unnoticed. It's payback time now. I seen all your lying ads. I know what you're tryin' to do. And I'm gonna getcha back this year."

"Charlie. What pack of lies are you talking about?"

"Oh, bull crap, honey—" He turned his head up and spoke to the unseen prison censor. "That wasn't profanity, not at all!" He turned back to Marilyn. "Bull crap, bull crap, bull crap. He's saying this time I'm getting out. Do you think that they're going to release *me?* They got the cards stacked against me ten ways to Sunday. I'm the only guy that was ever sentenced to death that didn't kill nobody. I got witnesses stacked a mile high who say I didn't hurt no one, but they won't let me use 'em. Who's Mr. Jew Ray Garvey to say I'm getting out?"

Marilyn nodded. "His name's James St. James, but that's okay. I don't mind what you call him. He truly believes that you're due to get out this time."

"And what fairy godmother is whispering in his ear?" asked Manson, poking out his tongue like a Maori warrior.

Marilyn pumped up the sincerity. "He agrees with you. He thinks you've paid your debt. He thinks it's high time you got out, and that's why he's doing this show."

"I know Mr. Jew Ray Garvey and I've seen what he did in the past. He's going to trot me out to scare all those mothers and fathers across America who know that their children love me better than they love them. He's going to put me up there and point at me and say *here!* This is the *bad guy!* This is the *evil man!*"

Marilyn shook her head. "Charles, that's just not the case.

James knows your case better than anyone. I can't pretend that last time we did a show he didn't try to make you look evil. But this time is *different*."

"Bull crap. It's payback time, and I don't want you making a TV show out of me."

Marilyn stared through the glass at Manson. She was in a hopeless position. But still she drew on the full complement of sales skills she had learned throughout the years. He was just another client. "Let's say you're right. Let's say we were unfair in the past. What is it you want? How can we make it up?"

Manson swept his head around, looking at every point in the room before responding. Marilyn could almost see the wheels and gears clicking. "A man in prison is used to being lied to in the morning, lied to at night, lied to by other prisoners, and lied to by people out in the world. I'm going to say that Mr. Jew Ray Garvey is a liar, too, and I don't have any reason to believe he's going to be true to his word. It's not what do I want, baby, not that at all. We got a saying, talk is cheap. It's what can you *do* to convince *me* that you're not lying scum! Prison house rules, baby, prison house rules." He raised his arms as high as they would go, about halfway up his chest, and shook the chains. His demeanor was taunting, unsettling.

Marilyn took a moment to consider her offer. In the back of her mind she realized the absurdity of trying to negotiate with Charles Manson. "Okay. What can we do for you? That's a fair question." She ambled on, trying to think of the magic charm that would make the deal work. "I know what will convince you. What if we have a tape of James St. James himself that you can use in your parole hearing? He'll speak on your behalf."

Manson stepped away from the glass for a moment and considered the notion. "What's he going to say that could convince anyone?"

"He can say anything you want. If you tell us what you want in the videotape, we'll get him to record it. I'm pretty sure he'd go along with that. And then you'll have your proof. No talk—proof."

"And what do you-all want out of the deal?"

"Just your cooperation. We just want permission to

broadcast your parole hearing. Nothing more. James St. James *cares* about you."

"You lay it on pretty thick, bitch." He yelled at the ceiling. "That's a kind of female dog, not a swear word!" He turned back to her. "I'll do it, baby, and only on one condition. I have to see the videotape here tomorrow. If he don't say every word of what I want him to say, no deal, no TV show. We got a deal?"

"We have a deal. Now, what do you want him to say?"

"Let me think. You got a tape recorder over there, right? Turn it on. This is what I want Mr. Jew Ray Garvey to say to the people of America."

Marilyn pushed record on her portable recorder and took down every word. Twenty minutes later she was out of the prison and on her way to the hotel. She called St. James at his personal number.

"Ray, I got the deal. Did you sign those contracts?"

"Yeah, I signed them. I sent them to your lawyer."

"Good. I got Manson to cooperate. There's only one condition."

"You what? You got the madman to bend to your will! You even astound me. You saved the goddamn show! What condition?"

"See, I told Manson that the reason you took out all those advertisements saying 'this time he might go free' is because you really believe it's true."

"So what if I do? So what if I don't?"

"Well, it matters to him. He said he would cooperate with us, but you have to say a few words on his behalf."

"On his behalf!" She heard the shoe-flying-hitting-something sound that was quickly becoming familiar. "If I get on the air and say Manson's innocent, there goes my credibility. There goes my audience!"

"Who said anything about 'on the air'?" asked Marilyn, with mischief in her voice.

"Yeah? I'm listening, I'm listening."

"We tape you saying whatever he wants. But it's not for broadcast. We make one copy of it. We show it to Manson to get him to cooperate. Then when the hearing comes, we just keep stalling and eventually say we forgot about it. He's the only one who's seen it. By that time it'll be too late. We'll have our show."

"You are the devil incarnate. That's why you're the tops! That's why you're getting a pilot! What's the little cretin want me to say?"

"That's a bit touchy. I'm going to play the tape over the phone. You've got to say it word for word. Those are his requirements. It's weird, so brace yourself."

She played the first forty seconds of Manson explaining what he wanted St. James to say. Marilyn heard another potted palm knocked over. He got back on the line. "Stop it! I can't say that!"

"Then you don't have a show."

"Christ!"

"It's all we've got."

"I'll do it. But if anyone except you, me, the cameraman, and Manson ever sees this tape . . ."

"Don't worry. I've got you covered. We'll have the only copy of the tape and we'll destroy it as soon as the show is over. There's no chance anyone will see it."

St. James knew it was risky, but he wanted that cute palace in Paris. This show had to go off without a hitch. Life without risks was not worth living. The show must go on.

23

FORTY-SIX MILES FROM CORCORAN, A PRIVATE ROAD JUTTED OFF the main highway. On either side of a wide gate, drivers were greeted with the following warning:

CAUTION: LOOSE GRAVEL NEXT SEVEN MILES
TULARE GRAVEL MINING COMPANY

There had once been a guard there, but corporate restructuring gutted the staff of Tulare Gravel. The station was now just an empty box, its green paint faded and peeling, its window cracked. The orange minivan drove unchallenged onto the quarry grounds.

The mining facilities regularly moved within the two-square-mile property. When a deposit became depleted, the mobile homes that served as offices were relocated to the next promising site. Mel Branch supervised the crew of fourteen that was working on the north end of the quarry, about half a mile from the main gate. His men shipped out one hundred fifty tons of gravel a day to a public road being built in Sequoia National Park. Branch and his newest crane operator, Carl Donnen, were discussing equipment purchases for the quarry when the orange van pulled up to the office, a cloud of white dust in its wake. The two working men wore jeans, flannel shirts, and gimme-caps. Branch had a potbelly from three years behind the desk, whereas Donnen was trim.

Branch had a thought who might be in the van, and grimaced at the thought of safety inspectors descending on his operation. He hurriedly gathered up the papers on his blotter, stuffed them in a drawer, and locked the desk. Then he reached behind him and turned off the radio, which had been playing nonstop country hits. Remembering the beer he'd had at lunch, Branch stuffed a piece of gum in his mouth.

The van idled in the driveway for several minutes before the side door slid open.

Donnen cracked a smile. "If it's OSHA, I'm in love."

"What the hell?" asked Branch.

Three beautiful young girls walked to the front door of the office and knocked. They all appeared to be sisters, with similar long brunette hair. The third was a slender beauty with short, blond hair. They all carried oversize women's purses.

"Come on in!" yelled Branch. Donnen ran to the door and opened it. The girls walked in.

"How can I help you?" asked Branch.

"Um, hi. I'm Peace, and these are my sisters Cleo and Silhouette."

"Nice to meetcha. I'm Mel Branch. This is Carl. As I said, how can I help you?"

"Um, we were just wondering if this is a real quarry."

Branch chuckled, slightly puzzled. "Yeah, sure is."

The girl leaned forward on Donnen's desk. He could smell flowers in her hair. She spoke in a soft, deliberate voice. "Um, we're doing a report? About quarries? And we wondered if we could ask you some questions."

"Sure. Don't see why not."

She continued. Branch hardly heard her. He was staring at her soft, white skin. "So how, um, do you get all the rock out of the ground?"

"Variety of ways. First off, we find a decent vein. We got a staff geologist who takes care of that. He's right more than he's wrong, but it's still a guessing game."

"Yes, but then how do you get it out?"

"This for school?"

"Um, yes. How do you get the rock out?"

"Crosscutter will work on certain gravel; if it's packed tight, we'll blast it out first. What kind of report is this?" he asked.

"College class," she said. "So you use dynamite?"

"Not dynamite, but same exact principal. They've got new blasting products just about every year, and we use the safest on the market."

"Blasting products? But I mean, do they blow up just like dynamite?"

"Just like dynamite."

Peace stepped away from his desk. She turned and made eye contact with her two companions. They withdrew guns from their purses. Branch knew his weapons: They each held a Heckler & Koch automatic rifle, guns that could cut off his head in an instant. Cleo covered Branch. Silhouette aimed at Donnen.

"Jesus God! What the hell is that?" yelled Branch.

Peace's manner abruptly changed. Far from the unsure student asking questions, she now shouted orders authoritatively. "Put your hands on the desk and leave them there!" She turned to Donnen. "Keep 'em where we can see 'em!"

"What do you want? We don't have no money out here!"

"We want your explosives."

"No problem! No problem!"

Donnen started to run for the door. Before he'd taken

three steps, Cleo cut him in half with a staccato burst from the automatic. He did not even have time to scream before he fell to the ground in a pool of blood. Cleo smiled sheepishly afterward, as if she had just burped. "Sorry. I was a little too quick?" she asked.

Peace shook her head. "Nah, sister, you did fine. The pig tried to run."

Tears started to well up in Branch's eyes and he wet his pants. "I have a kid and, um, two ex-wives." He pleaded, "I'll do whatever you want! Just be careful."

Peace shook a fist at him. "Listen, man, we don't give a damn for your kid or your ex-wives. We want your dyno. You don't dick with us, we don't dick with you."

"Okay. The HE is stored out at the worksite. It's about five hundred yards from here."

"Stand up," yelled Peace, reveling in her new role as leader. "Keep your hands where we can see them. Get up!"

Branch stood and walked toward the door. He dropped to his knees when he saw his co-worker. Donnen's right side twitched violently. The pool of blood around his body grew larger.

"Get moving, motherfucker!" yelled Cleo.

Branch ignored her and lifted his friend's head into his lap. "Carl, oh, God."

Donnen's eyes momentarily opened. "I'm hurtin', Mel."

On his knees, Branch turned to Peace. "Can't you get him a doctor? You can't just leave him dying."

Peace grabbed a gun from Cleo, shoved it into the dying man's face, and squeezed off three quick shots. They made wet *thud* sounds as the bullets penetrated Donnen's skull. She poked the gun into Branch's nostril. "There. He don't need a doctor anymore. Get off your knees. You look ridiculous."

Branch did as instructed. They marched him down a winding path through a thicket of trees to the area in the quarry where work was being done. As they grew closer, the whine of the gasoline-powered stone pulverizers grew to an overwhelming din. They came to a clearing where a small patch of level land hung at the edge of the ninety-foot-deep gravel pit. Four workmen were on break, eating out of metal lunch boxes. Two men operated a loader and were filling an eighteen-wheeler with gravel. Another man operated the massive pulverizer.

Peace yelled into Branch's ear. "Tell them to stop what they're doing and get us the explosive."

Branch waved at the pit foreman, Shane Parker. Branch caught Parker's eye, then made a cutting motion across his throat. Parker nodded, spoke into a walkie-talkie, and the machines slowly ground to a halt. The muscular black foreman walked forward, puzzled.

"What's going on, Branch?" asked Parker.

Branch looked left and right. Parker saw that the two girls had guns. "Oh. Jesus."

Cleo blurted out, "Oh Jesus is right!" then laughed to herself. Peace pointed a gun at the foreman. "Get everybody who's working on this site. I want every last one rounded up and put . . ." She surveyed the area. A large red crane stood on the side of the work area, on the very edge of the gravel pit, cables extending down into the deepest recesses of the hole. It had a large, air-conditioned cab that sat eight feet off the ground over the tanklike treads. "Put them into the cab of that machine. And lock it."

Parker shook his head, baffled. "Who are you?"

"What the fuck do you care who I am?"

Branch, now shaking with fear, spoke in a soft voice. "Parker, do what they say."

"Yeah, okay." Parker cupped his hands over his mouth. "Lance—get your crew and get over here. *Now!*" The men put down their sandwiches and slowly walked over to join the group. Parker pulled his walkie-talkie from his belt and lifted it up to his mouth.

Cleo knocked it out of his hand with the butt of a gun. "You're calling the cops, aren't you? Isn't that what you were going to do?"

"No, I was calling the water truck crew. They're down in the pit. You said everybody was to come up here."

"You better not be lying."

Parker leaned over to pick up the walkie-talkie. Cleo kicked him in the rear side, knocking him to the ground.

He called the water crew while the girls looked on, skeptical. A few tense minutes later, the bright green truck drove up and parked. Three men got out of the truck and joined the group of workers standing in the center of the work area.

"All of you!" yelled Peace. "Into the cab. Let's move!"

Nine of the men were forced to climb over the tractor treads and squeeze themselves into the tiny operating cabin of the crane. There was barely room to breathe. Branch and Parker started to follow their workers into the cab, but Peace pulled them to the side. Parker began to ask why, but was abruptly cut off by Peace. "Where's the explosive?"

The men remained silent.

"Now you can talk," she said.

Branch explained. "It's at the far end of the worksite. We keep it down there for safety reasons."

"Is it locked?"

"Yes, it is."

"And who has the key?"

Parker stepped forward. "I do."

She turned to her companions. "Cleo, Silhouette—which of you wants to stay and guard this collection of rockheads back here?"

"I'll do it," said Silhouette.

Peace bit her lip. "What would you do if they ran?"

"I'd shoot 'em."

"You wouldn't have the nerve."

"Yes I would! J'osüf taught me how," said Silhouette.

"Nah, you'd wimp out!" yelled Peace.

"The hell. Which of these guys has the keys?"

"The black guy."

"Then we don't need the white one. Watch this." She trained the gun on Branch. For several seconds she stood there, scared. Peace smirked. Embarrassed, Silhouette exhaled, then unloaded twenty-five bullets into Branch, blowing him backwards across the gravel lot. Parker screamed.

"Very special," said Peace. "Okay, you guard the truck."

"No problem."

Silhouette stood at the base of the crane, pointing the gun at the cabin.

Cleo and Peace kept a gun trained on Parker, who led them to a metal locker standing by itself in the middle of a flat, paved area fifty yards from the worksite.

"Open it," said Peace.

"Yes, ma'am." Parker pulled a key from around his neck and opened one of the nine separate compartments.

"Open them all."

"You can only open one at a time. It's so that any accidental explosion might be contained."

"Take out the explosive and put it on the ground."

Parker did as asked.

"Now open the next one."

He did as instructed. One after another, he opened the two-foot-square steel lockers, extracted a small bundle of paper-wrapped explosive, and gently set it on the ground. Each bundle was about twice as big as a shoe box. The last locker contained a wooden box, divided up into slots much like a box of wine bottles might be. Parker was especially careful setting it on the ground.

"That's all of it," said Parker. "Eight packets, each with twelve charges. The wooden box is caps. You gotta be damn careful with those."

"How good is it?" asked Cleo.

"What do you mean?"

"What can you blow up with this? You have to show us how to use it."

"Girls, you don't know what you're getting into. You ought to leave this shit and get out of here, and we'll forget we ever met."

"Fuck you," Peace said, and knocked him in the face with the butt of the gun. He fell to the ground, his forehead spouting blood.

Peace kicked him. "We wanna see how it works. Let's blow something up."

He stood up, slowly. "All right. Whatever." He unwrapped one of the paper bundles and extracted a fluorescent green stick about the size of a candle. "Hold this. This is HE Fifty-four." He handed it to Cleo.

"You mean dynamite?"

"It's like dynamite, yes. Be careful with it."

He opened the wooden box and pulled out a small piece of circular metal, about the size of a sink stopper, with two small wires hanging off its end.

"This is a blasting cap," he said. "You gotta be especially careful with this."

"Put it back in the box and we're gonna carry the whole box out," said Peace. "Do it! Cleo, give me the gun." Her sister handed over the weapon. "Now, get as much of that dynamite as you can carry."

Cleo stuck two bundles of explosive under each arm.

"Get more than that! We're gonna need as much as we can get!"

Cleo then lifted the hem of her dress and filled it with the deadly packages. The skirt stretched out of shape.

Parker stepped back away from her. "Be careful! That stuff ain't sticks of candy!"

Cleo stared him in the eye. "I'm not afraid of death. My time will come when my time comes. I won't drop anything."

Peace waved the gun. "All right, then. Let's blow something up."

They walked back to the work area. Silhouette paced back and forth in front of the crane, pointing her gun at the cab. The men inside stared out, helpless. Peace surveyed the area and pointed at a Johnny-on-the-Spot toilet.

"Blow that up."

"It'll blow plastic all over the place."

"I don't care. Blow that up!" she commanded.

"If I show you how to do this, you have to promise not to hurt any of my men."

"Maybe we will, maybe we won't."

"I want a promise from you that nothing will happen to my men!" yelled Parker. "Else, just kill me now. I won't show you a thing. You can blow yourselves up for all I care."

Peace smirked. "Isn't that cute? The noble boss watching out for his pig-workers. Forget it. I'm not making any promises."

"Then you don't learn how to use this."

Silhouette, fifty feet away across the lot, yelled over to her comrades. "What's the fucking holdup? Why can't we just get the dynamite and be on our way?"

Peace yelled back across to her. "Pig won't tell us how to use it."

"Get a move on before someone else comes!"

"I'm working on it!" yelled Peace.

"Okay, I won't hurt your men."

Parker eyed her warily. "How do I know you're sincere?"

"You don't. But if you don't help me now, I'll just kill them all right now." She yelled across to Silhouette. "Fire into the fucking crane!"

"Right now?" yelled Silhouette.

"Yeah!" replied Peace.

Parker held up his hands. "Don't do that! I'll show you."

Peace yelled to Silhouette. "Forget it! He's gonna help us! Don't fire on the pigs!"

Parker walked into the work shed and emerged carrying a bright red box. "This is a detonator," he said, softly.

"Yeah? You didn't say anything about that!" said Peace. "I thought we could use matches!"

"No, you can't."

He rolled out a coil of wire extending from the shed to the outhouse. "What's that?" demanded Peace.

"Just wire. We use special HE wire, but any kind of electrical wire will do, pretty much, fifteen amps or better."

"What's that mean?"

Parker was flustered. "It's an electrical term! I told you I'd show you how to do this! Just listen to me."

He buried one of the green sticks beneath the portable toilet and left one end sticking out. "It's going to stink like hell."

"We want to do it," said Peace.

He tore off an inch of paper from one end of the H-E 54 and twisted on the blasting cap. He touched the two ends of the long wire to his tongue, then fastened one lead to each of the terminals. "Pay attention. Secure the H-E. Attach the cap. After making sure there's no current in the wire, attach the wire to the cap. Got it?"

Peace nodded. "Yeah, I got it."

"Follow me. We wanna be in the shed when this blows," said Parker. The gash in his forehead continued to bleed, covering the left side of his face with blood. His hands shook.

Peace and Cleo followed him into the shed. He dragged the wire and the bright red detonator box inside.

"Make sure the detonator is set on 'Safe.' Now you fasten the opposite end of the wire to the detonator." He cut off the cord, stripped off about an inch of insulation on each of the wires, and hooked them to terminals on the red box. "Put the key in and turn it to 'Test.' The needle on the back side of the detonator should peg into the green, indicating the battery has enough juice." He pulled a key off of his belt and fastened it into the box, then turned it one notch to the right. The needle pegged. "Then turn the key the other way and lock it into 'Ready' position." He turned the key to the left. A red light lit atop the box.

He turned to the girls. "Are you sure you want to do this?" he asked.

Peace pointed the gun at his head.

He reached toward the box. Peace hit his hand with the barrel of the gun. "I wanna push the button."

"Go ahead," he said, putting his fingers in his ears and ducking down.

She pushed a switch atop the box marked "Fire." A moment later a resounding roar shook the shed. Bits and pieces of plastic and human waste rained down over the entire area for thirty or forty seconds. When it ceased, they ran outside, excited, and ran over to where the outhouse once stood, marching Parker in front of them. All that remained was a twisted pile of melted plastic and steel in a five-foot pit.

"Neat!" yelled Cleo.

"We blew something up!" yelled Peace.

They heard a cry from across the lot. Silhouette was lying on the ground.

The two girls ran to her side, keeping Parker in front of them. Scratches covered her right arm, and the right side of her face was bleeding. "I'm hurt," she said. Cleo helped her to her feet. Her injuries were minor, but the sheer quantity of them made her appear worse off than she really was.

"You okay?" asked Peace. "Can you walk around?"

"I guess so," said Silhouette.

Parker stood to one side. "I told you it could be dangerous," he said. He started walking toward Silhouette's gun, which lay in the dirt a few feet away.

"You asshole!" yelled Peace. "You hurt her on purpose!" She squeezed on the trigger of the gun and sent a hail of bullets ripping through his chest, then stood over him and put a final shot through his head. "You meant to do that! You motherfucking goddamn pig."

Silhouette was visibly spooked by the goings-on and the shock of the explosion. "Let's get our dynamite and get out of here!"

Peace pointed to the crane with her gun. "What about them? They'll point us out to anybody who asks, and then we're doubly screwed."

Cleo spoke up. "Why don't we blow them up?"

Peace smiled. "Good. Do it."

As the men looked on helplessly from the cabin of the crane, Cleo put down her gun and went through the steps that Parker had showed her. She unwrapped one of the sticks of HE, stuck it under one of the treads of the crane, twisted in a blasting cap, and ran wire back to the shed.

When the men in the cab saw what was about to happen, they began screaming and clawing at the windows. Cleo, Peace, and Silhouette hid in the shed and began attaching wires to the detonator. They heard a cracking sound and looked outside; one of the men had punched through the window of the crane and was starting to climb down. Peace picked up the Heckler & Koch and mowed him down. He fell off of the crane. He was followed by another worker.

"Get a move on!" yelled Peace. "They're getting away!"

Cleo twisted the wires and turned the key. They looked outside. The men were scurrying out of the cabin and climbing down the side of the crane. Peace hit the button atop the detonator. A great rush of air and dirt flew into the shed over their heads. They kept their hands over their heads for several seconds, then peered up and looked out. A secondary explosion rumbled through the cabin as the fuel in the massive crane ignited, and a blast of heat knocked them back down.

The crane heaved to the right, skidding clockwise on its skids. One end hung over the precipice, dangling over the hundred-foot drop. Abruptly a mammoth boulder beneath the exposed skid gave way, and the colossal machine oscillated back and forth, teetering like an oversize rocking horse.

Silhouette opened her eyes and watched. "Look! Cool!"

The three girls watched as the mammoth crane lurched first to one side, then to the other, then gave way and slipped down into the deep gravel pit. They ran to the edge of the hole and saw the machine roll end over end down the rocky wall until it finally crashed to a stop almost a hundred feet below. It ignited and was immediately consumed by flames.

On the ground in the work area, the two men who had managed to escape from the crane before it blew lay still. One had been decapitated, the other lay bleeding to death. Peace put a few bullets into the second one until he stopped twitching.

"Let's get the dyno and go. Don't forget the detonator!" yelled Peace.

Cleo and Silhouette piled the explosives into their skirts. Peace carried the box of blasting caps and the detonator.

Exhilarated at their newly discovered power, they sang to themselves as they walked back to the van. They piled the explosive into the back of the van and pulled out.

"It was pretty cool when that crane blew up! I mean, kah-boom!" said Cleo.

"Yeah!" said Peace, who then gave a rebel cheer. "Yah-hooo! I just want to blow something else up! J'osüf will be so proud."

Just before they got off the dirt road and hit the main stretch of highway, Peace stopped the van.

"High five!"

They slapped hands and drove home, triumphant.

24

TRUMBO'S FIRST ORDER OF BUSINESS WAS TO FILL UP THE TANK OF the Mazda without being recognized. If he was lucky, he might have twenty or thirty miles worth of gas left in the tank, or he could run out at any time, in which case he'd be stuck and very likely busted. There weren't a lot of places to hide in the rural area, especially so near a prison.

He headed north on the service road parallel to the highway for about fifteen miles, driving slowly to conserve gasoline and to keep from drawing attention to himself. He came to a highway exit with three gas stations. There was a Texaco, a Shell, and an independent gas station. He selected the third, suspecting that the chain stores would be more likely to hear about the murders farther down the freeway. He pulled in the back, parking at a pump not visible from the cashier's booth. *Just act like everything's okay,* he thought. He shoved a twenty through the booth and walked to the car. While he was filling up, two cars pulled up to the other pumps, a family station wagon and a black Ford. *Don't panic,* he thought, *don't panic.* After topping off the tank, he'd only used thirteen dollars and eighty-eight cents worth of gas. He got in the car and started to pull out. As he was driving across the lot, a man in a fishing cap ran after him and pounded on his trunk, yelling something at him. He stopped the car, but was prepared to speed out in a split second. He revved the engine and kept his foot on the gas as the man walked slowly around the car and approached the driver's-side window.

"Yes?" asked Trumbo, trembling.

"You forgot to get your change, son. Guy in the booth asked me to tell you so."

"Right." Suspicious, he stopped the car and walked over to the booth to recover his change. The man in the fishing hat walked with him.

"Son, you look pretty worn-out. Ought to give it a rest for a while, get off the road."

"Sounds like a good idea," said Trumbo.

"You could get hurt out there. Where ya going?"

"Just to visit some relatives."

"Right. Take care."

When Trumbo got back into the car, he caught his reflection in the rearview mirror and saw that he appeared completely strung out. His crudely cut hair was greasy and matted. His face and hands were smudged, and his clothes were smeared with dirt. If he was trying to be inconspicuous, it wasn't working. He got back on the highway and drove another twenty miles until he came to a roadside rest stop, an acre of grass with bathrooms, picnic tables, a phone, and a kiosk featuring scenic spots of California. Several other cars were parked there, along with a couple of eighteen-wheelers. At the far end of the parking lot was a "roach coach," a mobile grill that sold hamburgers, candy, and coffee. No cops.

He didn't have a clue about where to sleep. If he slept in the rest stop, surely a Highway Patrol car would recognize him sooner or later. He walked to a pay phone and called his lawyer at home. It rang several times before an answering machine picked it up.

"Clemenson, this is Trumbo Walsh. I'm in trouble. Pick up the phone if you're there."

A shrill shriek was followed by Clemenson's calm voice. "Trumbo. I was wondering what happened to you."

"Look, man, I can't talk long."

"Don't talk to me here. I suspect my phone is bugged. I've been defending some very hot, eh, political cases. Let me give you a number. Call me there in ten minutes."

Clemenson gave him a number, then hung up.

"Son of a bitch!" yelled Trumbo. He had no more change. He ambled down to the roach coach. A young Hispanic man stood in the window, next to a sign listing prices for various kinds of hot dogs and hamburgers.

"Can I get some change for the phone?" asked Trumbo.

"No, man, no change. That's the policy," replied the kid.

"Look, it's a real emergency. I've got to make a long-distance phone call."

"Sorry!" said the kid.

Trumbo then picked up a packet of cheese crackers. "How much?" he asked.

"Fifty-five cents."

Trumbo threw a dollar on the counter and got forty-five cents back.

"I'll take another."

He paid with another dollar. He continued buying items costing slightly less than a dollar—a candy bar, a Coke, a pack of gum—until finally the kid behind the counter gave up.

"Okay, man, it's really an emergency. How much change do you want?"

"Can I get about five bucks' worth of quarters?"

"It comes in ten-dollar rolls. That okay?"

"Sure." He laid a ten spot on the counter, and the kid gave him the roll of quarters. Then he went back to the pay phone and dialed the number Clemenson had given him. It rang forty or fifty times before Clemenson answered, out of breath.

"Trumbo?"

"Yeah."

"What's the haps?" The lawyer tried to sound hip beyond his years. "Staying away from that Alison character?"

"No, man. I'm trying to find her."

"You know what I told you!"

"I know what you told me. That's the least of my troubles. I hooked up with Barbara Thompson."

"The escapee?"

"Yeah."

"Goddamn. What's going on?"

"I'm going to turn myself in in a couple of days. Until then I have to stay out. Something big is going down. Alison's hooked up with these people who are going to try and break someone out of prison."

"Is Thompson looking for these same people?"

"Thompson ditched me, but not before robbing a gas station. You'll probably see it on the morning news. I was there, but I wasn't involved."

There was a long silence, followed by a worried sigh from the lawyer. "Do you know who Thompson is? Just who are they going to break from prison? Manson?"

"Yeah. How'd you know?"

"It just fits. Look, man, you've got to turn yourself in right now. Go to the nearest police station and tell them what you've told me."

"Forget it!" yelled Trumbo. "I've got to find Alison first."

"Listen, man, if you get busted, you'll be in very deep shit. Even a sharp lawyer—which I humbly admit I am—won't be able to help you then. What do you plan to do?"

"Lay low, look for her. I haven't slept in days."

"Where are you now?"

"At a highway rest stop."

"That's the first place they look for fugitives. After we talk you've got to get out of there, fast. What part of the world are you calling me from?"

"Kern County. Near Corcoran."

"Manson country."

"Yeah."

"Shit. The good news is that they probably aren't looking for you yet. Listen to me. I've advised drug dealers on the run, political fugitives, immigrants, refugees. I see how they get picked up. Do not, I repeat, do not try to check into a motel. Do not go to any more highway rest stops. Stay off the highway—they're the most heavily patrolled area in California. They run a license plate check on you and your goose is cooked."

"So what do I do?"

"Shit, I don't know. You say you're near Corcoran?"

"Yeah."

"Hold on a sec. I'm looking in my daybook. There's a guy up near there who owes me a favor. He was busted a while back for growing pot, looked like he was going to be sent up for twenty years. I found some irregularities in the arrest—civil rights case, you know, so I took it. He lives around there someplace. Just a sec—here it is. Marcus Hugo. Botica, California. It's about ten or twenty miles from Corcoran."

"What?" asked Trumbo, trying desperately to keep up with the lawyer's rapid-fire patter.

"Not as your lawyer, but off the record, as a friend, I'm telling you that if you're goddamned stubbornly determined to stay a fugitive, I know a pad where you can cool your heels. Dig?"

Trumbo chuckled at the neo-sixties lingo. "Dig? Yeah, I *dig.* You serious? Is this guy *cool?*"

"As a matter of fact, he's a jerk, but he owes me a favor. If it weren't for me, he'd be in prison by now. I'll give you his phone number. Call him in fifteen or twenty minutes; I'll talk to him first. Make sure to get the hell out of that rest stop. And if anyone asks—you never talked to me."

"Real 'Mission Impossible' stuff, huh?"

"No, it's just that I've given you the kind of advice that could get me disbarred. I trust you, though. Take care, and good luck. Whatever you do, do not call me at my home number. Every day around noon and again at six I'll be at this pay phone. Call me here instead."

"All right. Thanks, man. I owe you one."

"And I'll collect on the favor, Mr. Walsh," said Clemenson, with a chuckle. "I always do."

The line went dead and Trumbo found himself, once again, completely alone. He shivered violently, from cold and from lack of sleep, then got back into his car and drove aimlessly, killing time until he could call Hugo. The broad outlines of distant farmhouses and the red, flat farmlands glowed in the gray predawn light.

He found a pay phone outside a closed bowling alley and made the call. Hugo's voice was kind, though he didn't say much beyond giving directions to his home. A half hour later Trumbo arrived at the ranch-style suburban tract home at the back of a lower-middle-class suburb. Trumbo parked in the driveway and walked to the front door, wondering what to expect.

Before Trumbo pushed the bell, the door opened and a gaunt, pasty-looking man in his late thirties, wrapped in a flannel bathrobe, waved him in. Marcus Hugo had a pencil-thin mustache over a narrow upper lip which was working its way into a smile. Although he was bald on top, what little hair he had was long and tied behind his neck in a ponytail.

"You're Rhumba?" said Hugo.

"Trumbo. Trumbo Walsh."

"Marcus Hugo. Damn glad to meet you. Any friend of Clemenson's is a friend of mine, you know how it is. Before you come in, why don't you move that car into the garage? If they're looking for you, it's better to keep it out of sight, right?"

"Yeah, I guess," said Trumbo.

"I'll open the garage."

After Trumbo pulled the car into the cluttered garage, Hugo welcomed him into his home. It had the feeling of a bachelor pad: The furniture was the type provided by "rent to own" companies. Fast-food wrappers were heaped on a glass coffee table, and a healthy stack of empty Pabst beer cans were collected in a bucket at the end of the couch. A big-screen television dominated one end of the room.

Trumbo took a seat on the couch, and Hugo stood next to him.

"Clemenson said you were in trouble," said Hugo.

"Yeah. Thanks for taking me in."

"No problem, man. What kind of trouble?"

"It's better for both of us if you don't know."

"Okay." Hugo flashed his warm smile. Trumbo was beginning to like the guy. Once you got past his sleazy looks, he seemed closer to the Rotary Club type than the stereotypical drug dealer.

"You can stay as long as you want, Rumbo. Make yourself at home. Can I make you something? An omelette maybe?"

"You serious? I can do it."

"Nah. I don't get much company."

Trumbo started to stand.

"No, no no no. Stay seated. I'll do it for you. If you want to take a shower, have a beer, that's fine, whatever. But *I'll* do the cooking. You relax."

"Thanks." Trumbo leaned back on the couch, a bit uneasy. Something about Hugo did not quite add up, but he was too tired to protest and had nowhere else to go. Hugo brought him the omelette on a TV tray and engaged him in a brief conversation about Amway products, then showed him to his room. Unlike the rest of the house, the guest room was spotlessly neat, and Trumbo quickly fell asleep on the king-sized bed with unbelievably clean sheets. Nonetheless, he parked his wallet and the clip from the pistol underneath his pillow, just in case.

He was awakened at four in the afternoon by the high-pitched whine of the television. He pulled on his pants and wandered into the living room. James St. James's "Exposé!" television show was playing on the big-screen TV. St. James delivered a monologue about the upcoming parole hearing for Charles Manson, his voice ominous, his eyes unblinking. Trumbo watched from the hallway for a few minutes. Hugo sat inches from the television and took notes. He did not notice when Trumbo entered the room. Trumbo tiptoed back to the bedroom, put the clip into the handgun and stuffed it into his pants, then made a great deal of noise walking into the living room. Hugo spun around, caught Trumbo's eye, and waved. He folded the spiral notebook he had and pushed it under the television, then turned off the set.

"Sorry, I didn't mean to wake you up," said Hugo.

"It's okay. I should get up soon anyway. I have stuff to do. What are you watching?"

Hugo visibly twitched. "Oh, you know, just some afternoon TV garbage."

"James St. James?" asked Trumbo.

"Yeah, I guess. 'Exposé!' it's called. I've been looking forward to today's episode all week."

"How come?"

"'Cause our most famous local resident is on."

Trumbo played naive. "Who's that?"

"Manson! He's over at Corcoran State Pen, not far from here. Lots of my neighbors are screws."

"So it's just a sporting interest?" asked Trumbo.

"Pretty much. I'll put it back on if you want to see."

"Sure."

Trumbo was fascinated. Part of a three-part lead-in to the Thursday parole hearing coverage, today's episode was "Should Manson Be Paroled? You be the Parole Board." Filmed clips recounted the history of Charles Manson and his followers, including Trumbo's mother.

Much of the information was completely new to Trumbo.

Manson and his followers had murdered eight people in their homes in the summer of 1969. They lived an outlaw lifestyle, stealing food, taking drugs, and participating in orgies. They believed that a great race war was about to occur, and found prophecy in Beatles records. Trumbo could hardly believe what he heard, and suspected that St. James was exaggerating many details. Especially unconvincing to Trumbo was the part about the Beatles, whom he always thought of as Paul McCartney's old backup band. Who could possibly mistake the guy who wrote "Band on the Run" and "Ebony and Ivory" for some kind of prophet?

Trumbo was only half paying attention to the content of the show. He was mostly looking in the background of shots to see if his mother or father were visible in any of the footage. For most of the show, he watched in vain—she never appeared. But then at the very end of the program, St. James began making a pitch for the next day's installment in what he was calling "Manson Week." Trumbo sat bolt upright when he heard.

It started with a picture of the Family—the very same photograph that he'd found in the Pasadena Library. St. James spoke in hushed, ominous tones. "Tomorrow on 'Exposé!' we see what happened to some of the other Manson Family members." The television zoomed in on his mother's face until the grainy photo filled the screen. "We'll be leading the search for Barbara 'Black Magick Mimi' Thompson, who tried to murder a Supreme Court justice, and who escaped from a California prison last week. Where is she now? Could she be waiting for Manson to come out? To find out, tune in tomorrow for 'Exposé!' Good day. I'm . . . James St. James."

The closing credits started to roll. Hugo chuckled. "That's a pretty good show. I mean, *bad* good, y'know? Like bowling alleys?"

Trumbo sat in dumbfounded silence.

"Hey, what is it, man?" asked Hugo.

"I only wish I could tell you, man."

"Ma-an, I've had my run-ins with the law. Don't know what Clemenson told you, but I used to deal big-time. I got busted big-time. If they track you down, it's gonna be a lot harder to explain what happened than if you go to them now."

"That's what Clemenson said. Maybe I'll turn myself in. I don't know for sure. But I have to find a girl first. I think she's around here near Corcoran somewhere. That's why I came up."

"I'm not much help to you. I don't know anybody around here," said Hugo.

"I have some ideas where to look."

Hugo folded his arms defensively. "I'm on parole. If you get busted and I'm with you, they can send me up just for the parole violation. I'd go with you, but—"

"No, it's okay. It's enough just having a place to stay."

Hugo frowned. "No prob. Can't I do something else for you? You want to use my car? Your car is definitely on the cop hot sheet. Use my Toyota truck. It's ten years old, but it's at least street-legal." As an afterthought he added, "And the insurance is paid up."

Trumbo laughed. "Thanks, but won't you get in just as much trouble as I do if I get arrested using your car?"

"I didn't consider that, but I hope not! You'll at least have a fighting chance in my car."

Trumbo smiled. "Thanks, Hugo."

"No problem."

Trumbo took a quick shower, ate a frozen pizza that Hugo insisted on cooking for him, and hit the streets at dusk. He started looking for Alison in the downtown part of Corcoran simply because he had to start somewhere.

25

FROM THE TINY, HOT STOCKADE, ALISON WATCHED THE LAST RAYS of sun disappear like lost hope through the van's shaded windows. This marked the end of her third day of captivity. Today was her best friend's birthday. It was also Monday, the one day a week her shop was closed back in Ohio, seemingly a million miles away. She wondered how her shop was doing without her.

Her existence had become monotonously routine. During the heat of the day, she slept. Once in the morning and once in the evening she was taken out at gunpoint so that she could relieve herself in the Porta Potti adjacent to the van. When evening broke, she was allowed to wash up from a bucket filled with cold water. Sometime in the evening J'osüf Sunn would come in to talk with her. Usually at night Denise would smuggle in stale Pop-Tarts and water, the only food Denise could get her hands on.

The previous evening she had taken Denise's advice and played along with Sunn. He spoke at length about "Day One" and the "new revolution" and how he and his girls were part of an avant-garde political-musical-cultural-art-everything else movement. Alison smiled politely and encouraged him to elaborate his theories. Immediately afterwards she was given her first batch of "official" food: some raw vegetables, cold mashed potatoes, and the most welcome of all, half a bottle of cranberry juice.

Just after dark she heard the latches come off of the van, and the cabin light was flipped on. Sunn smiled and leaned over the rear seat of the van.

"How ya doing?" he asked.

"Bad. I feel kind of dizzy. I need to go to the bathroom, and I'm hungry."

"Sure. Let me arrange for one of the girls to take you out. I'll get you some food. How do boiled potatoes sound?"

"I'll take anything."

Sunn clapped his hands twice and Silhouette entered the van. Under Sunn's watchful eye, the chains fastening Alison were released. Silhouette let her wash up thoroughly, providing two buckets of water, one warm, one cold. She offered her a change of clothing, which, after some hesitation, Alison refused. She had to retain some semblance of her former self.

Back in the van, Sunn let her eat unchained. He took the opportunity to fill her in on his plans.

"Alison, you know you're a very special girl, don't you?"

She resisted her first impulse, which was to retort sarcastically, *What are you, Mr. Rogers?* and instead simply nodded politely. "Yes, I know I'm special."

"I mean, really special. I haven't told you everything you need to know. We had to gather you for your own good." Sunn continued, "At first I thought you weren't going to make it. Sometimes the people with the most power don't know how to recognize it and have to be dealt with."

"Dealt with?" She gulped down a mouthful of potatoes.

Sunn spoke calmly, like a country lawyer. "It's like an old sick dog. You know what they say, he's no good to himself. I began to fear that years of living in the world of consensus reality might have spoiled you for good. But you still have the light within."

She bit her tongue and agreed. "Yes, I know exactly what you mean."

He clapped his hands together. "Good! It's not long until the big day."

Sunn smiled brightly. "You're going to work out great!

Once you understand how things really are, you'll be truly free. Thanks, Alison." He kissed her on the neck, a wet one. She tried to hide her repulsion. He winked at her and left the van. She began crying.

Sunn strutted around, gathering his brood from their hideouts. Denise lay on her back staring up at the night sky. Silhouette and sisters Peace and Cleo were in the mobile home. Others rested in the lean-to next to the mobile home. He clapped his hands and called out to each of them by name, sounding like a camp counselor: "Let's go, put a move on it, we're going on a little field trip! Get it together, girls, and bring a sweater, 'cause it's gonna be cold tonight!"

He herded all of them—except Denise—into the back of Adelaide Naomi's ancient pickup. Denise asked why she had to stay behind.

"You've got to keep a watch on Alison Wonderland."

Denise kicked her feet in the dirt. "I never get to go anywhere! You've left me behind twice before!"

"This time I'm going to give you a gun. Does that make it better?"

"No! I want to go somewhere. I'm so bored, you can't even believe it."

"Diva—trust me. You don't want to come. Look. I'll give you my handgun. Here." He pressed a revolver into her hand. It was heavier than it looked. "Keep an eye on her. We'll bring you back something good."

Denise relented. "Okay. But if you don't bring me something, I'll be pissed."

Sunn lifted her off the ground and gave her a big, grandfatherly hug. "Bet on it. And if we don't, send me right back out and I'll get you whatever you want. Deal?"

"Deal." Denise shook hands with him.

"Now, run along to the van, okay?"

"Okay."

The girl took off.

Sunn went to the mobile home and yelled into it. "Magick Mimi? Where are you, love?"

The middle-aged woman leaned out of the mobile home's bathroom. "What is it?"

"We're going to secure some funds. I found a place in Bakersfield that will finance our efforts richly. I want you to come along and set an example for the girls."

"Sure."

The woman emerged from the bathroom and walked with Sunn to the truck. Mimi, almost the same age as Sunn, was the only person who didn't constantly show deference to him. The girls were fascinated with her. They speculated wildly about her special treatment. While they hung on Sunn's every word, Mimi Black took a comfortable seat inside the truck and completely ignored him. She chatted comfortably with Adelaide Naomi. They seemed to have a lot of catching up to do.

"Tonight there's a techno rave in Bakersfield, fifty miles from here. Adelaide investigated this one for us last week and reports that even though it's in a small town, it rivals some of the big L.A. raves. We will relieve them of some of their ticket money."

Sunn hopped onto the truck bed. The girls instinctively moved out of his way as he walked toward the front of the truck. He stopped upon reaching a built-in toolbox just behind the cab, reached into his pocket, produced a key, and removed a padlock from the box. By now the girls stood in the truck's back, curiously watching over his shoulder as he lifted the top of the box.

The fading sunlight reflected off of a variety of handguns and shotguns. Sunn pulled them out one by one, selecting a weapon for each girl.

"Peace—take this sawed-off twelve-gauge." The seventeen-year-old accepted the weapon with awe. She immediately held it up and gazed down the barrel.

"Goddamn it, don't point it at me," said Sunn. "Keep it pointed down!"

"Sorry," she giggled.

"When you get your tool, wait on the ground, okay?"

"Sure."

Peace hopped down out of the truck.

"Cleopatra—this is a Walther P-38."

"Thanks."

He handed out the rest of the weapons to his eager

followers: another shotgun, two Smith & Wesson .38s, and a Colt .45. For himself he selected the only automatic of the bunch, a Chinese-made faux Uzi. He hopped from the truck. Magick Mimi and Adelaide Naomi compared their own weapons as if discussing hand lotion.

"Come on." He led them to a flat area in front of the pickup truck, illuminated by its headlights.

"Listen up. First, don't ever point these things at each other. Understood?"

The girls all nodded.

"What we have to do tonight requires some precision, some concentration, and most of all, the good grace of your hard work. The rave ticket point is a small record shop in Bakersfield. Watch this."

He dragged his foot across the ground, drawing a twenty-foot line perpendicular to the truck. "This is the front of the record shop, right?" He led them in a collective visualization of the strip mall, rendered in the medium of dirt and imagination. "Next door is a sewing machine repair shop, and on the other side is a T-shirt shop. We expect that there will be two or possibly three armed guards. All we have besides the will of Jesus is surprise. That's why we're going to practice here until we can all learn how to put ourselves in place, guns concealed, until the moment the shit goes down. We'll start with Silhouette . . ."

26

THE TOYOTA TRUCK HAD ITS SHARE OF PECULIARITIES—LOOSE clutch, squeaky brakes, a tendency to idle too fast—but Trumbo was happy to be rid of what the radio reporters called the "cop-killer car" seen at the gas station. Just after dark he drove into Corcoran, then slowly worked his way into the rural area where he had dropped off Barbara, hoping to find Alison.

An hour investigating dozens of tiny country roads netted him only frustration. He found fields of soybeans, lettuce, and alfalfa, punctuated by the occasional fruit orchard; whenever he saw a farmhouse or ranch home, he slowly drove by, looking for any sign that it might be the right place. He only wished he could approach the houses one by one and see who lived in them, but he was a wanted man. He knew from a brief childhood stay in rural Iowa that farmers were suspicious of unannounced visitors, and he couldn't run that risk.

A tension headache was beginning to throb in his temples, so he decided to take a break and drive into town for something to eat. He exhaled deeply and massaged his neck, then turned on the radio to an oldies station. As soon as he relaxed for a moment he noticed something he had been looking at without really seeing for the entire evening. Stapled on every second or third telephone pole was a large poster with phosphorescent paint that reflected directly into his headlights. He passed several of the bills. Each featured reflective high-tech letters in a font reminiscent of computer bank symbols on the bottom of a check. They spelled CVR. His first half-conscious thought was that the signs must be related somehow to work the phone company was undertaking, but then curiosity got the best of him and he stopped to read one.

His headlights illuminated the frenetic, densely designed poster, and he realized at once that it was an advertisement for an underground party. His hunger vanished and he drove to a pay phone and listened to the recorded advertisement for the party. It was occurring tonight and tickets could be purchased at a record store in Bakersfield. An address and directions to get to the ticket point were given.

He encountered no traffic until he got within a block of the store, when suddenly it came to a standstill on the two-lane street. As he proceeded slowly through the traffic jam, he saw the eerie blue and red streaks of light reflecting off of a building ahead.

When he reached the corner he looked to the left and saw the sign for Inner Ear Records; yellow tape marked POLICE LINE: DO NOT CROSS crisscrossed the window. Four cruisers were in the parking lot, and three more on the street. *Busted the rave early, I guess,* he thought.

As he turned the corner, he saw that police were stopping every car, and two cops shined a flashlight into each vehicle. He gritted his teeth and proceeded ahead.

When he came to the checkpoint, one cop flashed a light into his car while the other asked for his driver's license. He pulled out the fake bought just a few days earlier and handed it to the cop.

"William Wachtler."

"Yes, that's right, sir."

"They call ya Bill?"

"Yes, sir."

"Whatcha doing in Bakersfield, Bill?"

"Just driving through. On my way up to Corcoran and I stopped for something to eat."

"Drive safely, Bill," said the cop. He started to give the license back to Trumbo, but something caught his eye and suddenly he snapped it back and scrutinized it closely.

"What's your birthday, son?"

"What?"

"I said, what's your birthday?"

He didn't remember what he'd told the forger to put on the license. "April eleventh," he answered truthfully.

"Very good. Your license expires this spring. Don't forget to renew."

"Thank you."

The cop waved him on.

When he turned the corner, Trumbo saw what all the fuss was about. Someone had been murdered. Two white vans marked COUNTY CORONER were parked in the lot, and at least a dozen uniformed cops swarmed around the area, along with ten or fifteen suits. His heart skipped a beat. He knew Sunn was behind the murder, even before he saw the dark graffiti splattered on the side wall of the establishment, which said only SKELTER. He figured it wouldn't be more than a couple hours before they realized that the same word had been written on a wall in Los Angeles just a month before. And pretty soon they'd be passing around a photograph of one of the only living suspects: him. He sped away, and was nearly hit by a news van making an illegal turn onto a one-way street.

"I'm driving as fast as I can," screamed the driver of the van, a man who was pulled out of bed with a promise of two hundred dollars for a couple hours of work. *These New York scum think they can boss me around, I'll show them,* he thought.

"Well, drive faster!" screamed James St. James—whose private jet had just arrived from New York and who now sat in the passenger seat, issuing decrees. "They're going to goddamn cover it up, that's what'll happen, they're going to cover up the splattered blood and then my ass is grass."

In the rear of the camera van was a two-man television team, rousted out of separate bars earlier that evening by Marilyn McLeod, who sat in front, taking notes from the frantic St. James. The local crew once considered Marilyn the biggest asshole in the world, but then they met St. James. Although Abe the soundman wanted to punch St. James, Fritz the cameraman, older and wiser, pointed out the flip side of working with St. James—he had money to burn. Marilyn agreed to pay them the unheard-of sum of four hundred dollars an hour for as long as they wanted to work, with a three-hour minimum. For that kind of dough, they could afford to be insulted.

"We're here!" shouted St. James. "Stop your dinkweed van and let's figure out how we can get the footage we need."

The driver balked. "We're on a one-way street."

"Did I ask you for a street map of the town or did I tell you to park, monkey boy?" shouted St. James.

"The only space is in front of a hydrant!" said the driver.

"What's a ticket in this burg? A hundred? Two hundred? Add it to your tab."

"They'll tow us!"

"Three hundred. Now, park the van."

Dave stopped the car. St. James stood and directed his wrath at Marilyn.

"How good is this crew?" he demanded.

Slightly bored, and immune to St. James's vitriol, she replied, "They're as good as you can get on thirty-minute notice in Bakersfield, California."

"Did you prep them?"

"When was I going to do that?"

"Move out of my way." He pushed past his second-in-command and faced the camera crew.

"Boys, lemme tell you what we're doing here. We want footage that no one else has. Someone wrote the word 'Skelter' on a wall, maybe in blood, and you goddamn better get that on tape, hopefully with a grieving widow or something in the foreground. No doubt they're gonna drape a cover over that any time now, so get that first. I want human interest stories—I want to hear from the next of kin. I want to hear from the cop who discovered the mess. I want to hear from kids who shop at this record store. And most of all I want a body shot!"

Fritz pinched his soundman. "Sir, I will get you anything you want as long as I don't have to violate the police line."

"What did you say?"

"We've been shooting video in Bakersfield for six years and we won't cross a police line. We got press passes. The cops respect us and we respect them. We can't cross the line."

"What'll it take to get it? Another hundred?"

"Mr. St. James, if I cross the police line, they could yank my press credentials. That kiboshes any chance I have of ever working for the news station again."

St. James went pale, as if encountering a threat to his life, then ratcheted down his rant to a clearer, inspirational tone. Suddenly he sounded like Knute Rockne. "There's no other way. Sure, the cops let you do some things—you scratch their back, they scratch yours—but we can't let that interfere with the *people's right to know."*

Marilyn watched St. James, amused at this strategy. It seemed almost as if he were ready to shed a tear for the dear old U.S. Constitution.

St. James put his hand on his heart. "Given free television news or a free citizenry, I'd take the television news; that's what Thomas Jefferson would have said if he were alive today. What separates us from the Russians and the Cubans is a little something called the First Amendment. I don't want to prevent you from getting work—I'm thinking of your career now, I want to help you. Someone has to stand

up and declare that enough is enough. You've got every right
to get in there and show the truth. More than a right—as a
member of the press, it's a responsibility. Can you let a
couple of local cops destroy the rights of the people of the
United States?"

Fritz laughed and replied, "I'll see what I can do. I guess
Thomas Jefferson would have wanted the body shot."

St. James nodded. He didn't realize that Fritz was making
fun of him. "Get it. Learn it. Do it."

"Sure."

"And after you get the body shot, I want to do a little
stand-up piece with the police cars in the background. Say,
about fifteen minutes from now."

"No prob."

Fritz and Abe quickly assembled the Ikegami camera and
deck and crawled out of the back of the truck. As soon as
they were outside, Fritz turned to Abe and whispered,
"What a bunch of bullshit. I ain't crossin' no line." Abe
laughed.

Inside the van, St. James grilled Marilyn. "How'd you
hear about this?"

"Local news radio. They reported about the word
'Skelter' on a wall at the scene of a quadruple murder."

"What a bonanza for my show."

"Four people died, Ray."

"I know. Isn't it great? Three and I would never have been
able to make this into a national news story. Four is the
magic number to get ABC, CBS, NBC, and every local-yokel
station in the U.S. of A. to run this story. This is bigger than
that girl in a well. Don't you see? Every time a news show
runs this footage, it's like a free ad for Thursday's Manson
show."

"But no one says it's related."

"They will now. Lemme get my interviews with the
police; we'll edit it *my* way and offer the free footage to any
station who wants it. It'll sound like Charlie himself robbed
this record store by the time I'm done with it."

St. James leaned out of the front window of the van and
surveyed the area. "Shit. Two yokel news crews are here
already, filming this shit. You got enough cash?"

"Enough cash for what?"

"Buy up the footage."

"I'll do my best."

"Don't overpay. Remember that Rodney King was the first video news superhero, and the cameraman only got five hundred bucks."

"I'll do my best."

"Swell."

Marilyn hopped out of the van while St. James primped and made himself up in the rearview mirror. By the time he got out, the bodies were on their way to the coroner and the news crew was waiting for him.

"Hey, boys!" he yelled as he hopped out of the van. His platform heels made a loud click on the pavement. "You got the body shot?" he yelled. A crowd of bystanders had formed, and many people looked askance at St. James.

Fritz nodded. "Got 'em loading it."

"Swell. Let's do the stand-ups."

"What do you want to do?"

"I'm gonna interview the cops. Let's go."

"Shouldn't you ask them first?"

"Hell no! This is national big-time television, boys. Full steam ahead—video blasting! Follow me."

St. James stepped over the police line without pausing and ran to the first cop he could find, a young man in uniform. Fritz reluctantly followed. Suddenly St. James's tone changed to the baritone he used whenever on-air, a voice halfway between that of a circus barker and a hanging judge. He spun around and stared straight into the camera.

"I'm James St. James, reporting from the scene of the tragic Bakersfield Helter Skelter murders. With me is"—he read the badge on the cop's chest—"Officer Sandler of Bakersfield's finest."

The cop squinted into the light and looked up.

"You're James St. James!"

"That's right, Officer Sandler. I'd like to ask just a few questions."

"Fire away."

St. James fired. "Why does your police force think this heinous and cruel multiple murder of innocent civilian citizens was related to the pending release of Charles Manson? Is it the word 'Skelter,' written in blood on the wall of this record shop?"

The young cop raised his eyebrows. "They think it's Manson doing this? Whadda ya know. Damn."

St. James raised his hand for Fritz to pause taping and spoke softly to the rookie cop. "I want you to look good on television for all those viewers. You see, my brother is a cop, and I try to look out for cops whenever I can."

"Yes, sir."

"So when you answer, try to use complete sentences. It looks much better on television. It's a small thing, but I want you to look *good* if we use this footage."

The cop straightened his hair with his hand and smiled broadly. "Yes, sir."

St. James gestured for them to turn the cameras back on.

"Let's try it out. I ask you your name, you answer in a complete sentence. What is your name?"

"Officer Dominic Sandler."

"No, no, no. Say a sentence, you know, 'My name is Officer Dominic Sandler of the Bakersfield Police Department.'"

The cop parroted him. "My name is Officer Dominic Sandler of the Bakersfield Police Department."

St. James patted him on the back. "That was great. Let's try some more. Is your department investigating why mass murderer Charles Manson, who will be released Thursday, is related to the slayings?"

"I'm not sure."

"Do the complete sentence. Say, 'Our department will investigate the connection between tonight's tragic slaying and mass murderer Charles Manson.'"

"Really?" asked the cop.

"Really," said St. James. "Try it."

The rookie deepened his voice and stared straight into the camera. "Our department will investigate the connection between tonight's tragic slaying and mass murderer Charles Manson."

"That's great! I'm going to talk to some other officers, okay? You did really good."

"Thank you. Um, is Manson involved?"

St. James shook his head. "You said so."

The cop shook his head, puzzled, as St. James hustled away.

St. James danced a little jig. The small-town cops were perfect fodder for his show. Within twenty minutes he had footage from cops, coroners, and detectives all unwittingly saying things that, taken out of context, would make the perfect intro to Thursday's show. By the time the Bakersfield Police press officer arrived, saw what was going on, and issued orders that no sworn officers were to talk to the media, St. James had all the footage he needed. St. James was in such a good mood that he even turned his persuasive powers on the press officer and persuaded him not to revoke the credentials of the camera crew.

After snatching the tapes from the crew, they dropped the cameramen off at the same bars where they had started their evening. St. James and Marilyn returned to the double suite that St. James had booked in the hotel, released only after management was bribed to kick out a newlywed couple. He pulled off his platform shoes—not throwing them at anything or anyone—fell backwards on the bed, and kicked his feet in jubilation.

"Marilyn, this is the story of the century. You're gonna uplink it to New York, and the editors there will have the video release cut by morning, ready for every A.M. show in America."

"Sure, right. It's the *Citizen Kane* of news stories," she said without irony.

"I like that. Maybe we can use it. Nahh. Not catchy enough. But I still like the phrase."

Marilyn sat in the only chair in the room. "We still haven't talked about Manson's cooperation. We really have to have that tape. He threatened to pull out unless we had it."

"I said I'd make the tape, you'll show it to Manson and no one else, and then we get it back, right?"

"If you're so worried, you can show it to Manson yourself."

"Can't we do something else besides that tape?"

"Not if you want Manson!"

"He won't accept something less?"

Marilyn stood up. "Jesus Christ, Ray, you remind me of an old joke. This mother is sitting on the beach and her five-year-old child disappears into the surf, drowns. She falls to her knees and prays, 'Dear God, please don't take my son! Please, just grant me this one prayer, bring little Bobby back.' The sky parts and winds wash over the waves, and a few minutes later, her boy emerges from the surf. She embraces the kid, who's alive and well, then suddenly gets back on her knees to pray again. 'Dear God, I forgot to mention, little Bobby had a hat.'"

St. James stared at her. "I don't get it."

Marilyn clucked her tongue. "You have to make the fucking tape."

"Okay. Let's get a crew out here in the morning."

"What time?" she asked.

"Seven A.M. What time are you supposed to show it to Manson?"

"Two P.M. tomorrow."

"I'll take it to the prison myself," said St. James. "Then I'll destroy the tape."

"No problem," said Marilyn. "I don't relish another visit with him." She stood. "I wanted to remind you about my show," she said.

St. James stood up and turned on the charm. "Marilyn, I'm giving you your show because you are the number one kick-ass producer I have on staff. Because you can put a show together. Not just anyone can do that. You can. You know how those other butt-kissing wimpoids operate; they're—"

Marilyn interrupted. "You're not gonna worm on me this time?" she said hopefully.

"I'd never do that," he said. Uncharacteristically, Marilyn took him at his word and made a mental note to get the contracts from him later. She had a lot to do right now. She began the arduous process of calling bars, trying to locate her overpaid local camera crew.

27

"YOU'VE GOT TO GIVE US THE SHOES," SAID THE YOUNG CORRECtional officer in the visitor relations office of Corcoran State Correctional Facility for Men.

"Excuse me?" demanded James St. James.

"Regulations prohibit platform shoes. We can provide disposable slippers to be worn while in the facility."

St. James growled, "These are *not* platform shoes."

The correctional officer pointed at a large sign on the wall listing regulations for visitors to the prison. "Any shoe with a heel of greater than three quarters of an inch may not be worn during prison visitations."

"Do you know who I am?"

The CO placed his palms flat on the table. "Your confidential visit with Mr. Manson is scheduled from three P.M. to four P.M. After that you'll have to wait another day because no space is available. You can argue with me until four P.M. or you can give me the shoes."

"This rule is clearly unconstitutional. I see no reason for it."

The officer blandly replied, "In the past, contraband materials including drugs and weapons have been smuggled inside platform shoes. That's why we have the rule." The officer glanced at St. James's shoes. "I think you could hide a *lot* of contraband in that particular pair, if you don't mind my saying so."

St. James pulled off the shoes, grumbling, "If I have to, I have to." He set the shoes on the desk. The elevator shoes added about three inches to St. James's height. He slipped on a pair of cotton slippers. The videotape recorder and videotape he carried were examined. Then he proceeded through two metal detectors, a personal search, and then a long, meandering path out of the first building, across a courtyard, and into the recalcitrant unit. He took a seat in a tiny room about the size of a freight elevator, divided down the middle with wire-reinforced Plexiglas.

Moments later, he heard a door clang closed. Manson was escorted to a chair in the other half of the room. Chains ran from his hands and feet to a metal band around his waist. His shirt was orange, which meant that he was an escape risk and required special handling. With a clamorous rattling of chains, Manson dropped to the stool bolted to the floor in the center of the room. He stared at the ground for a moment, then raised his head slowly, making sudden eye contact with St. James. No matter how many times St. James saw Manson, each time he was shocked at the threat and the power of his eyes.

"Hello, Charles."

"Well, if it isn't Mr. Jew Ray Garvey."

"I wish you wouldn't call me that. My name's James St. James and I was raised a Methodist."

Manson stared blankly ahead for a moment. "Ain't that unusual, you objecting to me calling you by your real name when you call me such sweet things all the time." Manson cackled. "Am I mistaking you for some *other* TV trash or didn't you call me Satan himself? Didn't you say I was pure evil? You know you did. You called me all that shit on nationwide television, and so I have the right to call you whatever I want to call you. I can give as good as I get, Mr. *Garvey.*"

"Charles, I came in to thank you for cooperating."

"I didn't say I'd cooperate unless you made that tape. If you do something for me, I do something for you. You screw me, I screw you."

"I know I said some harsh things in the past. But this time I think you'll get out. I really do."

Manson walked to the glass divider. "Listen, Ray baby, don't bullshit a bullshitter. You don't trust me, I don't trust you. That's the way it is. You can't come in here pretending you're my long-lost friend and defender. That's a pile of crap. Maybe I'm the Devil, maybe I'm Jesus, but either way, I'm not that stupid."

"Charles, I can understand your hostility."

"Stop the psychobabble, Ray; I get enough of it from the prison shrink. Face it: I'm a prostitute and you're a prosti-

tute. I'm getting something off of you, and that's the tape
you made for me. You get something off of me, and that's
your TV show. You're nothing without me, ma.. f I didn't
have something you wanted, you'd be acting lik ..e asshole
you are every time you make a TV show about me, running
around with your little microphone and calling me names,
and I play the evil crazy killer you want me to be. It's all
roles, man. Now we're in different roles—you're sucking up
to me. If only your TV audience could see you saying,
'Please, Charles' and 'I'm on your side, Charles' and 'I want
to help you, Charles.' This is my chance to get you to suck
up. So suck up to me, Ray, and make it good."

"I don't think I have to dignify that with a response," said
St. James. "Let's get right down to it. I made the tape."

"Word for word?" asked Manson.

"Word for word."

"And you'll play it on your show, right? During the
hearing, right?"

"I said I will play the tape."

Manson walked in a circle around the space like a horse
that had been cooped up too long. Then he leaned against
the wall and faced St. James. "Put up or shut up. Let's see
your cards."

"I'm sending the papers around to you. You'll sign them
after I play the tape."

"Do what thou wilst," said Manson.

"All right."

St. James pulled two personal-appearance releases and a
felt-tip pen from his jacket and rang for a guard. The officer
disappeared with the papers and reemerged a moment later
in Manson's half of the visiting room. Manson held the
papers at arm's length. He didn't have the benefit of his
reading glasses. "I don't know what half this shit means, but
show me the tape and I'll sign 'em anyway."

"Sure. You're sure no guards can hear us?" asked St.
James.

"Hell, I ain't sure of anything. This is the legal counsel
visiting room. They're not supposed to listen, but anything
is possible," said Manson.

"I'll take the chance."

St. James held the portable VCR/television to the glass,

inserted the videotape, and pressed the play button. For the next eleven minutes Manson watched the tape, chuckling at a few points, staring in disbelief the rest of the time. St. James nervously chewed on his lower lip during the entire presentation and tried not to imagine the consequences were the tape ever to be seen. After the tape stopped, St. James turned the machine off and placed the VCR/TV back on the table.

"Satisfied?" asked St. James.

"Man, you really did it," said Manson. "I thought that chick making promises for you was more of your bullshit, but you came through. I know we don't get along, but I recognize now that you're a real man."

St. James nodded. "Thanks. I told you I'd come through on my half. Now you be a man, too. Sign the release?"

"Hey, man, I'm taking my time. I'll sign it, don't you worry."

"I need you to sign it today. We have to get clearances to tape your parole hearing, and if we don't have that signed today, it won't be of any use."

Manson cackled. "I said I'd sign it, but I didn't say when I'd sign it. Maybe I want to take my time."

"You know as well as I do what that means."

"I'll sign it today if you do a couple more things for me." Manson sensed fear in St. James's eyes.

"What more do you want? I made the tape. Now you have to live up to your word."

"I'll do it, but first you gotta do a couple things. They're easy things, too, Ray baby. You can do 'em right here, right now." Manson's smile highlighted the deep wrinkles in his face.

"What? What now?" demanded St. James.

"Say, 'I am a prostitute.'"

"I'm not going to say that."

"Then I'll sign it next week."

"Why do you want me to say that?"

"I want our relationship to be clear," said Manson. "Nobody calls me the shit you called me without making amends. I'm signing some lawyer-ass form I don't understand so you can get what you want. I want you to say what I want you to say. Fair play, man."

St. James mumbled softly and quickly. "I'm a prostitute."

Manson raised his eyebrows. "Louder."

"Charles, do we have to do this?" asked St. James.

"Yes, we have to."

St. James cleared his throat. "Um, I am a prostitute."

"I know," said Manson with a chuckle.

"Now, sign the damn papers!" said St. James.

"One more thing, Ray. I really want to sign this form, believe me I do, and I want to do business with you, but first"—Manson twisted to the side, rattling his chains—"just for me, bark like a dog."

"What?"

"I want you to bark like a dog," said Manson.

"I'm not going to do that."

Manson lifted the contract to his mouth and bit a little strip of paper off, chewed it up, and spit the wad of wet paper on the ground. "Mmmm, good!" said Manson. His voice took on a commanding tone. He was in control and knew it. "I can keep chewing on your pissant contract till it's gone or you can be a good boy and bark like a dog."

St. James stood up. "Can anyone hear us?"

"Maybe, maybe not." Manson bit off a piece of another corner on the contract and spit it out. "Chewy delicious!" he yelled.

"Woof," said St. James, quietly.

"Louder!" shouted Manson.

"Woof!"

Manson balked. "Ray, you're just saying the word 'woof.' Put some heart into it. Really bark, man."

"Grrrr!"

"Louder!" yelled Manson, rattling his chains.

St. James looked to left and right, then put on a barking performance worthy of Rin Tin Tin, growling, snarling, and yapping into the air. For added impact he curled his hands so they looked like a dog's paws. Manson laughed so hard, he lost his breath, then applauded the bizarre performance.

St. James straightened his tie and sat down. He was blushing. "Satisfied?"

Manson nodded. "I just wanted to prove that even though, out there in the world, you may be some sort of hotshot TV star, in here I can make you do whatever I want." Manson signed both sides of the document with a flourish. "There, now you got what you wanted, Mr. Whoredog!" Manson rang for the guard, who promptly entered the visiting room and accepted the papers and the felt-tip pen.

"Take these back—to Mr. *Whoredog* over there," said Manson.

Without comment the guard took the papers, appeared in St. James's half of the cell, and gave them to him.

"You have five minutes," said the guard.

"I'm done here," said St. James. "I'm ready to leave."

"Fine."

As he left the cell, Manson's voice came over the speaker. "Woof woof woof! Made ya bark like a dog! Made ya bark like a dog! Whore-dog! Whore-dog! Whore-dog!" The laughing abruptly ceased when the metal door clanged shut.

St. James stuffed the papers back into his jacket, picked up his portable television, and left. As he walked across the yard to the visitors' center, he silently tried to recover from his humiliation by thinking about all the young French girls he met when he was last in Paris. It was worth it.

Things were falling into place for St. James. In the time he was at the prison, two of his assistants had arrived and set up an office in the double bridal suite. A stack of thirty or so message slips awaited him when he walked into the room. He flipped through them like a Vegas dealer going through a pack of cards while the assistants tried to keep up with him.

"Trash, trash, trash, call back say I'm unavailable, trash, send some candy to the hospital but don't spend more than twenty bucks, trash, trash . . ." His eyes grew large. "What the fuck is this? What. the. fuck. is. this?" He held the message slip at arm's length as if it were a rotting fish. The junior producer Wytowski and the slender receptionist Mark-Jon looked at each other, to determine who had to field St. James's fury.

Wytowski sighed with relief when Mark-Jon raised his hand halfway and extended his pinky finger. "Uh, I can answer that question. Wytowski took the message." Mark-Jon smirked.

St. James bellowed, "Well, what is it?"

"Some lawyer called. I was on another line trying to set up catering for Thursday's shoot."

"You were setting up catering? Read me the message."

Wytowski blushed and took the message slip. "It says, 'Attorney general's office wants to discuss improprieties concerning Clandestine Productions and parole board member Anton Lenski.'"

"Why didn't you beep me right away?"

"You left orders not to be disturbed. I thought you were meeting with Manson."

"I was. But you need to know when to disobey me."

Mark-Jon rolled his eyes. Wytowski grimaced. "Yes, sir."

"Get the AG's office on the phone now!" St. James stuffed the message slip into Wytowski's hand. It took Wytowski a few minutes, and during the interval St. James nervously paced.

St. James picked up the phone. Mark-Jon and Wytowski watched from a respectful distance as St. James talked. They saw their boss sweat, an unprecedented human reaction.

"James St. James. I understand you called us earlier in the day . . . What? No, sir, we had no idea at all . . . Of course we don't condone such behavior . . . I agree with you, we must stop this kind of thing at the source. You can count on our full cooperation . . . I'm only sorry it was one of my own employees. Yes, sir. Thank you for bringing it to our attention."

St. James replaced the telephone receiver gingerly, as if it were a time bomb. He sat in silence for a moment. When he resumed his usual speaking voice, it was so shocking, Mark-Jon jumped. "Mark-Jon, take a memo. And a letter. We have some work to do."

"Yes, sir."

"To the State of California Attorney General's Office. Date, today, from me, blah de blah, you know the drill." St. James leaped to his feet and paced across the room while he dictated. "Thank you for alerting our office about the unfortunate incident involving California Parole Board member Anton Lenski and my own employee Marilyn McLeod. Bribery is a serious charge. However, we would like to ensure you that such an outrageous and egregious breach of the law did not originate with our company, but with a rogue employee." St. James chewed on a pen while he talked.

"While our company makes its best efforts to adhere to the strictest journalistic standards of professional integrity, occasionally one lone employee will decide to take a short-cut. Clandestine Productions works in the field of broad-casting and always avoids even the appearance of impropriety. As such we will cooperate fully with the attorney general's office to get to the bottom of this affair. If it turns out to be false, we will be happy to know that is the case. If it turns out to be true, we will assist the prosecution in any way we can.

"You may be glad to know that effective immediately, the employee in question, one Marilyn McLeod, will be sus-pended indefinitely without pay."

St. James popped open a can of Diet Pepsi, gulped some down, then continued. "Put on the usual best regards, me, etc., and send a copy to our lawyers."

Mark-Jon and Wytowski stared in disbelief. Wytowski spoke first. "You're gonna fire Marilyn? What'd she do?"

"There comes a time when a man has to do what a man has to do. This decision is hardest for me. You know how much I respect and admire Marilyn. But we're talking about journalistic ethics. And she crossed the line."

Mark-Jon and Wytowski both spoke simultaneously. "What line?"

"The line. You young kids don't know about this kind of thing, but it goes to the roots of what we do. She tried to bribe a guy, that's what happened. I don't know why or how, but that's the kind of thing we just can't do."

Mark-Jon blurted out, "You sighed the check request!"

"I had no idea that's what she was going to do." St. James faced away from his employees. "Mark-Jon, see if you can get all copies of that check request and bring them to me. Call the East Coast office and get them to Fed Ex the original and all copies. We're, uh, going to need it. To help the attorney general, right? Wytowski—I have some urgent meetings to attend to around town. Why don't you wander over to Marilyn's suite and let her know what's happened. She ought to be on the next plane out of Corcoran."

"You want *me* to fire her?"

"Suspend, not fire. Get it! Learn it! Do it!"

"Yes, sir."

Wytowski got up his courage and walked down the hall to Marilyn's room. She was not pleased to hear the message from St. James.

"That midget cocksucking lying piece of human excrement!" She grabbed Wytowski by the lapels and lifted him off the ground. "When did he say this?"

"A couple of minutes ago."

"And the twit didn't have the nerve to face me on his own."

"Marilyn, I'm really sorry about what happened . . ."

"Are you going to keep working for that bucket of slime when you know what kind of tactics he uses?"

Wytowski worked his way out of Marilyn's grip and sat down on the side of her bed. "Marilyn, you knew what he was all about. It's never been a big secret that when the heat comes down, St. James fires the nearest person. As I recall, a certain producer got her first big break after the 'Inside Hitler's Bunker' producer was fired for participating in the forgery of those diaries, isn't that so?"

"But that's different! He was a stringer! That guy put himself out on a limb! He should have known better."

"Marilyn, *you* should have known better. Live by the sword, die by the sword."

"I'm completely screwed. What's he going to do?"

"He's going to hang you high and dry. The whole bribery thing is gonna look like it was your idea, that St. James was a saint the whole time, and he's already acting outraged that it could even happen at such a fine company as Clandestine Productions. My advice: Get yourself a lawyer, pronto, and cover your ass."

"Don't you know, Wytowski, you'll be the next sacrificial lamb when something goes wrong?"

Wyktowski grinned. "Sure I do. That goes with the territory. But no one else pays as well as St. James."

"I'm sure I'll have no problem at all getting another gig after the publicity surrounding the Clandestine series. Whatever happened to the 'Hitler's Bunker' guy?"

"Last I heard, he was a congressional lobbyist for an industry coalition of phone sex companies. You know,

'976-SUCK,' '1-800-BLOW JOB,' that kind of thing. Supposed to be very good at it, too."

The thought of losing her job with St. James depressed Marilyn more than she could say. "Want to go for a drink? You know, say good-bye?"

Wytowski shook his head. "St. James has me up to my ass in alligators this afternoon. First thing I gotta write, in fact, is the press release . . ."

"Blaming me."

"Marilyn, don't lay a guilt trip on me. What was *your* first gig with the dwarf?" asked Wytowski.

"'Inside Hangar Eighteen.' The aliens thing."

"It was the 'Hitler's Bunker' show. You made the weepy-eyed video with St. James professing not to know anything about the faked diaries. You were the one who got the bright idea to film St. James in front of the Supreme Court, hand on a family Bible, swearing he didn't know anything about the bogus stuff in his own show."

Marilyn blushed. "Okay, okay. I remember. You're right." She pushed him toward the door. "Have a good time. And don't look for cover from me when your turn comes."

She slammed the door behind him.

Marilyn sat down on her bed and stared at the ceiling for a while, then started to cry. St. James had always been contentious and he was a self-centered manipulator, but in spite of all her fights with him, he was her only true soul mate. For years before meeting him she had to contend with mushy limo-liberal journalists who didn't understand the joy of pure Machiavellian achievement. Then she met St. James and her life changed. He appreciated how she thought, and more important, he understood the magnitude of her achievements. She got her first job with him following her last local news gig: a staged reenactment of a gang-style execution killing pretending to be real news. While editorial pages and radio talk show hosts around the nation condemned her, her station, and telejournalism in general, only James St. James sent her a bouquet of flowers and an invitation to a friendly lunch. She accepted the invitation and was surprised at his reaction: That day, two years ago, he said, *Marilyn, you have created Great Television. You understand the medium in a way that few do. In my book, what you did with the gang shootout is a form of American genius. You truly speak the language of television. And you pulled a thirty-share in the ratings.* He hired her on the spot.

She would miss him, but he had forced her into an uncomfortable position. She would have to destroy him. He had forced her hand. And now she had to play the trump card, a weapon she had carefully and methodically stowed away just in case.

It would be lonely at the top.

Within a week James St. James would be nothing more than the punch line to a mean-spirited joke, marginalized as quickly as Pee-Wee Herman after the Florida masturbation incident or Rob Lowe after his sex tapes. She had the goods and she would use them.

28

DIZZY WITH FEAR AND DISGUST, TRUMBO SPED AWAY FROM THE record store. He had seen hundreds of accidents in his life—many of them fatal—but the twisted and burned bodies he dealt with every day had never disturbed him. They seemed victims of fate. In Los Angeles, a certain number of people are going to wreck their cars every day, and of those, a certain number will die. Trumbo never felt a personal bond with car wreck victims. It was something that just happened, and someone had to clean up. He liked to believe he was the go-between who shielded ordinary people from further death and disaster. When he arrived at crash sites, traffic was backed up, bodies, metal, and glass were scattered everywhere, and the normal rhythms of the city were knocked out of whack. When he left, harmony was restored.

These deaths were different. Not so much because he felt responsible. The thing was, *he couldn't restore harmony.* When Joi Wilmot was killed, when the men at the gas station were shot, when those poor souls at the record shop were murdered, he was powerless. But Alison was another matter. There was still time to help her.

He hightailed it back to Corcoran and drove aimlessly around the rural roads, looking in vain for the farmhouse or trailer or tract home where she was. He knew that the murder in Bakersfield had been committed by the same people. He only hoped that they hadn't hurt her. Trumbo opened the car window and let the cold night air blow in, drying his skin, making his eyes water. He drove past the patch of field where Barbara ran away and stared at the trailer in the middle of the field. He looked at his watch: a little past midnight. He was hungry. He pulled into a gas station, bought a pack of gum and some coffee, and asked the attendant if there were a late night coffee shop nearby.

The attendant directed him to a Denny's two stops back toward Bakersfield on the I-5, "probably the only place within thirty miles still open." He ordered a Grand-Slam Breakfast to go—no reason to take a chance on being recognized by a cop. They stuffed the pancakes into a Styrofoam box, and he ate in the parking lot, contemplating his next move.

His thought was disturbed by overamplified music coming from the opposite side of the parking lot. *drub drub drub;* one hundred twenty beats per minute, the rhythm of raves. He glanced in the rearview mirror trying to locate its source. A pickup truck was parked next to the Dumpsters in back. He couldn't see the driver's face, but he noticed several girls in the bed of the truck. One of them hopped out and walked into the restaurant. She was too far away to get a good look at her face, but she wore a bright orange cotton dress. He racked his brain to remember where the odd juxtaposition had occurred before. It was at the second Moon Man. The girls selling T-shirts with J'osüf Sunn dressed like that. He started his engine but kept the lights off, focusing his attention on the girl.

Inside the restaurant she bought something—pies, it looked like—paid, and returned to the truck. She handed the bag through the driver's window, then jumped into the back of the truck. The pickup passed him and turned right—toward Corcoran—onto a service road adjacent to the freeway. Trumbo pulled out, his lights off.

The truck with the girl drove so slowly that Trumbo had a hard time keeping an adequate distance. Several cars passed him, fell in between him and the truck, and then passed them. They didn't get on the freeway, although they passed two entrances. Just before Corcoran they turned onto a two-lane farm road. Trumbo stopped at the intersection, gave the truck a chance to get ahead, and then followed. No one else was on the road. He let them get about a half mile ahead. He had driven this road several times earlier that night looking in frustration for Barbara's hideout. Far ahead of him, the van took a sharp right and moved perpendicular to the road, leaving a trail of dust behind, illuminated by its red rear lights.

Trumbo found the turnoff, a dirt road accessible only after opening a chain-link gate. *No wonder I missed it,* he thought. So that he wouldn't arrive immediately after them, he drove a few miles down the road before returning to the spot. He parked a quarter mile away from the gate and quietly walked down the road. He jumped the chain-link fence and hiked down the dirt road. For about twenty minutes he saw nothing but dirt, stumbling on an occasional pothole in his path. At one point a second dirt road, even narrower, jutted off toward the center of the field. He followed it over a small rise and heard laughter and talking. Staying low to the ground, he reconnoitered the compound. Four or five girls and a gray-haired woman in leather sat around a campfire, loudly telling stories. Next to them was the pickup he'd seen at Denny's. In back of that was a massive trailer home on bricks, and behind that, the familiar orange van. He was certain that these people were responsible for the murders of Joi Wilmot and half a dozen others; they wouldn't hesitate a moment before killing him. He would have to search the area when they were asleep or gone.

He lay down on the soil and watched. Several additional girls joined the group by the campfire, and sang *a cappella.* They sang "Kum Ba Yah" and "Amazing Grace" and several other songs he didn't recognize. A man joined them; although his face was obscured in the dark, the distinctive voice belonged to none other than J'osüf Sunn. At his side was Barbara Thompson.

During all the movement around the camp, he noticed one constant: Someone always stood by the edge of the van. For a while a young girl leaned against the vehicle, conspicuously left out of the singing by the campfire. Trumbo's first guess was that she was being shunned for some misdeed. After an hour she switched places with another girl, and later yet another girl took sentry duty by the van. Whatever was inside was worth protecting. Money? Weapons? Then the girl standing watch leaned her head toward a window and carried on a conversation with someone inside. He strained to listen, but the distance and a slight wind kept him from hearing. Hope began to grow within him.

Finally the group began heading into the oversized trailer. The process took a long time; the girls took turns washing out of a large metal can full of water before disappearing inside one by one. He counted them; there was Sunn, seven girls, Thompson, and another older woman he had never seen before. Sunn was the last to wash. Afterwards, he extinguished the fire with the remaining water, sending plumes of smoke into the air. Then Sunn hiked around the campsite. His first stop was at the van, where he had a conversation with the girl standing guard. Sunn then walked to the pickup truck, looked inside the cab and then the flatbed. He went to the far side of the trailer, looked left and right, and, satisfied, headed toward the door of the mobile home.

Just before he went in, Sunn stopped in his tracks. Trumbo flattened himself to the ground, trying hard not to move a muscle. Sunn tilted his head back and cupped one hand over his ear. Then he walked directly toward Trumbo. Lying on his belly in the dirt, with no weapons and no cover, Trumbo held his breath. Sunn came within ten feet of him and stopped. Sunn turned to the side, unzipped his pants, and took a piss. After a moment he returned to the trailer and went inside.

Did he see me and pretend not to? Is he setting a trap? Trumbo lay still, watching the trailer for another forty-five minutes. He saw the girls moving inside, pulling out bunks, and climbing into them. No one was watching out the window. Finally, after about an hour, all activity ceased and the lights went out. Trumbo stretched. He had cramps from staying still for so long. He was cold. He lifted himself to his knees and dusted himself off, then pulled himself across the ground toward the van.

He could no longer see who stood guard outside the van. She had moved to the far side of the vehicle. But he knew *someone* was there. He got within a few feet of the van and then dropped to the ground and crawled underneath. There was barely enough room to maneuver. A greasy fluid dripped onto his neck. When he lifted himself over a stump, a sharp piece of metal cut into his shoulder. On the opposite side of the van he saw the sentry. Just one very young girl, judging by her tiny tennis shoes. She did not seem to notice him. He dragged himself backwards, crawled out from the opposite side of the van, and slipped around the front. When he moved around the corner, his cover would be blown. By his calculations he would be only a few feet from her. If she had a gun, she might shoot him; he listened to see if she had moved. She hadn't. Her teeth were chattering. He had the element of surprise.

He silently counted backwards from ten and then jumped out from his hiding place. In just a few seconds he saw the guard: a girl barely into puberty. Her arms were folded in front of her, and she shook with cold. Trumbo tackled her, throwing his full weight upon her and putting one hand over her mouth so she would not scream. They lay in the dirt together.

Trumbo was prepared for a good fight, but the girl surprised him. She cried. He held her to the ground, his hand tightly clamped across her mouth, while he whispered questions in her ear.

"Is Alison Wilmot in this van? Nod yes or shake your head no."

She nodded.

"Are you the only one guarding her?"

The girl nodded again.

"When will someone else come out? Soon?"

The girl shook her head. Trumbo hissed in her ear. "Are you sure?"

She nodded again.

Keeping his hand clamped across her mouth, he sat up and let her sit up in front of him.

"Is the van locked?"

The girl nodded.

"Give me the keys."

The girl violently shook her head.

He twisted a fist into her back. "Give me the keys to the van or I'll—" He stopped midsentence as the girl's warm tears fell on his hand. He couldn't bring himself to hit a little girl. "Ah, never mind. I'll just break a window."

The girl shook her head harder than before. She tried to talk; he kept her from speaking. She pulled one arm out from his grip and drew a circle in the dirt, with one line going out of it.

"What's that mean?" he asked.

She wrote the word "bomb" in the dirt.

"A bomb? Wired to the van?"

She nodded. Then she wrote another message in the dirt. "Help me get away."

Slowly he lifted his hand a quarter inch. If she tried to scream, he could stifle it in an instant.

She whispered softly, "You don't have to keep gagging me. I want to leave this shithole."

"What's with the van?"

"Look at this." She turned around and pointed to several wires dangling beneath the engine, attached to several sticks of explosive. "They put that on there in case Alison tried to start the van. Sunn swears it'll blow up if someone even opens the door."

Tentatively Trumbo released his grip on the girl. She didn't try to run away.

"You must be Trumbo," she said.

"How do you know?"

"I been talkin' with Alison. I didn't think I'd ever get to meet you."

"What's your name?"

"Denise. I want to leave here."

Trumbo nodded. "Do you have a flashlight?"

"No."

"Keep watch for me. I think I can detach the bomb."

He crawled beneath the van once again, and waited until his eyes adjusted to the dim moonlight reflected beneath the vehicle. Three sticks of explosive were fastened together with masking tape. Attached to them was a metal device about the size of a D battery. He assumed it was a blasting cap. Two electrical wires extended out of it. One wire extended into the engine compartment, connected to the starter or the battery. Starting the engine would send electricity down to the explosive. Another wire extended into the doorframe. He lay silent, wondering how someone would wire a bomb. He thought of all the car wrecks he had been to, and all the conversations he'd had with mechanics.

It must be wired into the door light. Open the door and it completes the electrical circuit that illuminates the inside light. Except in this case, the electricity was rerouted to a bomb. *Door is the juice. Engine compartment is the ground.*

He started to tug gently on the wire, then suddenly had second thoughts. Sweat ran across his forehead. *What if it's the other way around? What if the doorframe is the ground and the first connection goes up to the battery? If I drag a wire out of there and it touches the vehicle, it could blow the whole thing.*

Cautiously he pushed his arm along the wire that ran up to the engine compartment. With his fingers he felt the wire go past the engine block, past another metal object, and then his arm got stuck. He pulled his hand out quickly, cutting the side of his arm on the metal. Then he twisted his body around so that he could reach the other side of the engine block. He found the wire again, and pushed his arm as far up as it could go. He touched a familiar flat plastic shape. The car battery.

His second guess had been right: This wire was juice, the door wire was the ground. He exhaled sharply as he realized that he almost blew up the entire vehicle. *This* was the wire he should disconnect. He tugged sharply. It wouldn't budge. He pushed his arm up farther into the compartment, stretching so that his shoulder pushed directly into the engine block. The metal tore into his skin. With the tips of his fingers he reached as far as he could and was barely able to touch the contact on the battery. Holding his breath to stop the pain, he gently untwisted the wire attached to the battery terminal. When he pulled off the last bit of wire, he braced himself for the explosion that would end everything. Instead, the wire came off.

He lay flat on the ground and stretched the wire the rest of the way through the compartment, then laid it on the ground. Looking straight up, he then yanked the second wire out of the doorframe. No explosion. He was alive. He crawled out from beneath the van and pulled the bomb out with him. Denise watched tensely.

"You got it out?" she asked.

"I hope so."

"Fuckin' A!" said the girl. Trumbo could not restrain his smile. He carried the homemade bomb thirty feet into the field and gingerly put it down. Then he returned to the van.

"Do you have keys?" he asked Denise.

"Nope."

"Maybe Alison can open the door."

"Nope—she's chained in the back of the van."

"Goddamn." He kicked his foot in the dirt. "Denise— look in the windows of the trailer and make sure no one is awake."

The little girl ran across the dirt and ran a circuit around the trailer, then returned. "All clear, Kemo sabe," she said.

"Cool." He stepped to the spot where the campfire had burned. There were a number of large rocks around the fire pit. He selected a long, thin stone and returned to the van. "Here goes nothing," he said, then heaved the rock into the vent window of the van. It bounced back.

"Safety glass," he said. Then he held the rock in his hand and jammed it with all his strength into the same piece of glass. The vent window shattered but remained in the frame. He poked a few holes into the glass with the rock and then stretched his hand back toward the door lock. Grimacing, he flipped the lock on the door, pulled his arm out, and then opened the van.

"Alison!" he whispered.

There was no reply. He crawled to the back of the van and found her chained to the floor, dead asleep. He shook her several times. "Alison! Wake up!" With great effort she opened her eyes for a moment, but then she fell back into her deep slumber.

Denise whispered into his ear. "Sunn drugged her food, I bet."

"Shit!" Trumbo tried the cuffs fastening her to the floor of the van. "Do you have a key to this?"

Denise shook her head. "Sunn sleeps with the keys."

"Can we pry it off?"

"Alison pried 'em off last week, so Sunn got some new handcuffs and chains to make sure it wouldn't happen again."

Trumbo held Alison's chained hand in his own. It was sweet to feel her touch, to see her alive, even in these circumstances. The joy of seeing her heightened his frustration that he couldn't free her.

He whispered in her ear. "Alison, wake up. Just for a minute. It's me, Trumbo."

She remained silent.

"Alison." He kissed her forehead, then placed a dozen tiny kisses on her cheeks, her nose, her neck. He whispered in her ear, nibbling gently on her earlobe. "Alison, wake up. I love you."

She slowly opened her eyes. The total relaxation in her face, caused by the sleep and drugs, gave her features an angelic quality. She focused on Trumbo and let slip a tiny Mona Lisa smile. "Trumbo, I'm glad you're here," she whispered, then her eyelids slowly drifted downward and her head fell onto Trumbo's lap as she was sucked back into the abyss of sleep.

Trumbo looked up. Denise sat behind him, her hands on her hips, scowling impatiently. "We gotta get out of here somehow!" she said. "How come yer wastin' time talking to her now?"

Trumbo smiled at the girl. "Something I've wanted to do for a while. It's going to be risky getting out. I might not survive to see her again."

"Oh, bullshit," said Denise. "What're we going to do?"

"Are there any other cars here?"

"Like, what do you mean?" asked Denise.

"Someone who could follow us."

"Just one other truck."

"The one next to the trailer home?" asked Trumbo.

"Yep."

"Okay. You stand outside as if nothing unusual happened —in case someone comes out. I'm going to mess up that truck so they can't chase us."

"Then what?"

"Then we'll think of something."

"Okay."

Trumbo and Denise climbed out of the van. Denise stationed herself where Trumbo had first found her, leaning against the vehicle. He started to crawl towards the truck, twenty yards away, when she called after him.

"Trumbo!"

He walked back to Denise's side and whispered, "What?"

"What if someone comes out?"

"Pretend nothing has happened."

"What about that?" She pointed to the broken window.

The girl was scared. He patted her on the shoulder and tried to sound reassuring. "You're a smart girl. Steer them away from it. Make sure they don't see what happened."

"I'll try," she said.

"Good!" He patted her on the head, turned, and walked to Sunn's pickup truck. He crawled beneath, pulled out a few wires at random, then to make sure he hadn't missed anything, untwisted the tiny bolt in the bottom of the oil pan. Black, sticky oil dripped out all over the ground. Even if the car started, it wouldn't run very long before seizing up. Just to be sure, he pulled out a few more wires and stuck them in his back pocket.

When he crawled out from under the truck, he looked toward the trailer. Someone was awake. He turned and looked for Denise. She was no longer standing by the van. He crept silently around the trailer and saw Denise arguing with a much bigger girl in the courtyard.

"I don't believe you!" said the older girl.

"It just happened! I swear!" said Denise. She turned her head and caught Trumbo's eye.

"What are you looking at?" said the older girl.

"Nothing," said Denise.

Trumbo ducked into the shadows next to the trailer before the older girl looked over her shoulder. He heard something snap beneath his foot.

"Someone's out here, you little creep. I'm going in there and wake up Sunn."

Trumbo calculated his odds. He figured the girl was twenty feet away—five long paces. He did not know if she was armed. He ran at the girl and tackled her. He shoved his hand across her face before she had an opportunity to scream, pinning her to the ground with all his weight. The girl squirmed and struggled beneath him.

"Who is this?" Trumbo asked Denise.

"Silhouette. She came out to take a piss."

"That's it? No one else is awake?"

"I don't think so."

"Someone will come looking for her in a minute unless we get the hell out of here."

Trumbo cried out as Silhouette bit down, hard, on one of his fingers. "Goddammit!" He lifted her off the ground and carried her to the van. He tore off his shirt and quickly fashioned a gag, which he wrapped around her mouth. Then he took his belt and wrapped it tightly around her hands and feet, fastening the other end of the belt around the front seat panel. He calculated that even if she struggled, it should hold her for a few minutes.

"Denise, keep an eye on her. I'm going to hot-wire the van."

He flipped open the hood of the van and looked inside. He lit a match to see what he was doing, then took one of the wires appropriated from the truck and fastened it to a terminal on the starter of the van. He touched the opposite end of the wire to the battery. The starter whirred and the engine came to life. He twisted the wire around the battery terminal and slammed the hood, then jumped into the driver's seat of the van and closed the door.

Denise stared at him from the passenger seat. "She got out."

"What?"

"She pulled her wrist out of the belt. Sorry!"

He looked out the window just in time to see Silhouette disappear into the trailer home.

"Jesus H. Christ." Trumbo slammed the van into gear. The wheels spun on the dirt. He put it into reverse, rocked the vehicle back and forth, and got out of the dirt. On the flat ground he fishtailed the rear end of the van, and throwing a cloud of dust up behind him, sped toward the road.

In the rearview mirror he saw Sunn and Silhouette run from the mobile home. Sunn had a gun.

"Hold on and fasten your seat belt!" yelled Trumbo. Trumbo swerved the van right and left to make it a more difficult target and raced toward the main road, almost losing control when he ran over an unseen stump. He heard several shots and then a nerve-jarring sound as one of the side windows of the van took a hit and shattered. They reached the road and he saw that the gate was still secured. *Run it!* he thought. He pushed the accelerator to the floor and raced headlong toward the gate: forty miles an hour, forty-five—*I'll break through the damn thing and get out of here*—fifty, fifty-five.

The van careened into the gate; glass and metal flew into his face. The front of the van smashed directly into a metal post and crumpled with the force of the blow. Steam hissed out of the radiator, then something gave way and boiling water sprayed into the air as the engine died. The gate was bent out of shape, but held firm. Denise screamed.

Trumbo wiped shards of glass away from his forehead; a dozen tiny cuts covered his face.

"Denise, you okay?" he yelled.

She cried out, "I don't know, I don't know."

Trumbo put his hands on her face. The left side was a spider web of tiny scratches, but the right side was untouched. Her eyes were tightly closed. "Denise, open your eyes. Can you see?"

Panting, she opened one eye, and then the other.

"Trumbo, I'm scared."

"Lie down on the floor." He reached in the back of the van and found a blanket, then put it over her. "Be calm." He crawled over the backseat and knelt down next to Alison, who still was asleep. He inspected her hands and feet where the chains were fastened to her and found no major damage. Perhaps because she was so relaxed, she had escaped injury, he hoped. He opened one of her eyelids with his fingers. Her pupil contracted when the interior van light hit it. He knew from the many accidents he had attended that that was a good sign. He kissed her and hopped out the back door of the van.

The whine of an engine reverberated across the wide field. In the distance he saw the headlights of the pickup truck making its way toward him. *They must have started up the truck. Guess I didn't take the right wires out. Shitfire!*

He ran toward the fence and examined it. Even though it had stopped the van, one post was pulled out of the ground. He lifted one end of the deformed gate and pushed it out of the way into the road. He heard a terrible grinding noise and looked over his shoulder. The truck had stopped. Without oil, the cylinders had seized up and the engine block had probably cracked. Sunn and Silhouette jumped out of the truck. They were a few hundred yards behind. Two minutes, max, until they were there, less if they decided to shoot him from where they were. There was no time to try to free Alison from the back of Sunn's demolished van, no hope of getting the van to run again.

He ran down the road to Marcus Hugo's truck. He slammed it into reverse, cursing the clutch, and backed up to the van. Steam and water still sprayed from beneath the van's hood. He had no tow bar. No chains to fasten the cars together. Praying that there would be no traffic on the country road for at least a few moments, he threw it into reverse and drove backward as fast as he could, bracing himself for the collision. His neck snapped backwards as the truck met the van.

As he had hoped, the two bumpers had met, overlapped, and locked together. He leaned into the van and threw the transmission into neutral. He heard several sharp pings as gunfire hit the van. Sunn was only about fifty yards away and gaining, firing at them as he ran. For several moments the wheels spun. Then the truck suddenly gained traction and he literally towed the van away, with Alison and Denise inside.

He turned right on the road and sped away into the night. In the side mirror he saw several flashes from Sunn's gun, but there were no more hits. Now he held his breath and hoped the jury-rigged connection between the truck and the van held, at least for a couple miles until he was out of harm's way.

He proceeded for another three miles until he came to a train crossing. He stopped; the bizarre towing arrangement might not hold over the elevated crossing. He pulled off the road, dragging the van behind, stopped, and crawled into the van.

Denise was on her knees, sobbing uncontrollably.

"Keep it together, little friend," he said to her. In spite of the crisis, he took a moment to pat her arm and try to cheer her up. "You're okay now. Sunn's way behind us. We'll get you all patched up in a little while. I need you to keep control for a little while. Can you do that for me?" he asked.

She sniffled some more, then stopped her tears. "My knees hurt. I hurt all over."

"I know you do. I do, too."

With one final sob, she stopped her crying. "Okay."

"Go get into the cab of my truck. I left the engine running. It's a lot warmer in there. Take the blanket with you."

"Okay."

She hobbled to her feet and walked to the truck.

Trumbo opened the back doors of the van and tried to figure out how to free Alison. She still lay on her side, drugged into a stupor. Her wrists were secured in handcuffs; chains went from her feet to a bolt in the floor of the van.

He pried open the side of the van where the spare tire was kept. He threw the spare tire onto the road and found what he was looking for: the tire iron. He pulled it out and tried to jam it beneath the bolt holding the chains in place. Three times he tried, and three times the tire iron slipped out of place. The final time he tried, the iron almost hit Alison in the leg. *No good.* Then he realized it didn't matter what happened to the van itself. He peeled back the carpet and began pounding away at the entire floor panel. In a couple of minutes he pried up one side of the body panel, peeling it back like the lid of a giant can. He lifted Alison and moved her out of the way, then began working on the opposite side. He broke through one weld, then another, then pulled up the entire body panel. It was made of steel and probably weighed sixty pounds. He threw Alison over one shoulder, as a fireman might, and the four-by-three-foot steel hunk of van floor dragged on the ground. He set her down behind the pickup truck, lifted the metal into the bed of the truck, then put her into the flatbed, chains, metal, and all. She shivered and woke up for a minute.

"Alison, it's okay. It's me, Trumbo."

Tears fell down her cheek, but she said nothing.

"I'm getting you out of here," he told her.

He ran back to the van and got out the blanket, then threw it over Alison.

He knocked on the truck door. Denise rolled down her window. Trumbo put on his best big-brother voice and tried to soothe her. "Denise, I really need your help now. Alison's in the back of the truck. She could get cut on the jagged metal. I need you to ride with her and make sure she doesn't get hurt. Can you do that for me?" He forced a smile.

His appeal to her maturity worked. Denise climbed out of the van. "You need me?"

"I do. Sunn can't be far behind."

"Okay."

Denise climbed up into the bed of the truck by Alison's side. Trumbo patted her on the shoulder. "Keep yourselves covered with the blankets. It's only about fifteen miles."

"Okay." She hopped up into the bed of the truck and tended to Alison. He was glad Denise had something to distract her from her injuries.

He examined the linkage between the truck and the van. They were twisted together, the bumper of the truck hooked under the bumper of the van. He ran back and pulled out the tire iron and the jack. He stuck the jack under the van's front left side and jacked it up as high as it would go. There was about an inch of clearance between the bumpers on the left side, but on the right the metal was still twisted together. He hoped he could separate them.

He jumped into the driver's seat of the truck and spun the wheels as hard as he could. With the screech of metal on metal, the bumpers scratched and clawed against each other, then suddenly jerked loose. The truck was finally clear of the van. He sped down the road, away from Sunn.

As dawn broke, he drove to Marcus Hugo's house in the quiet little suburb. Sprinklers sprayed lawns. A newspaper boy threw papers onto people's porches. A woman stepped outside and watched her dog relieve itself. It was soothing to be surrounded by the tranquillity of a neighborhood filled with gentle people unaware of the trials he had suffered that night. He was often sentimental about the pleasures of families living in homes with lawns, fathers and sons who barbecued together, mothers dressing their daughters up for church. This morning, because of the stark contrast with his experiences of the previous night, he was almost teary-eyed.

Hugo greeted them in a bathrobe and fluffy slippers. The two men helped Denise get inside, found her a spot on the couch, and covered her with a blanket. She was in surprisingly good spirits. Trumbo wanted to keep her away from mirrors, at least for a while. The cuts on her face appeared worse than they were, and he needed to keep her calm just a little while longer. Hugo helped Trumbo carry Alison—still fastened by chains to the sharp metal panel—into the living room.

"Just what exactly were you getting into last night?" asked Hugo suggestively. "Some kind of S and M?"

"Long story. You got bolt cutters?"

"I'm on parole. I can't keep criminal tools."

Trumbo stared him down. "You got some anyway?"

Hugo scowled, disappeared into the basement, and returned with a four-foot pair of bolt cutters with a sharp stainless steel business end that looked like a wicked bird of prey. It took about ten minutes to remove the chains and handcuffs.

Trumbo gave Marcus a twenty-dollar bill, "for the long distance," then called a paramedic he knew named Doug Op. Op cursed him for calling so early, then gave Trumbo instructions on first aid. Trumbo checked both girls for concussions and was pleased to find out that they probably hadn't suffered any. Op told him how to clean and dress the cuts they had endured from the crash, then advised him to cover them both up and get them some bed rest. Trumbo was happy to comply and tucked Alison into one bed, while Denise rested on the couch.

Trumbo took Hugo out of the girls' hearing range.

"Can you watch them? I need to go out for about fifteen minutes."

"Where you going?" asked Hugo.

"Make a call. Gotta go out because the place I'm calling might have a trace on the line. If I call from here, they'll know where I am, and I need to lay low for another day or so."

"What's up?"

"Tell you later."

He didn't want to tell Hugo he was calling the cops, because it would merely make the parolee nervous. Trumbo drove to a convenience store about a mile away from Hugo's house and stood by the pay phone for a minute gathering his thoughts. He took a deep breath and dialed 911.

"I'd like to report, uh, a kidnapping and a stash of illegal weapons and explosives."

"Pardon me, sir?"

"I said I want to alert the police to a kidnapping. And some bombs."

He could hear the operator do a double take on hearing the inflammatory report. Kern County emergency operators probably didn't get many calls like that. "Yes, sir, what's your name?"

"I don't want to say. The man's name, the one who did the kidnapping, is J'osüf Sunn. He's out on the old Tower Road, in a mobile home—trailer park–type house—in the middle of a field about one and a half miles east of the railroad tracks. There's a dirt road leading to it. The fence in front, well, it's pretty smashed up. There is one man and about half a dozen women. They're all heavily armed. Machine guns, explosives, I don't know what else."

"Can you give a more specific address? Or your name, sir? Perhaps you could show the police where this is or at least talk to an officer."

"I'm sorry. I can't."

Trumbo hung up and quickly left the parking lot. He needed just one more day. He would spend a little time with Alison before turning himself in. He realized no matter how solemnly he proclaimed his innocence, they would hold him on half a dozen charges, probably without bail.

When he got back, Hugo was eating breakfast and Denise slept soundly on the couch, in spite of the "Today" show blaring from the big-screen television. Trumbo walked back and looked at Alison asleep on Hugo's bed, aglow in a saffron beam of morning sunlight. He quietly took off his shoes and lay down next to her. Unconsciously she reached out and put her hand on his. She turned her head to the side and opened her eyes. Whatever drugs they had given her were wearing off.

Startled, she jerked her hand away from Trumbo.

"Where am I?" Her voice was as soft as sleep.

"We're in a friend's house. It's Trumbo. I got you out, Alison."

"The chains are gone."

"Everything's going to be okay."

She frowned. "Is Sunn here?"

"No, he's not here. None of them are here."

"Are they still after me?"

"I called the police. They won't get far."

She sat up and tentatively stretched out her shoulders. "I'm all bruises and knots."

"How long were you in that van?"

"Too long."

"Here's some water."

She drank about half the glass, then leaned back onto the pillow. "You really came and got me?"

Trumbo nodded.

She stared at him. "Thank you." She reached out and touched his face. "You're all scratched up."

"Looks worse than it is. Don't worry about me."

Alison rocked her head around on her shoulders. "God, I'm sore and grimy. My legs are still all needles and pins."

Trumbo ran his fingers through her hair. "It's okay now. I'll go start you a bath." He stepped into the bathroom, started the water running, and returned.

Alison was smiling. "You're really taking care of me."

"Yeah."

"Thanks."

"No need to thank me."

Alison twisted around and sat up, dangling her legs off of the bed. Then she braced herself and stood up. Almost immediately she lost her balance and crumpled to the floor.

"You okay?"

"My legs are numb."

"I'll help you."

He leaned over the bed, put one arm behind her neck, the other in the crook of her legs, and lifted her. She wrapped her arms around his neck. Without saying a word, he carried her into the bathroom. He gently helped her to sit on the edge of the bathtub, and then leaned over and shut off the water. The last few drops splashed down in the tub, echoing through the bathroom as the two looked at each other.

"Help me get into the water," she said. "I'm afraid I'll fall again."

"Okay."

He unbuttoned her long-sleeve shirt and helped her slip out of it. Welts and blisters encircled both wrists where the handcuffs had dug into her flesh. Bruises covered her right arm. She clung to his neck for support while he pulled off her shoes and socks, and then carefully pulled off her blue jeans. When he saw the deep blue bruises on her ankles, he understood the savagery to which she had been subjected. He quickly slipped off her brassiere and underwear, and then lifted her in his arms and lowered her into the bathwater.

"You okay? Water all right?"

"You have no idea how good it feels."

"Should I leave you alone?"

"Never."

He kneeled on the floor behind her and helped her sit up in the tub. Trumbo squeezed some shampoo into one hand and rubbed it into her long, dark hair. She closed her eyes and slowly swayed her head, pushing it against his fingers as he massaged the lather into her scalp. She visibly relaxed beneath his touch. He rested her head on one hand and rinsed the soap from her hair.

Tears welled up in Alison's eyes. Trumbo wiped them away with his finger. "Are you okay?"

She bit her lip. "Nobody ever took care of me before. Nobody ever asked me how I was."

He found a clean washcloth beneath Hugo's sink, dunked it in the suds, and filled it with lather. Gently he rubbed it across her back, in wide, tranquil circles. She arched her back, and her breathing became deep and slow. "Oh. That's so wonderful," she purred. He rubbed the cloth across her shoulders and neck, then slowly washed her front, lingering for just a moment on her high, small breasts, her nipples small and dark like chocolate kisses. He took a long time with her hands and feet, gently pulling the slippery, wet cloth between them, massaging each finger and toe, warming them, bringing them back to life. She held on to his arm with both hands as she dunked herself beneath the water and rinsed off. The quiet splashing of the water was meditative and calm.

"I just want to stay here forever," she said. "Sit by me and hold my hand. Talk to me. Tell me a story."

As she lay with her eyes closed, luxuriating in the warmth, he gently stroked her arm.

"What kind of story?" he asked.

"Something pretty, faraway, something to take me away."

Trumbo didn't usually tell stories, but for her benefit he made one up. It was a tale of a boy who, from childhood, had been stowed away, alone, in the engine room of a luxury ship, never knowing how he got there, never knowing how to get out. The boy had never known any other life and he had free run of the giant ocean liner. He made his way through the heating ducts and secret passages, going from room to room, stealing fine food from the kitchen, bathing in ocean water overflowing from the engines. From his hiding place he watched the rich passengers at their fancy-dress balls and their captain's dinners, and saw them lying in the sun on the deck, but he never mixed with them, because he knew if he revealed himself, he'd be hauled off to an orphanage. He preferred his solitary existence on the margins of the ship, unseen and unheard, without an obligation to anyone.

When the boy grew older, pangs of loneliness set in; he saw that everyone on the ship had a wife or a husband or a girlfriend, and realized there was something missing. One day he started hearing unusual sounds. There was a separate set of secret passageways in the ship that he had never explored. He discovered a young woman almost the same age, who had been hiding in the same ship herself. Together they watched the parties and finery of the beautiful passengers, but they also saw the fights, the money changing hands, the misery of the ship's crew. The boy and girl debated revealing themselves but decided that they liked their secret existence better, and one day when the ship was passing an island, both of them jumped off of the boat and swam away.

The deserted isle was full of delicious fruit and friendly animals, and they lived a happy life together until they grew very old.

Alison smiled when he finished. "I know what you mean."

"It doesn't mean anything. It's just a story."

She leaned over and kissed him. "Help me up."

He lifted her to the edge of the tub, and then helped her stand. They kissed again. She tasted delicious, like grapes and strawberries. Her slender, wet body pressed against him, soaking him from head to toe. "Dry me off." He found the biggest towel he could and vigorously rubbed her dry. She set the towel on the floor and leaned against him as he fluffed up her hair. Her skin was pink and warm and glowed. He couldn't help staring at the curve of her breast, at her flat, pink stomach, at her long, trim legs, bent at the knee, at her tiny arched feet.

She leaned her head against his shoulder and closed her eyes. He kissed her again, longer and deeper. She put his hands on her breasts and he held her close.

"You get in. I'll wash you off now."

She was animated and lively as she scrubbed him down like a favorite pet; although it had only been hours since her captivity, she had regained her humanity and humor. She giggled as she splashed the water around, twisting the little patch of hair on his chest into a knot, biting his toes, letting her hands brush against his erect penis, protruding from the sudsy water. After she dried him off they went to the bedroom and made love for what felt like hours; playfully they touched and teased and bumped against each other, as if discovering the touch of skin against skin for the first time. They crumpled into each others arms. Just before they fell into a deep, satisfied slumber, Alison whispered into Trumbo's ear "Now we just have to find that island."

29

LLOYD P. LLOYD, A CORCORAN REGIONAL POLICE DISPATCHER,
looked at his log, trying to figure out where the hell Car 22
was.

He flipped a switch on the lighted board in front of him
and radioed one of his motorcycle cops. "Eleven?"

"Yes, Lloyd P. What's up?"

"Paul? Bobby's been missing a couple of hours."

"I haven't seen him."

"You want to go check on him? He might be at that
Basque restaurant he likes. Last he called in, he was on old
Tower Road, about a mile east of the tracks, investigating
some crank caller."

"Gotcha. I'll fill you in later."

Paul Mower was glad for the distraction. He was bored
after sitting by the side of the road for three hours, pointing
a radar gun from between his legs. He jumped on his
motorcycle and rode toward Tower Road.

He started at the railroad and drove east, but saw nothing
on his first pass. He banged a U-turn, and drove back a little
ways until he saw skid marks and broken glass next to a
chain-link fence that had been smashed to hell. He pulled off
the road and walked over to investigate. He squinted and
peered down the dirt road that ran perpendicular to the
fence. About a hundred yards in front of him he spotted
Bobby's cruiser. He unholstered his weapon and tentatively
took a few steps toward it.

He trotted back to his motorcycle and plugged in to the
radio. "This is eleven to dispatch, eleven to dispatch, over.
Dispatch, I have a possible OID situation, between the
forty-three- and forty-four-mile marker on Tower Road.
Send all available units." It was an officer-in-distress call,
words that struck fear into the heart of every cop. It meant
that a cop was in an immediately life-threatening situation.

"Eleven, do I read you correctly? OID?"

"Yes."

"Eleven, do you have more detail on that situation?"

Before Paul could answer, he heard the crack of a gunshot and was knocked flat on his face. In his disoriented state he thanked God for body armor; the shell had hit him squarely in the Kevlar vest. Staying on the ground, he rolled around and grabbed his service revolver, searching frantically for the source of the gunfire, without success. He spoke into the radio again. "I've been hit by gunfire. Goddamn it, I need backup!" A second shot struck his helmet and knocked his head backwards. He scrambled down into the ditch by the side of the road. As soon as he looked up, he saw the business end of a machine gun pointed at his face, held by a teenaged girl younger than his own daughter.

"Hello, Mr. Piggy. Good-bye, Mr. Piggy," she said.

"No, don't!"

Silhouette squeezed off fifteen shots in less than five seconds. She rolled his body over, took away his pistol, and then darted down the road away from the farm.

Mower's radio was stuck in the on position. At the Corcoran Emergency Services Dispatch Center, Lloyd P. heard the chilling sound of gunshots, and gasped. "OID! OID!" He stood and looked over the divider separating him from the other dispatcher. "Paul's been shot!"

Lloyd P. blocked his emotions and flatly broadcast the information to any units within hailing distance. "Two officers down, suspect or suspects unknown, Old Tower Road, all units please respond."

All across Kern County law officers dropped what they were doing—be it writing speeding tickets, eating lunch, or breaking up domestic disputes—and raced toward the location, lights flashing and adrenaline pumping with the horrible feeling that a fellow officer had suffered the fate every cop thinks about every day he's on the job. Within minutes representatives of the Corcoran and Bakersfield city police departments, the county sheriff, Highway Patrolmen, two ambulances, and a hook and ladder truck had converged on the rural road.

Twenty-six minutes later, the double-wide trailer home a quarter mile away from the road was in the crosshairs of a dozen police sharpshooters. At least one person—some thought many more—could be seen through the windows of the trailer. A plea from the commander in charge to abandon the facility and surrender was ignored. When a helicopter flew overhead to repeat the demand, it was greeted with several rifle shots.

All the makings of a standoff fell into place: hostile belligerents in a difficult-to-secure location with no intention of giving themselves up. The commander in charge told the officers around him to prepare themselves for a long wait. All that was missing for a full three-ring circus was the media.

It was fifty-five minutes before airtime for the first of James St. James's two warm-up live broadcasts from Corcoran, California. St. James had prepared a show to hype the upcoming "Manson Parole" episode, including half a dozen high-priced "experts" who would all solemnly testify that, indeed, this time Manson would go free. St. James had rented out a local warehouse to serve as a production studio for the two live programs. Actually, Marilyn McLeod had done all the leg work. Now that it was set up, he no longer needed her. He was making notes for incendiary language he could use on the show when Wytowski burst into his private office.

"Knock, Wytowski! Goddamn it."

"It's an emergency."

"Go back outside. Close the door. And knock."

"Yes, sir."

The new title of senior producer that Wytowski had inherited from Marilyn McLeod didn't buy him any additional respect. He stepped back into the hall, closed the door, and knocked. There was no answer. He knocked even more urgently.

"Just a minute," said St. James. Wytowski bounced on his heels while his boss laid a power trip on him by making him wait. After two or three minutes St. James finally said, "Come in!"

Immediately St. James laid into Wytowski. "What was so goddamn important? We go on the air in less than an hour, and I need my concentration."

"That's just it. There's a breaking news story just south of town."

"What do I care about some local-yokel news?"

"It's Manson people. They're in some sort of standoff with the cops."

"Jesus Christ, why didn't you say so?"

"I did try to say so. The local station is all over it."

St. James's platform heels clacked relentlessly as he ran behind Wytowski down the hall and outside. In the trailer that housed St. James's mobile broadcast equipment, three of the televisions were tuned to a local news station. A harried-looking newswoman stood by the side of a road and tried to describe what was going on behind her.

"Two police officers were shot and killed earlier today at the edge of this Corcoran County field. The perpetrators have barricaded themselves into a double-wide trailer parked at the center of the farm."

She gestured broadly and the camera turned to show a dozen CHPs, local cops, and sheriff's vehicles lined up behind barricades, guns aimed at the mobile home.

The reporter continued. "As you can see behind me, a substantial amount of firepower has been focused on this threat. Early reports that the Manson Family cult is behind this have not been confirmed . . ."

Suddenly a shoe flew through the cramped room. "God-damn it! Why aren't we there yet?"

"It just happened, James," said Wytowski. "I thought we ought to be there."

"Get me three camera crews and a chopper. We have to get out there in"—he looked at his watch—"forty-five minutes."

"Uh, sir, we don't have the list of local crews."

"What the fuck do you mean by that?"

"Marilyn had them."

"What does that mean, Marilyn has them? Are you a senior producer or are you an overpaid secretary? I want mobile crews! I want a chopper! Learn it! Do it!"

Wytowski pulled his cellular phone from his pocket and started calling through the yellow pages. Twenty minutes later he had one camera crew—not three—and had yet to locate a helicopter. He reported to St. James.

"Pull the fucking studio cameras out of the studio and throw them into the production van. The satellite uplink can be set up after we get there. If we have to, we'll run tape until the first commercial break and then go live. Get on it. I'm out of here," screamed St. James.

"Where are you going?"

"To the airport. To bribe a helicopter."

Wytowski went into overdrive, stuffing fifty-dollar bills into the hands of union television crew members. He found the driver of the mobile video van in a hotel room with a hooker, and paid her off, too. Seven minutes before the show was to begin, he was on-site, across the street from the fleet of law enforcement vehicles positioned around the perimeter of the rural enclave.

He found the local freelance camera crew and slapped a thousand bucks into each of their palms, then told them to figure out how the hell to get their cameras hooked up to the satellite remote, with promises of more cash the faster they could accomplish it. The yokels were simultaneously impressed and angered at the get-it-done-right-now attitude of St. James's crew. But they ran nonetheless. Wytowski was learning to enjoy the crisis atmosphere.

Three minutes before airtime, the camera crew had stationed themselves at the edge of the police line, their lenses pointed straight into the middle of the large field. The satellite uplink had been established and Wytowski had impressed enough police with his press credentials that the group wasn't immediately going to be thrown out. One problem: no sign of James St. James. Wytowski raced into the mobile van, talked to the studio in New York over the satellite, and told them to run tape for the first segment of the show—whatever rerun was handy, with first preference going to a Manson episode. The New York director swore and complained but promised to do the best he could on such short notice.

Wytowski was soaked with sweat. He stepped out of the mobile onto the street and immediately had a clipboard full of papers blown out of his hands by a powerful wind. He looked up and saw a tiny helicopter—marked CENTRAL VALLEY EMERGENCY MEDICAL TRANSPORT—land in the middle of the street. As soon as it had touched down, James St. James leaped from the chopper, as calm and composed as if he had just gotten home from church.

"Everything on the up and up, Wytowski?" yelled St. James.

"Yeah! Told 'em to run tape for the first ten minutes."

"Fuck that! We have forty seconds until air. Where's the camera? Point me in the right direction, run inside, and tell them we're live, live, *live* from Corcoran."

"Yes, sir."

St. James found the yokels, cursed at them for their poor choice of camera equipment, straightened his toupee, and waited for Wytowski's go-ahead.

"We're live. You're on," screamed Wytowski.

"This is James St. James."

30

WITH ONE LEG WRAPPED AROUND TRUMBO'S SLEEPING BODY, luxuriating in the delicious postcoital slumber, half-awake, half in heaven, Alison was jarred from her reverie by the unexpected sound of sobbing. Startled, she pulled herself away from him. Little Denise stood by the side of the bed, her hands twisted into fists, her face red with sobbing.

"Alison . . ." she cried. "Wake up. Wake up."

Alison pulled the sheet over her breasts and sat bolt upright. She poked Trumbo, who groggily began to pull himself out of sleep.

"What is it?"

"Cuh, come out to the living room. They, they're"— Denise grabbed a Kleenex and blew her nose—"they're going to kill them all."

"Who?"

"Silhouette and Cleopatra and Peace and Princess and J'osüf and everyone. They're gonna kill them!"

"Oh my God."

Alison pulled on one of Trumbo's long shirts and a pair

of underwear, then shook Trumbo awake. He sluggishly wrapped a blanket around himself and hurried to the living room.

Denise sat in front of the big-screen television, sobbing her heart out. "It's on all the channels. They're going to kill them all."

Trumbo and Alison watched, horrified. The television showed the mobile home as viewed from a helicopter. The trailer and truck were easily recognizable. It gave Alison the jitters seeing it again so soon. Thirty or forty police cars surrounded the trailer. Leaning on each car were two or three policemen in full riot gear, many aiming rifles at the broken-down trailer home. Halfway between the trailer and the road was another, larger group of vehicles. Trumbo immediately recognized the vans and trucks as media vehicles. The logos of television networks and local stations were emblazoned across them.

Denise shook with fear. Alison put her arms around the little girl to console her. "It's okay, Denise, it's going to be all right."

The girl shook her head furiously. "No it isn't. They're going to kill them all. I *know* those girls. It's not their fault, it's not their fault!"

Trumbo turned up the sound. James St. James's voice boomed from the speaker. ". . . FBI negotiators gave them until sundown to surrender before further action is taken. Death has visited this godforsaken swatch of land twice today, taking the lives of two officers of the law, and the Grim Reaper may descend yet again, as the showdown of the century continues between the upstanding citizenry of California's Central Valley and the deranged inhabitants of the Trailer of Doom." He stared into the camera earnestly while gesturing to the chaos behind him in the field. "Sunset is forty-five minutes away, and we will report live continuously until some resolution is achieved. Already at least one hundred officers of the law have surrounded the compound, and while we were on a commercial break, three bulldozers and two battering rams arrived. Just who is inside? Reports link the occupants of the trailer to the notorious Manson Family, but except for a few glimpses earlier this afternoon, no one has seen how many people there are. Is it a small army or one madman with an arsenal? All that we know at this time is that gunfire issued twice from the trailer, making a tense situation even tenser."

Trumbo turned down the sound.

"They're completely screwed," said Trumbo.

Denise protested fiercely. "They're not all bad. Any girl from any town could have gotten mixed up with J'osüf Sunn. He's the one pulling strings. He's the one who tells them all what to do. And now they're going to die . . . If only the cops knew the truth, they'd back off."

"We can call them," offered Alison.

"They wouldn't believe you if you called, and the message won't get there until it's too late. Look at what they're doing . . ." Denise pointed to the television screen. Dozens of sharpshooters aimed at the mobile home. A tanklike vehicle was wheeled into place in front of the trailer, its hardened steel tip aimed directly at the front door. "It's happening too fast."

Trumbo threw up his hands and caught Alison's eye. "What do you think?" he asked. "It's the same shits who chained you in the back of a van. I say they deserve whatever happens to 'em."

Alison shook her head and spoke softly. "If Denise were still down there, I wouldn't want them killing her just for being in the wrong place at the wrong time."

"You have a point. Let's go." Trumbo glanced around, slightly puzzled. "Where's Hugo? We should take his truck."

Denise shrugged. "I haven't seen him since I woke up. I think he has a job or something."

"A job! What a concept. We'll take my car."

As they drove toward the scene, they listened to radio reports. Every station was covering the situation. Alison switched from station to station, desperate for information. The stories were filled with frightening glimpses of pending violence:

Fifty troops from the California National Guard have arrived, armed with full combat gear and bearing M-16s and other high-powered weaponry . . .

All eyes are trained on the trailer, waiting for some evidence of compromise.

As Trumbo, Alison, and Denise raced toward the complex, the sun, burnished a brilliant carrot color by the Central Valley dust, slipped behind the mountains. They turned onto the old Tower Road, only about a mile away. Almost immediately they were stopped behind an enormous snarl of traffic: The crisis had drawn morbid voyeurs from miles around, all of whom were stopped behind police barricades.

Trumbo parked the car, and the three jumped out. Distant sirens distorted by the wind sounded eerie warnings. Four or five helicopters circled above the trailer. At least two hundred cars were parked in the middle of the road. Families stood by their cars and sat on the roofs of their vans, staring vaguely in the direction of the trailer, as if waiting for an outdoor concert or a Fourth of July fireworks show. Some had brought folding chairs. Car radios blaring from every vehicle created a cacophony of competing reports.

"We've got to get there, now!" shouted Alison. "Come on!" They weaved in and out through hundreds of spectators. At the front of the traffic jam four sawhorses and two cop cruisers blocked any passage. Beyond the blockade was a half mile of empty road, and then the convoy of police and military vehicles. Trumbo, Alison, and Denise attempted to dodge past the cops in the ditch next to the road, but were stopped by an oversized patrolman from the California Highway Patrol, resplendent in the standard knee-high black leather boots, pressed blue uniform, white helmet, and sunglasses.

"No getting through here, folks," said the cop. "This road has been closed off. You'll have to go back to your vehicle, please."

Denise shouted, "I *know* the people who are *in* there. You can't let them shoot them like dogs!"

"I'm sorry, but no one can get past here."

Trumbo spoke. "She really does know them. Maybe she could talk to the officer in charge and give him some ideas on how to get them to give up peacefully."

The Chip shook his head. "That may be, but nobody's going up there now. Believe me, kids, you shouldn't be out here. The people inside are cop killers and they're still shooting at us. Why don't you just go back to your car and listen to the radio?"

Denise couldn't contain herself. "I'm not lying, you dipshit! I've got to talk to them!" Denise broke from Alison's hand, skipped past the cop, and tore as fast as she could down the road. Alison and Trumbo followed her.

Before they'd gotten a hundred yards toward their goal, the Chip had caught up with them on his motorcycle. He skidded the bike to a stop in front of them, blocked their path, and climbed off, holding his baton at the ready. Moments later a cruiser from the roadblock pulled alongside him. Its driver had drawn his pistol. Trumbo, Alison, and Denise were trapped.

The Chip was pissed. "On the ground!"

They obliged him, lying facedown on the gravel.

"I'm going to place you under administrative arrest for interfering with an officer of the law in the performance of his duties. Put your hands behind your back and cross your wrists."

The second cop got out of the cruiser. "Cuff 'em?"

"Yes."

"The little girl, too?"

The Chip hesitated. "Yes. She ran first."

The cruiser cop slipped nylon restraints across Trumbo's wrists. The white saw-toothed band was similar in design to the plastic ties that fasten garbage bags. He pulled out a second pair and was about to place them on Alison's wrists when a mighty roar rumbled through the air, delivering a painful blow to their ears as a tumultuous wave crawled across the country.

"Holy shit," shouted the Chip.

Trumbo leaped to his feet, his hands still fastened behind his back, and looked in the direction of the trailer. Above the trailer, a massive orange fireball brighter than the setting sun shot hundreds of feet into the air, undulating and spinning across itself like a great unstable liquid. It was almost immediately followed by another blast even greater than the first, which shot thick black smoke straight up into the air.

The Chip and the cop jumped into the cruiser and

slammed the door. Alison and Denise stood next to Trumbo and stared in shock and disbelief at the destruction before them. Above the trailer a helicopter spun out of control, its tail gyrating hopelessly around the fuselage until it finally crashed with a dull thud in the field.

Suddenly black particles rained down from the sky upon them: bits and pieces of charred wood and still-burning plastic.

Denise screamed. Alison grabbed her hand.

"Let's get out of here!"

They ran past the barricade, past the convoy of thrill-seeking voyeurs, back to Trumbo's car, which was now surrounded by a crush of escaping onlookers in all varieties of vehicles. They watched in awe as the sooty smoke rolled into the twilight sky away from J'osüf Sunn's trailer. From the relative safety of Trumbo's car it was as distant and remote as watching a drive-in movie.

"They're all dead now," said Denise.

Alison pressed the girl's head against her and stroked her hair. "Yes, they are. You tried to warn the cops, you did everything you could."

"Completely gone. I can't believe it."

"It's okay. You'll be okay."

"Let's leave," said Trumbo. There's nothing we can do for them anymore." He took a deep breath. "It's over."

Denise punched him several times in the arm. With his hands still fastened behind his back, he couldn't stop her. "I know they were fuckups, but they took care of me! Sunn's one thing, but some of those girls were my friends!"

Trumbo bit his lip. "My mother was in there."

There was dead silence from the girls.

Then Denise asked, "Which one was she?"

"Barbara Thompson. I didn't know who she was until a couple days ago. I always thought she was dead, and now I wish I never met her. I don't want to watch this anymore. They're gone. Alison, there's some pliers in the backseat. Cut off these handcuffs and let's get out of here."

After two snips from the pliers, the nylon restraints were pulled from his wrists. He drove the car into the drainage ditch alongside the road, passing the dozens of cars parked behind him, and headed back to Hugo's house. They played the radio until they heard a report claiming the trailer had been reduced to "scrap the size of toothpicks," killing all occupants and injuring dozens of cops. Trumbo switched off the radio and they drove in silence save for the sound of Denise's soft sobs. Trumbo kept one hand on the wheel and held Alison's hand with the other.

"I don't know what I hoped for," he said. "It's hitting me kind of weird. I wonder if I'll turn out the same as my mother."

"You won't, Trumbo, believe me," said Alison.

"Thanks for saying so."

Alison squeezed his hand. "What do you want now?"

"Same thing I always wanted, but it just seems that much further away: a normal life, a decent job, a house where I can have a dog."

"That's it?"

"No." He drummed his hands on the wheel nervously. "There's something else. But sometimes, when you want something very badly, and you say it out loud, it suddenly becomes impossible."

"Say it to me."

He frowned hard at the road and said nothing for a long time, struggling with himself.

He turned to her and said, "I want you, too."

She smiled. "That's what I was hoping you'd say."

"When we turn ourselves in, it's going to be a living hell. Our faces'll be all over newspapers. The cops'll go apeshit. I'll probably be arrested and charged with everything they can think of."

"We'll go through it together—you'll need my help. I'll wait for you. I'll help you clear your name."

"Thanks."

Alison continued, "I'll find us a house to rent while you're in court. And I'll get a dog."

Denise leaned up over the middle of the seat. "I hear that mushy crap you guys are talking." She sneaked a smile out beneath the tears. "You make that Ozzie and Harriet bullshit sound great."

Alison looked at Trumbo. "Should I look for a house with an extra bedroom, near a school?"

Trumbo glanced at Denise in the rearview mirror, then at

Alison. "Only if we stay in one place for a while. I don't want her to have the same fucked-up childhood I had."

Alison smiled. "I'll get a long-term lease."

They pulled into Hugo's driveway. Trumbo pressed a button to open the electric garage door.

The garage door rose, and Trumbo drove the car inside. Immediately he sensed something different. Although Hugo's garage had been cluttered when he left, the clutter had been shuffled around. He glanced at a heap of tools in the back corner. *Wonder what that is.* The garage door whirred and began closing behind them. Trumbo only then realized what he was looking at: a heap of rifles, shotguns, and automatic weapons, dumped so carelessly in a way that indicated their owners must have plenty more where those came from. Earlier that day Hugo had been uncomfortable even admitting he had bolt cutters. Trumbo slammed the car into reverse and started to back out of the garage. The door came down behind him and the car smashed into it, throwing Trumbo, Alison, and Denise backwards. He pushed the accelerator to the floor and the engine whined while the rear tires spun furiously against the cement, throwing off thick, black smoke. When he realized that his car was outmatched by the garage door, he killed the engine.

J'osüf Sunn walked into the garage, followed by Silhouette, Peace, and Barbara. Sunn's chest was crisscrossed by bandoliers and he held an AK-47 in his right hand. Barbara and Peace each held a high-powered rifle. The heavy weapons looked peculiar in their thin arms.

"Hello, kids," said Sunn.

Alison gasped. Denise screamed. Trumbo merely sighed and gripped the steering wheel tightly. He wasn't surprised, because he didn't believe in good times or happiness. Only when things went to hell did he feel in his element.

Barbara opened Trumbo's car door. "Come out, son. I'm glad to see you met one of the other chosen ones." She spoke softly and deliberately. "Now all of the remaining Horseman's Clan is here. Cleopatra is inside making some popcorn. We have some videotapes and records, and we've got a day and a half to get to know each other all over again."

31

FROM THE SANCTUARY OF HER BATHTUB, MARILYN MCLEOD watched James St. James's show with the sound turned down low. She didn't even consider the program's spectacular content. What she noticed was the style, or—she smiled —the lack thereof. First off, the cameras should have been *much* closer to the explosion. St. James was removed from the action by at least two hundred yards. *Sloppy.* Second, St. James had nothing even remotely resembling exclusive coverage. A half hour earlier she flipped through the channels and discovered that every network and all the local stations had coverage as good as or better than James's. *Weak, weak, weak.* One of the local anchors, no doubt an ambitious man angling for national exposure, was doing a much better job of pumping up the hot-button words ("earth-shattering . . . Armageddon . . . showdown of the century . . . a Shakespearean tragedy") than St. James. If Marilyn had been there, she would have scribbled ten or fifteen words onto a cue card to keep St. James squarely in purple prose. Without her he sounded mush-mouthed, just another reporter in front of just another situation.

She didn't really care about the explosion, to tell the truth. She was waiting to see how well St. James distanced himself from the scandal that had led to her termination. She poured another glass of red wine, took a sip, and dunked her head under the water.

When she reemerged she saw St. James surrounded by other reporters; he was reading from a prepared text. *This is it.* She turned up the sound.

His five-minute statement was nearly flawless. Even as he heaped blame on her, she admired St. James for the craft that went into his bogus tale of woe. He promised to dedicate the full faith and resources of his staff to rooting out the guilty parties. He promised to help prevent such abuses in the future. Then he told the story of his dear sweet mother: On her deathbed, she had made him promise to always get to the truth no matter how difficult the investigation, regardless of personal sacrifice. He wiped a tear from his eye and thanked the other stations for allowing him to bare his breast in public. He slyly inserted a plug for Thursday's show, then turned away, apparently overcome with tears and unable to speak.

The speech was vintage James St. James, the kind of emotion-filled performance that earned his nighttime specials a thirty-share. Of course, none of it was true. For one thing, St. James's mother, Eleanor Garvey, was alive and well in a retirement community in Phoenix, Arizona. She hadn't talked to her son in over a year, still angry about his changing his name.

Marilyn pulled herself out of the tub and dried off. It was to her advantage that he had successfully extricated himself from the brouhaha. She wanted him flying high, believing himself free of any taint, when she shot him down. Thursday would be the right time, during the Manson parole show. He would have his biggest audience in years, and they'd eat it up like bacon and eggs.

She pulled the fluffy pink bathrobe tight and plodded from the bathroom into her hotel room. On the bed sat a Hi-8 video player and three VHS recorders, which she'd purchased that afternoon, along with a stack of thirty blank videotapes. They were wired up so she could make three copies at a time. She could have them all made by Wednesday's Federal Express cutoff and in the hands of various interested parties just about the same time that St. James's show went on-air. Her checklist of recipients included CNN, MTV, the three big networks, FOX, local news broadcasters in New York, Chicago, Dallas, San Francisco, Atlanta, and Los Angeles . . . and a Mrs. Eleanor Garvey of Phoenix, Arizona. Revenge was reputed to be sweet, but this was better than the best sex Marilyn had ever had.

32

J'osüf Sunn and Barbara Thompson escorted Trumbo, Alison, and Denise at gunpoint from the garage into the house. During the hour that Trumbo was away, J'osüf Sunn and his followers had transformed Hugo's abode from a dull suburban home into a fortress of insanity. Sheets of aluminum foil secured with black electrical tape covered the windows. Every lamp in the house was gathered in the center of the living room. The electrical cords were severed and fragments of smashed light bulbs covered the floor. Hugo's big-screen television had been unplugged and now dangled by its cord from the ceiling like a bizarre oversized piñata. Dozens of candles provided the room's only illumination, giving it an eerie glow. The room smelled of incense and melted wax.

As he was being escorted inside, Trumbo happened to brush against the wall and got fresh paint on his arm. The couch now rested in the middle of the living room, away from the wall, which was now covered with a freshly painted mural. Trumbo recognized it at once: an anthropomorphic sun surrounded by thirteen planets. It was the same twisted image he saw in the abandoned house in Los Angeles. The only difference was that each of the planets had a name attached to it. The second planet from the sun was clearly marked "Alison." The label on the planet closest to the fiery orb was clearly marked "Trumbo, The Inheritor."

He paused too long, and Barbara poked him with the barrel of a gun and pushed him toward the kitchen. Two ordinary kitchen chairs were now deranged thrones, covered with bits and pieces of Christmas ornaments, doll parts, and crepe paper. Denise was whisked off to the back part of the house, tears streaming down her face. Trumbo tried to stop her, but Barbara shoved the gun into his spine. Sunn motioned for Trumbo and Alison to sit, emphasizing his request with a flourish of his gun. They took their places in the bizarre chairs. Trumbo glanced over to Alison. Desperation and frustration filled her eyes. He reached under the table and squeezed her hand in consolation.

"Hello, Trumbo," said Sunn. "My name is J'osüf Sunn. We've met before."

"I thought you were dead."

"In the explosion? I'm not that dumb," said Sunn.

"Who was in the trailer?"

"Only one brave soul: Adelaide Naomi gave her life so that we could go free. And so that I might free you, and Alison, from the bonds of consensus reality."

Something inside Trumbo snapped as he listened to Sunn rant. It might have been the ugly beaded vest that pushed Trumbo to lose his temper, regardless of the danger. "Why are you assholes keeping us here? What could you possibly want from me or Alison?"

Sunn stood a few feet from them and rested his weight on his gun as if it were a cane. "You were *meant* to be here. You're one of the special ones. This is a reunion."

"This is not a reunion. This is perversion. You're a slimeball, and you're taking advantage of underaged girls."

Sunn didn't flinch. He paused and breathed a sigh of infinite patience. "When you do truly understand, when you trade facts for Truth, you'll realize that I'm taking advantage of nobody, that I'm a maker of opportunities, a giver of gifts. I'm giving you the chance of a lifetime, Trumbo. You are the leader of the chosen ones. You are *ours.*"

"I'm not yours and never was."

Sunn smiled enigmatically, leaned his rifle against the wall, then poured some water into a pan. He dumped a washcloth into the water, walked to Trumbo's chair, and knelt before him.

"What the hell are you doing?" asked Trumbo as Sunn sat at his feet.

He started to back away, but Barbara aimed her gun at Trumbo, muttering, "Don't try anything, son."

Sunn unlaced Trumbo's shoes and said, "I'm going to wash your feet, Chosen One, and anoint you to your rightful place." Sunn pulled off one shoe, then the other, and then removed Trumbo's socks. Trumbo clenched his fists in disgust.

When Sunn finished, he crawled to Alison's side and washed her feet, too. He pulled a blue glass bottle down from a shelf and rubbed some oil that smelled of sandalwood on both of their feet.

Sunn repeated several times the phrase "I anoint you and reaffirm your position in the universe as the chosen ones in the name of the Earth, the Trees, the Water, and the Air." Finished, he stood and casually lifted his gun. "Now you are truly one of the Horseman's Clan."

"Swell," said Trumbo, smirking. "What does that mean?"

"You have the power. You may not know it, but you can do anything."

"Anything, huh? What if I wanted to leave?"

"The power to do anything within the holy plan."

"That doesn't leave a lot of latitude."

Sunn shook his head. "You'll understand soon enough. You are a guest in this house, but you are also a guest here on earth. When you understand the truth clearly, it rains down on you all at once. You will soon understand. Sooner than you think. Until then we have to keep a close eye on you because the forces of evil would like nothing better than to use a chosen one for their own twisted consensus-reality ends."

"Yeah, right."

"We'll take care of you until you get the picture. Get comfortable, because you are not going anywhere for a while, at least not in your present incarnation."

"What's that mean?"

"You won't get out of here alive."

"Like Joi Wilmot. And the others who didn't do everything you wanted them to do."

"They chose not to cooperate. When someone is, er, recalcitrant in this lifetime, it's to their advantage to get a start on a new incarnation."

"You killed them."

"That's not what I said! It was their own doing."

"Like they killed themselves."

Alison kicked Trumbo underneath the table. He glanced

over at her. Subtly but firmly she shook her head as if to say, *Quit arguing with him.*

"You are not listening!" Sunn fired three rounds into the ceiling. Chips of acoustic tile sprayed down and the smell of grease and gunpowder permeated the small kitchen. Everyone jumped and stared at each other in stunned silence.

In a few moments the silence was broken by the cheery voice of Barbara, holding a plate of sandwiches in one hand and a .44 in the other. "You must be hungry! I made some sandwiches for you, son!"

"Thank you," said Alison, glaring at Trumbo.

"Thanks," said Trumbo, reluctantly.

Barbara scowled at him. "Thanks, what?"

He restrained himself and mumbled, "Thanks, Mother."

"You're welcome! They're tomato, avocado, and mayonnaise. Is that okay?"

"Fine."

With some ceremony she laid the sandwiches on the table between Alison and Trumbo, and then put paper napkins in front of each of them.

"I also made some tea." She poured two large glasses of iced tea and set them in front of them. Alison dug into the food eagerly. Trumbo, taking her cue, did likewise. In between bites he asked Sunn, "What exactly does a chosen one do?"

"You will lead a great tribe consisting of one seventh of the earth. There are six chosen ones and the Son of Man himself. Soon the Horseman's Clan will be free."

"You mean Charles Manson? Is that the son of man?"

"Horseman's Clan is all of us and Charles is all of us and all of us are the Horseman's Clan. When our leader is being held by the forces of consensus reality, all of us are held by the forces of consensus reality."

"Including me?"

"Everybody on the planet, but there are only a few leaders. When the apocalypse comes, there will be horsemen to lead the way. Jesus reincarnated as Charles is the leader, but all the horsemen are important. Rearrange the letters, it's no accident—the same letters that spell Charles Manson spell 'Horseman's Clan.' It's too important to be an accident. There's a reason for everything."

"When's this all happen?"

"Day after tomorrow."

"You have the apocalypse marked down on your calendar?"

"It's not like you think. The apocalypse will come after Jesus is freed. No one knows what precisely it will be like, but just that it will be."

Trumbo finished the sandwich and washed it down with the entire glass of iced tea. He then poured himself another.

To Trumbo's surprise, Alison continued Sunn's bizarre proposition. "You see, Trumbo, we're the good ones. We were born of the Horseman's Clan, and we are the pure ones."

Sunn clapped his hands together happily. "Your friend understands the Truth. Why can't you?"

Sunn and Alison chatted amiably for a few minutes, finishing each other's sentences as they laid out a bizarre plan for the end of what they called "consensus reality." Trumbo looked to Alison for some sign of skepticism, some hint that she wasn't taking this all in stride, but she did not so much as wink. *Is she in on this? Is everybody here crazy but me?* Trumbo closed his eyes and was shocked to realize that with his eyelids down, he saw everything in the room brighter than when his eyes were open.

He gazed across the table at Alison. At once she seemed to be right in front of him and also a thousand miles away. Her smile glowed with confidence and certainty. He felt himself being pulled toward her as if a magnet to metal. Her voice and Sunn's overlapped and commented on each other.

Trumbo shook his head and swore he could hear the blood swishing around in his skull. Nothing made sense. He heard Alison laugh as Sunn said that they didn't kill anyone, they just helped them make the right decision to die. He heard his father's name mentioned several times—*We helped Luther make the decision. Luther wanted it to be that way*—and slowly he realized that Sunn had killed his father. Sunn and his horde of maniacs had somehow killed Luther. Trumbo's pulse pounded with fury and the mental noise dissipated for a moment.

He rose, walked to the sink, and splashed some cold water on his face. He realized what was wrong: *The goddamn hippies drugged me.* A deep resentment welled up inside him and he tried to focus his thoughts, push out the drugs, get a grip. He concentrated on why he hated the flower children. *They all sold out. They promised to fight for peace and love to the good of mankind, but turned inward and became the most selfish people ever.* He tried to concentrate his thoughts like a laser, thinking about how he was the victim of the flower children: shuttled around throughout his childhood, never in one place, just because his father and his mother had pursued every selfish whim. *The drugs didn't make them selfish shits. They were selfish first, and took every drug offered because of it.* Trumbo was furious that Sunn had doped him up. *Don't let it take over, don't let it take over, keep in control. They killed my father.*

Splashing the water, he slowly came back to reality and gritted his teeth, determined not to hallucinate, not to let it get the best of him, not to fall into the trap his mother had fallen into. *Keep a grip. Think of Alison. You can't let anything happen to her.*

He exhaled forcefully, concentrated his thoughts, and closed his eyes again. Things went black, just as they were supposed to do when you close your eyes. He opened them up and he could again see the room. With sheer force of will he resisted the effects of whatever hallucinogen they had slipped in his tea.

Sunn and Barbara chatted cordially with Alison. Trumbo listened to what they said. It still made no sense. Mentally he split himself into two: The drugs were still in one part of his brain, but the hardened, tough voice at the back of his head could still distinguish fantasy from reality. *What they're saying doesn't make sense,* he thought, *and it shouldn't make sense. Sunn is insane.* He watched Barbara and Sunn each drink a glass of the tea. If they began to hallucinate, he thought, perhaps he could get himself, Denise, and Alison out of the house and out of trouble. He walked from the sink to the table. The drugs made it seem like a hundred-mile march, but he resisted and remembered *it's only a few feet.* His rational mind prevailed and he ignored the conflicting signals coming from his confused feet.

"Trumbo. Sit down. This throne belongs to you," said Sunn. Trumbo sat down slowly.

"It's not a throne. It's a chair decorated with party favors," he said.

Sunn grabbed Trumbo's forearm and spoke in soothing, lyrical rhythms, like a hypnotist. "I can see you're resisting. It takes too much effort. Relax, Trumbo, you'll be okay. You're safe with us. You're going to experience some special feelings. You're a chosen one who is going to have a place in the world like no other."

Trumbo clenched his jaw and reduced Sunn's words to meaningless sounds. He tried to think of something else, anything else.

Suddenly, silence. Sunn left the kitchen and Barbara followed him, leaving Alison and Trumbo alone. He pulled himself away from the reverie, grabbed Alison's hands, and stared into her eyes.

"Where'd they go?"

"Back of the house. There's still two girls with guns at the front door and in the garage," said Alison.

"They've doped us," he said.

She nodded and spoke in a whisper. "I don't like tea, so I only drank a couple of sips. It's not hitting me too hard."

"I drank two glasses," said Trumbo. "I feel like a schizophrenic. It comes and goes."

"If it's what they gave me last week, it'll wear off in about twelve hours."

"I'm resisting as hard as I can, but Sunn's bullshit is worse than the drugs."

"When they had me in the van, Denise told me how to get Sunn to lay off. Just pretend you agree with everything he says and he'll leave you alone. Argue with him and he keeps on ranting until he's blue in the face."

"So you're not buying into it?"

She smirked. "Hell, no."

"We have to get out of here," whispered Trumbo.

Alison nodded. "We do, but I'm not leaving without Denise. We made her a promise. We can't just dump her like so much baggage."

"I have a plan," said Trumbo.

Trumbo crept across the kitchen and rummaged through the broom closet until he found a bottle of rubbing alcohol, one-third full. He tiptoed into the living room and splashed the spirits until the rug was saturated, then poured the remainder onto the curtains. He kicked a candle onto its side so that in a minute or two the flame would ignite the alcohol. He replaced the bottle in the cupboard and sat down across from Alison. "We can only hope the neighbors call the fire department," he said. She smiled.

Sunn returned to the kitchen, visibly agitated. He shouldered his gun. "What was all that rumbling I heard out there?"

"Nothing," said Trumbo. "I got some water."

"Stay where you are. If you want water, I'll have someone bring it to you."

"Sorry."

A gentle popping sound, like a large Tupperware container being opened, came from the living room. Trumbo glanced over and saw a blue flame dance across the carpet as the alcohol was consumed. Moments later, the curtains ignited, throwing thick black smoke up to the ceiling. The smoke alarm sounded a grating warning.

"Goddamn!" shouted Sunn. He ran into the living room, realized that he had no way to extinguish the fire, then dashed past Trumbo and Alison to the back of the house. Seconds later Sunn returned, followed by Barbara and two of the girls, all armed with blankets. They darted into the living room and threw the blankets over the flames on the floor. They pulled down the curtains and trampled them.

Taking advantage of the distraction, Trumbo grabbed Alison's hand and the two of them slipped to the rear of the house. They opened the door to the room where they had stayed, searching fruitlessly for Denise. Then they went into the other bedroom. The room was a jumble. An electric clock and portable television dangled from the ceiling. Like the front room, the windows were covered with foil. Thrown on the bed were two M-16 rifles. Trumbo grabbed one and Alison grabbed the other. Emboldened by the weapon, Trumbo yelled out, "Denise! Where the hell are you!"

Her shout came from the bathroom. "I'm in here!"

The bathroom door was secured with a padlock. Trumbo

stood back and kicked the door as hard as he could, without result. He flipped the rifle around and jammed the butt end into the door several times, succeeding only in denting the wood. Finally he smashed the barrel of the gun into it, cracking one of the panels. He kicked the door with his foot and was able to open up a hole big enough to crawl through, although he scratched his back on the shreds of wood. He leaned back out. "Alison, there's hardly any room in here. Stay there and keep us covered in case someone comes in." She nodded.

Denise's wrist was handcuffed to the pipe beneath the bathroom sink. Her face lit up when she saw Trumbo.

"We're gonna get you out of here," he said. He examined the handcuffs and discovered they were made of hardened steel. The pipe beneath the sink was an inch in diameter and did not give way when he tugged on it.

"Shit!" He looked around for something that might break the cuffs. Discovering nothing, he placed the barrel of the gun against the handcuffs.

"Close your eyes, Denise. Look away and try to protect your face."

She did so. He closed his eyes and pulled the trigger. It made a pathetic click sound. He pulled it several more times; nothing happened. It wasn't loaded.

He yelled through the bathroom door to Alison, "Give me the other gun!"

She handed it through the door. He lined it up with the handcuff chain. "Cover your face again," he told Denise. He pulled the trigger. A loud report echoed through the tiny bathroom, and fragments of the compressed-wood sink cabinet flew everywhere. Denise's hand jerked backwards, but the cuffs didn't give way. Trumbo lined up another shot and fired again. This time water sprayed from beneath the sink, soaking him and Denise. Denise leaped up. The chain was broken, leaving jagged, hot metal where the bullet had severed it.

Still holding the military rifle, he forced open the bathroom door and helped Denise through behind him. Alison exhaled sharply when she saw that Denise was safe. In the other room, the smoke alarm still wailed.

"We'll go out here," said Trumbo. He peeled the foil away

from the window and discovered burglar bars blocking their exit.

Alison pointed to a metal lever on the floor. "That's the fire emergency switch." She kicked it, and the burglar bars outside tumbled to the ground. Trumbo rolled open the sliding glass window and helped Denise through. Alison climbed out after her, and then Trumbo crawled through, joining them in Hugo's small backyard.

Behind them, inside the house, the shrill smoke alarm suddenly ceased. Before they took three steps, Sunn's voice boomed behind them. "Hello, kids."

"Run!" said Trumbo. They raced across the backyard toward the fence that separated the house from the large dirt lot behind. They were nearly at the fence when several shots flew past them, splintering the fence.

A girl's voice yelled, "Hold it!"

Trumbo turned around and saw the girl aiming an AK squarely at Denise. She had been lying in wait for them. The three stopped in their tracks.

"Trumbo—have we met?" the young girl asked. She couldn't have been more than seventeen. "My name is Silhouette."

Sunn ran back to the fence and grabbed Trumbo by the shoulder. "You're a fucking chosen one!" he yelled. "You should know better! The time of apocalypse is nigh and you try to break up the Horseman's Clan and ruin everything! Get some sense, boy!"

Sunn pushed Trumbo to the ground and jammed his foot into his shoulder. He pulled a handgun from his pocket and jabbed the cold metal barrel into Trumbo's forehead so hard, it began to tear the skin. Sunn spoke in soft, lulling tones. "You have failed to understand why you are here. Are you a chosen one?"

Trumbo muttered "Yes."

"Say it."

"I am a chosen one."

"Do you understand that your cooperation is a matter of life and death? That you have the special power, and if you won't put it to good use, you will be destroyed?"

"Yes, I understand."

"You won't run off again like that?"

"No, I won't." Trumbo panted.

"Damn straight you won't."

He stood over Trumbo and stomped on his right foot twice, twisting it backwards. Trumbo gasped for breath, then screamed in pain.

"It's for your own good," said Sunn. "I hate to harm a chosen one, but one day you'll understand. You'll live."

33

ON THE MORNING OF THE PAROLE HEARING, PRISONER NUMBER B33920 ate an early breakfast, showered, and donned the bright orange shirt and pants that were standard issue for all prisoners in the recalcitrant unit. Like all potential parolees, he submitted to a body search, and was fitted with an iron band around his waist with chains leading to heavy cuffs on his wrists and ankles. Once he was in chains, however, his path varied from the other parole candidates.

While the other sixteen were placed into the regular holding cell in the administrative detainee unit on the Corcoran State Penitentiary grounds, prisoner number B33920 was escorted to the transfer station at the front of the building. He submitted to two additional body searches, and a hand-held metal detector was thrust into his armpits and up and down both legs to ascertain that he held no objects that could serve as weapons.

The three escorts took him to the parking yard and led him into what the bureaucrats referred to as an armored inmate transportation vehicle. The AITV was merely a school bus, painted black and labeled on the front, back, and sides with the legend PRISONER TRANSPORT and the seal of the California Department of Corrections. Heavy steel mesh covered all windows on both sides, and the driver sat in an isolated cage at the front. Each of the twenty-two metal seats was welded to the ground, and special studs allowed prisoners to be locked into position.

Number B33920 was the only prisoner. Three correction-al officers took great care in fastening him into position squarely in the middle of the bus. After locking him down, one of the officers asked, "Comfortable?"

"Nope!" said Manson.

"Good," said the officer. "That's the way we like it."

"Hey, man—am I the only lucky winner on today's luxury cruise?" yelled Manson.

The guard flinched. "You are the only inmate being transported today."

"What's the deal?"

"We just do what we're told." The guard knew very well what the deal was, but had no intention of discussing it with Manson. Some bonehead state judge had signed a special order demanding that Manson's parole hearing be open to the public. Another judge signed another order to get the venue moved into the Corcoran County Courthouse so that it could be broadcast live. Although nobody up high would talk about it, the rank and file knew the real scuttlebutt, and the scuttlebutt's name was James St. James. Not a day passed in a single prison in the entire state when someone didn't offer up the opinion that *if the muckety-mucks would just let us do our jobs, the system would work perfectly by now.* However, the feeling that they were being jerked around for political reasons was so familiar to correctional officers that they no longer bothered to ask questions.

Once Manson was secured, the bus lumbered to life and rolled out of the yard. It passed by the interior guard station, over the drainage canal that surrounded the prison farm, and rolled north toward the courthouse.

Prisoner number B33920 enjoyed the view during the six-and-a-half-mile ride. He hadn't seen much more than poured cement and a tiny window of sky in the two and a half years he had been in Corcoran.

Manson had read the many letters and cards that had come in from old friends in anticipation of the parole hearing. Most said "good luck" and "hope it all goes well," the usual. A few protested his innocence, and the writers offered to testify. He turned them all down. The letters that made him chuckle were the ones from his favorite fuckup, a guy calling himself J'osüf Sunn. Sunn was a character, all right. In 1969, back at the Spahn Ranch, Sunn showed up one day and just bought into every line of bullshit that anybody threw his way. Astrology? Sunn was into it. Past lives? Sunn ate it up. Vegetarianism, out-of-body-experiences, you name it, the dude believed it. Even though Sunn talked a good game, Manson never liked him: The guy was too much of a brownnoser. He had a different nickname out at the ranch, though Manson couldn't quite remember it.

Sunn wasn't heard from for ten years or so, then started up a correspondence with Manson, who kept writing back because Sunn was always good for a few bucks or some stamps or some paper. The guy's letters were usually a couple of clicks off of normal. Lately he'd been writing about the new beginning and how the family was getting back together and how Charlie was getting out this time. Manson wrote him back a few times, mostly in hopes of getting some new video games.

As they approached the tiny town of Corcoran, the streets were lined with flags and signs. Hundreds of cars and mobile homes were parked along the roads. Manson barked out at one of the guards, "What's going on? Town fair or something? Lots of people here, man!"

The guard behind the cage laughed. "They're here to see you, Manson."

"No shit!" He was genuinely surprised. The two Highway Patrol cars escorting the bus were joined by four more cops at the town line. Manson looked through the mesh windows at hundreds of men, women, and children lining the streets. People pointed and stared, and Manson obliged them by scowling and baring his teeth through the metal cage of the bus.

All traffic was blocked off from the block surrounding the middle of town. The bus paraded up Main Street, through a checkpoint, and stopped in front of the courthouse. While the guards on the bus made his transfer legal and official, Manson stared at the gaudy scene outside. Giant banners hung from every light post, with a studio-retouched portrait of James St. James side by side with a fifteen-year-old snapshot of Manson. The picture graced the front and sides of a video truck bigger than a moving van parked in front of the courthouse. Most interesting to Manson were the armed guards lined up across the street. First off, their uniforms were ill-fitting. Second, a lot of them were women. Third, the great majority were joking and laughing with one another, as if it were some kind of Sunday picnic. But the most unusual detail was that they were *across the street* from the courthouse, making it unclear what they were protecting. He just shook his head and wrote it off to the strange changes that happen in the outside world while a guy is locked away.

Wytowski had slept four hours in the past three days. His time was consumed putting out fires and unraveling the many mysteries left behind by Marilyn McLeod. As the full scope of her efforts became clear, he briefly wondered whether she had lost her mind. He had a list of questions and no way to answer them. While pounding on James St. James's locked door, Wytowski glanced at his notes.

The first note simply said ELEVEN!, underlined, boxed, and circled on the legal pad. McLeod had apparently contracted for eleven three-man camera crews—easily eight more than would ever be useful—and had not bothered to tell anyone why. The first camera crew arrived at seven A.M., and the eleventh apologized for being there late when they showed up at five after eight.

Second, why on earth was Greta from Upper Atmosphere Casting calling, claiming that the "thirty atmospheric personnel" were in place awaiting direction? Extras were for movies; Wytowski had never heard of reality television using them.

Then there were the little things: Three catering companies? Four electrical generators? Six satellite dishes? And why did someone deliver via Federal Express twenty-five hundred tickets to a Parole Board Fraternal Organization ball, when the ball was last week? That one could slide, but for some of the other weird problems, he needed St. James's assistance. St. James wasn't answering his door. Wytowski pounded extra hard.

Inside the hotel room suite, James St. James read the pages from the fax machine as they rolled onto the floor.

Paris real estate is taking a nosedive! he thought gleefully as he read the real estate pages from the Parisian newspaper. He ignored the pounding at the door until the last of the fourteen pages came through. When the fax stopped whining, St. James tore off the pages, jammed them under the bed, and opened the door.

"What?"

"James, there's a dozen problems we have to go over before this thing can go on the air."

"Why can't you deal? Isn't your job to keep me from having to concern myself with the stupid little things?"

"It's stuff left behind by Marilyn."

"Come in. Close the door."

"She hired eleven camera crews."

"I okayed that."

"Eleven?"

"We couldn't get a true exclusive. So we bought up every camera crew in five hundred miles, which won't exactly make it exclusive but will make it hard as hell for the other networks to hire locally."

"Fine. Same with the satellite dishes?"

"Yep."

"Okay. There are other problems."

"Like?"

"An extras company demands to be paid. Three caterers demand to be paid. An old lady who said she can channel ancient spirits showed up—"

"Demanding to be paid. Pay, pay, pay. Pay whoever comes in hailing distance. If it looks like we can use them, put 'em to good use. If it looks like they're just some poor sucker Marilyn tied up so they won't work for someone else, send 'em off on a wild-goose chase."

"Like what?"

"Use your imagination! Make up a map. Send 'em off somewhere fifty or a hundred miles away, and then get one of those temps to answer phone calls for them and keep 'em driving around all afternoon. I don't care."

"Let's do your schedule, James."

"Fine."

"Noon—record promos in front of the courthouse. One

o'clock—lunch. Two o'clock—makeup. Three o'clock—a run-through for technical. Four-thirty, on the set. Five o'clock exactly, we're on the air."

"See you at noon for the promos." St. James hustled the producer from the room, slammed the door, and returned to his Parisian newspaper.

Marilyn McLeod walked leisurely through the town of Corcoran, inspecting the festive decorations. *Wytowski did a tolerable job picking up where I left off,* she thought, *although I would have done it better.* She saw the extras drilling across the street from the courthouse, the dozens of camera trucks and electrical trucks and lights and the hundreds of people running through the streets, and became somewhat giddy. It was a typical out-of-control, over-the-top television show, there would be dozens of headaches in the hours ahead, and *none of them were hers.* She felt like an adult returning to high school with memories of times filled with emotional turmoil and discovering that it was just a place. If she were still on the payroll, she would be frantic and crazed, ensuring things went smoothly. Today her goal was the exact opposite. At precisely the time when they were going on the air, she planned to bring the whole circus to a crashing, embarrassing halt.

That morning she had taken a massage, gotten her hair done, and had a facial. Then she bought a new business suit for her unscheduled airtime later that afternoon. Now she had to wait. Waiting was always the hardest.

The correctional officers who took charge of Manson inside the courthouse were accustomed to absurd bureaucratic demands, but this one took the cake. They looked at the schedule:

9:00 A.M.: Inmate B33920 transported to courthouse
10:00 A.M.: Prehearing arguments
12:00 P.M.: Lunch
1:00 P.M.: Witness testimony
2:00 P.M.: Afternoon break
3:00 P.M.: Makeup

* * *

"What the hell is this?" asked the guard. "Makeup? *Makeup* for an inmate?"

"Don't even ask. I don't want to talk about it."

34

Day One

LYING ON THE CARPETED BATHROOM FLOOR, TRUMBO SLOWLY blinked his eyes over and over again. Each time he opened them, he focused on a few objects just long enough to recognize them and think of the proper name: That's a faucet. *Blink.* That's the sink. *Blink.* A bottle of Osco baby shampoo. *Blink.* A shag carpet. *Blink.* Each time he closed his eyes, images from the irrational drug-induced fantasies exploded onto his retina like a silent fireworks show, distant and distracting.

A sharp cramp in his foot jolted him awake. He used the pain to pull himself from the drug's grip. He clenched his teeth and stared at his swollen, discolored foot. He groaned like an animal in a trap, but he welcomed the suffering. It was *real,* it was *his,* and the jabs in his leg helped force the hallucinations from his mind.

For just a moment he let his eyelids droop. *Blink.* That's Dennis Clemenson's head, bleeding onto the radiator. The lawyer's lifeless face stared back at him, the mouth fixed into a scream. *Blink.* It was not a hallucination. A rush of adrenaline washed out the last vestiges of sleep, and with a gasp he recoiled from the macabre artifact. *That's how they found us here. They found Clemenson first.*

Barbara sat on a folding chair behind him, a machine gun comfortably slung across her lap.

"Your lawyer was very brave, son. He didn't talk until the very end. It was sad what happened to him."

Trumbo cleared his throat. "Why did you do it? Why do you need me?"

"Today is Day One. The chosen ones will acquire their

powers today. Jesus will be released. It's only a few hours until the glorious moment."

"You're crazy," he muttered.

"That's what they said about Einstein." She bit her lip. "Do you want something? You've been asleep for more than a day. Are you hungry?"

"I want to see Alison and Denise."

"That can be arranged. Alison's doing fine. She understands. Perhaps she can explain the miracle to you."

Barbara stepped out of the bathroom. When the door opened Trumbo noticed that Silhouette stood in the hall, holding a rifle. She waved at him, then closed the door. A few minutes later the door opened again. Barbara led Alison into the bathroom. "I'll leave you two together for a bit," said Barbara, in her cloying mother voice. "Don't do anything I wouldn't do! Denise will be along in a moment."

Alison sat down on the edge of the bathtub. Trumbo was shocked to see that she wore a long, flowing cotton dress and had flowers and beads woven into her hair, just like Sunn's true believers. A moon and star pattern drawn with makeup covered the left half of her face.

"Alison—you're one of them?"

"No," she whispered. "They're listening outside the door."

"Yesterday and last night they 'initiated' me into the Horseman's Clan thing. They said I had many special powers. They spilled the plan—they think Manson's getting his parole this afternoon. We're going to go there and pick him up, and the new revolution starts sometime after that."

Trumbo shook his head. "What do you think they'll do when Manson doesn't get out? They'll kill *us*. We've got to get away before all this comes down."

The bathroom door opened. They abruptly stopped talking. Denise sauntered in slightly sheepishly. "Hi, guys," she said. "I was really worried about you, Trumbo."

"C'mere," he said. He gave Denise a big hug. "Thanks for saying so. I'm better now." He whispered into her ear. "We're gonna try to get out."

The three huddled together. "They have burglar bars on the big bathroom window," said Trumbo. "But there's the ventilation window over the shower." He pointed to a two-by-two-foot screen high off the ground. "I think we could get out there."

They scrutinized the window. Alison shook her head. "Denise can get through it, and maybe me—but you'll never make it through that tiny window."

Trumbo smiled, projecting a sense of security. "Don't worry. I'll get through."

"What if we get out, but you don't?" asked Denise.

Trumbo bit his lip. "I'm a big boy. If we stay, then we're all screwed. Look, our only hope is for someone to call the cops. One of us has to get out to do it."

He surveyed the cramped bathroom, then pointed to the shower. "Pull down the shower curtain rod."

Alison removed the rod carefully so as not to rouse Silhouette, then handed it to Trumbo.

He pushed the curtain rod against the sink and bent one end to form a crude handle. He stood in the bathtub; the pain was sharp when he put his weight on his injured foot, but he was able to stand. Using the rod as a wedge, he drove it between the edge of the screen and the wall. He pushed on the screen until it dropped to the ground outside. Trumbo stood on limped and peered out the window. It was about an eight-foot drop to the ground. None of the Rebirth girls were standing guard.

"We have to move quickly," said Trumbo. "They could discover us at any time. Denise first."

He knelt on all fours in the tub. Denise stepped on his back, and was just able to reach the frame of the vent.

"Hang on for a sec," he said. He stood and gave her a boost up into the vent, saying encouragingly, "Go for it. When you get out, run as fast as you can. Don't wait for Alison or me."

"Okay."

He hefted her up and she squirmed through the hole, then Denise dropped to the ground outside.

"Okay, Alison, you go next."

Again he knelt down; Alison climbed on his back and pulled herself into the hole. He stood up. "Alison, I love you."

"I love you, too, Trumbo," she said.

"Don't wait for me."

He pushed her through, face-first. When she tried to pull her hips through the vent, she got stuck. Trumbo grabbed her waist and twisted her forty-five degrees, so she could fit through on an angle. With great effort, she just wriggled through.

"Run!" said Trumbo. "I'll catch up later."

He watched through the vent as they disappeared around the corner of the house, elated at their escape. He sat down on the edge of the tub, knowing, as he had known all along, that he could not get through the vent.

Moments later the door to the bathroom flew open. Silhouette waved the rifle when she saw Trumbo. "Where are they?"

"Don't know," he said.

Silhouette, furious, fired two rounds into the ceiling, then leaped into the hallway. "Escape! Diva and Alison have escaped! Diva and Alison escaped!"

He heard footsteps stomping toward the front room from every section of the house.

"What?" screamed Sunn. "Find them, goddamn it!"

From the bathroom Trumbo heard the front door of the house bang open and much commotion outside the house. He inched toward the bathroom door, which now hung open, using the shower rod as a makeshift crutch. The hallway was empty. He limped toward the front room and glanced to the front door. Only one girl remained guarding the house. Little Panda stood near the front door, anxiously gazing out. She held a pistol at her side.

Trumbo figured this was his best chance. Panda remained focused on the scene outside. With effort, he threw himself across the living room and brought her crashing to the floor. He twisted the pistol from her hand. She started to scream, "Trumbo's getting—" but before she could say "away," he had socked her in the jaw.

He grabbed his crutch and darted out the front door. Outside, the suburban street was oddly quiet. He looked one way, then the other, and ran directly across the street, between two houses. He planned to cut between the houses and get to the next street before summoning help, but was stopped by a fence surrounding a pool. He turned and started to go around the house, but saw that Sunn and several girls had gathered across the street in front of Hugo's house.

He watched them from behind a toolshed. They talked amongst themselves for a moment, then he saw two girls lead Alison and Denise by the hand to the front door. Trumbo's heart sank. He waited a moment until they had all gone inside, then ran around the house. He hobbled past several suburban homes until he found a yard with no fence, then ran through the yard to the next street and up to the first house he saw. It was a single-story stucco affair, much like Hugo's.

He rang the doorbell but got no answer. He put his ear against the door and heard footsteps. A Mexican maid answered the door.

"Meester Shaver not home," she said. "He not home."

"I need you to call the police," he said. "Call the police!"

Scared of the strange intruder, she gasped and slammed the door in his face. He pounded on the door repeatedly, but got no reply.

He raced to the next house. Through the front window he saw a middle-aged woman watching television. He rang the doorbell. A moment later she opened a tiny peephole in the center of the door.

"Can I help you?"

"Ma'am, I need to call the police."

"Who are you?"

"My name's Trumbo Walsh. There are two women kidnapped on the next street over—"

The little window shut. He rang the doorbell again and pounded on the door. "Open the goddamn door! I need to call the police!"

He listened through the door. She talked to someone on the phone. "Well, he seems like a rough character, Marge. I'm not going to let him in. There have been all of those incidents lately where people get robbed in the middle of the day."

She was chitty-chatting with a friend! He couldn't believe it. He pounded furiously on the front door. "Call the police!"

He stepped into the yard, picked up a large rock, and threw it through her front window, which shattered all over the pink velour couch. He kicked the glass out of the way and crawled into her living room.

The woman screamed and dropped the phone. "Don't hurt me! I'll do anything you want!"

"I just wanted you to call the police, goddamn it!" said Trumbo. The woman cowered in a corner. Trumbo hung up on Marge and dialed 911.

"Emergency."

"I'd like to report a kidnapping."

"Is this a serious call, sir?"

"This is serious."

"We'll send out a cruiser. What is the address?"

"I don't know the address. It's a block away from where I am now. Damn it, send out a cop, send out a dozen cops. They're armed to the teeth and they have two girls hostage." He cupped his hand on the phone and asked his unwilling host, "What's the street that runs parallel, two blocks over?"

"Cherokee Row," she said, sobbing.

"It's on Cherokee Row."

"What is your name?"

"Trumbo Walsh."

"We'll be right there."

Trumbo sat down on the woman's couch. For the fifteen minutes before the police arrived, Trumbo tried to explain to her what had happened.

Finally three cruisers pulled up in front of her house. Four cops got out, guns drawn, and approached the house slowly. Another cop sat in a cruiser and talked on a megaphone. "Trumbo Walsh, come out with your hands up."

"Nice talking with you," said Trumbo before getting up off the couch. He opened the front door and stepped out slowly, his hands raised above his head. Two cops tackled him and handcuffed him, facedown.

"Jesus Christ!" he said. "You've got the wrong one! It's a block over! You've got to go over there! I was kidnapped."

"Yeah, sure. We ran your record. You're under arrest for suspicion of murder."

The cop dug his knee into Trumbo's back. "You have the right to remain silent, ya cop-killing fuck." He read Trumbo the rest of his Miranda rights, spit into his face, and then they dragged him into a patrol car. The cop hissed, "A lot of the boys in blue seen the videotape where your old lady killed two Highway Patrolmen. You're not gonna be a popular guy."

Out of breath, Trumbo tried to tell them what had happened. "A man named J'osüf Sunn has two girls kidnapped. Listen, arrest me, I don't care, I didn't do what you think I did. But just stop and see what I'm talking about before you take me in! Please, you've got to do it! It's only a block away."

"We don't got to do anything for you."

"Will you just take a look?"

"Yeah, what the hell."

Trumbo was in the backseat of one police car, another led and one more followed. He guided them to Hugo's house.

"That's where I was held. There. In that house."

The cop got on the radio. "Sergeant Pelt, the suspect alleges that a kidnapping has occurred in the house at 20255 Cherokee. Investigate at your leisure." He turned to Trumbo. "He should look it over, oh, sometime today. Even if he had Mother Teresa boiling in oil, it doesn't mean we will go easy on you."

The driver turned to the cop in the passenger seat. "They're not going to find anything in there."

Trumbo remained silent. They drove straight past the Corcoran State Penitentiary without slowing down.

"Where are you taking me?" he asked. He knew what cops might do to the people they arrested; he was from L.A.

"We're taking you to the county jail for booking, you worm. You'll get to prison soon enough, though, if that's what you're worried about." Both cops laughed.

When they got to downtown Corcoran, hundreds of spectators crowded the central square. The driver asked, "What the hell is going on here?"

"The Manson parole thing," replied his partner. "It's gonna be in the courthouse instead of at the prison."

"Yeah, right, I forgot. We'll take this little shit in through the back door."

Trumbo asked, "The parole hearing is in this building?"

"Don't ask questions, cop killer."

The county sheriff's office was in the basement of the Corcoran County Courthouse. It consisted of a small office with several desks, two interrogation rooms, and a small holding tank with three cells. After Trumbo indicated that he would not talk without a lawyer present, they finger-printed him, photographed him, and placed him into a room about six feet square at the very back of the sheriff's offices. About twenty minutes after they left him there, the arresting officer came in and knocked on the glass.

"Hey, cop killer," said the officer. "We checked out your so-called kidnapping. Looks like you really messed up that house with all that Reynolds Wrap. Unfortunately for your lame alibi, nobody is there. Just thought I'd tell you. The place is deserted."

"But I was just there an hour ago!" yelled Trumbo. "They were holding two girls prisoner!"

"And I'm the pope," said the cop. "We're adding breaking and entering and felony vandalism to your jacket. Your bail is gonna look like the national debt. Have a nice day, pond scum!" said the cop, slamming the cell door.

J'osüf Sunn's minivan cruised along the country road slightly slower than the speed limit. Anyone passing the strange group might mistake them for a church youth choir or a Girl Scout troop. The cheerful voices of seven girls sang their favorite song, "Kum Ba Yah." Their angelic faces offered no indication of the destruction they planned. Barbara Thompson sat in the passenger seat, her hair freely blowing in the wind, contemplating the tasks that lay ahead. In the middle of the cargo van, the girls seated on packing crates swayed with the verses of the song and clapped their hands in time. All in all, a very happy group.

But the crates the sweet-looking girls sat on contained automatic weaponry, ammunition, plastic explosives, and detonators. Hidden beneath a Mexican blanket in the back of the van rode two unwilling passengers: Alison and Denise, handcuffed back to back. Gags stifled any attempt they might make to cry for help.

The van stopped by the side of the road and Sunn jumped out.

"We'll break for ten minutes," said Sunn, sounding a bit like a drill sergeant. "Anybody who wants to stretch out better do so now."

Several of the girls piled out. Sunn pulled two of them aside.

"Panda, Princess. You know what to do, right?"

"Yes," said Panda.

"Sure we do, J'osüf," said Princess. "We been practicing all week."

"Okay, I just want to make sure you have everything you need, because we aren't coming back."

"All right," said Panda.

"Let's unload your equipment now."

Sunn called off the items as Panda and Princess pulled them out of the cargo van. "Plastic explosive. You girls get eight bricks."

"Got 'em."

"Detonators—get nine, in case one goes bad."

"Right."

"Battery-operated TV, extra batteries."

"Check."

"Train schedule."

"Got it right here."

"Let's take a look," said Sunn, peering over Panda's shoulder. "This is the one," he said, pointing to the timetable. "If things go wrong, this is the train. It's hauling fuel from L.A."

"Duh!" said Panda. "We practiced, remember?"

"Good. Picnic basket."

"Check."

"Water, soda, and a blanket to sit on."

"Got 'em."

Sunn hugged Panda, then Princess, one last time. "Remember, everything you're doing will please Charlie. You're very important, and he loves you, and I love you."

"We love you, too," said Princess.

Sunn got into the van and watched the girls as they hauled the boxes toward the intersection of the highway and the railroad. He felt a certain wistful attachment to Panda and Princess, and wasn't sure he would ever see them again. He thought, *It was great with those two; I sure hope they don't have to die.*

After four attempts to engage the jail guard in conversation, Trumbo gave up on communicating with the man. The cops who booked him indicated that his hearing would be within twenty-four hours. In the meantime, there was nothing to do but wait. They offered him one phone call, but with Clemenson dead, he realized sadly, there was no one to call.

At two o'clock the guard switched on a television bolted to the wall above his desk. James St. James's special report began with the history of the Manson Family and continued up to the present day. Every few minutes St. James appeared on-camera, promising "live coverage from Corcoran, California, of the parole hearing of the century." During one of the commercial breaks the guard grunted at Trumbo, his first time acknowledging his presence.

"Hey, kid, that's all gonna happen upstairs at the courtroom. If you hadn't a gotten arrested today, nobody'd be in the lockup and I'd be up there watching. Manson's an animal. They ought to gas him like a sick animal. Supreme Court said they couldn't, though."

"Swell," said Trumbo.

"Of course, times are different now. Cop killers like you can still get the gas. Different Supreme Court said the new law was A-okay."

"Do you think I could get some water? I'm dying of thirst."

"What? I didn't hear you; could you speak louder?"

"I've been in here for three hours and haven't had any food or water."

The guard laughed. "Still can't hear you."

"That's cute," said Trumbo.

"I figure we'll get you whatever you want . . . just about the time they hold the winter Olympics in hell."

"Forget I asked."

"Forgotten," said the guard. He walked to a water cooler, poured a tall glass for himself, stood in front of Trumbo's cell, and drank every drop. "Just delicious on a hot day like today," said the guard. "Oops! Show's back on. Gotta watch."

At 2:23 P.M. a train carrying automobiles, agricultural products, and building supplies rumbled north on the railroad tracks just two miles from the Corcoran County Courthouse. Concealed in a thicket of weeds beneath the highway bridge and overlooking the railroad, Panda and Princess compared its arrival with a printed timetable.

"It's a minute and a half early," said Panda.

"Depends on whether you time the first car or the last car. I say it's just about on time."

"There's just one more train to go through before we have to get to work."

"The three fifty-two train."

"Yeah." Panda pulled a miniature television from her bag. "Should we watch something?"

"Does it get cable?" asked Princess.

"Nah."

"Forget it, then."

The girls had been waiting by the side of the tracks nearly an hour since Sunn left, and had turned a pile of weeds into a comfortable hideout.

After the 2:23 freight train disappeared beyond the horizon, Panda put her hands behind her head and pondered their mission. "Now that we've been learning about trains, I think they're kind of cool."

"Me, too. I hardly ever paid much attention to them. Now I know the different companies, and count to see how many engines and cabooses there are, and look to see if there's any hobos riding, and all that."

"It's kind of sad, what we're gonna do."

"That's only if the Man doesn't let Jesus free. We probably won't have to."

"That's what J'osüf said. But if he was so sure about that, how come we're out here sitting under a freeway?"

"You know. Just in case."

They both leaned back and listened to the freeway traffic for a little while. After a pause, Panda reflected, "I'm not *a-scared* of doing it. There's gonna be some casualties of the revolution, that's what J'osüf said. If we *have to* do it, I want to be the one who presses the button."

"I want to do it," said Princess.

"We can both push it at the same time."

They giggled and slapped a high five.

An eighteen-wheel truck roared over their heads on the freeway. When it passed, Princess smiled. "I like having something important to do."

"Yeah. Sure feels good."

"I feel all worked up. Either way, I can hardly wait. If we get to blow up the train—have to, I mean—that's a pretty cool thing. But if we get to meet Charlie—that has me totally jazzed."

"He's so handsome," said Panda.

"He's so wise," chirped in Princess.

"I haven't felt this excited since the first time I saw Kurt Cobain on MTV."

"Charlie's way hotter than Kurt Cobain, and besides, Kurt Cobain is dead."

"I know, I know. I'm just saying it's the same feeling. Kind of a buzz all through me, except better than drugs."

"What are you going to say when you meet him?"

"I've thought about it a million times and I'm not going to tell you!"

"You suck!" She laughed. "I've thought about what I'm going to say to him."

"Tell me!"

"You tell first. You were the one with the big secret."

"Okay. I'm going to just make eye contact with him—you know, he can see right into your soul—and catch his eye and for a minute I'm just going to look at him. And let him look at me. And then when I'm good and ready, I'm going to say, 'Panda. At your service.'"

Princess shrieked with laughter. "That's pretty cool! But it's something a stewardess would say."

"So what were you going to say?"

"First I'm going to touch his hand. And then I'm going to touch his face. And then when I can't stand it any longer, I'm just going to say one word. 'Love.' He'll know what I mean."

"That's so rad, Princess!"

They giggled with renewed excitement.

"What if we get killed?"

She blushed. "I think that's the coolest of all." She folded her arms across her breasts. "Then he'll know we *died* for him. Isn't that the ultimate sacrifice for love?"

"Yeah!"

"Want an apple?"

"Sure. They're under the 'splosive."

Without saying another word, they ate their apples and waited for the 3:52 train to pass, daydreaming about meeting Charles Manson and blowing up trains.

What's that smell? Parole Commissioner Carl Benning inspected his temporary office in the Corcoran County Courthouse and was displeased. Benning, for eight years the California parole commissioner, had never encountered as many irregularities in a parole hearing as he had with this one. He opposed the change of venue and lost. He opposed the television cameras and lost. To add insult to injury, his temporary office belonged to the director of recreational activities for the City of Corcoran. *They put me in the office of a gym instructor!* The cramped room stank of mildewed sneakers, and the walls were covered with posters promoting the benefits of vigorous exercise.

Whatever corruption at the top may have motivated the change of venue, the order was legal and properly filed, so he agreed to abide by it. However, the fifty-four-year-old commissioner would not allow the media circus surrounding the hearing to alter the seriousness of his courtroom one iota. He tore down the exercise posters and rustled up a janitor to spray Lysol in the room so that it would have some semblance of dignity. He had several short meetings before the parole hearing proper got going at five o'clock in the adjacent municipal courtroom. His basic strategy was to scare the fear of God into all participants. He asked a bailiff to round up the assistant parole commissioner, the Los Angeles DA, and Manson for a four-o'clock meeting.

Leo White, the thirty-eight-year-old assistant parole commissioner, arrived on time. Kevin Gee, the DA from Los Angeles, strolled in at five minutes past four. Gee, a tall, thin-framed man in his early forties, had Grecian Formula bluish-black hair, wire-rim aviator glasses, and an off-the-rack blue suit that lacked a tie. He was out of breath and sweated profusely.

"Good afternoon, Mr. Gee. You're late."

"I apologize, Mr. Commissioner. There were some complications getting here."

"I expect there were. You will not be late this afternoon. This is not L.A."

"Yes, sir."

"In L.A. they might get away without ties. I expect you to be properly attired for the hearing."

"Yes, sir, I was planning to put one on."

Benning casually asked the DA, "How many television shows have you been on, Mr. Gee?"

Gee exhaled sharply. "I never quite counted."

"Make a guess for my benefit."

"Eighty? A hundred?"

"And you often get paid for those appearances," continued the parole commissioner, tapping a pencil against his desk.

"Yes, sir."

"You could say it's a second income."

"To some degree."

"And you're comfortable with television cameras."

"You could say so."

"And you know what 'plays' on television, and what doesn't 'play' on television, am I correct?" Benning smiled, drawing the DA out.

"Yes, sir."

"And you know that, against my wishes, today's hearing will be broadcast?"

"Yes, sir."

"Perhaps you plan to hone your testimony so that it makes you look good to the viewers? Make it television-friendly, I believe that is the term?"

"I had considered it, yes, sir."

Benning suddenly stopped smiling and slammed his fist down on the table. "That's what I was afraid of! Mr. Gee. We may be in an unusual venue, but this will be my hearing! If you so much as glance toward the cameras or alter your behavior one iota, it will be noted. Am I understood?"

Gee nodded.

"I have read your prepared comments," said Benning.

"You have? I mean, of course you have."

"Some of us prepare better than others."

"They were just notes."

"They are not just notes. Get yourself a pencil. You will excise the following portions, which have no place at this hearing." He put on a pair of half glasses for reading and held the lawyer's comments at arm's length. "Strike the reference to Mr. Manson as 'the most dangerous man alive.' That is a generalization. Strike all references to the book and the motion picture *Helter Skelter*, which are popular entertainments and not legal records."

Gee blushed. "That takes out almost half of my prepared commentary!"

"You will still have half an hour to prepare new comments. I am not done yet, Mr. Gee. You will make no reference to the 'people watching at home,' nor *The Silence of the Lambs*. You will confine your comments to the subject at hand, which is the inmate whose application for parole is being considered and the *legal record* of the crimes for which he was imprisoned."

"Yes, Your Honor."

The door to the office opened. Two guards stood by the door, while two other guards escorted Charles Manson up to a chair in front of the parole commissioner's decrepit school desk. The chains clanked and clanged against the desk.

"Mr. Manson," said Benning, removing his glasses.

"Yeah?" said Manson, squinting his eyes as if he had just woken up.

"The reply is 'Yes, sir.' "

"Well, I don't know all that—"

"You have asked to represent yourself. If that is the case, I strongly advise you to follow the customs and conduct of this courtroom. If you do not, you will not be heard."

"That's bullshit!" protested Manson.

Benning stared him down. "If you use that kind of language in the court, it will be the last thing you say."

"Isn't this whole thing a charade, anyway? You people have no intention of putting me back out on the streets, so you may as well admit it," said Manson.

"I will treat you no differently than any other prisoner who is brought before me. And if you insist on acting as your own counsel, I will treat you no differently than any other lawyer. I recommend you take a crash course in courtroom behavior before the hearing begins in forty-five minutes," said Benning.

"Yes, sir," said Manson.

"One more thing. If you so much as acknowledge the presence of cameras, I will end the hearing prematurely. Am I understood?"

Manson shook his head. "It's your court, Your Honor. That don't make it right, but it's your court."

"Thank you. That will be all."

"Don't I get to say anything?" shouted Manson.

"At the hearing, Mr. Manson. Officers, take him out, and please close the door behind you."

Manson and Gee left. Over the next half hour Benning reviewed Manson's file and prepared the same way he had prepared for the thousands of other parole hearings. At a few minutes past five o'clock, the bailiff leaned into his office. "Your Honor, the hearing is ready to begin."

"Thank you," he said. Benning straightened his robes and walked down the hallway toward the courtroom. He walked through the entrance marked JUDGES and waited until he heard "Hear ye, hear ye, please stand for Parole Commissioner Carl Benning." He walked through the doors and assumed his position at the head of the courtroom. He quickly surveyed the room, and noticed Manson and three guards on his right, Gee and an assistant on his left, the five members of the parole board sitting directly across from him. Then his eyes were drawn inexorably to the two cameras in the back of the room. Just as he had ordered, the cameras were in the farthest corners of the room, and the operators remained completely silent. Just as he had ordered, James St. James himself was outside, banished from the inside of the courtroom and reporting from in front of the courthouse. In spite of his orders to Gee and Manson not to play to the cameras, he could not ignore them himself. He was being watched and analyzed by guys named Biff who lived in trailers and people who might vote for him if he ever ran for an elective office. He reached for a glass of water and took a long sip, deathly afraid he might dribble. He stared into the camera for what felt like hours, then instructed the bailiff to begin.

The bailiff read the case numbers and legal particulars pertaining to Manson's case, as well as a synopsis of Manson's previous parole hearings. Benning barely heard a word, and didn't notice when the bailiff sat down. Only the stony silence reminded him that he was required to do something.

"Uh, that is all?"

"Yes, sir," replied the bailiff.

"Well then. Good evening, ladies and gentlemen. We have a really big hearing today," said Benning, shocked to hear himself starting to sound like Ed Sullivan. "I mean, we can proceed with the hearing." His mind was a total blank. Though he'd done thousands of parole hearings, he simply could not remember what to do next. All he could think of were the people watching him make a fool of himself. Sweat dripped down his forehead, and he wiped it off with the sleeve of his robe. "I guess we start with, uh, the applicator—applicant—for parole, Mr., uh, the most Dangerous Man Alive, you know, Mr. Manson."

From his seat in the courtroom DA Gee glared at Benning. *Benning is stealing my best material!* he thought.

Benning stopped dead midsentence and closed his eyes. *Just don't think about the cameras,* he told himself. With his eyes tightly closed, he continued. "Uh, Mr. Manson, you have petitioned for parole. Do you have a statement why you are a suitable candidate?"

Manson, seated only a few feet away, squinted at the parole commissioner and said, "You got a problem, man?"

With his eyes still closed, he said, "You will address me as Mr. Benning or just as 'sir,' Mr. Manson."

"Mr. Benning sir, then. How come your eyes is closed?"

Benning blushed. "Just something in them." He opened his eyes halfway, just enough to see Manson, but not the cameras behind him. "Continue, Mr. Manson."

"All right, then. Yeah, I want to get paroled."

Benning squinted. "Do you have a statement?"

"Yes, sir. I have a lot I need to say."

"Say it, then."

"First off, the reason I'm here in the first place is not reality." His spoke with a southern Ohio accent filtered through forty-one years in jail: slightly nasal with a defensive edge. "They put me up because they say I killed some people. That, I have to say, is not real because I didn't ever kill nobody. The DA knew it, the judges know it, everybody knows I wasn't even at some of the places where those murders took place. That's the main thing. How can you convict a guy of murder when he never murdered anybody?"

"Mr. Manson, this hearing accepts the findings of previous courts as fact."

"Well, that's the real problem here. You look at the court records and it shows that I never killed anyone. Y'see, the world needs a villain and they picked me. I'm the lowest of the low. I'm lower than a snake. I'm the unwanted person. And because you accept your court records as reality—which I don't accept as my reality—you think that it's true. I'm saying I should get parole because I should never have been here in the first place."

"Is that your statement?"

"I could tell you about the traffic ticket I got in San Diego on the night that your reality says I did all this bad stuff and I could tell you about the difference between what happens in a court and what really happens on the street, but yeah, I said my piece." Manson pulled a pair of glasses from the table in front of him to get a better look at Benning.

"Thank you," said Benning. "District Attorney Gee, would you like to rebut the prisoner's argument?"

Gee stood and outlined his disagreements with Manson, and the facts in the original case against Manson. It was his forty-sixth time testifying at a hearing for one of the seven people convicted in the 1970 murder trial. He spoke without notes, beginning with a description of the relationship between Manson and the six who actually carried out the murders, and continued all the way through the murders themselves and the original trial. When he began his spiel, he directed his comments toward Parole Commissioner Benning but quickly noticed that, strangely, the man had his eyes closed. He subtly turned to face the cameras, listening for an objection from the bench. When there was none, he began pouring on the hype. He used the term "most dangerous man alive," since Benning had. When there was no objection, he reverted to his original notes and put on a full-on performance, ending with a nearly Shakespearian flourish as he waved his arms dramatically and yelled, "This man does not belong in society! This man belongs behind bars! Gentlemen of the parole board, if ever there were a reason to build secure prisons, it is Charles Manson. If ever there were one person deserving of lifetime imprisonment, if ever there were a dangerous maniac requiring all the protections of maximum security, Charles Manson is that man. Thank you."

Gee's heels echoed in the courtroom as he walked back to his desk and sat down. Manson, the parole board, and the various bailiffs and secretaries all looked to the bench for guidance. After a long pause, Gee spoke softly. "Your Honor?" he said, getting no response. He walked directly to the front of the courtroom and spoke loudly. "Mr. Benning. That concludes my statement."

Benning opened his eyes a crack and peeked out. "Oh, very good. Thank you. Mr. Manson, would you like to make a concluding statement before the parole board renders its decision?"

"I'm not done yet, sir. I have a lot more I need to say and I have a witness."

Benning spoke slowly, as if to a child. "You have had your say. The district attorney has had his say. The parole board has reviewed the written record of your time in the penal system, and now it is time for closing statements."

Manson shook his head furiously. "I have a witness! I have a witness who will testify for me!"

"The time for witness statements has come and gone. I warned you, Mr. Manson, that if you chose to represent yourself, I would hold you to the same standard as any lawyer, and I cannot make an exception because you were ill prepared or unfamiliar with the procedures of this hearing."

Manson leaped from his chair. "I have not presented my key witness, Your Honor!" he yelled.

"Mr. Manson, you will sit down," said Benning.

"I have a tape which proves everything! James St. James agrees with everything I said! I'm innocent and shouldn't be held in your prisons any longer!"

"Mr. Manson, you will be ejected from the court if this continues!"

"That's bullshit, man! This time around I had an ace in the hole. I have a guy willing to go on record supporting me, and he said he'd prove that everything I said is true!"

"Bailiff, please restrain Mr. Manson."

Two correctional officers raced to Manson's side and forced him to sit down. Manson was undeterred. "Your courts is the most corrupt in the world, pig! I gotta be allowed to state my piece, and my piece includes a videotape presentation from James St. James. He agrees with everything I say, and I ought to be able to include that testimony in this phony mockery of a trial—"

Benning slammed his gavel repeatedly, yelling louder than Manson. "That's all we will hear from the prisoner. Bailiff, please escort Mr. Manson from the court. This hearing is over!"

In front of the courthouse, James St. James sprang into action. He stood in front of a camera, facing away from the courthouse, waved to the director to switch him on, picked up a microphone, and began speaking. Behind him each of the thirty-three phony security guards hired by Marilyn jockeyed back and forth for position, each hoping to be in the shot.

"There you have it. In the conclusion of the parole hearing that may yet free mass-murdering maniac cult leader Charles Manson, he lost all control and mentioned your humble reporter, James St. James, by name, as the courtroom degenerated into chaos. Never before in the history of television has a parole hearing of this magnitude been brought into the homes of so many citizens. Let me go on record here stating before you, the American people, that no such videotape exists. Perhaps the sick, twisted devil was provoked by insanity to suggest such a thing, the same insanity that led him to murder *innocent citizens* in the privacy of their suburban homes. Perhaps this Guru of Gore was grasping at a last desperate straw to prove his innocence, and thought to take advantage of the situation to besmirch my reputation. Now that the hearing has officially ended, the parole board will reach their decision any time now. Remember, until they vote, the possibility exists that Manson will be unleashed. You can still vote whether *you* think Manson should be released by dialing the nine-hundred number at the bottom of your screen. When we come back, the sensational outcome of this sensational hearing. 'Charles Manson: This Time He Might Go Free' is brought to you by Kimberly-Clark Corporation, makers of Kleenex brand facial tissues, and by Kohler, the first name in bathroom fixtures."

He drew his finger across his throat, the indication that the camera should be turned off, and immediately began yelling at Wytowski. "What the fuck was that?" asked St. James. "Do you think anybody believes the nonsense about me on videotape supporting Manson?"

Wytowski shrugged his shoulders. "Is it true?"

St. James replied quickly; perhaps too quickly. "Of course it isn't."

"Then I don't think anybody believes it's true," said Wytowski halfheartedly.

Guerrera heard a loud argument and spun around. Behind him the faux guards pushed each other back and forth, jostling to get in camera range. They looked more like a drunken geriatric rugby team than a show of force. "What is going on with our security guards?"

"I'll get right on it, boss," said Wytowski.

"How're the ratings?"

"We're drawing a thirty-two in Washington, D.C."

"Yes!" Guerrera slammed a fist into his open hand and danced a jig of celebration. He was already thinking of a certain Louis XIV chair.

As the television coverage switched to a commercial message, Panda and Princess, secured in their hideout beneath the bridge, considered what to do next.

"Charlie looks so helpless in all those chains," said Princess.

"I think they're kind of cool. Sort of like he knows they're consensus-reality chains but he could really get out of them any time he wants to."

"It looks like he's not going to get out."

"Not through the regular system."

"What'd J'osüf say?"

"He told us if Jesus isn't free before the six twenty-three train comes by, that's a sign that we're supposed to blow it up."

"That's just a couple minutes."

They surveyed the afternoon's handiwork. Two wires ran from their hiding place atop the bridge down the steep incline to a spot next to the railroad tracks where they had concealed four bricks of explosive. It had taken almost an hour to wire the detonators and the plastic explosive, and they had to double-check every connection. Aside from what they'd learned at the quarry, their knowledge of explosives came from a book stolen from the public library, which was long on theory and short on practical advice. Still, it seemed like it should work. The blasting caps were connected in parallel. The wire ran up the hill to the battery and detonator. They had taken turns handling the detonator and pretending to press the button. Now it was time to put up or shut up.

"Hear that?" asked Princess.

"What?"

"It's the train. Look down the track." Far to the south Panda saw the light of the oncoming train. According to the helpful guy at the train station, the 6:23 carried almost exclusively petroleum products: seventy cars full of fuel oil, gasoline, and natural gas, destined for the far reaches of Northern California.

Princess excitedly grabbed Panda's hand. "That's it! That's the train! I can't believe it's almost time."

"It's so amazing. It's just going to go by, no one thinking anything bad's going to happen, and then . . ."

"I know. I know."

The slow-moving train rumbled closer every minute. Panda held her breath. Princess clutched the detonator lovingly in her right hand. "Put your finger on top of my finger, and then when it comes we can both press it at the same time. J'osüf's going to be so proud!"

"Okay," said Panda.

Soon they could see the entire train rolling toward them,

until at last the noisy iron monster was directly in front of them. Through the window of the engine, Panda saw the conductor.

"Let's wait until the tenth car. That way the conductor has a chance to live."

"Okay."

They counted cars in unison. "Five, six, seven, eight, nine, *ten!*" They jammed the button down. Nothing happened.

"Oh shit! Something didn't work!" yelled Princess.

"I'll go take a look," said Panda. She scurried down the track, following the wires to the C-4. One after another, she scrutinized the electrical connection. On the fifth brick of explosive, she noticed that the blasting cap had been knocked loose by the rumbling of the train. She twisted it tightly on. When she looked up, there were only fifteen cars left.

"Blow it!" she yelled to Princess. Princess couldn't hear her. Panda ran up the ravine, pulling herself up with all of her strength. "Push the button! Push the button now! It's fixed! It's fixed!"

Finally she held her hand up in the air and pantomimed pushing the button. There were only six cars left. Princess pushed the button.

In the first half second the force of the blast ripped through the side of a container filled with liquified natural gas. The white car was hurtled a dozen feet into the air, sending shards of metal flying across the freeway. The gas car was wrenched forty feet off the track, and the five cars behind it, also filled with liquefied natural gas, folded up behind it. The cloud of gas ignited on contact with air and flame, and the secondary explosion blew out two of the pillars supporting the freeway. Panda and Princess were crushed beneath sixty-two tons of reinforced concrete. Six unlucky drivers, unable to stop, smashed over the edge and were consumed in the hellish flames.

The shock waves ripped through Corcoran, a mile away. It began as an eerie wind blowing swirls of dust into the air. Spectators, camera crews, and the just plain curious looked up from whatever they were doing at the same moment. A split second later a sonic boom caught up with the wind, rattling windows. When the blast from the larger, secondary explosion rolled through, dozens of windows shattered and fell into the street, and the bell high atop the courthouse hummed and clanged.

Rupert Earsy, the unofficial commander of the faux guards hired by Clandestine productions, knew the sound of an explosion all too well from his time in Korea. The seventy-one-year-old man reflexively threw his arms in front of himself and hit the ground, screaming, "Incoming!" About half of the other guards saw Earsy dive and did likewise, resembling nothing so much as bowling pins toppling. One fake guard, a thirty-two-year-old woman, fell down the stairs and bumped her head. When she stood she screamed, "I've been shot! I've been shot!" at the top of her lungs. The hundreds of spectators in the streets took her erroneous claim at face value and ran for cover in doorways, under cars, behind trees. The town square devolved into chaos.

As quickly as it began, the rumbling stopped. People eased out from behind pillars and realized there was no bombing and probably no sniper. But in the distance, above the intersection of the 5 freeway and the railroad tracks, a thick black cloud of smoke rolled into the air.

One of eight *real* cops assigned to crowd control for the Manson hearing radioed in to headquarters to find out what the fire was. Lloyd P. Lloyd took the call.

"All units report to the intersection of the railroad tracks and the five freeway near Corcoran. Immediately!"

The cop replied, "All available units? We're doing crowd control for the Manson hearing."

"Repeat: all units. A preliminary report indicates that the freeway overpass is gone."

"Totally gone? Hasta la bye-bye, Lloyd?"

"Correct. The bridge is gone. Over."

"Ten four."

Within minutes every policeman left the area, sirens blaring, racing toward the freeway overpass. Not one legally invested officer remained behind to control the crowd in the town square. On the short drive to the site of the explosion, not one policeman took note of the orange cargo van driving slowly in the opposite direction toward the Corcoran town square.

35

The Standoff

"Merrily we roll along, roll along, roll along, merrily we roll along, Charlie will go free!" J'osüf Sunn brought the song to a big, happy finish as they rolled into Corcoran. At the perimeter of the town square, sawhorses and yellow crowd-control tape blocked their way. Sunn stopped to consider the obstacle.

James St. James, poised above the courtroom steps, breathlessly filled the airwaves with his special brand of hyperbole. "We await the verdict on the mass-murdering maniac of the century. Just a moment ago a massive explosion rocked this tiny town, shattering windows and sending smoke and dust high into the air." He pointed into the sky, and the camera followed. "Was the explosion related to the parole of Charles Milles Manson? Was it another in his series of atrocities, begun more than twenty years ago?" He turned to stare directly into the camera, and said earnestly, "This reporter thinks so."

St. James heard a crunching sound, followed by yelling, and glanced off camera for a moment. A van drove directly over two sawhorses that supported the police line keeping vehicles out of the town square. He quickly integrated the van into his rap.

"Can we get a shot of that? Behind me you'll see the broken glass . . . Now a van is driving into the middle of the town. What are they doing here? Could they be outraged citizens coming to lodge a formal protest against the potential release of the Maven of Mayhem? Stay with us live as we discover who the mysterious visitors are."

Inside the van, Sunn yelled to his passengers. "Hang on tight!" He jammed the accelerator down and tore through the second line of barriers, then skidded to a stop at the foot of the courthouse steps. Bewildered spectators around the square eyed the van suspiciously.

"It's time to do some good. You know what to do!" said Sunn to his followers. "Remember the rule of thumb—head shots and body shots only." He hopped out of the van and flipped open the side door.

Barbara and Silhouette leaped from the van and quickly spotted the thirty or so guards across the square. Each woman pulled out a machine gun, steadied it against the edge of the van, and casually aimed toward the faux security force. Simultaneously they fired twenty rounds a second at the extras. Several of them toppled down the steps, some dead, some wounded. The rest ran for their lives in every direction, screaming.

"Problem solved," said Barbara. "Let's go in."

With practiced precision, Barbara, Sunn, and three of the girls ran up the steps into the courthouse. Only Cleopatra stayed behind, to guard the van and keep an eye on Denise and Alison. The well-armed posse passed St. James on the way up the stairs. Silhouette hesitated for a moment and took aim at St. James's head. "Does he live or die?" she asked Sunn. "I need a quick decision."

Sunn grabbed St. James's ear and tugged on it, hard. "You broadcasting live, man?"

Atypically, St. James found himself at a loss for words. "Uh, yes, I mean, I could if you wanted me to. Or I could stop," he said.

"If he's broadcasting, take him hostage. If he's not, kill him and let's get on with it," said Sunn.

St. James yelled, "Yes, I'm broadcasting, it's live, trust me, live as live gets, going out all over America."

"He's a hostage, then. Take him. Kill the cameraman. Get the camera."

Silhouette pumped five quick shots into the cameraman, spraying his brains over St. James's suit. The cameraman's lifeless body fell down the stairs. St. James wet his pants. "Get in there," said Silhouette. "Carry the camera with you. And don't fuck with us."

"Yes," said St. James, terrified. He lifted the camera onto his shoulder.

The girls fanned out through the courthouse building. Cleopatra hustled Alison and Denise into the building at gunpoint. Periodic bursts of gunfire echoed through the empty hallways. Sunn and Barbara raced straight for the courtroom. They pulled open the door. Because the session was in a recess, only a bailiff, two journalists, and St. James's two cameramen were still inside. Within seconds Sunn took out the bailiffs with quick bursts from a machine gun. Barbara squeezed several shots into one of the cameramen, who was blown back into the corner, leaving a smear of blood on the wall as he fell to the ground. The other cameraman fell to his knees.

"Don't hurt me, oh please, oh please, don't hurt me!"

"Yeah, you may be useful. Get up!" He jumped to join the hostages. "Just keep taping, and I won't harm a hair on your head."

Three print journalists had taken refuge beneath a table. "Get the fuck up," demanded Barbara. The writers, all men, crawled out and held their hands over their head. "Who do you people work for?" she yelled.

"Los Angeles Times," said the first one.

"Shitty paper!" said Barbara, gunning him down and turning to the next writer. "C'mon—who do you work for?"

The second man stuttered, "Uh, uh, *Time* magazine."

"Consensus-reality bullshit." She wasted little time in popping eleven bullets into his head.

The third journalist, sobbing, blurted out, "I write for *Prison Times.*"

"The prisoners' rights mag?" she asked.

"Yes! I'm an ex-con!"

"I like *Prison Times.*" She lowered her gun. "You guys tell it like it is. You'll live, man; just quit sobbing."

"Thank you!" said the man, drying his eyes.

"Don't thank me—get out of here now." He sprinted out of the courtroom.

"Courtroom secured!" yelled Barbara.

"Let's find Charlie," replied Sunn. "Room-by-room search. Now!"

Barbara grabbed a pair of handcuffs off of the body of the dead bailiff and handcuffed St. James to the brass rail in front of the witness stand. "You try to split, we'll find you and kill you."

Peace and Silhouette walked arm in arm down the main hallway of the court building, stopping to open each door. The first room they came to was a smoking lounge for court reporters and other clerical workers. They kicked open the door and saw four women and two men huddled behind a couch.

"Hello, hello," said Silhouette. "Is Charlie Manson in here with you?"

A woman of about fifty, dressed in a plaid suit, answered her. "No! He's not here!" These were her last words.

In the subsequent four rooms the girls killed two bailiffs, a janitor, and five lawyers preparing for cases unrelated to Manson's parole hearing. They sang in jump-rope cadence as they walked between rooms; "Charlie, Charlie, wherever you be, we're gonna find you and set you free!"

Finally they approached a room labeled CORCORAN COUNTY RECREATIONAL ACTIVITIES COORDINATOR, which had on its door a poster of Arnold Schwarzenegger. The door was locked. Silhouette quickly fired several shots into the handle until the wood splintered away and the lock fell off. They kicked open the door.

Inside, Parole Commissioner Carl Benning was halfway into a heating duct. The grate lay on the floor. Silhouette grabbed Benning's legs and dragged him out onto the floor.

"Hello, hello! You are the pig parole commissioner!"

Benning gasped for breath as Peace shoved the barrel of the gun into his throat.

"So where the hell have you hidden Charlie?"

"Oh God, oh God, please don't hurt me."

"Answer my question and maybe I won't."

"He's two doors down."

"Thank you, piggy! And now you die."

Sunn burst into the room. "Don't shoot him. He's a good hostage."

"Your sentence is temporarily suspended," said Silhouette, laughing. "Get on your feet, ugly pig." Benning stood up. "Lead us to Charlie."

Tears rolled down Benning's face. "I have a wife and two daughters. I'll cooperate, I swear I will."

"Stop talking and start walking."

Benning led them into the hallway and stopped in front of a wooden door marked TRAFFIC VIOLATIONS. "He's in there."

"Stand in front of the door and tell them to open it. If they shoot, they shoot you, *capice?*" said Sunn.

"Yes." Benning knocked on the door. "It's Parole Commissioner Benning. Open the door—don't shoot."

There was a rustling sound inside.

"Open the door!"

Silhouette, Peace, and Sunn stood back from the door. It swung open. Inside, two prison guards stood with their weapons drawn, ready to fire.

Sunn yelled at Benning. "Tell them to drop them or we blow your head off."

"Drop the guns. Do what they say. *Do what they say!*" commanded Benning. The two guards dropped their weapons to the ground. Sunn walked into the room with a swagger.

"Thank you for your cooperation, gentlemen," he said, then fired three bullets into each of the men's faces, sending them sprawling backwards.

"Charlie—are you in here?"

There was no answer.

"Charlie—it's J'osüf Sunn. Are you in here?"

The room was momentarily silent. The eerie rattling of chains broke the silence, and then, from behind a counter, came Charles Manson, in the flesh. A strange smile worked its way across his elfin face, and he snorted. "Didn't expect to see any friendly faces today," said Manson. "What are you doing, man?"

Sunn replied. "We came to set you free."

Manson nodded his head, as if this sort of thing happened every day. "Cool. Let's get to it, then, man. Good to see you."

Peace stared in awe at the man she had been learning about for months, the man they called Jesus and Charlie and the New Leader and the Founder of the Revolution. She had never known quite what to expect. After all the buildup, she was speechless. Her first impression was, *He's shorter than I thought he would be.*

Her reverie was broken by Sunn. "We've found the prize,

Peace and Silhouette—go get Cleopatra and the other prisoners and bring them into the courtroom. Do it quick! Then plant charges at the exits. There's six doors around the building—make sure you get 'em all. Go get Cleopatra. Bring Diva and Alison in with her."

"Right."

"Find Barbara and tell her to secure the basement. There's a sheriff's office and a jail downstairs. Be prepared for some resistance."

"Got you."

"Get on it."

Manson shook his head, amused and surprised. "Man, you got a system for doing this shit, don't you?"

Sunn smiled broadly. "We did it all for you." Sunn flipped over one of the dead bailiffs and found a ring of keys. "Put out your hands." He tried several keys before finding a fit. He removed the manacles, then unfastened the chains from around Manson's waist and ankles.

"Twenty pounds lighter!" yelled Manson. "All right!"

"We're going to the courtroom. We'll secure all doors to the building, and then barricade ourselves in there. Then we'll trade Benning and the other hostages for a ride out of here."

"Where we going?"

"Somewhere without an extradition treaty. I was going to ask for the Baldenese Islands."

"Where's that?"

"Off the coast of South America. English-speaking, former British colony, good weather, pretty girls."

Manson clapped his hands. "You are one crazy motherfucker."

"To the courtroom."

"Following you, man," said Manson. "Hold up a second. I wanna get a gun." Manson pulled the service revolver from the body of the man who had previously been guarding him. He weighed it in his hand. "Wow. Feels good. Been so long since I had a piece, I can barely remember. Let's split."

They moved into the courtroom, where Barbara waited. Silhouette gleefully pushed Parole Commissioner Benning into the room.

"What should we do with the pig?" she asked.

Sunn considered her question. "Cuff his left hand. Keep his right free." Peace fastened the commissioner to the railing. Alison, Denise, and the other hostages looked on with horror.

Sunn smiled. "Hello, Commissioner. You're going to help us out of a tight spot, right?"

Benning, sweating profusely, shrugged. "What you want? What can I possibly do?"

"Oh, I think you can lend us a hand." Sunn grabbed Benning's right wrist in his hand. Benning struggled. Sunn clamped down hard.

Benning's whimpered, "What are you going to do?"

"Get you to help us out."

Sunn waved to Peace. "Come over here and help me for a minute." Peace skipped to his side.

Sunn said, "In my pocket is a jackknife. Pull it out, will you, and flip open the large blade."

"Oh God, no," said Benning. "Please, don't do it. Don't kill me."

Sunn shook his head. "I'm not going to *kill* you. What use would there be in that, if you're our hostage?" He turned to Peace. "Go find some bandages. There ought to be a first aid kit somewhere around here."

"Jesus Christ!" screamed Benning. "I've done you no harm! Don't do it! Don't do it!"

Sunn jammed Benning's hand backwards against the railing. In a doctor's bedside tone he said, "This will only hurt . . . *a lot.*" He cracked Benning's thumb backwards and jammed the jackknife into the thick tissue, cutting quickly until he reached bone. Blood gushed down Benning's arm.

The parole commissioner screamed at the top of his lungs.

Sunn jabbed the knife several times into the bone, then twisted the thumb around until it came off in his hand. Peace returned with a first aid kit. Sunn jammed the severed thumb into his pocket, then wrapped up Benning's bleeding hand.

"There, that wasn't so bad, was it?" said Sunn, releasing the hand.

Benning passed out when he looked at the bloody amputation.

In the courthouse building's subbasement jail, the officer guarding Trumbo did not immediately notice the sounds of gunfire coming from upstairs because he was too busy fiddling with the television set, which had inexplicably gone black.

"Dang it. You'd think they could spring for a decent television in this joint," said the guard.

Trumbo rapped on the Plexiglas window of his holding cell, trying to catch the guard's attention. The guard barked at him, "Forget it, kid. I'm not gonna get you any water. You just have to tough it out."

Trumbo rapped furiously. Finally the guard turned up the speaker that allowed them to speak. "Yeah? What's the problem?"

"I heard gunshots."

The guard shook his head. "Go back to sleep, punk."

The picture on the television suddenly came back to life. The network logo was broadcast on the screen, accompanied by an orchestra playing "Greensleeves." Every ten seconds or so a recorded voice announced, "We are experiencing technical difficulties. Please stand by."

Trumbo yelled at the guard, "If you'd turn off the television, you would have heard the shots! I'm *not* bullshitting you."

"Shut up." To spite Trumbo, the guard cranked the volume on the television as high as it would go. He turned and raised his middle finger at Trumbo. Moments later, a rain of lead propelled the guard backwards until he collapsed in a pool of his own blood.

Trumbo dove underneath the cot in his cell. He heard two sets of footsteps, then girls' voices, giggling with delirious glee. *Sunn's girls,* he thought. *Holy shit, they've done it, really done it. Alison and Denise must be with them.*

"Nice shooting," said one of the girls.

"I think you got him first," replied the other.

"Yeah, but you got the body shot and the head shot. I think I only got him in the arm."

"Any other pigs back here?"

"Take a look around."

Trumbo held his breath and pulled himself as far underneath the cot as he could.

"Nah. Just that one. I think we've got the basement pretty secured. Back to the courtroom."

"Cool."

Trumbo waited several minutes before pulling himself from beneath the cot. The television test pattern ended, and was replaced by a local television anchor. "Terrorists have stormed the county courthouse building in Corcoran, California. They hold as many as six hostages, including convicted mass murderer Charles Manson, television personality James St. James, and several other county officials and employees. They are demanding the right to broadcast their demands on television, and in just a moment we will begin broadcasting those demands live."

J'osüf Sunn appeared on the TV screen. He stood in a courtroom. At his side, Barbara held a gun. Sunn read from a prepared text. "This is J'osüf Sunn, second-in-command of the Rebirth Fellowship, devout follower and believer in the Horseman's Clan, and messenger of Charles Manson, the bringer of truth to the unenlightened world. Consensus reality is over. The lies perpetrated by the Man are over. The new revolution is here, and the reunited Horseman's Clan shall give peace unto the world. While our methods may be violent, our ends are peaceful."

He stumbled backwards. "We have six hostages. They will be returned safely once the consensus-reality pigs have obeyed our simple demands, which are: one, the delivery unto us of the sixth chosen one, a man named Trumbo Walsh; two, sixty-six million six hundred sixty-six thousand dollars in cash, to be delivered unto us; three, our safe passage to the Baldenese Islands; and four, fulfillment of the promise by the consensus-reality networks to play the videotape made by James St. James, who is now our prisoner. The videotape will prove Charles Manson's innocence."

He held his hand up to the camera. For a moment the image blurred, then clearly visible was a bloody severed thumb. "This is the thumb of the consensus-reality parole commissioner, Carl Benning. We will continue to remove his fingers, one per hour, until our demands are met. When he has no more fingers, we take his toes. When those are gone we kill him and begin on James St. James."

He lowered his hand. "Do not attempt to storm the building. Each of the exits has been wired with plastic explosive. If you doubt we have the will to use them, consider the train which was blown up just a half hour ago by our fellow believers. None of our demands are negotiable. That is all. Turn off the camera." The picture went blank for a moment, then the local news anchor returned.

Trumbo was shocked to hear his own name among the demands. He briefly considered what would probably happen: Sunn's demands would go unmet. Sunn would realize that his entire scheme was merely a deranged fantasy, and then anything was possible. Disillusioned messiahs often turned on their own, as was the case in Jonestown and Waco. Trumbo had to get out.

A quarter-inch plate of mesh-reinforced Plexiglas was all that separated Trumbo from the key to his cell, which dangled uselessly on the hip of the dead guard. Trumbo looked for something he could use to break the Plexiglas. He took off one shoe and pounded on the Plexi, giving up after about a minute. If it were that easy, every crook who was ever booked would break out in minutes. The cot was welded directly to the floor; useless. The television reporter droned on as Trumbo searched for a way to escape. They confirmed that all armed guards in the building had been killed or otherwise knocked out of communication. Then they showed a police and FBI barricade erected around the courthouse.

He glanced up and saw two water pipes jutting across the ceiling of the cell. They were about an inch in diameter, painted the same color white as the ceiling. He stood on the cot and felt them: one hot, the other cold. He pulled himself up on the cold-water pipe. He fastened both hands around the pipe and pulled down on it with all his weight. It didn't budge.

The cot was by the edge of the cell; he reasoned that if he could pull himself to the center of the pipe, he would have more leverage. He pulled himself up on the pipe and then climbed hand over hand to the center of the cell. It flexed just a little bit under the strain of his weight. He bounced up and down on the pipe; it flexed a little farther down on each successive drop.

He dropped to the ground and let his arms rest for a moment. Then he thought about Denise and Alison, helpless, at the mercy of J'osüf Sunn. Trumbo climbed back on the bed and worked his weight to the center of the pipe. Dangling from the pipe, he bounced up and down as hard as he could, grunting with each successive drop. His efforts were paying off. At the right wall, the pipe began to slip the tiniest bit; a fine mist of water sprayed out of a crack that had appeared. He grunted as he bounced harder and the pipe finally gave way. He dropped to the ground, landing on his injured foot. A torrent of water sprayed from the pipe, soaking Trumbo and filling the floor of the cell with water.

With the added leverage, pulling the pipe from the opposite wall was easy; he grabbed the broken end of the pipe and pulled back and forth across the room until the copper on the opposite end heated and gave way.

He caught his breath. Now he had a tool. The most primitive possible, to be sure: a six-foot piece of pipe, jagged at both ends. As water poured down on Trumbo, he gripped the pipe and smashed it repeatedly into the Plexiglas window. A small hole gave way; he jammed the pipe through and used the leverage to pry it into a larger hole. The metal mesh bent out of the way until he had a hole big enough to stick his arm through.

Soaking wet and shivering, he reached down through the hole toward the keys on the dead guard's body. The keys were just a few inches beyond his grasp. He pulled on the guard's tie and lifted the body to a higher sitting position, then yanked the keys off of his belt. He tried fitting keys into the cell lock. On the ninth one, he heard a click, and the door unlatched. He pushed it forward.

Trumbo was soaked to the bone. Water continued to gush uncontrollably from the broken pipe. He sloshed back past the cells to the rear area of the holding tank and discovered a cinder block wall with a bright yellow sign, emblazoned with three red triangles nestled inside of a red circle. FALLOUT SHELTER, said the sign. He tried the door. Locked. He quickly found the appropriate key on the guard's key ring.

The door creaked open. Fallout shelters, most built in the early sixties, were supposed to provide safety in case of a nuclear attack. These walls were two or three feet thick, and steel plates had been bolted to the area around the door.

He flipped on the light. The dank room looked like it had not been cleaned or maintained in years. Spiderwebs and dust were everywhere. Eight cots were arranged around the perimeter of the room. Shelves held army surplus food, labeled variously 144 MEALS READY TO EAT, EMERGENCY WATER, FIRST AID KIT/FIELD KIT, and so on. He found a bundle wrapped in olive drab paper labeled CLOTHING, tore it open, and unrolled it on the floor. Inside were ten gray cotton jumpsuits, surprisingly clean considering the state of the room. He stripped off his wet clothes and put one on. It felt good to be in dry clothes again.

He returned to the dead guard and pulled a police radio off the man's belt. He flipped it on and monitored the chatter. Most of what he heard was indecipherable cop codes, but he got the general idea—they were bringing every cop in a hundred miles to the situation. He flipped the broadcast lever.

"Hello? Hello? Does this thing work?"

"This is a police emergency frequency," said the voice, belonging to Lloyd P. Lloyd. "Please desist using this frequency immediately."

"I'm hidden in the courthouse. I am not a hostage."

Lloyd P. dropped the lingo for a moment. "Who is this really?"

"I'm serious. I'm in the building with the . . . uh . . . Manson Family."

"What kind of radio is that?"

"It says American Radio Works 133."

"Okay. Listen to me. You want to talk to the officer in charge. See the little buttons on the front?" said Lloyd P. Lloyd.

"Yeah."

"Okay. Push in two-two-five-one, then hit the 'CF' button. That stands for change frequency."

"What happens then?"

"You'll be talking to the situation commander. I'll tell

him you're going to contact him. Wait one minute, then switch frequencies like I told you to."

Trumbo did as instructed, then tried the radio. "Hello?"

"This is Special Agent Vincent of the FBI. I understand you are in the building."

"Yes, I am."

"What can I call you?"

"They might be listening, too," said Trumbo. "I'd rather not say. Call me, oh, Brave."

"Brave. Like it. How do we know you are not one of the hostiles?"

"Well, I'm scared to death—is that good enough?"

"Where are you in the building?"

"I said, they might be listening and come find me."

"We have to know who you are first, and confirm that you are not one of the hostiles. I recommend that you find a safe place to hide and stay there."

"Thanks a fucking lot," said Trumbo. He turned his attention to the television, a superior source of information. Cameras showed dozens of police cars, and even a tank-like battering ram, assembled in the town square. It looked like they were preparing to storm the building. He knew if that happened, Denise and Alison were as good as dead. They were his only friends, his only family. He had to do something.

He rummaged around to find needed supplies. He took the guard's handgun, a gas mask, and a canister of tear gas, put on a bulletproof vest and a helmet that he found in the police locker, got three pair of handcuffs, and stuffed the police radio into his pocket. Then he slowly headed upstairs, uncertain of what he would find.

In her hotel room just outside Corcoran, Marilyn McLeod watched the bizarre disarray of James St. James's show on television. When the gunfire broke out, the show was immediately replaced by a test pattern. Moments later, network news anchor Clifton Bernard appeared on-screen. He had no suit jacket or tie, and the newsroom was in the chaos that accompanies unexpected disasters.

"This is a UBC Special Report. Reporter James St. James

has apparently been taken hostage by Charles Manson in the town of Corcoran, California," announced Bernard. "It is not clear what happened in the small California town and we are awaiting further information." He put his finger to his ear. "This just in. About five minutes ago gunfire erupted in the courthouse where Charles Manson's parole hearing was taking place. Uh, we're going to play a tape of an earlier meeting between Manson and St. James . . ." They started to play a tape from three years earlier when St. James had visited Manson in prison. Marilyn flipped through the other channels, eager for information. All of the stations had preempted programming to bring live reports. As she channel-surfed she saw Dan Rather, Tom Brokaw, and Peter Jennings presenting summaries of the situation. In every case pictures of Manson and St. James were superimposed behind the network anchors.

She flipped back to the local UBC affiliate. They had stopped playing the tape and had Bernard back on the air. "I'm getting reports that the camera feed is still live. We're going to switch to that broadcast immediately. You're watching live coverage of the hostage crisis in Corcoran."

A grainy, dark image came on the screen. St. James had been bound with the same chains that once held Charles Manson, and stood in the witness stand of the courtroom. His face was twisted with fear. Worse, his makeup was running from an earlier crying jag. McLeod felt a twinge of pity, which quickly passed when she remembered how St. James had treated her.

"Send help, please send help. If this is being broadcast . . ."

The camera whipped away from St. James and settled on the face of Charles Manson, apparently talking to the unseen cameraman.

"Hey, man. That thing on? It is? You think people can hear what the hell I'm saying?" said Manson.

"Yes," came the voice.

"So I'm on TV, then?"

"Yes, I think you are."

Manson grinned. "Let me rap a little bit to the people out there. Your reality out there in TV land is that I'm some kind of murdering maniac. That's your reality, and that's what you've been taught. I could be whatever you want me to be." Manson sneered and snarled. "But that's not my reality, man. Lemme tell you the straight story of what went on. First off, I didn't kill nobody, and that's the way it is. They fixed it so they picked me to be your Devil, your Satan, your worst nightmare, but I'm not really like that at all. I wanna tell you all about myself.

"Before I do, I wanna let y'all out there know one other thing. I didn't have nothin' to do with gettin' out of jail today. Nobody's gonna believe me 'cause nobody ever believes Charles Manson, but that's the way it is. We got a judge here and a couple of kids hostage, and we'll maybe talk about lettin' 'em go once we gets some demands made up. First thing we're gonna demand is that every TV network shows a little tape that Mr. Ray Garvey, known to you better as James St. James, made up explainin' my reality."

Manson rambled about his childhood, prisons that he had seen from Washington, D.C., to Ohio to Indiana to Mexico to California, and his warped perspective on the 1969 murders.

Marilyn flipped through the other channels. NBC, ABC, CBS, and St. James's own network, UBC, all were broadcasting the feed from the courthouse. She shuddered and considered the unique position she found herself in. She pulled on some running shoes, grabbed the infamous videotape, and raced out of the hotel room, headed for the Corcoran town square.

Twelve minutes later she reached the center of town, videotape in hand. Two buses and a police van blocked the street. Behind that were dozens of sawhorses strung with yellow police tape. Fifteen police cars and Highway Patrol vehicles were parked behind that. A firing line of two dozen sharpshooters aimed at Sunn's yellow van, which was forty yards away on the opposite side of the barricade.

Marilyn ran to a uniformed cop performing crowd control at the perimeter of the police staging area.

"Ma'am, you can't go any further. This is a restricted crisis area."

Marilyn smiled. "Yes, I know that. Listen to me. Charles Manson demanded that before hostages would be released, a certain videotape must be played."

The cop shrugged.

"You haven't been watching TV?"

"I'm out here doing crowd control, ma'am."

"Listen to me!" she yelled. "I have the videotape that Charles Manson wants played. I have it with me!"

"I'll give it to the hostage negotiator if you want, ma'am. That's all I can do."

"Can I talk to him?"

"No, ma'am, this is a restricted area."

She yelled at the cop as if he were an eight-year-old boy. "This is crucial to the safety of those hostages! If you don't take me to someone in command, you could endanger all of the people in that building!"

The cop nodded. "I'll give it to him."

"You've got to take me there. I have to explain what it is."

"Yes, ma'am."

She watched as he disappeared into an unmarked car with the tape. Moments later a man in his mid-forties, dressed in a blue suit, emerged from the car and walked over to where Marilyn was standing.

"Special Agent Mark Vincent, FBI," he said. "This is the tape Manson's talking about?"

"You got it," said Marilyn.

"We'll take a look at it. How did you come into possession of this tape?"

"I worked with St. James until two days ago."

"Very good," said Vincent. "Come with me and we'll look at it immediately."

Trumbo crept up the staircase from the basement to the first floor of the building. On the stairs the corpse of a young sheriff's deputy stared at him, his hand hovering in front of his body, as if to stop gunfire. Trumbo averted his gaze and continued upstairs.

He came to a long hallway. The smell of gunpowder hung heavy in the air. They had been doing a lot of shooting. He was at the very back of the building. The emergency exit was blocked with heavy electrical tape. Attached to it were several wires, which led to a car battery and a gray brick that looked like modeling clay. He leaned down and read it. Plastic explosive. They really had booby-trapped the doors. He worked his way down the hallway to the front of the courthouse building. He stepped gingerly around a corner and immediately heard a blast of gunfire.

His breath exploded out of his chest and he felt a terrible aching sensation across his body, as if he had just endured a dozen body blows from a prizefighter. He fell onto his back, and reached in front. *No blood.* The bulletproof vest had done its trick. Trumbo pulled himself to his feet and retreated around the corner, out of the direct line of fire.

Footsteps approached. He removed the safety from the police revolver, and aimed. Moments later Peace stepped around the corner. He fired once. The slug ripped through her arm. Her machine gun fell useless to the floor. She stared at him a moment—as if to ask, *Why me?*—before falling to the ground.

Trumbo was suddenly sickened. He had been around death and dying for years; but he had never shot anybody, never willingly used force against another human being, much less a young girl. Yes, she had been trying to kill *him,* but now she lay on the ground, bleeding. "Don't die, don't die," he muttered. He dropped to his knees. The girl bled severely from the wound in her arm and was unconscious, but still alive. He tore off a section of her skirt and twisted a tourniquet around her upper arm, above the wound. He dragged her back into an office and closed the door. Then he picked up her machine gun.

Moments later he heard footsteps approach in the corridor. He opened the first door he saw: a janitor's closet. He hid among the brooms and chemicals, and closed the door.

Sunn's voice was outside. "Where's Peace? Peace!" he called. "Where are you? Why did we hear gunshots? Peace!"

He heard Barbara's voice next. "Maybe it was an accident."

"Could have been. She'll turn up."

"Did she have enough ammo?" asked Barbara.

"Probably. If we get split up, everybody needs to be able

to get to the ammunition and extra explosives. You know where they are?"

"I was on a different detail," said Barbara.

"It's all in the staff lounge. That room right there."

"In there?"

"Yeah. If we come under fire, anybody can get to it."

Barbara asked, "Why isn't it in the courtroom with us?"

"They know that's where we are now. If they come in through the roof, we need the ammo somewhere else."

"Okay." Barbara yelled, "Still wonder what happened to Peace."

"That girl is unreliable," said Sunn.

The footsteps faded away down the hall. Trumbo waited a moment and then let himself out of the janitor's closet. He looked around; the hall was clear. He flipped on the police radio and played it quietly. First he heard the usual coded gibberish, but by playing with the channels, he finally found a source of useful information. It was communication between a helicopter and the FBI. The helicopter was positioning itself above the courthouse. Trumbo discerned that they planned to drop several canisters of tear gas onto the ventilation ducts above the building, to put pressure on the "hostiles," as they called Sunn, and to cause confusion.

Then the cop on the ground stopped talking. All Trumbo heard was the roar of the helicopter and the pilot's voice. "Chopper in place. Forty seconds until gas insertion. Thirty seconds. Twenty. We're hovering above. Canisters released. We're out of here."

Trumbo's sinuses quickly became swollen. The gas was invisible. He pulled on the police gas mask and fastened it around his chin. It stank of black rubber and sweat, but after a few moments he found he could breathe again.

He darted down the hallway toward the main courtroom. Through the tiny glass window in the outside door, he could see Sunn, Barbara, and everyone else gasping for breath and rubbing their eyes.

Sunn dropped to the ground, as did several other of the cult members. Trumbo looked around until he spotted Alison on the opposite side of the room, weeping uncontrollably as the gas burned her eyes. He couldn't see Denise.

He pushed open the back door to the courtroom and got a closer look. Handcuffed, Alison sat in the jury box. Sunn and several of his girls writhed in agony on the floor. Trumbo closed the door. *If I can find the jury entrance, I can get her out before they notice.*

He ducked into the hallway and found a fire exit map. The juror's entrance was about forty feet away, through an office. Holding the gun in front of him, he raced down the hallway. He stood back as he pushed open a door marked JURY DELIBERATIONS. No one was inside. Even through the gas mask his sinuses swelled and his eyes began to water.

At the opposite end of the deliberation room was a door labeled COURTROOM. He peered through the tiny window atop the door. Sunn and his followers were still at the opposite end. Alison lay on the floor in the jury box. Trumbo, low to the ground, crawled into the jury box, concealed from Sunn by a wooden panel.

Trumbo helped Alison to her feet and dragged her into the deliberations room. By the time Sunn noticed him, they were almost to the door leading to the hallway. Sunn picked up a rifle and fired a few shots in their direction. They tore into the wood paneling next to the door.

Alison, still ravaged by the gas, could not stop the watering of her eyes, but she squeezed his hand in recognition. He squeezed back, and pulled her after him down the hall.

A pile of wires, timers, and switches blocked the front door to the building. Trumbo quickly saw that they were rigged to two blocks of explosive, set to explode if the doors were touched.

"This way," he said.

Alison, out of breath from the tear gas, could barely move. Trumbo lifted her in his arms and carried her across the hallway and down the stairs. There was a foot of water on the floor of the basement, from the broken pipe. He cut through the sheriff's office, passed the cell where he had been held, and used the keys to open the farthest back of the three holding tanks. He laid her down on the cot, then went to the sheriff's locker and pulled out another gas mask. He dashed back to the cell. Alison put on the rubber mask and pulled it tight. She continued to wheeze and breath heavily for several more minutes. Finally she caught her breath and relaxed.

"We're as safe down here as we could be anywhere," he said. "Until the cops get them out of there."

Alison shook her head. "What about Denise? She's with the hostages near the witness stand."

"We can't leave her."

Alison suddenly pointed toward the television, which still played the scene from the courtroom. "Look!"

Sunn's image stared out from the television. He faced the camera in the courtroom. His eyes were red and swollen, but the effects of the gas seemed to have worn off. "Consensus-reality vermin," he said. "We did not ask to be gassed. This is the penalty for your mistake. You did this. Not us."

Sunn grabbed Parole Commissioner Benning by the hair and dragged him on-camera. He stuffed a pistol into Benning's ear.

"I have one bullet in the chamber," said Sunn. He spun the revolver around several times. Benning braced himself for death. Sunn pulled back the trigger slowly. The hammer slammed into the chamber with an empty click.

"He lives this time," said Sunn. "But you still will pay for gassing us. Barbara, hold his hand."

Benning sobbed, sputtering, "Don't do it, please, don't do it, I didn't mean any harm," gasping for breath between each phrase. Barbara grabbed Benning's hand. Sunn pulled out the bloody knife and jabbed it into Benning's index finger a bit. Then he stopped and addressed the camera, yelling over the parole commissioner's screams.

"I said one an hour. But you violated my space. We take two for punishment."

He bent back Benning's hand and sliced through his index finger, then continued to tear through until the middle finger was partly severed. Benning gasped and looked away. Sunn pulled the fingers, attached only by a swatch of skin, and severed them. Blood specks splattered across the camera's lens. Sunn held the fingers up to the camera.

"Do it again, and I take out his heart."

He pushed Benning to the ground and spoke to Barbara. "Take him away. Bandage him up."

Sunn continued to rant at the camera. "None of our demands have been met. We fear you're not serious about fulfilling them. We will do everything we must to demonstrate our seriousness."

Over the public-address system in the courthouse came a booming voice. "Sunn. This is Special Agent Vincent of the FBI. We are prepared to meet some of your demands. You must promise that if we do, you will release at least one hostage."

On the television, Sunn looked all around to see where the voice was coming from. "Where are you?"

"We've tapped into the PA system of the courthouse."

"Let's talk, then."

"You mentioned a videotape."

"Yes. That is to fulfill a promise made to us by James St. James."

"If we play the tape, will you release St. James?"

Sunn rubbed his eyes. "Why don't you play it and we'll talk further?"

"We need to see if you can keep a promise, Sunn," came Vincent's voice over the PA.

"Okay. You play the tape, we'll let the weasel go. But we still need our other demands fulfilled."

"We're working on them. These things don't happen instantly. We're looking into every one of your requests."

"Play the tape, then," said Sunn.

"Do you have a television to see if we keep our word?"

Sunn nodded. "Yes, we do."

"Then we'll proceed."

Inside a broadcast truck parked outside the courthouse, an engineer slipped the videotape into a player and sent it out on a feed that went to all four networks.

Instantly, in living rooms and bars and in front of electronics stores and everywhere else that television was broadcast, James St. James's image appeared. Sunn watched it in the courtroom. Alison and Trumbo watched it from the jail downstairs. On the tape, St. James sat behind his usual desk, reading from a prepared text. His voice was slightly stilted.

"This is James St. James reporting. My closest personal friend in the whole wide world, Charles Manson, asked me to read a statement on his behalf. Let me say that first of all . . ." St. James squinted at the handwritten pages. "First of all, Charles Manson is completely innocent of all crimes ever attributed to him. I should know. I am a news reporter and . . ." St. James picked up the paper and scrutinized it closely. "I guess it says I know everything in reality, and my reality is your, uh, your reality. And what I say is reality is, uh, really reality." He turned and spoke to someone off-camera. "That's what it says!" He turned back to face the camera.

"The American media reality machine is packed with lying dogs, bark, bark. I am a lying dog. I am a prostituting lying dog. Bark, bark. The time is now to check out the real reality and ignore the lying dogs like me." Again he consulted someone off-camera. "It says here, 'Take off your pants.' Do you think I ought to?"

Marilyn's voice from off-camera said, "It depends on how bad you want him to be on your show."

"Yeah, right. This tape goes to no one except him, see?"

"Whatever you say."

St. James chuckled. "Don't look!" On the videotape, St. James stood and removed his trousers. He wore red satin bikini underwear, which dug into his gut. "Okay. I'll keep reading. I have lots of proof that Charles Manson was never a murderer and never killed anybody and was set up by the media and the justice system. He never should have been put in prison in the first place but the system was down . . . the system was down on him, uh, the lying dogs put him where he is because they're scared of him.

"Everything you think you know is a lie. Everything the media tells you is a lie. Everything you know about Charles Manson is a lie . . . I am a liar. If there was . . ." He turned off-camera. "It's his grammar and it's bad!" He turned back to the camera. "If there was murders that happened by other people that's a sad thing and I feel bad about that but I didn't do it. I am not lying now."

St. James again turned off-camera. "It says, 'Kneel on all fours on your desk and bark like a dog,' and then double-underlined in his chicken scratch it says, 'It better be real good barking and for a real long time or I ain't going to do your show.'"

McLeod's voice replied. "Well, you better do it, then."

"Yeah?"

"You wanted to do this show, not me."

St. James screeched with laughter. "Damn. Nobody better ever see this."

"You better hope not," said Marilyn.

"Okay. The show must go on."

St. James climbed up on the desk. In profile his platform shoes looked even bigger than usual. When he leaned over, his toupee canted at an unnatural angle. His shirt fell forward, emphasizing the red bikini underwear. Then he gave the performance of his life, barking up a storm, alternately howling like a lonely coyote, growling louder than a pit bull, and barking, lots of barking.

He crawled off the desk and sat back down in the chair. "That's all of it, right?"

Marilyn's voice off-camera said, "No, there's one more little bit on the back of the page."

"Oh, right." St. James stared into the camera, lifted his middle finger, and pronounced in his best announcer voice, "America, I give it to you up the ass." He laughed hysterically. "That's it. There's a grain of truth in it, don't you think?"

He turned to face the camera. "Okay, cut. Turn it off. And if you *ever* tell anybody—" The screen turned to static. By the time the bizarre broadcast ended, Marilyn McLeod was already back in her hotel suite, faxing resumes to every network, letting them know of her immediate availability.

By the time the broadcast was over, the gas in the building had dissipated and Alison and Trumbo were able to remove their gas masks.

Trumbo turned the sound on the television down low. He picked up the police radio and dialed in the frequency that Lloyd P. Lloyd had told him would connect him with the FBI.

"This is me again," said Trumbo, speaking into the radio. "I'm still in the courthouse. I'm the one who you didn't believe a little while ago."

After a few moments of silence, Vincent's voice came over the radio. "How do we know you're not a hostile?"

"If I were, you'd see me on the television camera that's in the courtroom, don't you think?"

"Identify yourself."

"Can Sunn hear me?"

"Maybe he can. I don't know," said Vincent. "If you're going to help us, like you say you are, we need to first know that you're not lying to us."

Trumbo hesitated. He had to run the risk. He needed their help to get Denise and Alison to safety. "You'll know I'm telling the truth because I am one of their demands."

"What do you mean?"

"My name is Trumbo Walsh. When Sunn read his demands on television, he said that he wanted you to give him Trumbo Walsh."

"Yeah, right," said Vincent. "Where are you?"

"I am in the basement of the courthouse."

Outside, in the barricade surrounding the building, Vincent scribbled a note to one of his aides. The aide ran to a computer in the FBI van, and came back a few moments later. Meanwhile, Vincent strung Trumbo along with pointless chatter.

"Walsh?" said Vincent.

"Yes?"

"My records indicate that you're under arrest for murder. It also shows that you are an accomplice in crime with one Barbara Thompson, one of the hostiles."

"I'm not—"

The radio went dead.

"Shit!" said Trumbo.

"What happened?" asked Alison.

"He thinks I'm with Sunn."

"So what's that mean?" she asked.

"I have to try to get Denise on my own." He handed her one of the guns he'd taken from upstairs. "This is a machine gun. It works just like you think it does. This is the safety switch." Trumbo pointed to a black metal lever. "When it's off, all you do is pull the trigger. I'm going upstairs to get Denise. If anyone tries to screw with you down here, fire first, ask questions later."

"Be careful," said Alison.

"I will be."

"I'm scared," she said.

"Not half as scared as I am."

Trumbo crept up the stairs. If he could get to the staff lounge, he could destroy the ammunition dump. Then they would only have what was in their guns already. He would still have the upper hand. He tightened his body armor and slipped down the hallway.

He reached the ammo room without incident. There were heaps of machine-gun clips, several huge boxes of ammunition for the handguns, and several army hand grenades. He wondered where they got the hand grenades. The ammunition was scattered all over the room. Trumbo pulled the heavy boxes to the center of the room so that one grenade would detonate every box of ammo, leaving Sunn with nothing.

Suddenly the public-announcement system came on. It was Vincent talking with Sunn. Trumbo only heard Vincent's half of the conversation, separated by long pauses.

"Sunn—you lied to us. You did not release St. James as you promised . . . Yes we did . . . Yes, it was on every major network . . . No, it does not prove anything . . . Sunn, you sound irrational. Hurting the little girl will not accomplish anything . . . I showed you I was a man of my word. Now I need you to release St. James . . . Yes, I called you a liar. You cannot continue these fantasies . . . No, that's not the only time you lied . . . No, in fact, one of your demands was fake and you know it . . . You know which demand it was, too . . . Trumbo Walsh. He's in there with you already. That was a bogus request and you know it . . . Don't pretend he's not with you. You had him talk to us, trying to fool us . . . Yes, he is. Don't lie to me, Sunn, and I won't lie to you."

Trumbo flushed with fury. The FBI agent had sold him out. Now Sunn knew Trumbo was in the building. Trumbo heard footsteps.

He had just heaped the last box on when Cleopatra ran into the room, holding a rifle at arm's length.

"Drop it, Trumbo," said Cleopatra.

"No."

"Drop it now. If you don't, I'll shoot you on the count of three. Sunn said I could if I wanted to."

"No."

"One, two . . ." Trumbo braced for the bullet. She had aimed at his head. The body armor would do no good.

Before she said "three," he heard gunfire from the hallway. A bullet ripped through Cleopatra's shoulder. She spun around, firing as she turned, spraying the hallway with bullets. Trumbo dove behind a desk, hiding from the unseen assailant.

Barbara Thompson walked into the room. "Drop the gun, Cleopatra. Don't hurt my son."

Cleopatra leveled the gun at Barbara. "We have to bring him back, dead or alive! That's what J'osüf said. You were going to help!"

"I changed my mind. Drop it."

Cleopatra stood upright, holding her machine gun with her uninjured arm. "You are one of the bad ones now, Barbara," said Cleopatra. "If you're not, prove it by shooting Trumbo."

"Back to hell, then, bitch," said Barbara. Both women fired simultaneously, filling the room with the staccato furor of gunfire. Cleopatra was knocked instantly against the back wall, her body shredded beyond recognition, her face a bloody pulp. She slid down to the floor, dead. The oily smell of gunpowder hung in the air.

Barbara dropped her gun. She bled profusely from several wounds. "I been hit, son," she said. "I been hit." She lay down on the floor. "I couldn't let that girl kill my only son. I couldn't do it. No matter what, I wanted to save my only son."

She lifted a walkie-talkie to her lips. "Sunn?" she said.

Sunn's voice came over. "Barbara?"

"Sunn, Trumbo's dead. I killed him. You can stop looking."

"Did you have to?" asked Sunn.

"I had to."

The walkie-talkie dropped out of her hand. "My boy, I can't let you be part of the madness anymore. You're such a sweet boy. I'm sorry for everything."

Trumbo knelt next to her and held her hand, which was sticky with blood. "I'm sorry, too," he said.

"Go on, get out of here, son. Save your girlfriend. I don't

want you to make the same mistakes I made." She gagged as her lungs filled with blood.

"It's okay," said Trumbo.

Tears welled up in her eyes. "Call me Mom." She gagged and coughed up blood. "Just say the word, just once."

"Mom."

"Son."

Her head fell to the side, limp, dead.

Trumbo looked away from her face as he took away the walkie-talkie she used to talk to Sunn. He ducked into the lounge and pulled the pins out of three hand grenades atop Sunn's pile of ammunition. He slammed the door and ran down the hallway as fast as his feet would carry him.

The explosion blew the door off of its hinges. Flames and smoke flew out of the room. Then there was a deafening cacophony like popcorn from hell as hundreds of rounds of high-powered ammunition exploded in rapid succession. Trumbo raced down the hall, ducked into an office, and slammed the door. The building filled with thick, acid smoke.

He ducked beneath a desk and flipped on the police radio. A voice repeated, "Walsh . . . Walsh . . . Walsh . . . Come in Walsh . . . We want to talk to you . . . Walsh."

He spoke into the police radio. "Yeah?"

"One moment." Vincent's voice came onto the radio. "Walsh. I blew your cover. A policeman from Los Angeles contacted us."

"Who?"

"Lieutenant Pete Mazer."

"Petey's there?"

"Yes. We now know who you are," said Vincent. "I personally saw the videtape of the gas station. It's clear that Barbara Thompson is at fault."

"I'm not talking to you, Vincent. Put Mazer on."

"I really want to help you now, Walsh."

"You sold me out, Vincent. Put Mazer on the line."

The crackle of static was followed by the familiar voice of Lt. Pete Mazer, Trumbo's friend from LAPD. "Hey, Trumbo, tough situation, huh?"

"No, Mazer, it's a picnic in here."

"What was the explosion?" asked Mazer.

"Their ammo dump. They kept it all in one room. What they have left now is just what's in their guns."

"Good job."

Trumbo whispered into the radio, "Let me give you the layout. Sunn and the hostages are together in the main courtroom. The west wall of the courtroom has some tiny windows at the top, not big enough to get out, but I think it's an outside wall. Right?"

"Yes, it is," said Mazer.

"If we can get the FBI to draw their fire, they might run out of ammo."

"They still have the bombs," said Mazer.

"Sure. But their guns will be useless."

"And then what?"

"And then . . . if they have no more ammo, it makes my job that much easier."

Mazer continued. "What else do you know? Are the hostages safe?"

"I've been watching them on the TV, just like you," said Trumbo.

Mazer replied, "Vincent says the FBI has an armored vehicle. They'll assault the west wall in two minutes. See if it draws their fire."

"One more thing," said Trumbo.

"Go ahead."

"There's about a twenty-foot drop from the biggest window in the building, by the judge's chambers. Put an air mattress down there in case I have to jump. It's the only place someone can get out without going through the courtroom. And the doors—well, you know about the doors. They're wired with some pretty funky-looking bombs."

"Gotcha. Affirmative on the air mattress, Trumbo."

"I'm turning down the radio so they don't find me."

He hid beneath the desk and waited for the sound of gunfire.

The shock wave from the ammunition explosion rumbled through the courtroom. James St. James fainted. Denise screamed uncontrollably. Benning, gray with shock from loss of blood, lay quivering on the floor. The situation in the courtroom was out of control. Smoke poured in beneath the doorway leading to the hall.

Sunn stood at the front of the room and raised his hands above his head. "Please do not get upset! This is the beginning of the revolution. We may encounter some small setbacks, but the greater good as the Horseman's Clan is reassembled will more than compensate for any small problems we encounter today. Concentrate on the good. The smoke is not real. The fire is not real. All that is real is our love for Charlie and our quest to make the world a better place after the revolution."

Manson walked to the front of the courtroom and grabbed Sunn by the lapel. "Just what in the fuck are you talking about? What's all this shit about the fire isn't real? It's real, boy! Get a handle!"

"But, Charles, I don't believe in consensus reality."

"Do you believe in this?" Manson slapped Sunn across the face. "Is that real? Man, I thought you had some kind of plan to get me out of here. But now we're dead meat as far as I can tell. What were you doing anyway, boy?"

"I was going to reunite the Family."

"What family?"

"You know, the Manson Family. The Horseman's Clan. The ones who are going to bring the end of the world."

"That's bullshit! There never was no Family. Where did you ever get such an idea? Watching TV shows?"

"Uh, I was at the Spahn Ranch."

Manson tilted back his head and stared at Sunn. "I don't remember you."

"Sure, I was there in sixty-nine."

"D'jou have the beard then?"

"No, not exactly."

Manson slammed his fist into his hand. "I remember you now. We always called you some other name, though. It wasn't J'osüf Sunn, it was somethin' else."

"Uh, yeah."

"C'mon, what'd we call you?"

"Red Ryder. Remember?" said Sunn, hopefully.

Manson squinted. "There was no Red Ryder that I remember."

Sunn blushed. He had always imagined himself the new

leader, the second-in-command to Charles Manson. He liked to believe that Manson respected him, had somehow *chosen* him to continue the job. And now Manson couldn't even remember his name.

"I guess some of you called me by another name."

"Yeah? What?"

"Not many people, but some, called me, uh, Dhhrrtb," grunted Sunn.

"What?"

Sunn lowered his voice. "Dirtball."

"Yeah! Dirtball! Dirtball, I remember you now! You was always diggin' these tunnels and saying we should live in 'em, and we teased you about it! That's you?"

"Um, I did dig a tunnel."

"Yeah." Manson frowned. "Well, what gave you the idea t'take over a courthouse?"

"All those letters you sent me. They were all about how there's six good ones and six evil ones, and one leader, and how you have to kill the bad ones and get the good ones together—"

Before Sunn finished, Manson slugged him in the face, knocking him backwards. "I asked you to send me batteries, you fool! I was talking about a video game! Not a lot else to do in solitary, man! That's what the good ones and evil ones was. I didn't say to storm a courthouse like some kind of half-baked commandos! You are just plain fool stupid—the dumbest, craziest son of a bitch I ever saw."

Sunn was shaken more by the words than by the punch. His voice was abnormally high and nasal, a panicked difference from his usual authoritarian pitch. "It can't be! It's not right! This is the way it was meant to be! Today is Day One. This is the beginning. All the signs are right. We freed you! We did everything we were supposed to do for the Rebirth to happen!"

"Horseman's Clan? Horseshit! You are crazier than I am, Dirtball! Thanks to you, now we're really screwed, and all the fool cops and judges is going to think this was *my* idea. I'm never gonna make parole."

Suddenly the entire room rumbled ominously as if an earthquake were tearing through the building. The west wall shook unnaturally. After a pause, it rumbled again and the metal edge of the police battering ram smashed through the building, sending splinters of wood paneling flying. FBI negotiator Vincent's voice boomed over the public-address system. "Sunn, give yourselves up. We're coming in."

The battering ram backed up and rammed a larger hole into the wall. Sunn grabbed his rifle, leaned it against the judge's bench, and started firing on the vehicle.

He lifted his arms and yelled into the courtroom, "Shoot at the great dragon which is destroying our paradise! Fire on it! We can prevail! We have the power!"

Fire and Silhouette lifted guns, took aim at the battering ram, and fired. The noise was deafening as dozens of rounds per minute were expended uselessly against the armored vehicle. After pounding a fifth hole into the wall, the battering ram pulled back and parked a short distance away from the building.

Sunn drew his finger across his throat, indicating for them to stop firing. Seconds later, several bullets smashed into the wall over his head.

He whipped around just in time to see the door to the courtroom close. He swung the machine gun into position and blasted several bursts of fire toward the doors, splintering them. "Who's there?" he yelled. "Who the hell is firing on us?" He walked toward the front doors. Fire followed him, gun at the ready.

Before they reached the door, several more shots rang out, originating from the *opposite* end of the courtroom, behind the judge's desk. Sunn whipped around, took aim, and fired into the rear doors. "We're surrounded," said Sunn. "Fire —you take the front door. Silhouette—you and me cover the back door here."

Silhouette asked, "What about the side doors to the courtroom?"

Sunn considered the question for a minute. "If they fired in from there, they run a chance of hitting one of their own."

Fire stood just inside the front door, her rifle ready. Sunn and Silhouette cautiously pushed open the back door of the room with the barrels of their guns and peeked into the empty hallway.

Trumbo, secreted in the hallway, heard every word. He slipped down the hallway and walked directly to the side doors, the only entrance not under guard. Quickly he un-threaded a shoelace from his sneaker and fastened a slip-knot around the trigger of the machine gun he had taken from Cleopatra. He put in a full clip of ammunition, aimed the gun at the ceiling, and tightened the shoestring. A deafening hail of bullets sprayed the room. Trumbo darted down the hallway in the opposite direction.

Inside, Sunn screamed, "They're firing from the side doors, dammit! Take it out, take it out!" The two girls and Sunn aimed at the side doorway and fired continuously. Sunn ran out of bullets first, then Fire. Finally Silhouette's gun ran out of ammunition, and the *click, click, click* of empty chambers reverberated throughout the courtroom.

Sunn raced to the side doors and kicked them open. When he saw the machine gun rigged up with a shoelace, he screamed, "The pigs! Those fucking pigs! No one is out there!"

He stepped into the hallway. Silhouette and Thursday followed, unsure of what they might find.

Trumbo immediately crawled through the rear door and into the jury box. He glanced around, then ran to the witness stand, where James St. James, Denise, and Parole Commissioner Benning huddled together.

Trumbo whispered to them, "Follow me. I'll get you out of here. Do it!"

He took Denise's hand and led her through the jury deliberation room into the back hallway; Benning, now conscious, and St. James followed. He whispered to them, "The doors are wired with explosives. Can't use them."

He led them through the thick smoke to the little room marked JUDGE'S CHAMBERS. He tried to lift the window, but it was rusted shut.

"Stand back," he said.

Trumbo lifted a large leather chair over his head and heaved it through the window. The glass flew everywhere. The chair tumbled twenty feet to the ground. Using a heavy lawbook, he smashed out the remaining fragments of glass, then peered outside. The FBI had erected an air mattress below, as requested.

"Denise, you go first."

"You coming out?" she asked him.

"Go!" He lifted her over the ragged glass. She leaped down onto the cushion and was quickly escorted away by FBI agents. Benning jumped next. St. James hesitated.

"Get going!" said Trumbo.

"I'm scared of heights," he said.

"You want to stay and get shot?" Trumbo pushed the newsman with all his might. St. James screamed all the way down to the air mattress. Two FBI men lifted him off the mattress and whisked him away.

Mazer, down on the ground, yelled to Trumbo through the megaphone, "Jump, Trumbo! It's your only chance!"

"Things to do, Mazer," said Trumbo.

Alison was still in the building. He had to get her out of the sheriff's jail in the basement. He choked as soon as he turned in to the hallway. The smoke was thicker than ever. Staying low to the ground, where there was slightly more air, he crept past the courtroom. He heard Sunn's voice ranting obscenities. Then he heard him say, "We're doomed. We will go down fighting and make our way into heaven the promised way, through death. Detonate the bombs."

The sulfurous smoke was now so thick, Trumbo could barely see two feet in front of himself. He thought he heard a door open. Was that someone running past him? He couldn't make it out completely. Whoever ran by was too short to be Sunn. He thought he caught a glimpse of a bright yellow shirt, but couldn't be sure. No matter. He had only minutes to get Alison. He ran down the stairs two at a time toward the jail in the basement.

The water in the small jail downstairs was now almost a foot deep. He sloshed through, trying to find his way in the smoke.

"Alison! Alison! It's me! It's me!"

He felt his way past the desk. The fire door separating the sheriff's offices from the jail had automatically closed. He used his last rounds of ammunition to blow off the lock. A torrent of water gushed out from the jail area.

"Alison!" he yelled. He felt his way through the ever-darkening room. "Alison! We've got to get out! Where are you?"

His heart sank. *They found her.* Blindly he pushed his way back to the farthest cell. Then he heard her voice reply, "Trumbo. Over here."

He ran his finger along the wall until he came to a desk. "Here I am," she said.

He turned around. She stood right next to him. "You're all right?"

She nodded. He grabbed her hand.

"We've got two minutes, maybe less," he said. "Sunn's gonna blow up the whole building."

He led her out of the sheriff's office and back up the stairway. They were almost to the judge's chambers when he smacked straight into J'osüf Sunn.

Holding a knife.

"Won't you die with me, O Chosen One?" said Sunn. His eyes were bloodshot. His voice rasped from the smoke. He held the knife to Trumbo's throat. Trumbo instinctively kicked Sunn in the balls. Sunn toppled to the ground, but not before he jabbed the knife into Trumbo's thigh.

Alison screamed.

Trumbo yelled, "Alison, get out. Go to the second door. Jump from the window. Now!"

She disappeared into the thick smoke.

Trumbo leaned down and yanked the knife out of his thigh. The pain was overwhelming. Sunn pulled out another knife, even bigger than the first, engraved with icons representing the sun and planets. He jabbed at Trumbo. Trumbo deflected the blade with the knife in his hand. Sunn made another thrust. Trumbo locked the blade with his own.

"You were one of the bad ones," said Sunn. "I should have known. Now you will die with me."

"Like hell," said Trumbo. He attempted to dart around Sunn and make a break down the hallway. Sunn blocked his path, swinging his knife in front of him. Trumbo ducked, threw his arms around Sunn, and knocked him to the ground. They wrestled. Sunn got the upper hand and pinned Trumbo to the ground. He held the ceremonial knife at Trumbo's neck.

"Die with me, evil one. Die with me now."

For a moment Trumbo thought of Denise and Alison and

the fantasy life they had helped him create. The image of the two of them alone, suffering in the cold world, galvanized him into action. As quick as a snake he threw his right hand into the flat side of Sunn's blade, knocking it across the room.

Sunn kicked Trumbo in the knee, then jumped on him, knocking him back to the floor. They wrestled again, Sunn on top. Trumbo jabbed his knife against Sunn's throat.

"Get off me!" screamed Trumbo.

Sunn cackled. "No. You were evil. I knew you were evil."

Trumbo scratched Sunn's neck. "Get off me, you crazy son of a bitch!"

Sunn shook his head. "Kill me," said Sunn. "Please kill me. We're going to die in seconds. Release me. I want to die. End my life. I want to die!" yelled Sunn.

Trumbo, still pinned to the ground, couldn't make himself do it. "No, Sunn, that's not my way. I was never a killer like you. I know that now."

He dropped the knife, gathered all his strength, and pushed Sunn off of him, then ran. After a few steps, the first bomb went off, directly between Trumbo and the judge's chambers. The exit through the window was cut off. Flames shot down the hall toward him. The heat singed his hair. He turned on his heel and dove down the stairs, plunging head over heels toward the basement, now nearly waist-deep in water. A second blast rolled through the halls as a bomb exploded in another part of the building. Trumbo scrambled backwards toward the jail, certain he would die in the inferno.

Denise and Alison, covered with soot and bruises, held each other, tears streaming down their faces. They stood across the street, behind the barricade erected by the FBI, staring toward the courthouse, when the first blast shook the ground.

Part of the roof flew into the air, hurtling end over end before the flaming timbers crashed into the ground. A second, larger blast ripped through the west wall. The second story of the building collapsed, showering sparks into the twilight sky. Then the main charge detonated. Fire shot out of all of the windows. The explosion ripped through the building from back to front, sending shreds of wood and concrete into the air like fireflies from hell. The bell atop the courthouse flew off, ringing a final death knell as it slowly tumbled to earth. It landed several hundred yards away, ripping the roof of a police car like so much aluminum foil.

Like a dying beast, the building leaned over to one side, fire and smoke spewing from a dozen openings. A support gave way somewhere within, and the entire structure heaved and toppled to the ground.

Alison gasped as if she had been physically struck. "Oh my God. He's dead. He's dead." She hugged Denise and hid the girl's eyes from the devastation.

Deep in the fallout shelter in the bowels of the building, Trumbo sat in the pitch-black darkness, listening to the eerie hissing sound of the building burning above, separated from the inferno by only a few feet of reinforced concrete. He touched the wall. It was as hot as boiling water. But miraculously the air in the shelter was breathable, and he was relatively insulated from the fire raging around him. At one point there was a terrifying booming sound as a beam crashed down on the shelter. He braced himself for injury, but none came. He was safe.

He lay down on a cot and listened to the raging fire. Then, inexplicably, he heard what sounded like someone else breathing. At first he took it for some odd sound that came from the fire; but the regularity was too great to ignore.

"Who's there?" yelled Trumbo.

There was no reply. Trumbo stood and walked along the line of cots lining the perimeter of the room, touching them one after another. On the fifth one, he touched a man's face.

"Who are you, man?" asked a familiar voice, an accent that was a strange mixture of hillbilly, mean old man, and California New Age.

"Manson? Charles Manson?" asked Trumbo.

"Yeah, hell, yeah. Who are you?"

"Trumbo Walsh."

"Man, I heard you fighting with Sunn when I was trying to get away. You're right, man."

"Right about what?"

"You're not a killer."

"What?"

"You're not a killer. You said it to Sunn. You're about peace, man. I knowed when you was a baby."

"Where?"

"Spahn Ranch. Luther Walsh took you away. I told him to. After the murders and all that. I didn't think a baby should get mixed up in that shit. I told Luther Walsh to take you away, as far away as he could. I guess he done that. Luther was a damned good guy. He showed up after you was borned."

"After I was born?"

"Yeah. He was trying to talk your mother into splitting from me. I told her to do what she wanted, man. But she stayed. Lotta kids stayed that shouldn't have."

"Luther's my father," said Trumbo.

There was a long pause. A few moments later, Manson lit a match. The eerie light played across the cracks and crags in Manson's weathered face. "Well, Luther's not exactly your father. He raised you. I'm your father. Barbara was hanging with me almost from when I got out of jail in sixty-seven. I knocked her up."

"Oh my God."

"It's not that bad, kid. You're not a killer. You're not evil. You're not like your mom, you're not like me. Each of us makes our own way in the world, man. Each of us does what he has to do. I wished I didn't do half of the things I had to do. I was thrown out at age nine. I spent most of my life in jails and reform homes. I spent the last half of my life bein' the most hated man in the world. People puts all their fears on me. Other people like that nut case Sunn sees me as some kind of messiah or leader. I get letters, phone calls, people wantin' my autograph. What people sees in me is whatever they wanna see. But I ain't the Devil and I ain't no messiah and I ain't no leader. I'm just a burned-out old ex-con. I'm gonna die in jail. It's a miserable thought. You don't want that, boy."

"No."

"Boy, you gotta just try to make something of your life.

Get a little job. Stay out of trouble. If you gots a girl, that's good. You got a girl?"

"Yeah, I do."

"Take care of her."

"Is it true? Are you really my father?"

"Don't worry: I ain't gonna tell anyone else. I think about you sometimes, wondered where you was, wondered if you went good or bad. I tell ya, I'm glad you went good. I'm pissed at that asshole Sunn for fucking things up for you."

They heard a roaring sound as burning wood above them hissed and split in two. The room was becoming hotter. Manson continued, "So I won't tell nobody. I want you to have some advantages I didn't have. I don't want you having the baggage I had to carry around—reform school, jail, trouble every minute of my life. But I want a couple things in exchange. First, drop me a line every now and then. Tell me how you're doing. Use a made-up name—call yourself, I don't know, Lost Child or something. I'll know it's you."

"What else do you want?"

"We're gonna be in here awhile, man, waiting for that fire to burn off. Just tell me what it's like."

"What *what's* like?"

"The world, man. I ain't been out since 1970. What's a young man do in the world? What's out there? Everything I know, I know from TV and letters. Nobody ever just tells me what it's like. The kids I meet your age here in the joint are thugs and creeps. What's a real guy like in the real world?"

"That's all?"

"Yeah. Just tell me."

The match went out, and they sat in darkness. Trumbo lay down on the cot and took a deep breath. "Okay. That's fair. First off, I drive a tow truck. When there's an accident, I'm the guy who cleans up the wreckage so life can get back to normal . . ."

An emergency crew treated Alison and Denise for cuts and bruises. The paramedics wanted to put them into the hospital immediately, but Denise insisted they stay until the fire was put out, or until there was incontrovertible evidence that Trumbo was dead. The fire raged most of the night, sending sparks and thick black smoke into the air, while nine fire engines poured water onto the flames.

Shortly after midnight, the central beam in the building split in two. Visible in the subbasement was a cement cube, sixteen feet on a side. The four major networks, CNN, and dozens of local news stations speculated on the meaning of the box. Was it the jail? Was it some kind of vault filled with city documents? No answers were forthcoming until three in the morning, when one of the town's old-timers drove in and explained that it was a bomb shelter, built soon after the Cuban missile crisis, maintained until recently with a full store of provisions.

On hearing this news, the firefighters concentrated their efforts on extinguishing the flames surrounding the bomb shelter. The fire captain claimed it was highly unlikely that anyone was in there, and even less likely that anyone had survived.

Denise, exhausted, cried herself to sleep in the ambulance. Alison was still wide-awake. She heard about the bomb shelter and stood by the main fire truck, as close as she could to the flames without being burned. The water sprayed frenetically across the concrete structure, blowing back soot and timbers until the gray cube, smeared with ash, was clearly visible.

Alison dared not consider the possibility that Trumbo had survived. Disappointment had followed her in life, and tonight would probably be no different. She thought of all the plans she and Trumbo had made. Even if she only knew him a short time, she felt a powerful bond to Trumbo. The little things he said to keep her spirits up, and the moments they shared, would stay with her the rest of her life. She was too depressed to cry, or scream, or yell. She stood stone-faced, like the statues on Easter Island, staring, waiting. She missed him. She loved him.

When dawn broke over the Central Valley, three firefighters were lowered into the steaming pit of ash. Alison wanted to look away, but could not divert her eyes from the site. The firefighters, dressed head to toe in protective gear, worked their way slowly across the basement floor, testing the ground with each step to keep themselves from falling into some unseen hole. The minutes it took them to cross the pit felt like hours to her. One fireman lifted a huge ax and pounded on the door. Sparks flew as steel met steel until the vaultlike door finally slid open.

A figure stepped out, silhouetted against the blackened wreckage.

Charles Manson peered into the sunlight, rubbing his eyes. He was alone. Alison's heart sank.

A firefighter escorted Manson across the charred wasteland and deposited him on the edge of the wreckage. A half dozen cops rushed to the site, and Manson was handcuffed and led away. An entourage of law enforcement officials and television cameras chased him to the paddy wagon waiting at the edge of the police blockade.

Only Alison kept her eyes on the bomb shelter. One of the firemen returned to the shelter. Alison crossed her fingers; *hope to God, hope to God, please let it be, please let it be.* The firefighter walked out alone. A few seconds later, Trumbo emerged: limping and covered with soot, very much alive.

Tears filled Alison's eyes. She ran past the police tape and stood at the edge of the pit. The firefighter helped Trumbo crawl up the ladder, and lifted him out of the basement onto the ground above. He was hurt. He stumbled onto the ground. Alison ran to him.

"Trumbo!" she yelled.

"Hey, Alison!" he said casually.

She hugged him. He cracked half a grin. "Pretty bad fire, huh?"

"It's over now," she said.

"Yeah. It's over," he said. "Time to rebuild."

They kissed, then turned their backs on the smoldering wreckage of the Corcoran County Courthouse and walked toward the rising sun, which brought warmth and light to the Central Valley of California.

EPILOGUE

From *The Venice (California) Weekly Gazette Shopper*

MARRIAGES
WALSH-WILMOT WEDDING

Trumbo Walsh, 28, owner of Venice Towing and Repair, and Alison Wilmot, proprietor of the Cut-N-Run Hair Salon, exchanged vows Saturday in a nondenominational garden ceremony held at sunset on the Venice Beach pier. The bride wore a tea-length white silk dress, of her own design. Denise Walsh, their adopted daughter, served both as flower girl and maid of honor. Denise has recently been in the news as founder of Teens Heal the Bay, an environmental advocacy group.

From *Phoenix Daily Journal*
"Whatever Happened To . . ." Column

JAMES ST. JAMES

In the eighteen months since the abrupt cancellation of his television shows, "Exposé!" and "Suspect at Large," controversial reporter James St. James has undergone a lot of changes—beginning with his name. He now prefers to be called Ray Garvey. "St. James was a stage name," he says. The ex-newsman is heavier and considerably balder than you may remember, but beneath the crow's-feet around his eyes you can see some of the spark that once drove him to the top of the tabloid TV business. In an interview conducted in his mother's Phoenix, Arizona, kitchen, Garvey described his downfall as "a learning experience—a hideous, hellish learning experience."

Last year, seven business partners and the television network won a class action suit against him resulting in the personal loss of more than eleven million dollars. In addition, the Federal Communications Commission filed an unprecedented motion against the newsman, banning him from the airwaves for seven years. (Garvey's latest appeal was rejected by the Supreme Court last week.)

Yet the Phoenix native remains optimistic. "There's more to life than work, work, work," said Garvey, who briefly sold group life insurance until his license was revoked for "gross irregularities." "I'm in a healing process right now. Without the demands of the daily grind, I've been sampling all the things I denied myself so long: riches, women, politics. It's refreshing."

Asked about a possible return to television in the year 2003, when the FCC ban expires, Garvey laughs maniacally. "I have some ideas, yes, it's something I've been thinking about." He sighs. "I've got plans for a classy show, something completely different than 'Exposé!' In the year 2003 they'll have cameras the size of wristwatches. Without tipping my hand, imagine the unique possibility of arming drug gangs with live television cameras. It'll turn broadcasting on its ear."

Garvey is currently completing his memoirs.

From *TV Guide* (cover story)

EMMY-WINNING "MARILYN MCLEOD INVESTIGATES" SEASON STARTER A SMASH: DON'T MISS IT

Tonight all of America is asking the same question: How can the self-styled "Queen of Investigative Journalism" top herself? Last season, viewers were glued to their sets as Marilyn McLeod built a reputation for

bare-knuckled TV news with a heart. Who can forget
the groundbreaking report on tax law changes that
forced a Wisconsin dairy farmer to kill two thousand
calves rather than declare bankruptcy? Or her heart-
rending story of the housekeeper who committed suicide so that her four Salvadoran children might be
adopted by her wealthy employer? McLeod has rock-
eted to the top of the Nielsen ratings—handily beating
"Sixty Minutes." Even the First Lady admits to being a
loyal viewer.

Tonight ratings giant "Marilyn McLeod Investigates" enters its second season, with a fast-paced,
tear-jerking true story told as only McLeod can tell it.
The stunning account of six South Carolina cheerlead-
ers kidnapped by an oil-rich third world dictator and
forced to join his harem—while the sheikh hid behind
an outdated international law—methodically uncovers
corruption in the corridors of power from Wall Street
to the United Nations. McLeod's latest brims with
phenomenal revelations that showcase her trailblazing
talents as the first feminist of tabloid television. Don't
miss it!

From: *Inmate Personnel Files,*
   Corcoran State Penitentiary

TO:
Manson, Charles
Inmate B33920
Corcoran State Penitentiary

Dear Inmate *MANSON:*
By *UNANIMOUS* vote the Parole Commission of the
State of California has determined that *INMATE
NAME: B33920, MANSON, CHARLES* shall remain in
the custody of the California Department of Correc-
tions.

The Commission has determined that you are not
eligible for parole for the following reason or reasons:

X Inmate does not show sufficient signs of rehabilita-
tion for release.

X Inmate's behavior during incarceration was below acceptable penitentiary standards.

X Inmate's original offense not amenable with parole release at this time.

X Inmate may pose danger to others if released.

X Other: *SEE ATTACHMENTS (EIGHTY-TWO PAGES).*

You may reapply for parole in *AUGUST 1997.*

(Signed)

Carl Benning

Parole Commissioner

California Department of Corrections